Conten

Book 1

Book 2

Diary Entries

Book 3

Isobel of Glenmoriston

Zaynab El-Fatah

Published with the assistance of Angel Key Publications

https://angelkey.com.au

Isobel of Glenmoriston

In the format of letters and diary entries
This is Isobel's Story
1759, Scotland

Contributions
and maps
by Fatima
Zayn al-Abidin

Illustrations by
Halima Karger
and Fatima
Zayn al-Abidin

An historical fiction compilation in the form of letters and diary entries, where in the Eighteenth-Century Scottish Highlands, all around Isobel is death, rape and burning fires. Her Mither is lost as well as her home and livelihood. Isobel takes shelter in a shieling with her three children and her grieving father in the aftermath of Culloden. Her soldier husband Padruig Dubh, in escaping execution, leaves the family to fend for themselves while living in Coiraghoth cave as one of the Seven Glenmoriston Men. Their farm is burned down as well as their crops, and the coos and Clydesdale horses are stolen. Years go by, and eventually, she begins to see crops replanted and a new home partially built, but once again, her beloved husband is taken from her and forced into military service for the British in a foreign land. Finally, despair sets in. Will romance help her survive this time? Will new love save Isobel?

This is Isobel's Story.

Dedication

To the wives, mothers, sisters and grandmothers
of the slain clansmen on Drumossie Moor and
their descendents,
wherever they are in the world.

To dear Daniel Whyte
Happy reading.
Zaynab El-Fatah

List of illustrations

List of maps

Map 1. Historical Clan lands, Scotland

Map 2. Glenmoriston and Inverness shire

Map 3. Approximate escape route of Prince Charles Edward Stuart and his guides – April to September 1746

Map 4. Escape route of Prince Charles Edward Stuart – April to September 1746

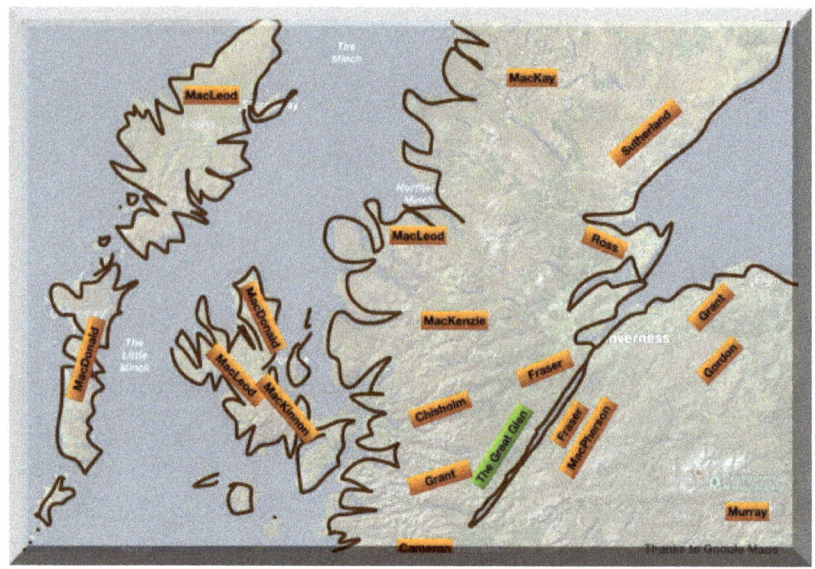

Map 1. Historical Clan lands, Scotland

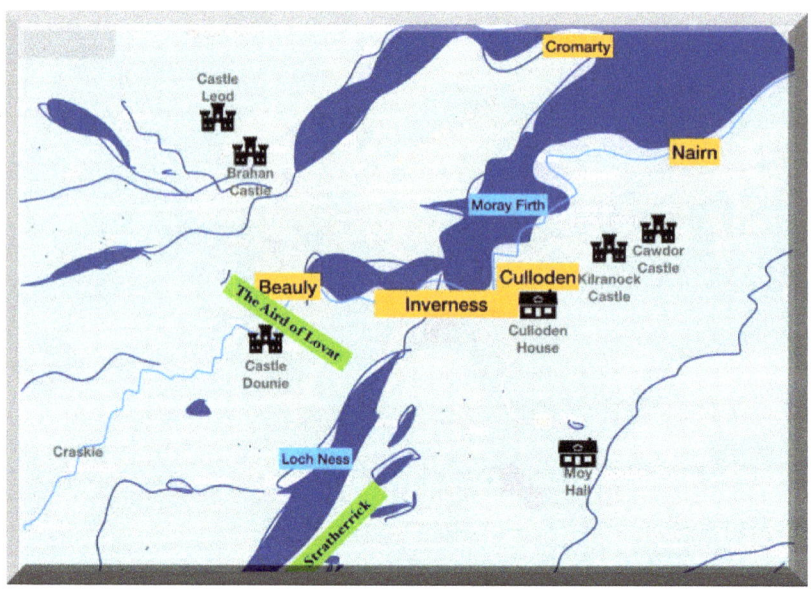

Map 2. Glenmoriston and Inverness-shire

**Map 3. Approximate Escape Route of Prince Charles
Edward Stuart – April to September 1746**

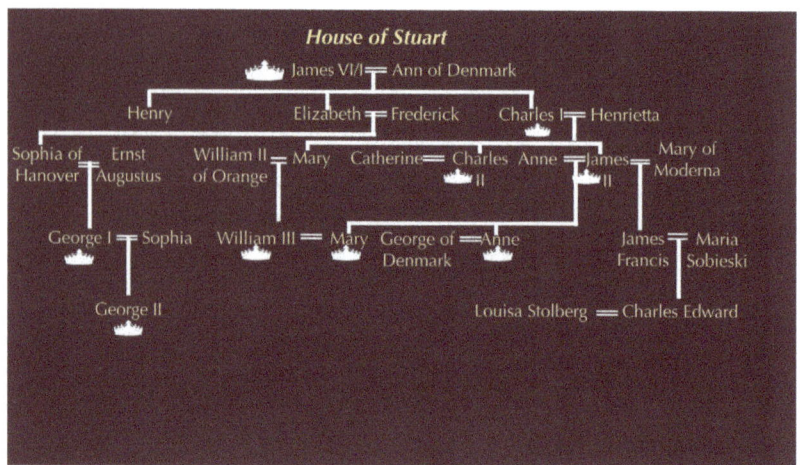

Family Tree of the Stuarts

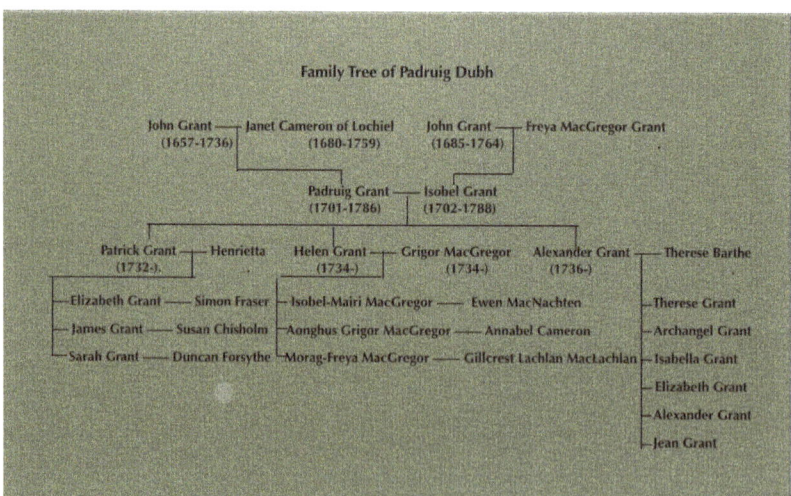

Family Tree of Padruig Dubh Grant

Prologue

This personal, fictionalised story, **Isobel of Glenmoriston**, tells of a heart broken wife whose soldier husband has to escape the British forces dealing with the time period after the Battle of Culloden in 1746 through to when the British Forces had given up looking for the Prince. Isobel's Mother, Freya is murdered in that time, by British Forces and the farm burned down. Her husband, Padruig, tells his story five years later in 1751, to Bishop Robert Forbes as documented in *The Lyon in Mourning*. Before that decade was over, he was forced into Military Service [14] upon a ship bound for New France (Canada) with the 78th Regiment of Frasers, leaving Isobel and his family again to cope with the continued rebuilding of their lives on a remote farm in the Highlands of Scotland, without him, until his eventual return almost four years later. Two of Isobel's adult sons and their wives abandon her, leaving her alone with her grieving father and her daughter, still living in a tiny shieling. Facing another freezing cold winter and still awaiting her home to be rebuilt after it had been burned down by British troops, she has neither Padruig nor her sons. Despairing, three of the Glenmoriston Men and one of their wives come to her aid, as well as Padruig's Uncle Allan MacDonald.

The Battle of Culloden was the last of the Jacobite uprisings in Britain, resulting in catastrophic losses to Scotland in 1746. The Jacobite Scottish clans involved were led by Prince Charles Edward Stuart, son of the exiled James Francis in Italy, who was attempting to win back the throne of the British Isles. Despite the Catholic faith of the Stuarts being politically unpopular, the Episcopalian Church was also a target of the government. Many of their Ministry were arrested and imprisoned, such as Bishop Robert Forbes of Leith, who went on to compile and write the **Lyon in Mourning.** Kept secret and not published in its complete form until about 140 years later in 1895, this *"Collection of Speeches, Letters, Journals Relative to the Affairs of Prince Charles Edward Stuart"* is key to an accurate understanding of witness statements from those directly affected by these horrific, graphic truths those many years ago. Without manuscripts like this, these events and the cruelties of that prevailing government may well not have ever been known.

In 1746, Prince Charles Edward Stuart had a price of £30,000 on his head, so the intensity of the search for him after his escape from the Culloden battle field led to the deaths of many innocent people uninvolved with the Jacobites or politics, as well as their livestock and their livelihoods. Homes were burnt to the ground, and both women and girls were raped on the mainland of Scotland as well as on the  Hebridean Islands, like the Isle of Raasay, by British troops. People were shot, imprisoned naked on ships where scores died, hung, hung drawn and quartered, beheaded [17], transported to the colonies or sold as slaves in Barbados.[12] This marked the end of Highland life as they knew it. A culture and a people were successfully crushed. Some would argue it was an attempted genocide on the part of the Duke of Cumberland, the third son of the reigning monarch, George II.

Isobel of Glenmoriston was the wife of Patrick Grant, known as Padruig Dubh of Craskie due to his black hair. They both lived in Glenmoriston, which was an area severally affected by the Scorched Earth Policy of the prevailing government. Padruig fought in the Battle of Culloden along with six of the men mentioned next in the Forward. All of the Glenmoriston men and himself, were betrayed by the  Laird of Grant, who advised them to give up their arms and stand down, then they could all *"go home in peace"*. Hundreds believed that man and were subsequently shipped in the prison ship *Furnace*, first to London and then onto Barbados. Only two men returned alive [13] reporting that another six men were still alive in Barbados. All the other prisoners died in the most horrifying conditions imaginable. Because of this betrayal, one man left the British side, named Grigor MacGregor, under Lord Loudoun and joined with the six men who chose not to give up their arms or Highland dress and took a pledge of allegiance one to the other and to that end, escaped to live in a cave on the Hill of Lundy, between Corri Dho and Glen Affaric, called Coiraghoth. They became famous as the Seven Glenmoriston Men.

While living in their large cave, they were surprisingly visited by Captain Alexander MacDonald of Glenalladale of Skye accompanied by none other than Prince Charles Edward Stuart in need of help and guidance through the tough terrain unknown to them, in order to reach their destination in Badenoch to two of the leaders of the Rising being, Ewen MacPherson of Cluny  and Donald Cameron of Lochiel, known as the gentle Lochiel. Lochiel had been badly injured in both ankles on the day of the battle and was being hidden and cared for as the leader of the Camerons. "Dr Threpland waited on Lochiel after the battle of Culloden and dressed his wounds for him, so that when the Doctor left Badenoch, Lochiel needed only to keep his wounds clean and to apply dry dressings to them." [14]

The Seven Glenmoriston Men were tenacious as to how to care for the Prince and how to keep his location a secret despite the bounty offered for his capture by the Hanoverian government. Of the Seven Glenmoriston Men, Prince Charles Edward said that they were his first Privy Council sworn to him since the Battle of Culloden and that he should never forget them or theirs if ever he came to his own. "I find that Kings and Princes must be ruled by their Privy Council, but I believe there is not in all the world a more absolute Privy Council than what I have at present," [14] he said. They succeeded in their duty as it fell under the Highland law of hospitality, to which they adhered. Additionally, they all took an oath not to disclose his whereabouts. They reached Badenoch, and the Prince was handed over to Lochiel via Cluny, after which Lochiel and the Prince escaped on a ship to France via Lochaber.

Forward

The Seven Glenmoriston Men:

Patrick Grant - Padruig Dubh of Craskie - nephew to Allan MacDonald

Hugh Chisholm		Alexander MacDonald (d.1751) of Aonach
Donald Chisholm		Grigor MacGregor
Alexander Chisholm (d.1751) (sons of Paul Chisholm, tenant at Blairie/Blame)		John MacDonald (Campbell) of Craskie [Oes Iain]

The Oath of Fidelity and Secrecy

(Translated from Erse)

*"Their backs should be to God
And their faces to the devil:
That all the curses the Scriptures did pronounce
Might come upon them and their posterity
If they did not stand firm
To the Prince in his gravest dangers
And if they should discover
To any person, man, woman or child,
That the Prince was in their keeping,
Till once his Person should be out of danger, etc."*

The Seven Glenmoriston Men kept to their Oath of Fidelity and Secrecy and it was not known to anyone until about a year after the Prince's eventual escape to France, that they had had any knowledge whatsoever about the Prince's whereabouts.

The Seven Glenmoriston Men previously had been famous for refusing to give up their arms, which was required by a new law after the Battle of Culloden. They had taken an oath one to another and held to their Highland way of life. They were all very strong and courageous men, Hugh Chisholm only being seventeen at the time. A famous incident occurred where British troops were being guided through Glenmoriston by Donald Fraser stealing sixty Highland coos belonging to Padruig's Uncle Allan MacDonald. Although they were only seven men and the British forces outnumbered them with sixty soldiers and thirteen Scottish militia, the British became so frightened of their fierceness, that they threw down their weapons, and many ran away in fear. Padruig Dubh communicated with the leader of the Militia and decided not to harm them. After the coos had run away, the British Major gave in to their demands and ordered the militia to round up the coos and hand them over to the Seven Glenmoriston Men. The British Major was quoted as having said, *"they weren't men, they were devils"*. Padruig also demanded some of their food, which was given to them.

Book 1

Letters between Isobel and Padruig

Letters

An historical fiction in tumultuous 18th Century Scotland where a broken-hearted wife and husband from the Highlands are once again separated. Padruig is forced into service with the English armed forces to fight in Quebec against the French. Left with only the remnants of the farm that once was, Isobel, with an unfinished home and only three crops, faces another freezing cold winter without sufficient food for her aging father and her dependent daughter Helen. This is Isobel's story.

Isobel of Glenmoriston
Isobel's Story
1759, Scotland

Craskie Farm

Glenmoriston

Scotland, 1759

To my dearest Padruig,

My heart is breaking as I try to keep my hand from shaking at the most dreadful news of your unplanned departure from Scotland to a foreign frozen land far from me and our family.

On the first day, when you did not return from your visit to Bishop Forbes in Leith, I asked all of your friends if they had seen you on the off chance you were nearby. On the second day when I awoke, my tears flowed freely and I knew something terrible was before us and I could lose my one and only Padruig Dubh. By the third day, Donald Chisholm, Hugh Chisholm and Grigor MacGregor all gathered here to reassure me that whatever had befallen you, they would finish the house for me, my Da and Helen, before the winter snows, so that we could move out of the shieling.

I have never been inconsolable in my life before. While I felt my heart breaking, although grateful for their help, your friends looked on helplessly, so Grigor's son, Grigor Og, went for his Mither and Uncle Allan, sensing the urgency. I am not sure what they all arranged, but they sent someone on a fast horse up to Inverness to enquire after you and demanded the Post Office send any news immediately to us.

Morag was as patient as anyone could be, as she sat quietly knitting beside me, speaking soft words in Gaelic of lovers reuniting. God bless Morag. If I hadn't heard word of you, I wanted to walk to the loch

3

and drown. If I had never seen your face again, looking at me as your wife, I wanted to join you wherever you were. She must have passed on to her husband Grigor, just how serious my situation was and the Glenmoriston men got very busy finishing the house that you had been building, but with an altered and improved design. They had all agreed to work on Craskie for as long as it took and at the same time, Uncle Allan and Morag made sure I didn't go near the loch and that food was still cooking. Neighbours brought food over and there was an overwhelming sense of help and support. There were stews and parritch and bannocks, so that all of the hungry workers, as well as us, stayed fed while I lay useless. I'd finally given up in despair, may God forgive me.

Woe to me and Da and to our family and farm and to finishing our home. I am now without my husband. As a mighty storm came rolling in over the North Atlantic onto our north Scottish coast, the rain fell down incessantly and the heavy clouds were unable to completely pass the peaks of our Highland mountains. I thought of our old friends and crofters who had lived here as tenants on our land, but like us, their homes were burnt down and those who survived the burnings were forced to move to where there was work on the coast. I thought of them as the rain came down and I missed them, as our bairns had grown up with their bairns, many of whom I had delivered, but more than anything, right now still living in our tiny shieling with my sweet old Da and our grown Helen, I was more than anything missing you, my darling husband. I was not expecting to lose you too.

With our Patrick having already moved out, not being able to stand the confines of the shieling with his wife and bairns, he is now rebuilding her family's farm. How is that fair? How will I do this alone? Since your departure, after a blazing stramash with Da just yesterday, our youngest son Alex and Therese decided to move to her family's farm as well. We all knew the shieling had its limits, but in losing both of my sons because I could not adequately provide for them, had a particular kind of misery all of its own. However, if we had never lived there Helen may never have fallen in love with Grigor Og. I loved my wee Alex dearly no matter how much you and he argued or he and Da argued. Sleeping in such a confined space was always difficult and Helen and I frequently slept very closely to give the growing

4

men more space. When you finally joined us, I had to sleep sitting up sometimes.

The smell got worse as the family bathed less and less in the freezing cold burn and urinated into two chamber pots that Helen and I would empty each morning. One morning she climbed out the wee door first with one chamber pot and disposed of it, waiting on me. I saw her look to her left at another person coming along the path. Before that day no one had known we were living in there. She looked particularly pretty with her long black hair flowing in the breeze, I had thought. Whoever it was mustn't have been a threat and she had taken on a shy looking appearance until I came through the wee door with the second chamber pot. I said, "Helen can you please empty this one too?" and came out. A skinny but very handsome, tall young lad was staring at us both, then covering himself he turned and ran back in the direction from which he had come. The next time we saw him was with his Father Grigor Mohr. They smiled very shyly at each other and now they're betrothed. Grigor Mohr looked questioningly at the young couple that day as he was unaware that they'd met each other before.

My memories were interrupted then when suddenly, bursting through the rain, came a rider galloping fast, on what seemed to be one of the biggest horses I'd ever seen, with news of you having been forced onto a ship near Leith to be a part of the 78th Fraser Highlanders headed for New France. Da explained to me and Helen where that was in the world, for I had never heard of it. He explained that the British wanted to defeat the French in New France under General Wolfe.[15] I thought I recognised that name from Culloden.

Helen suggested that I have a nice hot bath because the men had already put on the roof, over what was to be our new bedroom with a working chimney. Then as my mind worked its way out of the fog of grief and disbelief, I felt for you, my dear love, how you must feel fighting for the English after all we have been through. All I ask of you is to stay alive and come home to me and my dear Father who needs you. All three of our children and your dear sweet grandchildren need you too. Helen is distraught though my love, because she fears that she can't marry her betrothed Grigor Og, now that you are gone. What should we do? Da suggested they hand-fast and marry in the

Kirk when you come home. What do you think? It's a big decision, as Grigor Og would have to move in with us once the house is completed and we need at least one strong young man on the farm. I need Helen to help me with Da and she still makes all of the soap and the candles, so I can finally get myself together and continue building up our farm on my own without you. I am going to have to rethink our whole farm strategy.

Da said not to worry about the slate roof you were going to build on our new stone home, because the men have nearly completed it and it will be finished before any heavy snows. There will be some new additions and alterations from the first plan taken on the advice of your friends. They have suggested that we make the house much bigger, with two additional rooms and two more fire places, making the house more fire retardant and stronger to prevent another destruction of our home. God bless our friends.

After last night's severe storm, three of our huge oak trees from the tree line fell down. I thought it was a gift from God, so we are also going to use the timber from them. Grigor Mohr is widening the front doorway and building a beautiful oak door and the Chisholms, being so clever with their timber work, want to build a new wooden addition to the front of the house to keep the snow and rain from the windows and doors.

Patrick and his wife and the bairns are coming over tomorrow to help finally. I think he is keen to be here helping instead of helping his father in law all the time, or at least go between us both. It is my opinion that Alex and his wife, however won't ever move back in with us, because the work over on that property is all but finished, except for the crops.

God bless our friends for helping me so much my love, so let your mind be at ease for us. They are keen also, to build a two story addition to the back of this stone home, as overall, they say it is still too small if everyone decides to move back home and they can use the oak. There'll be enough left over to make more beds too. The additional window frames are from the oak trees, but Da has to go to Inverness for the glass windows, the locks and other bits and pieces.

Morag and her friends came over again with pots of soup and stew this time to feed the hungry men who have offered to bring in the corn when it is ready and the ladies have offered to help me with the grinding.

They are all growing potatoes as well and suggested that we do too. I hope you don't mind eating potatoes like the Irish. I have agreed to this. Hugh said he would build the storage place for the potatoes and add on the enclosure to the house for the donkey before it gets too cold and whenever he came over, he was accompanied by his two beautiful Scottish Collie sheep dogs [45] and their puppies that he was breeding. I wondered if one day they could be useful on

the farm, those sheep dogs. Morag continued to sit beside me, knitting quietly, whilst I adjusted to the new reality.

You'll be wanting to know the news about a certain person who lived with you in Coiraghoth cave. Apparently, news has it that he is no longer Catholic. He is Protestant now. Maybe because of those dreadful meetings in Paris in '46 and '48 with King Louis of France that upon hearing that all of their pleas were rejected for Scotland and that the French King no longer recognised the Stuarts, that it was all just too much for them. I am still so sad about the passing of Lochiel in France back in 1748.

We heard that Ewen MacPherson of Cluny was called to meet your special friend over in Switzerland somewhere. Last I heard he didn't want to go, for fear of being caught as there is still a price on his head, but apparently Prince Charles insisted and he has left, or so I heard. I'll let you know if we find out what comes of the meeting between them if we ever hear back from the MacPhersons. I am not fae, but it feels ominous.

You will remember, my love, Ned Burke who led the Prince off the field after his horse was shot in the shoulder [17] and the groom was decapitated? Like you told me, that brave Ned led the confused Prince to safety and travelled through Stratherick to consult with Lord Lovat, God rest his soul, at Gorthleck House.

Ned passed away about eight years ago and his epitaph has only just reached us with your rider and it reads thus: [12]

To perpetuate the memory of Edward Burke

Who died in Edinburgh, 23rd November 1751

Born in an humble Cottage,

And of mean parents,

In the Island of North Uist;

Ignorant of the first principles of human learning;

Doom'd to converse with the meanest

Of mankind,

And exposed to the various temptations

Of poverty.

Happy in these disadvantages

Since thereby

His given worth

Was the more conspicuous

Fidelity

And disinterested Friendship

Eclips'd his other virtues

Let the venal tribe behold and admire,

And blush,

If yet a blush remains!

Learn by his example

O ye great!

He preferred a good conscience

To £30,000

Perhaps in the reading of it, your new companions there will reminisce about those times.

I had wanted your permission on buying goats, but as you're not here, I am going to have to become accustomed to making independent decisions or decisions with advice from your friends, Da or Uncle Allan. I want to buy two nannies and a billy, which Da said I would need to comb daily, so that we could replace our mattresses and pillows in no time as well as have delicious goats' milk again. I have missed the milk.

John MacDonald, Os Fain, visited this morning, but being in poverty himself, could not assist us but he sends his kind regards to you and hopes you return safely. I mentioned his visit to both Donald and Grigor and they were none too pleased. I admit to feeling uncomfortable with him here without your presence and knew he was begging. How different he is to the rest of you. The Reverend in Inverness, Rod John Stewart, was hoping to talk to you about John MacDonald, but Da and I were obliged to tell him that you were on your way to New France. Perhaps when you return you could visit him in Inverness. Forgive me please if I have spoken out of turn to him, but he promised to maintain our privacy concerning the matter. He voiced concerns over Donald Fraser and wondered if he was still bitter about you and your Seven Glenmoriston Men causing him to lose face and the tobacco you took lawfully from him. That story of you retrieving your Uncle's coos [14] is still told around firesides and we still grieve the loss of both Alexander MacDonald and Alexander Chisholm, may God rest their souls.

Oh, how I wish you were here to talk to about more coos. I think we should be increasing our breeding herd. At the first opportunity, once the goats are sorted, I'll put the word out that we are in need of coos now, preferably a breeding pair. They are such pretty beasts. I feel so sorry for them being  sold to the heartless Northumbrians, who don't understand how to care for them. I hear they have become rich over our goats, our highland coos and our horses. [11]

The MacKinnons [12] have suffered much. The Old Laird who spirited your special friend back to the mainland with redcoats in hot pursuit, I heard recently finally passed away in 1756. [11] John MacKinnon had to be hospitalised in Bath and taken from the Isle of Skye leaving his wife and four children. Donations were sought, but he chose to be hospitalised so as not to cause anyone any financial trouble. When he was captured just after the Old Laird in '46, they were both tortured. Did you know that? John was stripped and flogged, causing permanent lameness in his legs from his thighs down. Both these lovely gentlemen, like you and Ned Burke, refused to give up the Prince despite the £30,000 reward offered. This still shocks the Hanoverians. I did not know, till Da told me, that the Old Laird was kept in the "Furnace" prison ship and the Tower of London, where he expected the traitor's death, like Lord Lovat. [17] But oddly, he was pardoned by the Court. His advanced age was one reason given for the pardon. I'm just pleased the dear sweet old man died in his own home on Skye.

Such contrasts there are, my dear, the sweet old Laird of MacKinnon and the evil Laird of MacLeod. [12] I hear more Lairds have sold their tenants as slaves to Barbados, just as Norman MacLeod did on the Islands. [17] Our Highland culture had already begun to break down early in the 1700s when Norman MacLeod saw his people as a commodity. Some of the lairds have started calling themselves "landlords." Thank God the Laird of Glenmoriston could never be accused of the like, but how sad that the Laird of Grant sold his soul to the Devil too, along with Sir Alexander MacDonald of Skye.

I feel both relieved and devastated right now. How relieved I am to know the reason why you just didn't come home, but how devastating it is to contemplate just how long we may be separated. When the summer comes again, in the middle of May, and the wild bluebells carpet the woods and the yellow irises flower along the banks of our burn and I take my new beasts to fatten, only then will I console myself with the memory of you when you used to court me and say such sweet things. When just fourteen, you asked me to wait for you and wait for you I did and will do again and again. I will keep you in my prayers morning and night and tell the children and the grandchildren of their brave Father and grandfather, who saved a Prince with his devoted and loyal friends.

Hoping peace and strength will come to you and safety and good health my dearest Padruig Dubh.

With all my love,

Isobel of Glenmoriston

Isobel of Glenmoriston
Isobel's Story
1759, Scotland

Somewhere out at Sea
78th Fraser Regiment, Highlanders
1760

To my dearest, my precious heart, love of my life, Isobel,

I can honestly say that I had never felt fear until I was taken onboard this ship thinking you would never know where I was. Praise be to the Almighty God that somehow it was known and the word given to you where I was. I was so distressed sitting on deck, listening to the endless creaking of this huge wooden vessel, imagining that at any time it would all fall to pieces and we'd all drown and be eaten by sharks or freeze to death.

After reading your beautiful words, I felt myself back in the Braes of Glenmoriston, smelling the woods and breathing in the Highland air. Despite having to wear the 78th Fraser Highlander plaid, I will do as you have asked of me and I promise you all that I will do you proud and return to you. I understand how you feel, I too cannot bear this separation. We've been together since we were wee, admittedly I was away for military reasons but we never expected at our ages to be parted again. I am so sorry, I was looking forward to this time of my life. Please forgive me for being the cause of so much grief to you. I will do what I need to do to return to you, my love, and I am confident that Uncle Allan, Grigor, Donald, Hugh and Morag will help you, Da and Helen get through this sorrowful time. Please advise Helen and

11

Grigor to handfast until I return and I agree for my new son-in-law to move in with you in the new house.

More ships have joined this one, so it appears that I am to be involved in a major operation. The Admiralty hasn't told us anything, so I don't even know where we are headed, other than New France. I just hope the English don't use us Scots as cannon fodder again. But don't worry Isobel, I am very good at dodging cannons. Many of the Frasers want to stay in New France, if it is successful and obtain free land on offer. They all lost their homes and land in Scotland, but I sense the main reason for them leaving Scotland for good, was the tragic beheading of Lord Lovat. [17] While there is a sense of shame amongst some that he was beheaded, by far the majority are still incensed at the unfairness of it. After all, Lord Lovat only gave the Prince a glass of wine on his escape from Culloden and being so old and infirm, he was physically unable to do anything for the cause.

It has become known that Simon Fraser Master of Lovat did not arrive at Culloden field on time for the battle and instead guarded the bridge into Inverness, but the question remains — for whose side? There are a few embittered men here that he has since become the government's best soldier and is leading us here now in his own Fraser Regiment, despite what they did to his father. The government had wanted to be seen as proactive in searching for so called traitors after Culloden, given the great embarrassment of losing the Prince, but I always say that Lord Lovat was an innocent man. The Frasers do look miserable about this topic if it ever comes up, but I just say that they could think of him as a martyr to Scotland.

I do remember Ned Burke in his role in taking the Prince quickly off the field of battle and leading the way to Lord Lovat, followed by a few others as well as a young lad on foot running for his life and them galloping. Ned was the only one who knew his way through

Fraser lands to Gorthleck House, where Lord Lovat was. Apparently, the Master of Lovat, Simon, had already seen Lord Lovat there who had sent word to abandon the battle [17] and take to the mountains to restrengthen and gather numbers once the "Black Prince" had left Scotland and gone back to Flanders. This message was either ignored or the Master in fact never intended on delivering it. We'll never know and I am not about ask him.

The Master of Lovat went to Castle Dounie to get more men and Lord Lovat sent the same message to the Prince and it was considered, but word has it that it was an Irishman close to the Prince who refused that plan as they didn't know their way around our mountains. That was probably O'Neil. Drumossie should never have happened, for it was doomed to fail. It gave that butcher every excuse to massacre everybody, including innocent men, women and children in the Highlands. Then our titles and lands were laid waste. We had too many traitors amongst us, like President Duncan Forbes, [12] who lived to regret his part, but the wicked Laird of MacLeod had no regrets.

Both Donald MacLeod, who we knew as Palinurus, God rest his soul, and Malcolm MacLeod of the Isle of Raasay, would most likely have said that it was O'Neil who influenced the Prince in that fatal  decision. Palinurus experienced O'Neil first hand in the eight-oared boat as the Captain [12] when asked by the Prince to take him from the mainland to Stornway on the Isle of Lewis with his son, a Priest, O'Sullivan and the rowers. In fact, I have a list of those men. O'Neill wasn't trusted by those two faithful MacLeods, for many reasons, one of which was because he failed to offer assistance to Donald when imprisoned in London and another, because, despite not knowing the language and being a complete stranger to the country, he gave himself false credit where it was not warranted.

Anyway, Palinurus' son, whose name is Murdoch MacLeod, being only fourteen years old at the time, had to row as hard as any other man on that boat like Rhoderick, John and Alexander MacDonald, or Lachlan MacMurnich and Rhoderick MacGaskill. Even Duncan Roy and Ned Burke were rowing that day in a violent storm.

You would not believe the ignorance on this ship about the true story of how the Prince actually escaped to France. These Highlanders actually believe that somehow, by some miracle, that Flora MacDonald, [2] single-handedly "spirited him away" without the rest of us having anything to do with it nor question why Raasay was burned to the ground as well as us in Glenmoriston laid waste. It is like they think Flora got him all the way to France on her own! One good thing I'll say about Flora though, is that she told O'Neil that he couldn't get into her boat with them and she left him on the beach just standing there with O'Sullivan.

One thing the Irish dreaded, was being left alone in Scotland and there they were, O'Neil and O'Sullivan, standing alone on that cold, dark, windy beach watching Flora's boat row away. At least O'Sullivan had the sense to row out to a French ship that appeared, to seek help in France. Redcoats advanced onto that beach and O'Neil ended up imprisoned in London with Flora anyway, along with Malcolm MacLeod of Raasay, Palinurus and a mysterious Doctor John Burton from York. [13]

My dearest love, I do not object to your great plans regarding the goats or increasing the number of our small herd of coos. I just had one question. Where will you get the coin to buy the goats? I understand you might be "given a breeding pair of Highland coos" since we saved sixty of Uncle Allan's Highland coos from the Redcoats. Please tell Uncle that I said it would be a fair price for our labour that day.

Potatoes are a bonny idea. I have talked to a few Irish here and have asked how to cook potatoes and it seems there are many ways to cook them and they are easy enough to grow. I am confident you can do this and I will return to a well-run farm in Craskie by Isobel of Glenmoriston. God bless my good and clever wife.

There is something you may not know about the old Laird of MacKinnon and Palinurus and while I have the time while waiting to arrive in New France, I want to tell you some of these stories. Yes, I did find out where we're going eventually. It will be very cold there. Anyway, on the day that Inverness fell to the Prince, the Laird of MacLeod from the Islands was with Donald MacLeod of the Isle of Skye and asked him where he was going. Donald (Palinurus) said, "to Inverness to get me horse". Old Norman MacLeod replied, "You can't go there! It is full of rebels!" Palinurus said, "No mind, I don't want to lose me horse." As soon as Norman MacLeod saw "rebels" coming toward them and heard the Prince's pipers, he turned and ran in fear, but Palinurus kept on walking till surrounded by the MacDonalds of Glencoe who were ready to arrest him. Whereby, the old Laird of MacKinnon took Palinurus' hand and said, "Never mind lads, he's wi' me. I'll be bail for him. Come on Donald." The Glencoe MacDonalds had been going to remove his broadsword from his person, but after the Laird of MacKinnon's intercession, he commented that he, "was unco unwilling to part wi', it for it was a piece of verra good stuff." After that, Palinurus fetched his horse and wandered around amiably chatting in his native tongue. [12]

As you ask my dear, I will drop in to visit the Reverend John Stewart in Inverness upon my return, but I have misgivings about visiting Reverend Robert Forbes in

Leith again. Maybe after his house was ransacked for the papers about all of us, the constabulary kept watch on who was visiting him. After all, who gets a long stream of old Jacobites visiting? Even though he hid the papers securely, somehow that mysterious Dr Burton I mentioned, obtained information about all of us that could have only come from Robert Forbes. Dr Burton published a wee book, I forget the name, which put many of us at risk. Palinurus died, [13] God rest his soul, soon after this widely distributed publication naming him.

I will miss my dear little grandchildren. Will Patrick teach his bairns how to ride a horse without him or I being there? Da is too old and I haven't seen you near a horse. In your bargaining for beasts, please look out for two smallish Highland ponies for them and ask Grigor MacGregor to teach them, especially my grandson, all about horses. Grigor is a wonderful horseman. I am very disappointed in my sons and hope it doesn't remain permanent. I know how much you love your sons, especially Alex. You are the only person Alex felt happy with, so I am surprised he has left you. I hope you are still teaching our grandchildren their numbers as you taught Patrick, Helen and Alexander and please never let them forget our Gaelic. I suppose they'll have to learn English now too.

The best poetry in Erse is written by Captain Alexander MacDonald of Glenalladale of Skye, who brought the Prince to our cave. If you wanted his wonderful poetry in the Old Language, you could write to him. I dinna want our grandchildren to grow up ignorant of our culture, illiterate or lacking in skill and knowledge, but you're the best Mither, grandmother and teacher. Please tell Da also that it is even more important now that he has to pass on all his knowledge of the history of Clan Grant to the grandchildren while I am gone.

I did hear a rumour that the Prince turned Protestant, but I don't believe it. Maybe losing his sweetheart in the

French Court turned him against the religion too? The Pope will be none too pleased if this is true. The Prince was such a religious man. Every morning he went outside to pray, so I simply cannot imagine his change of religion. Us Glenmoriston men even asked him at the time whether he should consider changing from being Papist in order to improve his chances at becoming King and his response was to ask, 'would this protect him from being exiled to a foreign land?' He knew the answer and so did we. This is why I don't believe it.

Please let me know if you hear anything about what transpired between Ewen MacPherson of Cluny and the Prince because Cluny was given the value in gold of his Clan MacPherson lands by the Prince upfront and told no one where he hid it in '45. He didn't spend it on the tenants was the observation, unlike the Camerons of Lochiel. Being the chief of the whole of Clan Chattan would have had its complications especially with the MacKintosh's. The Prince's apparent dislike of Cluny, however, was likely born from his former association with John Campbell, Lord Louden. You are right, it feels ominous and I don't envy poor Cluny. My opinion on it, knowing the Prince could get no money from the King of France, is that he might press Cluny on this topic. It has always been a mystery to me also, what happened to Lochiel's clan land money, because he too was paid through the young Lochiel and to my knowledge, when he died in France, he was penniless. Nobody could find any coin there in Badenoch and his brother Dr Archibald Cameron, even stated upon his execution day in 1753,[14] that he had no money to leave his son. That having been said, the Camerons of Lochiel were well cared for, that I could see, after their shocking losses at not only Culloden, but every other battle in the previous year such as Prestonpans and Falkirk, the difference being that after those battles their homes and crops weren't burnt down. Maybe some of these Frasers here might know, because Cluny was a relative of theirs through marriage as he was Lord Lovat's son-in-law [17]

After arriving back at the cave, I gave Grigor, Alexander and the other men their share of the twenty four guineas (14) payment we got from Cluny. We all then talked about the entire episode from the night when Glen brought the Prince there to when he insisted on going to Badenoch. Despite the time spent with us being memorable, we questioned why he had wanted to go back to where he knew where the money was and we concluded that he was expecting to get that money back. Obviously, Cluny didn't give him any of it back in '46, nor did he reveal where it was hidden. Rightfully so, given that it was compensation for a potentially failed campaign, and the campaign did fail. It would've been uncomfortable for those two men to be staying together in "the cage". We also found out later that he had used his Mithers crown jewels to secure a loan in order to fit out the ship that was turned around and sent back to France. That ship, the Elisabeth, had the weapons on board that were intended for the rising. Grigor concluded that the Prince was in debt and needed to repay the loan and his Father would have been furious and also would be insisting on getting both Cluny and Lochiel's money back.

Soon I must do some work here on this wretched ship my dearest heart and leave my paper with great regret. They expect us to clean the deck of this floating tinder-box. I really hope the French don't have fiery weapons. I can't swim and the very idea of falling into that freezing Atlantic Ocean does not appeal. I pray that your spirits will be lifted after receiving my letter and that your happiness returns once again because you have a mighty burden on your shoulders now and the grandchildren depend on you, as do Helen and Grigor and your father. I've always known you to be the strongest of women. That's why Grigor thinks you are Pecht. Just putting up with me is proof enough of your strength and patience. May the Almighty God give you abundant rewards for all of your good deeds, my precious wife.

Holding you in my heart as a flame, never to be extinguished,

from your loving husband,

Padruig Dubh.

Isobel of Glenmoriston
Isobel's Story
1759, Scotland

Craskie Farm

Glenmoriston

Scotland, 1760

To my dearest Padruig,

Oh, the excitement to be given your letter into my hands. I was shaking all over and began to cry, knowing you were alive and writing back to us all here in Craskie.

In the letter you sound so strong and if you are swapping potato recipes with the Irish contingent, you must all be missing home. Please forward their recipes in your future letters, because I am sure their Mithers would have better recipes than I for cooking potatoes. I am so happy you love our

farming plans, even though you are not here, but I like to talk to you out loud sometimes as if you were still here and I tell the goats all about you. Helen sketched this lovely picture for you. They are such lovely goats and we have milk every day from them and as Da said, we'll have enough goat's hair for the pillows and mattresses in no time. So far, we have one big mattress for Da because he is feeling pain in all of his joints.

You'll be wanting an update on the house building progress. Praise the Almighty God, the roof is finally finished and so are the extra stone rooms as well as their fire places. They are beautifully built. After all these years of living in the shieling, I feel quite spoilt. We also have an abundant supply of peat to keep the house warm and there is always a pot boiling or a stew cooking thanks to a hart recently given to us by your friends. The front and rear wooden additions being built by Donald and Hugh Chisholm are looking bonny. The front is finished and Grigor Mohr's front door has been installed, but the rear will take at least another month as we get all the bits and pieces needed. Da bought the two extra windows just in time because it is raining heavily and Patrick, Henrietta and the bairns are visiting here now, so they are in the new rooms and using the new fireplaces. Patrick has been a great help. It was so wonderful seeing them all arrive. How I've missed them so. They have asked me if they could leave the bairns here when they return to his father-in-law's farm and they hope to go equally between the two homes. Naturally, I said aye.

Hugh Chisholm, God bless him, has also built the potato storage shed and the potatoes are planted all in rows. They look so neat and tidy. The soil is perfect for potatoes, according to Hugh and they are sprouting already. The corn was all harvested and we spent days both cooking and grinding it. There were so many bannocks and all our friends came over. Uncle Allan slaughtered a coo and we all cooked it along with venison and one of our geese.

Both Helen and Grigor Og looked very shy, but decided to hand fast for twelve months in front of witnesses. They knew their Fathers would take them to a Priest as soon as you were both available. Morag and Grigor Mohr were both very proud of them and their decision. They've occupied the room next to ours for now, but when the rear of the house is complete, they will get the entire bottom floor.

Everyone at our gathering read your letter and laughed about you wearing the 78th Fraser plaid. You would have loved the atmosphere here, even Alex and his wife, Therese, came over with all their bairns. They've grown so much, but didn't sleep the night. This occasion has to have been the happiest that I've seen everybody in years. There was even music, Gaelic singing and Da played his fiddle with a smile on his face and Donald Chisholm surprised everyone by playing his flute. We all miss you terribly, but you would be pleased to know that Patrick and Alex both admired our new home and I hope you will like the new additions too. Everyone has worked so hard here on this our future home and I know they are doing it for you.

While Grigor Mohr was here, I nervously asked him about the riding lessons for Beth and James, who will remain living here and he has offered to take over that role for you until you return, provided the bairns follow his instructions. I sensed a sternness in him and I hoped they were going to be obedient. I certainly was. He knows where he can get the wee Highland ponies, but is currently building a yard and a stable for them first in case a Campbell comes and tries to steal them, he explained. Grigor Og is going to help him build all of that and will work with his Father in purchasing the ponies with my coin. God bless them both.

Uncle Allan MacDonald smiled broadly at the mention of the coos and he is happy to give us a "breeding pair", but he wants to build an enclosure first for them for when it is snowing. So, that is going to happen. Of course, this began a whole jovial conversation  again around the fire about the seven of you terrorizing the Redcoats.

In the meantime, we have enough food. Guess what we have now? Fluffy, small, short legged chickens who lay smallish eggs. They're called Scots Dumpies. They were a present from Morag, who said they would bring a rooster next time so that we can breed up the numbers. The bairns slept with the chickens in the house, much to Da's disgust, but it is too cold outside for the wee creatures and we don't yet have a dedicated chicken coop and the geese won't let them sleep with them.

The chickens have, however, triggered some old memories. I've been avoiding the task of feeding chickens and when I was given our cute Scots Dumpies, I gave the job of feeding and caring for them to Helen. I knew if I picked up the chicken feed, I'd transport myself back in time to the day when I was feeding the chickens in June '46 and there are some details of that day that I've never told you, my dearest. With you having been snatched away from me now, I regret not having told you more, so I will do my best in this letter.

At first on that fateful June day, I heard an horrific spine-chilling scream echoing through the braes and the sounds of heavy hooves of many horses coming our way. I'd heard from a panicked neighbour earlier to be ready in case the dragoons came to our part of Glenmoriston because our Laird's house had been burnt down in the early morning with his wife helplessly watching on. The Laird of MacLeod and Sir Alexander MacDonald had slept overnight there [12] but at dawn, despite the pleadings of our Laird, the beautiful home and all its outbuildings were burnt to the ground. All on the orders of the Duke of Cumberland. John Campbell Lord Louden was there too, but it was the two lairds who enjoyed the total destruction of our Laird's home. All of his crofters were burnt out as well.

In preparedness, I'd put blankets, a chamber pot and some food, including cheese, bread, parritch and cold meat, in the old shieling that no one used anymore, deep in the heart of the forest away from our home and the outbuildings and hoped we could hide there if they came to my door, which they did. The smell of acrid smoke had started to fill the air, I dropped the chicken feed and grabbed young Helen in my arms and told Patrick to grab Alex our youngest and run like the wind to the shieling that Helen used to call the fairy house. Ma and Da were close behind, but I didn't turn to see how far behind they were. Inside the shieling, I covered the bairns' mouths and told them to make no sound at all. A while later, Da staggered in breathless and dazed, but without Mither. We didn't speak, but I knew Mither was dead. We just listened to the joyful whoops of the dragoons burning down everything and killing our livestock, except the coos and Da's prized Clydesdales. I heard the leader telling them to round up our forty head of frightened coos, the eight Clydesdales and Da's carriage and steal them away. Everything else, including our chickens, were slaughtered or thrown onto the fires, including my cat. The dragoons chased our tenants up and down and we heard the horrified screams of a ravished woman tenant of ours and tears rolled down my face uncontrollably, but silent. Poor Alex was holding his wee hands over his ears.

After you had fought at the Battle of Culloden, I knew you were safe in a cave with your friends, some of them our neighbours, thank God.

A woman's screams came again from another direction. It was Grigor MacGregor's wife, Morag, I knew her voice.

That day we lost Mither and three of our women were raped, including Grigor's wife, along with Alexander MacDonald's wife, Isabel MacDonald and Flora MacDonald, wife of John MacDonald.[14] Grigor doesn't know — Morag has never told him to my knowledge. All of our crops were destroyed, as you know and I looked helplessly around inside the shieling at the one kettle and saucepan and the little food I had put in there earlier. I thanked God that there was peat aplenty to light a fire once the dragoons were all gone. There was an eerie silence at their noisy departure. I heard one of them say, "Where is that slimy Italian?" and I assumed by that they meant Prince Charles Edward Stuart. The response was, "At least we've got that old Lord Lovat". My heart sank knowing Lord Lovat had been captured. Please forgive me for not imparting more of the details while we were still together, but it was just too hard losing Mither and the Clydesdales and so very difficult to talk about. One day I'll be able to tell you more about Mither.

Da just interrupted my letter writing to you my love and spoke to me about a field that's fertile enough to grow oats too if I could arrange to grow it there in order to have homemade parritch, so coming out of my old memories, I just thank God the dragoons didn't get their hands on our precious Helen all those years ago. The oat field will only be possible if I can acquire the seed, source an unbroken plough and an ox. Maybe Grigor Mohr could fix one? There are plenty of broken ones, but no oxen. I'll pray for an ox too. That particular field is covered in bracken and stones, so the four of us will have to clear the field for planting.

I know you used to have a big stable for all our horses before the English burned it all down. Do you want me to make any preparations to rebuild that in the way of gathering building materials? I also haven't wanted to grow barley as it will attract thieves looking to cook up whiskey. If we get another flock of anything, other than goats, a few sheep would be sensible for both the meat and the wool. I love spinning and sewing.

You asked how I would get the coin for the goats and this is my story. I'd heard talk that some wealthy women were wanting dresses identical to the one that the Prince wore when he was disguised as the maid named Betty Burke and there have been some expensive ones made and sent to Edinburgh. [11] I have the exact print, but not the same expensive fabric and I copied the pattern including the bonnet and called it "Betty's Dress". When Da was in Inverness, he took it to a shop for them to sell for us while earning a small commission and it sold that very day. It was with that coin, my dearest, that I bought the nannies. So, I made another and it sold too. And I bought the billy with enough coin left over to purchase more material each time. So, my sewing ambitions are to make Betty dresses for the big things, like maybe the two wee ponies and then material for men's shirts, so that our men can all start to look smarter with at least six shirts per man and some of them will have the Prince's style in the cuff and collar for special occasions. I'll make Da one first to see what it looks like and ask our friends what they think and make any suggested changes. It would be wonderful to get orders for the Betty dresses and the shirts. I can't afford good boots or shoes yet, but I am looking around. They are scarce and so many were taken off the deceased folk and I don't want to bring a ghost into the new house.

What are all of your ships going to do when you get to New France? Da wants to know the name of the nearest river in the Americas to where you are headed. So far, there is nothing in the local newspapers here about your ships, so it might be a secretive attack on the French. So much for the peace. France kicked out the Prince for nothing if a battle takes place between England and France. Da also wants to know what the role of the Highlanders is in this expedition. Da also said his friends told him that General Wolfe was a bit crazy because of the effects of consumption and the laudanum that he is consuming and he frequently vomits up blood. [5] Is he strong and sane enough to lead all of you?

I have a question about "spoils of war". Do those laws still apply to you in New France? Are any of you allowed to bring home "spoils of war?" If you are, I have heard that the French have some lovely silks and fabrics for their fancy clothing including buttons. If you see any, can you please bring me some fabric home, love, to make clothes to sell here if it is legal for you and if you can acquire a trunk to transport it all? I'd love one of those beautiful French gowns, but I'd have nowhere to wear it. So long as you think I am still pretty even at my age, I am happy when I close my eyes to sleep.

I have heard some news from Grigor Mohr for you concerning Ewen MacPherson of Cluny's visit to see the Prince, who was himself asking for money. Cluny's wife, and his daughter Margaret joined him in France, leaving his son Duncan in Inverness. [11] You and your men were right. Evidently, this story as Grigor said, is mixed up with Spanish gold too. Grigor Mohr believes it is at the bottom of Loch Arkaig and a lost cause. He has it on good authority from Jenny, Cluny's wife, that it was as we suspected, a very unhappy reunion with the Prince who was demanding the money back from him which was for the value of his estate. The Prince might be spending up big in Europe, how would we know? We do know that he is never coming back but I didn't know he already had a debt. That explains a lot. Although, another rumour is circulating that his father, James Francis, was trying somehow to retrieve the gold also and ultimately cost the life of Donald Cameron of Lochiel's brother, Dr. Archibald Cameron, may God rest his soul. France must be sinking in debt or James Francis is.

I was horrified to hear from Grigor Mohr that the Prince then went on and accused Cluny of embezzlement. I don't believe Cluny is an embezzler. Lord Lovat completely trusted him and so did Lochiel. Do you know what I think? Do you remember that creepy man, Robert Grant, [14] whose head you cut off and left above the road, as he had been a spy? I think that man was looking for Cluny's gold as well. I've concluded that the Prince can put a curse on a person, like King Louis of France, and he may have cursed poor Cluny, who may well be sick as we write. Do you think the Frasers there on your ship have any knowledge of the gold? After all, Lord Lovat was Cluny's father-in-law and Jenny Fraser is Cluny's wife. Surely someone there knows something? Best we keep Cluny in our prayers.

So now I know what some of what you men folk talk about. Thank goodness I can escape to my beasts and your beautiful kale field, which thank God you prepared years ago for us. Both the turnips and the kale in your fields are doing well. We eat neeps nearly every night, but Da is tired of neeps, so when the potatoes come, he might take to them.

27

It's getting harder to get him to eat his kale too. He is losing weight, as some old men do and I keep encouraging him to eat his kale. What do they feed you on the ship? I miss you hunting a beast for us, but occasionally one of your friends drops in part of a hart they've hunted, which is so kind of them. How I miss you in so many ways my precious husband.

We all pray for you every day, fearing what you might face in New France. While we all know you as a well-trained soldier when you were with Lord Lovat's company, we also dread a repeat of the horrors we have seen here in Scotland. I don't know what it is or how it is that you draw on something greater than yourself to achieve what seems to an ordinary person as impossible, but somehow possible to you. Just like you convinced the coo thieving Redcoats that the seven of you were seventy, [14] so you will again and the French will fear the bravery of our Highland men. [5] God be with you my Padruig Dubh and let them think of you as "devils not men" as the Redcoats here did. [14] If anyone can achieve whatever it is the English is planning with brilliance, it is indeed you my brave love.

Your grandchildren sing songs of the Seven Glenmoriston Men [54] and when they ask when their Grandda is coming back, I tell them that you will return when the next winter comes then passes into spring, if they have pleased their Grandda with their horsemanship, if they've pleased me in the fields with Grigor Og, helped with their Great Grandda and most importantly, if they have learned Erse poetry and song only then will you return. Aye, my love, I have written to MacDonald of Glenalladale on the Isle of Skye for the book.

I wish you good health, strength and all the happiness this world can bring you my dearest. I am forever yours and missing you so much that my heart aches.

Your beloved wife,

Isobel of Glenmoriston

Isobel of Glenmoriston
Isobel's Story
1759, Scotland

78th Fraser Highlanders
Quebec
New France, 1760

To my dearest, most faithful wife, Isobel,

Forgive me, my love, for not replying to your letter these last several months. I am well enough, God be praised, I am strong and the battle is over. Generals Wolfe and Montcalm are both dead and Quebec is now in the hands of the British. The young Simon Fraser was with us, God bless him, whose French language helped us succeed.

Once again, us Scots have found our-selves on both sides of the French and English wars and whilst the Royal Navy might have had some clever tactics, in the form 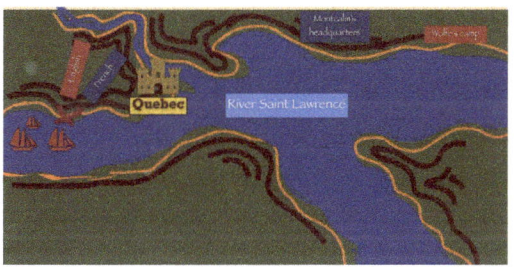 of an amazing sea navigator and cartographer by the name of 1st Lieutenant James Cook, the army had nae skill at all, just brute force. Cook used an army navigation tool, the Plain Table and Alidade triangulation method and applied it to naval charting [23] in order to carefully direct the flotilla down the narrow and precarious river system. And guess what? His father is a Scot! As Da may have predicted, us Highlanders were the only reason Wolfe's side had any chance of succeeding in this terrain.

Imagine a sheer cliff face with the Fraser Regiment climbing it in our plaids with the English regretting having looked up from below, leaving them rather red faced. We were then burdened by needing to pull them up the 150-foot cliff along with their artillery. Much to Montcalm's horror, by morning his "impénétrable" Quebec faced about 5000 British against his poorly managed 1500 French, costing them the city, the Colony and ultimately his life on the River of St Lawrence.

Seeing the Redcoats performing their "scorched earth policy" on the local population of innocent crofters was a terrible sight, bringing back so many horrific memories of the wholesale mass destruction of all things, living and non-living, in our Highlands after Culloden as perpetrated by the English and their Hanoverian masters. With Wolfe being dead and the Frasers being my main companions in this fight, I managed to distance myself from any such shameful act of wastefulness and cruelty and instead negotiated some lovely items for you, my love, from grateful locals in New France to whom we had shown mercy. Communication was a bit difficult though, as none of us spoke French and they didn't speak Gaelic.

After the battle on Abraham's Field, I had collected a few handy items to my benefit. As we are still not permitted to carry arms back home in Scotland, I had to get creative in order to get another set of weapons. After stashing my own blades, I presented to our armourer with a broken broad sword, two halves of a targe, a snapped dirk and a missing long rifle and pistol, thanks to a few unfortunate Redcoats that would not be returning to the British Isles. He questioned my legitimacy at first, once I claimed I needed a whole replacement set. My friend Colonel Robert Fraser and our junior officer Seargent John Fraser, backed up my claim, stating that as I had been up that cliff face first, I had lost both my pistol and long rifle whilst hauling up all the English. Robert added that my fierce fighting during the battle resulted in my Claymore being dashed and the targe split in half.

I was then duly reissued with new weapons, which I have attempted to draw for you my love - a dirk, a hilted broadsword, a new targe, a French pistol and a long rifle. The  British pistols were apparently susceptible to backfiring. I saw an old trunk in the room where the armourer was working and managed to negotiate a pretty price for it. The wood is old and has been long water proofed by oiling. The hinges work well and are made of brass, as are the clawed feet and once Robert laid a false bottom in there for me, I thought it would do nicely to conceal the weapons upon re-entry to the British Isles. I happily stowed my new weapons at the bottom of the trunk, intended for my new son in law, Grigor Og.

Your wish, my love, for French fabric and buttons was my command and legally negotiated and I expect you to make yourself first and foremost a gown from the purest silk I have sent you pretty wife. The other five rolls of raw lace can be used in your dress making cottage industry and the three bolts of linen can be used for your planned shirts for our Highland brothers to wear with their plaids once again, when the law no longer stands against our Highland dress. I will bring the goods along with me in the trunk when I return.

Our beautiful home in the Highlands of Scotland is truly cold and it can snow heavily and at times you think the rain will never stop, however it ultimately does and the birds sing only the tunes that greet a Highlanders' heart. However, here in New France, or maybe they'll change its name, the cold here is very different and even with its many forests, it doesn't have the same feel of our cold days and nights, nor does it have the beautiful smells wafting through the Braes.

After reading your last letter, I missed home even more imagining the whole family gathering together with our neighbours and friends for such a happy occasion for sweet Helen. Please congratulate Helen and Grigor Og and welcome him for me into our family. I am so happy that his Father is now officially part of the family, as I have always felt a strong brotherhood with Grigor Mohr.

I really miss you, my dearest wife, our children and all our grandchildren. I suppose I have another son now.

Your heart-felt story leads me to ask you, my dearest, which of course you don't have to answer. You've never told me how Mither died nor have you described the departure of the crofters. Could you bring yourself to confide these very sad memories in your next letter, if you so wish?

I am confident that our culture will never be completely destroyed despite the English efforts to do so. But I do so pity the future here for the indigenous Indian peoples. Some of them fought for the French and may have been responsible for the death of Wolfe.

The news in your letter was so comprehensive and I doubt I have the time to equal your efforts. Firstly, thank you for the wonderful job you are doing with our house design because you are the lady of the house and the lady has to be the happiest with her home. It sounds like Grigor Mohr and the Chisholms and even Patrick are doing wonderful work. My heart is with you all and I am quite excited to have the bairns living with us full time now. I think Alex could have helped out more, but his father-in-law is a grouchy one, so I guess he is just keeping the peace. Hopefully now he has seen the new home, it will encourage him and his wife to visit more often.

I met the most remarkable man a little while back. He is from a people called the Algonquian, who travel over vast tracks of this frozen land-scape to survive and thrive. He has the most remarkable skills for track-ing beasts and he has happily traded pelts and leathers with me. With my share from the Campaign, I was able to buy leather goods from him,  some of which are beautifully and skillfully deco-rated in traditional patterns of the Algonquian nation. For the grandchildren at home, I have a pair of boots each. For you I have a pair of fur-lined leather socks, as I know how cold your feet can get. For the horses, I have two small ornately decorated saddles and two more adult sized, but less embellished than the first two. I managed to get three bridle sets, all about the same dimensions. For Da, I have bought a decorated leather waist coat to keep the chill out of his chest. For Grigor Mohr, to whom I owe so much, I have a belt to accompany his plaid. For Donald and Hugh Chisholm, I also have belts, which can easily be used to hang the necessary weapons of self-defense. To Patrick and Alex, I have purchased handmade knives of the Algonquian people and for the married couple, I have purchased a Polar Bear skin for their bed. This animal had to be killed in self-defense as it attacked our friend's family while fishing out on the ice.

The animals in the drawings I have included are the purest white, except for the wolf which is grey. The

Arctic hare, the Arctic fox and the polar bear. They truly are a remarkable sight. The Frasers captured a hare for dinner one night and it must be an acquired taste.

Do you recall as bairns just how many grey wolves there used to be in the Highlands? I haven't seen many for a long time in Scotland, but here in New France, the grey wolf is prolific in numbers. They seem a little larger than ours are but I really enjoyed seeing them again in their family packs. It brought to mind a poem we all learned as bairns.

"On Ederachillis' shore,

The grey wolf lies in wait-

Woe to the broken door,

Woe to the loosened gate,

And the groping wretch whom sleety fogs

On the trackless moor belate,

The lean and hungry wolf,

With his fangs so sharp and white,

His starveling body pinched

By the frost of a northern night,

And his pitiless eyes that scare the dark

With their green and threatening light

He climbeth the guarding gate,

He leapeth the hurdle bars,

He steals the sheep from the pen,

And the fish from the boat-house spars,

And he digs the dead from out of the sod,

And gnaws them under the stars

Thus, every grave we dug

The hungry wolf uptore,

And every morn the sod

Was strewn with bones and gore

Our Mother-Earth had denied us rest

On Ederchaillis' shore." [37]

One of the French crofters gave me a bag of oat seeds as we were just about to depart. I just hope they remain in good condition until I return to Scotland. Hundreds of the men from the Fraser Regiment have decided to remain here in New France and settle on land offered to them by the English. Those of us returning home may be iced in here if we don't sail as soon as possible. Apparently, the ice is bad and we'll have that problem, but we also might encounter French troops down river in wait for us. Please pray for me my darling, that we overcome both the ice and the French. So, I bid you farewell for now my love, until I have you once again in my arms.

Yours forever, from your devoted husband,

Padruig

Isobel of Glenmoriston
Isobel's Story
1759, Scotland

Craskie Farm
Glenmoriston
Scotland, 1761

To my darling, the bravest of men, Padruig Dubh,

My husband, I have received your most recent letter telling of the shocking battle in New France. Praise be to God that you survived this and we all pray that you make it safely down river and navigate the ice successfully to make it home to us. I don't know if you'll get this letter, but I thought you'd be home by now. We all wait anxiously each day my dearest love. Even the bairns ask every morning if Grandda is coming home today.

Your friends have all been informed of your success and your narrative of climbing the cliff like a mountain goat at your age has everyone talking. I don't mean you're old, but you are not the young man who fought in the Battle of Culloden anymore. Oddly, there are mixed feelings about the French losing their colony. But is it possible the English have more to lose with their colonies further south in Virginia and the Carolinas? The French will have a cunning plan to retaliate, you can be sure, unless they run out of money. What do you think? Da is familiar with that river on the map that you have mentioned and is most surprised at the success of that sickly Wolfe. Da has the world map out every day now, trying to anticipate the ice the ships may encounter. He misses you so much, but when he talks to his friends about you, it is like he is speaking of "Fingal" himself!

Delays are a fact of life in such a precarious place, but I am so glad that we don't live there. Just the same, we wish those Frasers in the regiment who chose to stay well, but I do not envy their choice in such a place as you have described with bears and so many wolves. Of course, I remember the poem of that scary wolf and Da recites it perfectly in Erse. He did something in answer to your poem that might surprise you and it is published already in the local newspaper.

The Red Wolfe is Dead

"No more do we see the grey wolf
On Glenmoriston Braes
It is said they are all dead,
But the wolves in colours red
Were here in numbers abound
The red wolf dug up our dead
Frost or rain, they stripped them all
Their bodies lay frozen, no rest for them
And us to mourn
The red wolf stole our sheep
And our fish and cattle and goats too
No gate or door could stop
The red wolf but death
In a frozen land
Called "Abraham's field."
The red Wolfe is dead.
Some peace is afforded us as we lay
Them all to rest again"

-Anonymous

Isn't is beautiful, but so sad? Did you know Da was a poet? And it is his way of saying that General Wolfe is dead, as well as referencing what the Hanoverians did here to our dead after Culloden. [13] God bless Da and his beautiful heart.

Oh, please come back soon my love.

You have asked me a question regarding Mither to which I will answer as best I can, as I knew the day would come when I would have to be strong enough to impart the horror of it. We had already buried the dead the day after the burnings, although afraid to go outside incase there'd be Redcoats in waiting. I knew they'd been searching for Grants as well as the Prince, so I was worried about you my beloved and hoped that nothing could entice you out of hiding. I told myself that I could cope with the departure of our crofters and our lost income, but I couldn't cope, my love if you had been captured.

As Mither was buried, I buried a part of my heart. Da and her were running behind us with Da's arm outstretched to his beloved wife of so many years, when the first dragoon flew into our property wielding a very sharp broadsword from on horseback and cut off Mither's arm. Da said that at first, he didn't know what to do as he held Ma's severed arm, but then he saw that the sword was coming again for his neck and he ducked instinctively. At that very instant, Mither had run to be by his side with blood gushing from her severed arm and the sword struck her neck. The force of the blow nearly injured the horse as well. Da said her head fell instantly to the ground, but her body seemed to go down in slow motion with her skirts billowing out. Her feet were crossed somehow underneath her body, so that her torso just sat upright. The dragoon then angrily kicked her to the ground and galloped off to burn down our home. Da put Ma's arm beside her body, said a prayer and silently snuck into the tree line, but too afraid to come directly to us immediately in the shieling at first, in case he had been seen. From behind trees and bushes, he could still see Mither, but he knew she would want him to help us and so stealthily he went through the forest and eventually came to us hiding inside the shieling.

The horror of what had happened couldn't be expressed until the moment we put her in the ground and we wept like many others too who were burying their dead. A total of five died on our property that day.

As our surviving crofters all left after the burning, some began to wail as if in a funeral procession. We gave them our only surviving cart, as some were old. There were men, women and children clutching to what remained of their meagre possessions, found amidst the ashes. The children's faces were wide eyed with both confusion and grief. Only one child turned to wave to Patrick, Helen and wee Alex. As another wail could be heard, I knew I would never see them again. They had all collected a handful of sand[v] each, with which to be buried in the land of their destination by the coast. Told to farm kelp, the husbands had made the decision to go where there was work. The sounds of the wailing echoed all the way up to the top of our mountains, where Uncle Allan and his wife watched on as the procession left us. Bairns that I'd delivered were gone, dear friends whose voices would never be heard here again and their menfolk, left me feeling the absence of you my love. My bairns and I were alone on what was left of the farm, with only a shieling in which to live, accompanied by my grieving father.

On that day I had said, "Well, Patrick lad. I hope your Da taught you how to catch rabbits, red squirrels and pheasants. You'll have to teach Helen how to skin and gut them. Da can tan the hides to eventually cover the sandy floor in the shieling and there are wild berries and wild plums that are a bit tart, but edible." Fortunately, Patrick had his pocket knife and Da had a nastier sharp skein dubh. And so, my dear, it began.

When the bairns and I surveyed the landscape of our land where once their homes stood, we saw only six dark black burned patches where their crofts once were. We didn't go near them until after they had left, but after they'd gone, we then looked through the ashes. It was hard to imagine that in some of those crofts had lived four adults and three or more children. All that remained was the circle of stones in the middle where they'd done all their cooking. There was an odd smell coming from those old stones and I'd recognised it as burnt milk. Milk had been used to put out their cooking fire by the dragoons. One pale of precious goats' milk to these families was a huge loss, not to mention the goat and the chickens, who were burned as well.

Patrick walked through the ashes with a stick poking at it as if he would find something but nothing was left of three generations of crofters. I asked both him and Alex if they could find a rake, shovel and maybe a wee cart so we could start the clean up. Patrick came back very happily with both rake and shovel as well as a broken cart. So, we started from the first to the last of the crofts saving all the ashes and putting it on a pile near where I had chosen our new home would be. I wanted the new home further away from the Drover's Road and not to be built on top of our old one. Wee Alex asked me why we were saving all of the ashes and I told him that when his Father returned home, he would need it for the new privies or if not, I would use it in my new herb garden or Helen could use it for making soap. Helen was impatient to search through the ashes of our home. I asked her to wait until we had cleaned up all of the crofter's areas first. Alex did a good job of raking it all and then suddenly we had an almighty downpour and we all ran back to our shieling. Later that day, when we came out once the rain had stopped, we saw that the rain had washed the last of the ashes away, as well as that awful smell and it was like no-one had ever lived there. The rain had also washed the soot from our two remaining chimneys in our burned-out house and I'd wanted to preserve all of the good stone for our new house.

Patrick's job everyday was trapping our food and Da skinned and cleaned the rabbit or red squirrels that he'd trapped and both Helen and I cooked it without much seasoning, other than what we could find in the forest or by the burn. There was a nice mushroom that we found a lot of, that we added and some plants from the burn, as well as vegetables that had started to grow, like onions that we added to the squirrel and rabbit stew, but without salt.

I had almost finished cleaning up our old house site when Uncle Allan visited to ask how we all were. I told him about Mither and he wanted more details, which I didn't have at that stage. Da was still unable to tell me what had happened. When he saw Uncle Allan, he looked a little relieved and they greeted each other warmly. "I am sorry about Freya," said Uncle Allan. I had some clean stones from the fire place and offered them as something to sit on, as I did also. We told Uncle Allan everything that had happened and what had been stolen. He had taken his coos high up into the mountain, to stay in the winter shieling with Aunty Margaret. They couldn't be seen from there and they didn't lose any coos. He offered to slaughter a coo for dinner that night, up at his house. We all bathed that day in the cold burn and dinner that night was truly wonderful. We were all so hungry, despite Patrick's efforts. Margaret gave me some salt, vegetable seeds to plant as well as some vegetables that she could spare. Their house was not burned down, luckily, but they didn't know why. I only had the one long dress and a blouse and an arisaid, so she also gave me five plaids, two dresses, two blouses, some soap and candles and flint. She also

43

gave Helen two blouses and a dress and Uncle Allan gave Da a pair of breeks and a warm coat and a coo hide to cover the shieling floor. Giving us some of the meat and a pale of milk, we were very grateful and went back home to our wee shieling and lit the fire to try and warm it up. I asked wee Alex if he could take everything out of the shieling the following morning and rake the floor and put down the coo hide that Uncle Allan had given us and then put it all back. I gave us all a plaid each from Aunty Margaret to wrap ourselves in to sleep better that night. As I was falling asleep, I wondered where you were, if you were safe, if you had food and then I left it with God for another day.

The following day I asked wee Alex, after he'd finished his chores, if he could get all of the horse or goat manure that he could find on the property so that we could plant our seeds and off he ran. Helen came to me and said, "Ma, where's Da? When's he coming back?" I explained that you had to hide from the Redcoats because of Culloden and you weren't sure when it was safe to come back." Patrick was listening after returning from his trapping with two rabbits and said that it wasn't safe for us either, "But we're not hiding in a cave. We're trying to fix the farm, aren't we Ma?" he said. "Your Da is important to them to catch" and I explained that they wanted to hang you, "so for now it is just us," I said.

My darling, I hope this explains more of the early story before you returned home to us and what it was like for the bairns. I hope this answers your question, sad though it is, it is the reality of the Glen. It is not stopping. More and more people leave every day.

You'll be pleased that we received the lovely Erse poetry book from your friend Alexander MacDonald of Glenalladale in Moydart. Please be prepared for some bad news concerning Glen though, because he does not keep good health and may leave this life soon. I am sorry you may not have time to see him once more and swap your adventurous stories of saving the Prince. Wasn't it Donald Cameron of Glenpean who led Glenalladale to your cave and was very keen to hand over the Prince to you and get back to his wife in case his house was to be pillaged and burned that night? The poor man didn't make it in time and all was lost. Just the same, at first, Glen was wary of the infamous Seven Glenmoriston Men and went to your cave in the early hours of the morning when only three of your number were there. [14] When he took the Prince there, you said he was keen to leave without the rest of you, being out foraging as you were, so it was fortuitous of you and your devoted friends to have had the pledge of allegiance, one to another, or you may have returned to an empty cave. God forbid. Instead, you increased your number with Glenalladale, his men and the Prince who wanted to be guided to Donald Cameron of Lochiel in Badenoch. I am still in wonder at the achievement of your success in keeping every one alive and well, my love.

My heart leapt, when I read in your letter, that you actually did get the French fabric. Thank you, my darling love. The bairns can't wait to receive their boots. They have grown a lot, so I hope they fit. Da is thrilled with the fancy vest you have bought him, but as usual he is cautious as always and he says, "Only if he gets here safe and sound with that heavy trunk." He can't believe you bought saddles. I am so proud of you not harming the poor crofters. In our own experience here, it takes forever to rebuild from nothing and start all over again with the house, the crops and the various livestock.

Incidentally my love, Uncle Allan finished building the enclosure for the coos that he promised and then brought over the breeding pair. A beautiful bull and coo. I had insisted that I didn't want black, brindle or yellow, as you know I prefer the orange colour. On the first night in their new home, they were very busy with each other and I think we'll have a fluffy calf not too far along as the bull is very energetic. I am quite happy with our wee herd now. I know you don't usually put cow bells around their necks in the daytime, but I have, so that I know where they are at all times. I don't want them getting into the kale. Do you think we'll have to put up palisades, stone walls or hedges so that their wandering is controlled? Helen has taken to them and leads them around on a rope and tells them where they can't go, especially my new herb garden. Thank you for the seed, by the way and I really hope the sea air doesn't spoil them.

The farm is going well, in fact better than I had expected. I have two more nannies, paid for by myself. Uncle Allan has also built the goats a secure place at night. He is one of those who still believes wolves might come and take a goat. They are breeding, giving us milk and cheese and we have all the goat's hair we need now for mattresses and pillows. I think the goats are very fond of me, as they call out to me each morning when I go to feed them and let them out into an external enclosure. I only just learned how to make goat's cheese and it is quite a process with Helen's help. Now with Helen and Grigor Og here, we have the tasks for all of us divided up evenly with Grigor Og dealing with the heavier jobs. He insisted on clearing that oat field of stones alone and is working with his Da to fix the plough to start ploughing it by hand until we get an ox. He wants to seed it first, so that the soil is fertile enough to grow oat crops.

You'll love our herd of coos. They haven't done anything like I feared. Maybe they don't like kale. The bull doesn't like his bell, so I took it off him in case he became grumpy. The hardest part is to choose an animal for slaughter and I always took it for granted when you did this or carved it up and skinned the hide so skillfully. I am sorry for the things I took for granted and I never will again. Today I am choosing a goat for slaughter and I am afraid that I will cry. But Grigor Og will help with the slaughtering and all the rest. Da said he would help too, as he is a very skilled tanner. Hugh said he'd be able to do a better job next time. We will be able to eat well tonight and store some and dry some. A calf is due in a few days, so our livestock numbers will continue to grow.

We learned some bad news yesterday I am afraid. After receiving that lovely poetry book from Glenalladale, we were then informed of his passing, may God rest his soul. This was printed in the local paper.

January 30th, 1761, died in the 49th year of his age, Alexander MacDonald of Glenalladale, in Moydart, a man well known for being proof of the gilded dust when no despicable quantity thereof, and his own personal safety, with that of his helpless family, the weeping mother and the hungry babes, stripped of everything, tempted his acceptance. Firm to his word and steady to every trust, his soul was impregnable as a rock amidst all the storms and tempests this fluctuating state of things could dash against him. [14]

Let all the world say what they can,
Glen liv'd and died the honest man.

Donald and Hugh Chisholm told me that Glen saved the Prince from a great fall off a cliff.[14] I understand now why he sought you out. It must have been nerve racking trekking over our treacherous mountainous and almost impassable terrain.

I felt shy when you said to make myself the first dress with the French silk. I felt shy when I first saw you at the age of six and again when you were courting me. When I married you here in Craskie, the place of my birth, I never wanted to leave Craskie and I still don't. I have always wanted to grow old with you here and all that entails, until we both die. I just pray that miraculously we can die together and stay together in the Afterlife, for there was no one else but you in my heart as a young lass and that will never change, whilst I draw breath. I will make you a beautiful shirt and we can have a lovely wedding for Helen and Grigor Og in the Kirk. I will also be able to make Helen the most beautiful wedding dress now with that French lace. I wish you were able to wear your plaid to the wedding, but the law is unlikely to change any time soon, but you could still wear those beautiful belts that you have described.

How fascinating to meet Indians and see how they live? You must have so many fire-side stories to tell us all when you eventually get back home. I can't help but feel angry sometimes that my husband was ripped away from me. Forgive me my selfishness. I never want you to go to Leith again after you've returned home. I suppose you will have to hire a pony and cart to bring the heavy trunk straight to Glenmoriston. You can visit other people later. I need you so much, not because we all work so hard, but just because you are my soul, my heart, my everything.

We heard a dreadful banging on the door last night and a howling in the woods. Da was sure that it was a wolf after all the talk of wolves lately, so he left the house and went straight out into the freezing cold night to check on all the animals and the chickens and the geese and ensure they were all safe and secure, all without a thought to his own wellbeing. The fire had already been smoored, so I got it going again in wait for him. When he came back, he was so pale and freezing cold to the touch. I led him to the fire and rubbed his legs and arms, but he didn't respond or speak, so I called Helen to help me warm him up. We both rubbed his feet and hands to restore his core body temperature and Grigor Og

suggested we put a mattress by the fire, with a grate of course. All the while, I was praying for his health. I made him a hot boiled bone broth and his colour slowly returned.

"What was it out there Da?" I said. He responded, "Nuckleevee." I had to tell him that the Nuckleevee folktale was from the Orkney Islands and it was an ocean spirit, so it couldn't possibly be that, but he said it again. "Nuckleevee..." he repeated. It was creepy and I still don't believe it, but maybe Da is getting sick or just old. I really hope not. He has been teaching Beth and James about the history of the clans, especially Clan Grant, but then I noticed he was rambling a bit about Scottish folklore. Most of it was harmless, but I draw the line with Kelpies, Silkies and Nuckleevees. I don't want Beth and James to tell Henrietta, their Mither, that Da is scaring them with tales of the sidh. We grew up listening to all of Mither's and Da's superstitions that might be true, but the Nuckleevee?

My main concern now is Da's health. We are all fussing over him a bit and giving him soups, hot drinks and so far, his chest sounds well. Please keep Da in your prayers. Sometimes he just goes and sits by Mither's grave and puts a small cairn atop it and talks to her in the Gaelic, just the way I talk to you I suppose. Grigor Og is very grounded and is just concerned as to who was banging on the door.

Grigor Mohr and Morag are staying to dine with us tonight because Grigor Og wants to tell his Father about the incident last night, just to get his opinion. As we were drinking our hot tea, Grigor Mohr's face grew thoughtful at the story and his wife and son sat silently and waited for his opinion. Helen and I watched on at the family dynamics. Both of them were wide eyed when he said, "I agree. It's not the Nuckleevee, who are an ocean spirit and don't live around here.

My opinion is between two possibilities." Grigor Mohr named the "Baobhan Sith" [26] which is a vampire like beauty of the Highlands, which can "shape shift" into a wolf. That would account for the door knocking and the howling. They are also attracted to fresh blood and we had just slaughtered a goat, leaving the scent of blood in the air. He then turned to his son and asked him if he had cleaned up thoroughly after the slaughter or not. Grigor Og cast his eyes down and replied, "Not as well as I should have Da, I am sorry." Then Grigor Mohr, realising he had an audience, said, "Or it could have been Cu-Sith, [27] the faerie dog of Scotland". He then turned to Da, who was listening intently and asked two questions. "Da, did you see what kind of feet it had and what colour its eyes were if you were close enough?"

I shuddered to think that Da could have been near a vampire-like woman or a green wolf. The attention was on Da then, who casually replied, "It were noth'n bar the mist play'n tricks wi' mi eyes." Becoming uncooperative, we still don't know. We offered a room to both Grigor Mohr and Morag, so they wouldn't walk home through the woods in the misty cold darkness, to possibly meet one of these scary Scottish mythical creatures. I was glad they accepted for our sakes as well as theirs and thankfully it became a quiet and uneventful night. With no explanation of the knocking. Whatever it was, I felt it wasn't coming back, not to say it hadn't left an uneasiness.

We have the two new beautiful sturdy wee Highland Ponies now and Grigor Mohr is teaching both of the bairns how to ride and how to care for them, including brushing them down. Like you said, he is a true horseman and has given them both a drawing each of the horse with all of the names of the horse's body parts. He said they must learn their names and one day he will test their knowledge. He explained all about the horses' hooves and how to keep them free of small stones. At present we are borrowing his saddles and I told him that you have bought two saddles, so hopefully he won't have to lend them for too long. I'm listening in to the lessons and enjoying it.

As my letter comes to a close, it pains me to break away from you, my precious darling love. I am holding you forever in my heart and wishing you a safe passage back to Scotland. I must leave you here my love, with everyone sending you their best wishes, including Grigor

Mohr, Morag, Helen and your son-in-law Grigor Og as well as Hugh and Donald.

From your beloved wife, wishing you good health, safety and happiness in this life, affectionately yours,

Isobel of Glenmoriston

Isobel of Glenmoriston
Isobel's Story
1759, Scotland

Province of New York
Royal British Colony
New York Naval Base, 1761

To my dearest wife, Isobel,

I am writing to you from a British naval base in the Province of New York. We were forced to detour here due to a frightful weather incident in the North Atlantic and I hold out no hope for that wretched ship that we were on, but be assured that I am safe and well.

Don't let your heart grieve my love, I have arranged passage on a 40-gunner that has a scheduled crossing to Plymouth in the South of England, early next month. As my reluctant passage from Scotland took nearly seven weeks to arrive here on this continent, I am expecting at least a two-month miserable return journey at this time of year. I have been warned of illness on board ships for journeys of this duration. I am so sorry that I have been away for this long and praise God that my captors are not forcing me into another campaign in this place, as I can feel the seeds of discontent are well and truly sown here and I am eager to be removed from any further conflict as soon as possible.

Da's Red Wolfe poem is so vivid an image in my mind, especially as I hear the wolves howling now as I write this letter. The wolf numbers certainly haven't diminished here and each night there is an opportunistic attack on a naive Redcoat who wanders too far from his tent. No worries for me though, as I keep my dirk, my skein dubh and my claymore on hand always and I haven't actually seen the wolves actively hunting, but in the daylight, there is ample evidence. It is obvious, however, that they have a taste for human flesh, so the aftermath of any battle here would be quite gruesome. The wolves are helping the Americans by killing a few Redcoats and it makes me wonder if we made Scotland too comfortable for the English, by having completely wiped out our wildlife population, so that they could march straight in without any threats at all, other than from us. If James IV hadn't decimated our forests, we would at least have maintained their habitats and it was compulsory three times a year to go on a wolf hunt. There are many claims in Scotland as to who killed the last wolf one being a relative, Ewen Dubh of the Camerons. My Mither said I have his black hair.

I am really sorry to hear that Glenalladale passed. He was a brilliant scholar and unrecognised in his time. I will never forget those weeks he spent with us and the Prince, as he was so good at interpreting between our languages. The Prince had apparently been taught Gaelic before, but he really didn't understand a word of our Erse, so Glen made sure we all understood every-thing each other was saying. Do you remember me telling you that the Prince even cured us of our habit-ual cursing? [14] He was inspirational and I am happy to maintain his higher standards even though I am not likely to ever see his majestic self again. May God grant him a long life, Amen. Oh, how at one stage I was so willing to follow him to the continent. Forgive me my darling Isobel, for that weakness in myself. I've never asked you if you had forgiven me for wanting to follow him. With the Prince's attempt at getting renewed French support for our cause having failed miserably though, I knew we were on our own more than ever. This broke so many of our hearts, including Lochiel's and I think that's what caused his fatal apoplexy. No one could have expected the Black Prince to change the rules of war and declare "no quarter" against all of us. If we knew this beforehand, a good many of us would have deserted Culloden field.

When I was in Leith last, Bishop Forbes read to me an excerpt from one of his papers and said that "without exaggerating, I do not think there were ever greater, inhumane barbarities and cruelties of all kinds perpetrated in any country, either Christian or Infidel." [12] Only the strongest amongst us can survive such a determined enemy. You and I, Isobel, are among the strong ones and we will survive.

There has never been anyone in my heart but you from the moment we met, my love, and following you up the mountain that day with your coos, I felt nervousness for the first and only time in my life, but I knew that you were my woman and I was your man and that you'd definitely wait for me. You were so sweet when you shyly said aye. I'll never forget it. I knew you were the one for my whole life. So, I too pray that we live and die together, many years from now. Your lovely plans for our lass Helen and Grigor's wedding clothes sound perfect. What a wonderful Mither you are. I can only hope that they will be as happily married as we have been. As for wearing my plaid again, I will keep my tartan colours close to my heart until a time comes when I will not be transported to the colonies for wearing my own cultural dress. I don't take kindly to being told what to do.

Your Da is right being concerned about icebergs in the North Atlantic. We set sail from Quebec after getting free of the River St Lawrence and the dispossessed French, who were waiting for us at the mouth of the river. The captain of our ship believed it was early enough in the season to be free of icebergs, but not only did we narrowly miss two medium sized ones, but the ship was also broadsided by a huge freak wave. I am no seaman, but none could have predicted that wall of water coming in on that angle! Needless to say, that old vessel couldn't withstand the pressure and we had to limp to the nearest British held port. I overheard the Admiralty discussing port choices. Nova Scotia was too close to the French, Boston was too busy, Halifax is apparently difficult, if not impossible and so that left New York [1]. We've been here a fortnight now and I have taken to reading the daily paper. It is filled with complaints against their colonial rulers, especially over taxation.

The Algonquian language is spoken here as well as in Quebec. Dutch is quite common too, as the city used to be called New Amsterdam as it was a Dutch Colony and the Governor Cadwallader Colden has written a book on the 5 Native American Indian Nations called "History of the Five Nations." [7] I might try to get a copy before we set sail, as I relate to them from one indigenous people to another. Their connection to their lands reminds me of my home, my heart. I will always belong to Scotland and Scotland is mine.

You've asked what barriers would be best for our beasts. Our Highland coos have freedom stamped on their hearts, so palisades won't contain them, nor should we try. To protect your garden from deer, definitely have the men put up palisades and if we want to limit any loss of our wee herd, I think stone walls would be better, which I can help with when I get home.

I can't tell you how much it means to me that you are happy with the French fabric that I have for you. I have enclosed a wee square so that you can knit a matching shawl for yourself. The weather will turn cold again soon. Also, whilst I have put the bulk of our potato recipes in the trunk, I have enclosed one of them here with this letter that I think you'll like. The Irish have told me that you can boil the potato right through so that it's soft or if you have a lot of labour to do, you only partially cook it, so that it is still hard inside. In my opinion, that last one sounds disgusting and I like the sound of a soft potato with butter and salt. The other thing that goes really well with potatoes according to them, is milk and cheese. I was thinking that we could use some of your goats' cheese to make them tastier.

New York Province is a manufacturing hub and I have managed to examine a deep plough that has a slightly different design, which would be perfect for our rocky terrain in Glenmoriston. I will work with Grigor Mohr to make these adjustments to the plough he has fixed for you. They make tools, nails, kettles and lots of other products that are exported by merchants, so much so that there are pirates out in the bay. Station Ships have to guard the coastline and usually have to winter in the Caribbean due to the ice. I'll come home with as many farm machinery engineering ideas as I can.

I can't say that I am too happy about something banging on our door at Craskie. Oh, if I could be there with you. Grigor Mohr coming around was a good idea. Whether it was of this world or not, he is the best man to deal with a problem like that when I'm not around. When we were staying in our cave, he was the one we all relied on for all things other-worldly. He is very knowledgeable about Scottish folk lore and knows all of these ghostly apparitions by name, which gives me the creeps. I could only name half a dozen, like silkies and the sidh, but Grigor is a walking encyclopedia on ghosts and goblins. I hope Da is alright after this experience and I am sure that you will all be safe now that Grigor Mohr has been there and slept there. I can guarantee that it will never happen again. Please send my love and gratitude to him, Morag and especially Da. Keep an eye on Da's health.

I am pleased with how the horse riding lessons are coming along. It is so important that the youngsters are all as skilled as possible, so that we can be ready for whatever the future brings.

You'll be happy to know that I am eating very well in preparation for the harrowing journey ahead. There is bread and vegetables aplenty, as this is known as the "breadbasket" of the colony and I am eating as much fresh food as possible, especially greens, to build up resistance to the possibility of scurvy on board with all that salted mariner's diet. I'll tell you though, I am really not looking forward to it.

Take care of your precious self, my dearest love and always know I will be forever grateful to you during this time of heartbreaking separation while you have to work so hard to continue rebuilding our family's lives without me. I will try and make it up to you.

I am yours forever, the light that never dies, the poem that never ends and I am so proud that you are my 'Isobel of Glenmoriston.'

Yours forever,

Padruig Dubh

Isobel of Glenmoriston
Isobel's Story
1759, Scotland

Craskie Farm,
Glenmoriston
Scotland, 1761

To my dearest Padruig Dubh,

We had all surmised by now that your ships were delayed for one reason or another. We hoped you had pulled into one of the British colonies for safety. Once again, Da had to explain to all of us what an iceberg was and that your ship could've hit one. The tidal wave that hit your ship must have been terrifying. I can't imagine what that must've been like. Praise God you are safe and eating well and now preparing for your journey home. We are all horrified at the hazards you have faced at sea and Da has decided to put the map away now. Before he did that, he showed me where the British colonies were located closest to New France in case you had to go there, so I know where New York is on the map. It's all so strange to me though and I wish this wasn't happening.

We have had no more weird happenings in the night and it's not even a subject of jest if Da did actually come across either one of those nasty apparitions. You were so right about Grigor Mohr, he is so knowledge-able concerning folklore. My question is, however, why it happened at all? I can't talk to anyone else about it now but I will talk to you. Do you think that the poem Da wrote drew angry ghosts from their graves? Ones that had been dug up, stripped and left out in the freezing cold in '46? There are so many stories of dead bodies found after Culloden a month later, who had crawled from the field of battle to a cave and yet their bodies were still intact, as if they had just died![13]

The story of Alexander MacIntosh of Stratherick still sickens me to the stomach. Covered in wounds in a pool of his own blood, he overheard the Redcoats coming as they were stripping the wounded naked and executing them, man after man. They said, "Let us try if this dog be quite dead," [17] and they actually bayonetted his buttocks and he was said to be happy to receive it and concealed any reaction or emotion. It was most fortunate that he fainted, so they were sure he was dead. Several hours later, in the dead of night, he dragged himself on his hands and knees, where the two sentries of the battle field stepped into his path. He handed them 2/- sterling each in exchange for his life, which they received and he crawled twenty miles all the way back to Stratherick. That story never ceases to astound me. Can you imagine his wife's face when she saw her husband in that condition? But thank God, he was alive.

You'd be pleased to hear that Grigor Mohr's riding lessons are going very well with Beth and James. You will be so proud of both of your grandchildren, although I think it will be Beth who becomes dedicated to horses in some way later on. I am glad you have boots for them both to protect their wee feet. Grigor Mohr is the epitome of patience with the Highland Ponies and the bairns. He is growing fond of both Beth and James and I'm glad about that because Patrick doesn't come here as often now and when he does, he doesn't bring Henrietta anymore, much to my confusion and their disappointment. The poor wee bairns miss their Mither, but not enough to ask to go back to her with Patrick when he leaves. They really don't want to return to live on that other farm. I think something is amiss over there.

I could do with more help here on Craskie Farm from Patrick and so next time he comes, I am going to press him to stay a while longer to help Grigor Og with the hand ploughing and then I might just get the story out of him over his favourite dinner. He doesn't realise how much his bairns miss him and need him and yet I know him to be a kind and sensitive person, who would ordinarily respond to another's needs, especially his bairns. I just thank God every night that we all have Helen's Grigor to do the heavy tasks and to depend on. Grigor Og seems to have boundless energy, which surprises even other men.

You'll be pleased to know that the timber rear of our beautiful home, as well as the front in stone, has been completed now by Donald and Hugh Chisholm, may God bless them both. They have work of their own to complete, I am sure, but they have made our home their priority, God bless them. The rear has two levels, with a stair case to the upper level. There is also an attic with a window that opens outward with a view to the path leading down to the Drovers Road. All the windows have shutters for our very bad storms. I've tried to draw the pattern on our windows for you. I could not afford the most expensive windows so I hope you like this pattern.

From the attic, we can also see if anyone is moving cattle along the old drover's road or if anybody's entering our property. Do you want me to draw you a very bad sketch of the house also? The wooden rear is so beautiful. There is a huge fire place on the ground floor, centrally located which goes right up to the next level, where there is another fireplace. They have built the fireplaces in beautiful Caledonian Granite stone and there is a large hearth in front of each one embedded with iron. I bought fire pokers and grates for each one as well. On the second floor there is a very large office and library where we can do the books, but where we could also educate the bairns until we get a school again locally. Opening into the next room is my sewing room. Both of these rooms have beautiful outlooks over the property as far as the oat fields. Opposite those rooms on the other side are bedrooms, which could facilitate Patrick and Henrietta in one room, if they moved back and Beth and James are in the other one.

I forgot to mention also, that the men built a priest hole in the floor of the front stone room, which is our room. It's quite large if ever we do need to hide in there, but really cold. So, at present, I am storing neeps and corn in there.

The first potatoes were picked, but there's still more in the ground and it was easy to cook them. I kept the skin on because Hugh told me that it was medicinal and so I just scrubbed them well. Helen and I boiled them first, then fried them in butter with some salt and Da loved them. We were so relieved to see him eating again which was a big meal of beef, potatoes, neeps, onions and kale.

My last two Betty Dresses paid for the two ponies and this time I also bought home supplies of rolled oats, bees wax, salt, sugar, flour, honey, tea and the luxury of coffee. I'm thinking of getting my own bees. There was coin left over for cotton and silk to sew with in preparation for the lovely silk that you are bringing, my love.

Helen also made her shroud and I showed her how to embroider it. She chose to sew all of our local bird life on it and it is truly beautiful. Of course, when Grigor Og walked in, he asked why she was making a shroud as he didn't know the custom, poor lad. When Helen explained to him that it was to prepare for death in child birth, he went pale and shyly left the room. Between you and me, I don't think they are as active as you and I were when you couldn't keep your hands off me. Maybe Grigor Og is a bit shy, do you think? You'll have to get Grigor Mohr to chat with him so that they can have bairns. Maybe he doesn't even know how bairns are made. Shall I ask his father or leave it alone?

I had a most welcome visitor yesterday morning. Do you remember Mairi from the wool waulking group of women, including Arabella? I used to join them in making the plaids and it was great community fun as well as very productive. I made you a plaid, do you remember? Our wool waulking group stopped, of course, once our traditional Highland dress was outlawed, as you know, so she came around and suggested that we get together again after the wool clipping season this year. Instead of coloured tartan, she suggested we could make the same length of plain wool in one colour like grey, blue or brown. The men in Edinburgh need the wool for

woolen English style suits. So, her plan is that once we've made several lengths of various colours and thicknesses that she takes it to Edinburgh to sell. I said it was a bonny idea, but we'd need the wool-len lengths first to make our own long dresses being that none of us had sufficient clothing yet, then what was left over could go to Edinburgh.

Mairi then saw the fairness and necessity of clothing every-one first and said whatever we all needed was a priority, then if Helen and I would join in, Mairi would bring her daugh-ter Cora along. I offered up our house as the venue and our fast-flowing burn for washing the sheep prior to clipping, if all the

ladies agreed and if they wanted to bring their sheep here. I listed what Da, Grigor Og, Helen and yourself needed as well as myself and the bairns. She was surprised that I was going without. After that she said I could have all of the lengths that I needed, as would everyone else. I must admit, it would be nice to once again wear a thick woollen dress and arisaid after having gone without for so long. Maybe this year, if there's none to sell to Edinburgh, we could wait till next clip-ping season and at least we would all be warm and neatly dressed.

The conversation with Mairi went well and I asked Helen, who had joined us, if she'd like to learn wool waulking with its many songs because, as you know, she has never done it before and she is enthusias-tic to learn. Isn't that wonderful darling? I am so pleased our skills are not going to be lost. The other thing Mairi said was that she'd seen my Betty Dresses for sale in Inverness and that had been the inspiration for starting up the wool waulking group again. I listed how many beasts I had bought so far with the coin from the dresses that I had made and she was visibly shocked.

Of course, she asked when you were due back and I just told her I wasn't sure. She said she would keep you in her prayers and hoped you weren't being subjected to anything untoward. We drank our coffees, which she really loved and asked if I needed anything. I told her we were managing, but if she ever had a spare loaf of bread, I would exchange it for a jug of goat's milk and she went on her way. Now, my dearest, I have to buy a few sheep and maybe I'll teach the bairns how to knit as well. I'll need my own spinning wheel again someday soon.

We all keep so busy to stop thinking too much, but sometimes I find myself crying uncontrollably when I am telling our goats your story. The bairns found me crying one day and I blamed the goats and said that the billy had trodden on my foot. Forgive me God for lying, but I don't want them to worry too. Our friends, Grigor Mohr, the Chisholm brothers and Uncle Allan have all been lifesavers to us and I am forever so grateful. I made Uncle Allan his favourite cake yesterday and he ate the whole thing. I've never seen a man eat an entire cake. He said his late wife Aunty Margaret wouldn't make him his favourite cake for some reason. Uncle Allan always checks the coos while he's here and makes sure their night time enclosure is still secure. "Their horns can do damage," he said, but I think he just likes to procrastinate to spend time with the family. It must be lonely up there at MacDonald Farm.

Two lads, commonly known as the Fisher Lads, Hugh Og Chisholm and Hamish Chisholm, have chiseled "Craskie Farm" onto a log at the entrance of our property. There's room under it also for our name but they thought they'd best let you decide if you want Grant on there too. One of the lads made a present for me and chiseled into a small piece of wood, "Isobel of Glenmoriston." It's so lovely. I don't know where to put it yet, so for now, it's on the mantlepiece above the fireplace with Helen's drawings of all our projects, including when the goats were new. It's like an historical story in picture form. The loveliest drawing she has done is the day they hand-fasted. She really does love Grigor Og.

You'd be proud of your daughter and how she has matured into a young woman, always willing to assist, especially Da now that he has difficulty getting himself out of bed in the mornings. Grigor Og helps him with some private matters and getting dressed, God bless him. I am worried about Da though. The pain in his body is worsening and none of my herbal remedies seem to help anymore. The coffee perks him up a bit to give him enough energy to still walk to Mither's grave, but much slower. He refuses to go to any hospital for help or modern medicine because he is sure the English would only poison him. He will never trust the English until his dying breath. He told me one day just to bury him next to Mither if he doesn't wake up one morning. He's none too cheerful these days. I think he is just worried about you and that he may improve upon your return, God Willing.

I agree with your characterisation of our lovely coos and I'll wait for your return before any permanent structures are built. We have already put palisades around the kale crop and the herb garden to keep deer and coos out. If you get this letter before you leave New York, can you get a new plant that I have heard of called the "tomato" in seed of course, if they have it there? It is a red fruit and it is good to improve the taste of stews. The Spanish eat them a lot, so it must be good for you but we don't have any here.

New York sounds interesting. What kind of dissent do you mean? Are the Indians unhappy or it is the Colonials? I know nothing of the American colonies except that they grow tobacco in Virginia. Your return journey home from New York does not sound pleasant at all. I suppose you'd much rather spend an afternoon fishing on Loch Craskie than being on an endless sea for months with seasick men vomiting.

Speaking of fish, the lads I mentioned are fishing in Loch Craskie and taking them from farm to farm to sell. I told them I'd buy them next time if their catch was fresh, straight from the loch. It would be nice to cook us all fish for a change and easier on Da's loose teeth. Better for Helen too if she falls pregnant. Do you remember how much fish I ate when I was with child? Our diet is improving a lot now that the farm is flourishing compared to those miserable days after the '45 when we were near starving. [12] Grigor Mohr made a strange

63

comment one day that we are stronger than the average because there is Pecht in our ancient history. I hope he explains that one day.

My darling, I don't know how we can repay Donald and Hugh Chisholm and Grigor MacGregor for all they've done. Donald and Hugh Mohr even use homemade nails here when building. Do you think you could buy a bag of nails from New York for them to replace theirs? Uncle Allan suggested that we celebrate the new extension and invite everyone over again, and to say our prayers in every room in appreciation of our new home.

There is enough room here now for both Patrick and Alex and their wives and families. I told Uncle Allan that I thought something was amiss with Henrietta's family and he suggested that I visit Reverend John Stewart in Inverness, because he would know the back story and then Uncle Allan offered his assistance if a bit of force was needed to bring Patrick and Henrietta back home to Craskie to live here permanently. I hope when you eventually arrive home here, that your oldest son and his wife are reunited here with us all.

This weekend is the celebration for this wonderful new home and everyone is coming including the neighbours. In my next letter, I'll let you know what happened with the Reverend in Inverness and how the celebration went because Grigor Og and Helen will hand fast on that occasion. Praying for you always across the sea.

Your beloved wife,

Isobel of Glenmoriston.

Isobel of Glenmoriston
Isobel's Story
1759, Scotland

Plymouth Dockyard,
Plymouth, Devon
England, 1761

My dearest love,

HMS Panther

By now I am sure you would believe me either dead or never returning. For this I beg your forgiveness as I have no control over this army or this navy. It is to the Almighty God alone that I owe my thanks for keeping me alive thus far and well enough to this point and I only implore Him to return me home to you and the family as soon as possible.

The greatest delay is owing to the limitation of transportation vessels available to return soldiers home from the Americas. The 40 gunner I had mentioned to you couldn't be spared, as it was needed to protect two inner bays of the town called Sandy Hook Bay and the main New York Bay. Finally, after seeing ship after ship taking refuge in the calm waters to the north of Long Island, a 50-gunner called HMS Panther became available to load those of us wishing to return to England and Scotland along with our belongings. Do you like my attempt at drawing the ship? It was actively involved in the French and English and Spanish conflicts, so we ultimately had to make quite the detour.

Needless to say, after travelling what seemed like thousands of miles across seas and oceans, our vessel engaged in armed conflict with a Spanish galleon commonly known as "The Mighty" and gained dominance over her, her crew and the $1.5million worth of coin aboard.

As we once again headed northward and as the temperature dropped dramatically, the tropical diseases we had had onboard quickly changed to one of terrible misery, stench, vomiting, seasickness, headache, dysentery, fever, constipation, boils, scurvy, malnutrition, mouth rot and in some cases starvation. The smell of it all was the hardest to stomach. I even saw two men deliberately abort overboard to escape these horrors, only to be seen sinking beneath the waves.

I feel confident to share these horrific details with you only, my love, because I sit here now in England, writing to you in relatively good condition — albeit thinner — but with the unyielding constitution of a Highlander. I did suffer from seasickness and dysentery on the voyage though, but am a wee better now that I am back on land. I don't have my land legs yet, so I am a bit wobbly. It has permanently put me off sea voyages however and the conditions on board were not conducive to me being able to write and for that I beg your forgiveness.

Our trunk full of goods from the Americas has securely arrived with me into Plymouth. The temptation was too great for several thieves on board ship and after fending them off several times, I ended up sleeping on or next to our trunk for the entire journey. These men soon learned not to mess with me.

I plan to travel onto London, where I beg you forward your correspondence to Bishop Robert Gordon of the Episcopalian Church, an acquaintance of Rev. Robert Forbes, who has heard about us and will no doubt accommodate me and my needs. I will go to write to Bishop Gordon now to let him know that I am on my way and to expect your letter. I hope to stay with him and his wife as I am a little poorly and don't want to arrive home looking unwell or disheveled.

From London I will seek passage on a merchant vessel up to Leith, where I will do as you asked — not stay to visit anyone, but instead head overland straight home to Glenmoriston.

With much affection,

Padruig

Isobel of Glenmoriston
Isobel's Story
1759, Scotland

Craskie Farm,
Glenmoriston
Scotland, 1762

To my loving husband, Padruig Dubh,

It seems so long now since I last saw you, but I will never give up hope that the Almighty God will restore you to myself and our family.

I followed your directions and have addressed this letter via Bishop Gordon in London and I pray you are in the best of spirits when you receive this. I hope the long and dreadful journey hasn't left you too unwell. Perhaps the good Bishop could feed you up and give you a comfortable bed for the night if there's time with the shipping timetable. Please send him my best regards, although I know him only by reputation in aiding our folk down that way. Perhaps his wife could launder your clothes for the last part of the journey. Will you still be wearing the Fraser plaid? Because if not, perhaps you'd better buy a new pair of those English breeches in case you are stopped. They are still very strict here in Scotland about wearing tartan. Bishop Gordon might even have a second-hand pair to give you. The boots you left in must be totally worn through. Don't be shy to ask the Bishop for a bit of help if you need it because that is what he does.

The news here at home is really quite extensive, so I'll start with Reverend John Stewart's visit in Inverness. Uncle Allan picked me up with his horse and cart and we left the bairns with Helen and Grigor Og and Grigor Mohr to mind everything while I was gone for the day. It was a fine day to start with and I quite enjoyed the ride up to Inverness chatting to Uncle Allan and looking around at the scenery through the Great Glen. Loch Ness is looking as beautiful as

69

ever and the birds were making quite a lot of noise and I even spotted two Ospreys. A big Irish Setter dog decided to follow us, but we don't know who he belonged to. Arriving at Reverend Stewart's Manse, it was nice to see it all rebuilt and the white roses all growing again out the front. When we arrived, the Reverend's wife made us both a cup of tea while he finished up with someone else. Then he sat down and we had a long conversation.

First of all, he asked about you and told me that you are entitled to the Chelsea pension now that you have served in a British battle, so to apply for it. Then I asked him, could he please explain if there was something amiss at Henrietta's parents' farm and why they weren't coming to our farm so much anymore, but leaving the bairns with me. I was a bit shocked at his candid reply. In truth, Henrietta's father is a drunkard and not kind at all to his wife and those around him. So, in response, Henrietta feared that if she left her Mither, harm would come to her from her Father and therefore stayed. The Reverend' wanted the children safe with me and out of harm's way as a compromise in leaving Henrietta behind. It wasn't an ideal solution I thought, so I explained to him that I needed Patrick on our farm and with the house being completed now, there was room for them both and the bairns. While I respected Henrietta's fears, I conveyed to the Reverend that her priority had to be her bairns, as well as her husband. I wanted them both to come home today with Uncle Allan and I and leave her parents to their drinking problem. "She is not her Mither's Mither, she is the bairns' Mither," is what I said. I also expressed to him that I should have been told of their arrangement. I don't think he agreed but there it was.

I asked the Reverend if he could talk to her Father about his bad habits. He agreed to do that and all four of us, including the Reverend's wife, took two carts and two ponies and went to Henrietta Father's farm immediately after that conversation. I was determined to bring my son home, no matter what, with his wife and their belongings and he saw that both myself and Uncle Allan were going to achieve it.

When we arrived there, it appeared quiet but someone in the stables opened the door out of curiosity and it was none other than our son Patrick. His face was full of both joy and shock then quickly switched to fear. "Ma", he said, "what are you doing here?" It was easy. I just said plainly, "I am here to take you home son with Henrietta, to join your children. You'll be living with me now, not here." At first, I thought he was going to cry, but he went inside the house and packed up their things obediently and told Henrietta how it was and they scurried quickly with packing their belongings and loaded them on board the cart. He nodded to Uncle Allan with a knowing glance that there would be consequences if he didn't. Henrietta was flustered, but didn't put up an argument either and kept her eyes down. We must have all looked a bit threatening. We then left the Reverend and his wife behind to "talk" to her Mither and Father and trotted off home.

When we arrived at Craskie Farm with Patrick and Henrietta, the bairns came running full of joy to see both of their parents. What a relief that was. I've moved them all into the top floor of the wooden extension and they are happy. I can't wait to put them all to work. All we need now is a miracle for Alex to come home and you and the family will all be reunited once again.

I am a terrible sketch artist, but I have enclosed this humble drawing of our new home to give you some idea of what it looks like. Helen must get her artistic talents from you, because I can't get the dimensions right. In actual fact,  the front is much wider and the windows are all the same size, except the elongated one near the donkey house. The windows are very pretty and are made of an opaque glass with coloured geometric patterns in red, green, yellow and blue. I really like these ones because they let in enough light. All the windows have shutters too for the stormy weather. The front door is Grigor Mohr's perfected beauty and I love it, with its two huge latches and a doorknob in the middle with a big key. He really doesn't want anyone breaking in. I've also tried to sketch one of the latches on the door. Off the front porch, there is also a planter box that the men built for me for flowers and the like. I hope you like it darling.

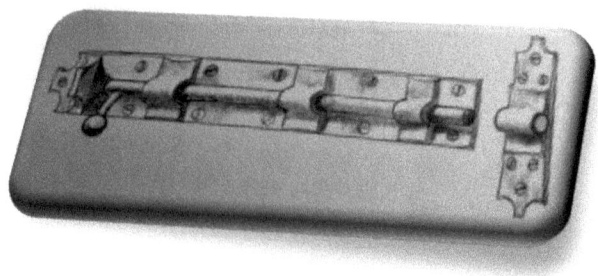

I had already moved Helen and Grigor Og into the wooden extension and they occupy the entire ground floor, east-side nearest the burn with a big spare room for their future children. Their bedroom is near the door that leads outside to the laundry. The bedrooms in the stone home are still allocated to yourself, myself and Da, a wee guest room and a wee servant room. There's a wee corridor in between our big room and the other three rooms with light coming in through the window at the end of the corridor.

I forgot to tell you about the privies. In total there are four at the rear of the wooden building, but if you want to build another closer to the house, then I'll leave that up to you. I think the men have done a good job with one of the privies, enabling two children to use it at the same time with an additional wooden plank that covers the existing holes with smaller holes so they don't fall in.

I've decided to put Henrietta in charge of both lighting and smooring the big fires in the wooden extension, as well as the kitchen and getting breakfast started every morning with Helen and the two of them will work together on breakfast. Grigor will still top up the peat daily. Patrick lets the coos and the donkey out and seems to be happy being involved with our wee herd, but our standards are higher than his father-in-law's farm. He must now clean out their enclosures, refresh their water and feed and check each animal, including their teeth, eyes and hooves.

My jobs are still my precious goats and their milk and cheese as well as my garden with all its medicinal herbs and I am proud to say we have another new baby goat. In total now, we have four nannies, one billy and five kids. Helen still collects the eggs for breakfast and feeds

the chickens and lets them out for a wee
roam too with the geese and she loves
her responsibility for the ever multiply-
ing chickens.

Uncle Allan surprised me and came
over for breakfast to check if all was
going well with Patrick and he spoke
to him in length about how to care for
each coo and to fetch them back each evening. Grigor Mohr had heard
of the intervention to fetch Patrick back also, so he and Morag came
over to give his list of expectations concerning the wee horses. Patrick
said that he was happy to feed them and clean their stalls, but he'd
prefer it if Grigor Mohr would still teach the bairns the horsemanship until you came back. He wasn't confident that he would be good
enough to do that. He thinks of you, Grigor Mohr and the Chisholm
brothers as Masters of the Horse. Grigor Mohr agreed to continue for
the bairns' sake, but he may have been a bit disappointed in Patrick.
We were all very hungry by the time we came back inside to eat
with Grigor Mohr, Morag, Grigor Og and Uncle Allan joining us.
Breakfast was a feast really and both ladies did a fine job learning to
work together and the men were all happy once again. Henrietta was
looking around at her new surroundings, but I believe her assessment
was one of admiration.

Uncle Allan said that he wanted to stay longer to speak to me privately. He has been concerned that you may have died, could die or go
missing and may never return and so with Da's health deteriorating
also, he wanted me to ensure that I'd still be able to inherit Craskie
Farm if both of you were deceased. Either way he said, I'd need a new
Will drawn up. I reassured him that you had directed me to mail this
letter to Bishop Gordon in London, so I was certain that you were
alive, albeit poorly and coming home soon. He still thinks we should
see our lawyer, Mr. David in Inverness next week to clear the matter
up and I agreed. I respect your Uncle implicitly and have always
taken his advice, so I will see the lawyer with Uncle, but I know you
are alive and coming home and God willing, Craskie Farm is safe. He
does have a point, but too scary to contemplate. It was an arrow to

my heart which he could see, so he tried to focus then on the upcoming happy celebration, which is this weekend. God bless Uncle Allan.

Everyone is coming with their wives and their children, the neighbours and even the lads who catch the fish from the loch are coming. We didn't invite Henrietta's parents in case her Father became drunk. It really is my opportunity to thank and praise everyone from the bottom of my heart for building this our wonderful home. When you get home my love, we will have another celebration with our inner circle and you can tell your men all about the fierce fighting on the Plains of Abraham and the horrendous wave that crashed against your first return ship. Their curiosity is beyond measure, but what unites Uncle Allan, Da and your men is the absolute loyalty and love that they share for you.

I feel you close my dearest. Stay safe and healthy and warm. May God grant you every happiness in this life.

All my love and affection,

Isobel of Glenmoriston

Isobel of Glenmoriston
Isobel's Story
1759, Scotland

My dear,

I am Bishop Gordon's wife and you may call me Margaret. At first appearance, your truly humble husband was emaciated, very thin and gaunt, pale and generally in a poor state. I insisted on caring for him before he attempted to travel up to Scotland with that heavy trunk. He still had the bloody flux that he had contracted on the ship, but we are dealing with that. His skin has a rash for which the doctor has given me a cream to be applied daily. He had several boils, which the doctor lanced, but his fever was still high, so the doctor asked him if he'd been injured in any way in any of the battles. The response was that he was injured and treated by an English doctor in New France. Apparently, a bullet did hit your poor man in the right lower calf muscle. The blood loss wasn't serious, but in treating the wound, that doctor left behind remnants of the bullet and dirt, then stitched it up, so in all of this time he has been in pain and developing an infection in turn causing a fever. Our good doctor reopened the wound and had to cleanse an extensive area. Your husband was very brave throughout. The doctor then stitched it back up again so now it should begin to heal properly. I think the doctor was glad the cause of the fever wasn't malaria; however, he has left me treatment for malaria if the fever worsens. Today I would say it has improved slightly, but he needs to stay here for at least three weeks if that is alright by yourself?

I am giving him regular honey water mixed with salt to replace what he is losing from his bowels and lots of fluids. Before small meals I give him charcoal, hoping the food will finally stay in his body and little by little, with the small meals, he'll be able to hold onto it better.

He enjoys coffee each morning and grilled bread with honey while chatting to my husband. He seems to keep the bread down the most, so you might want to keep some bread and honey at home in case the flux returns.

My husband is asking our parishioners for donations to fully clothe your husband as his clothing all had to be burned. We've been astounded at the generosity and with the money so far, we have purchased for him:

1. 2 sets of woolen breeches
2. 3 linen shirts
3. 4 pairs of woolen socks and 2 silk stockings
4. 2 sets of under clothes (the men wear them under their breeches)
5. ¾ length woolen coat donated by one man
6. 2 woolen vests knitted by the ladies of the Church
7. 1 elegant pair of leather knee high boots from one donor

I understand this is not Highland dress my dear, but I am sure the law will change one day and he will be able to wear his plaid once again. The parishioners have also collected enough money for your husband's fare back to Leith by merchant ship and enough left over to hire a carriage from Leith to Glenmoriston.

Now my dear, I must go and attend your good husband. May the Almighty God return him to full health and strength.

My husband will take him for a walk in the park tomorrow to slowly build up his strength, but he still may need to do exercises when he gets home. May God grant you patience and all the blessings this World can give such a wife as "Isobel of Glenmoriston".

Our best regards,
Bishop and Margaret Gordon

P.S. I have repacked your trunk in case it had been water affected, but all is good except for the oat seeds, which we are replacing for you.

P.P.S. My husband has put in the application for the Chelsea pension for your husband, which you will receive soon

P.P.P.S. My apologies for his short hair, but we had to shave his head for lice.

P.P.P.P.S. I have written to Reverend John Stewart in Inverness informing him that your husband should be home soon.

Isobel of Glenmoriston
Isobel's Story
1759, Scotland

Craskie Farm,
Glenmoriston
Scotland, 1762

To dear Bishop and Mrs. Gordon,

Thank you for your kind letter informing me that my husband is with you and in your trusted care in London. Please also thank the good doctor who discovered the cause of my husband's fever and his treatment of him. You are all most welcome to visit our farm in Scotland one day if ever you come here.

With the Parishioners' donation of clothes, I would like to humbly offer in return, a Betty Burke dress for you Margaret, if you could send your measurements with my husband. My husband must be most grateful indeed, especially for the fare to Leith and Glenmoriston.

I could only guess at how hard you have both worked to restore my dearest husband to good health and I hope he can write to me himself when he is well enough to notify me of his date of departure from London and expected arrival in Leith, Scotland.

May God bless you both, your good doctor and all of your Parishioners. I am eternally grateful. May the Almighty God reward you all for your blessed deeds.

My sincerest regards,

Isobel of Glenmoriston.

Isobel of Glenmoriston
Isobel's Story
1759, Scotland

Padruig Grant
C/o- Bishop R. Gordon
Episcopalian Church
London, England, 1762

To my dearest wife Isobel,

Forgive me please my love for the time that has passed since I could last write you a letter. Bishop Gordon has informed me that you know I have been here in London for some weeks now, convalescing with them.

It's hard to put into words how I have longed all this time for our home, our family and our friends in Scotland.

"I have met the battle in my youth,
My arm could not lift the spear when danger first arose,
My soul brightened in the presence of war as the green narrow veil
When the sun pours his streamy beams, before he hides his head in a storm
The lonely traveler feels a mournful joy
He sees the darkness that slowly comes" ....
"we are in the land of foes; the winds have deceived us Dar-Thula!
The strength of our friends is not near nor the mountains of Etha
Where shall I find thy peace, daughter of mighty Colla".

My dear Isobel, please tell my friends how much I have missed them and I'll never leave Glenmoriston by choice in this life again or their company, or yours Dar'Thula.

Thank you for writing back to Mrs. Gordon as she is very excited about getting a Betty Burke dress and I'll bring the measurements with me.

The days here seem long and could get boring, so I borrowed some poetry books in Gaelic from Bishop Gordon to pass the time. This Sunday I am attending their church to thank the parishioners for their donations. The fare is booked for this Monday. I am not sure how long the ship takes to get to Leith, then the carriage to Glenmoriston, but I estimate a week from Monday, God willing.

Please ask Helen and Grigor to wait a wee bit longer and we'll have their wedding in the Kirk when they decide. Grigor can call me Da.

Give my love to our Da too and thank him for his support of me.

"Thy face is like the light of the morning
Thy hair like the raven's wing
Thy soul generous and mild like the hour of the setting sun,
Thy words the gael of reeds...
Dar'Thula with the dark black hair
Thou art lovely as the sun beams of Heaven." [31]

Thank you for being my most precious in this world.

I am forever yours,
Padruig Dubh

P.S. This doctor's name is Dr. Browne and he will contact our family doctor for ongoing treatment if necessary.

Book 2

Isobel's Diary

Diary Entries

Isobel of Glenmoriston
Isobel's Story
1759, Scotland

Craskie Farm,
Glenmoriston
Scotland, 1762

Dear Diary,

After the initial shock of reading Bishop Gordon's letter that my husband was in England but sick and not yet coming home to Scotland, I decided to walk off my misery and keep the letter's contents to myself for now. Walking across to the bubbling burn by my house was always calming. Watching the early morning light dance off the creek stones as the cold-water

stream moved along on its way, momentarily I was peaceful. I stood still for a while until I noticed movement in the woods beyond the burn. It was the Irish Setter again. It had followed us home, which made me worry about our chickens and the new goat kids. Walking briskly back to the house, I called to Helen to put the chickens all back inside in case the dog was hungry, then walked the familiar path to my goats and picked each one up into my arms with a little kiss and called to their mums to go back inside until we were sure of that dog's intentions. The proud and protective billy sensed the danger and hurried them up and they were all happy to be inside their enclosure, safe and sound.

The birds were noisier today and the farm was busily working as it should with Patrick doing his work and Grigor Og up in the field perfecting the soil. 'No one will know that soil better than Grigor Og,' I thought, with the additional horse, coo and fowl manure. He really is a perfectionist like his Father. I was proud of my achievements here at Craskie Farm although I was facing the possibility that my husband could still die, but they just weren't saying it. I had just wished he'd told me about his leg wound, but I suppose he didn't want me to worry. My dear husband was thinking of everyone else except himself and now so close, or at least on the same island and I can't help him, but Margaret is tending him. Was I jealous? No other woman had ever touched my husband's skin but me and his Mither. My dear God, he had been covered in lice and had the bloody flux as well. I couldn't imagine my tall and broad Highlander husband emaciated and pale and my heart bled for him.

As I strolled down the farm deep in thought, I was getting nearer the oat field and our dear Grigor Og was hard at work. I tried to walk in another direction before he saw me, but then I heard, "Ma," I looked up at Grigor waving, so I walked across to where he had a big rock that he sat on occasionally. "You've something on your mind Ma. Can I help?" he inquired. Such a dear lad and patiently still waiting to marry Helen properly in a Kirk. Twice hand fasted and not complaining. I thought about the letter in my apron and decided to tell him. I showed him the envelope and said I had received a letter from Bishop Gordon in London. "Is everything alright with Da then?" he asked. "Not really," I responded, "but I hope with the Almighty's help it will be. He is a stubborn man and has endured the horrors of Culloden, having to live in a cave with your Father and the others, then saving the Prince without so much as a scratch. He escaped the Redcoats at every turn then, until a decade later he was put on that accursed ship to the Americas. His stubbornness and strength have got him this far, to London at least and they're caring for him, but my dear Grigor, he was wounded in New France and it became infected, so the wound site had to be reopened and cleaned out." Grigor's face changed from the young happy farmer to a graveness I'd not seen on his face before and I realised that I'd scared him too much. "I'm sorry Grigor, I didn't mean to worry you, but can you mind the farm until late tonight because Uncle Allan is coming to take me into Inverness soon? I'll leave it to you what you tell Helen about her Da, but please don't worry her too much," I said. "Ma," he replied, "you know I'd do anything for this family and I believe that Da will make it through this difficulty and soon we'll all see him again and what a joy that will be," he said. "Aye, you are a good lad Grigor. In addition, would you mind please giving this letter to your Father today because I won't be here to see him personally?" I asked.

I went back to the house to change and ready myself for Inverness. Uncle Allan and I didn't talk much on the journey this time, but the dog followed us again. Uncle had a lot on his mind and wasn't saying what it was.

At the lawyer's office I was surprised to see the short stout man was wearing a wig. He was a serious older man who demanded "proof of life" where Padruig was concerned. I still had the letter from Padruig, so I produced it much to Uncle's shock. "Here," I said "he's in London, alive and staying with Bishop Gordon. They've got his fare and he's coming back, so don't suggest to me that he's dead!" I then stood to leave when Uncle Allan beckoned me calmly to sit down and finish the Will. "Okay. It's like this," I said, "Craskie Farm belongs to Padruig Grant and should he pass on, it comes to me, Isobel Grant, or vice versa. Then when we are both dead, it goes to both Patrick Grant jointly with Helen Grant and her spouse. Privately though, I have to let you know, that due to proscription regarding the MacGregor name, Helen wishes to be known as Helen Grant and for your information only, her husband is Grigor MacGregor, who can't yet have the land in his name, if I understand the law correctly and that is why I have said "her spouse". When that law changes, I wish the Will to reflect that. Craskie Farm will then be a Grant-MacGregor enterprise and then Helen will wish to be known as Helen Grant MacGregor and her spouse would be named as Grigor MacGregor. Where do I sign?" I asked.

After I had signed the papers, the lawyer stood and apologised and said he had nothing but admiration for me and what I had achieved in my husband's long absence, unlike many others who had given up with our many hardships. As for Padruig, he said that he'd always be a hero and with that said, he intended to write to the powers that be in

London and lodge a complaint at the treatment of such a valiant hero after the Quebec campaign and expected his pension to be paid forthwith with backpay and an apology with a Certificate of Valour.

He went on to say, "All the folks around here know who Isobel of Glenmoriston is and I am honoured to have met you and wish you and Padruig a long and happy life. Good day my dear," he said.

It was hard to respond to that, so I just said, "Thank you and good day to you Sir." Uncle then piped up inappropriately and asked if anyone was missing an Irish Setter that had been following us. No, was the reply. He put a few posters around in shops, asking the owner to come forward and get him before someone found him to be a nuisance to their chickens.

I asked Uncle if he wouldn't mind taking me to the dress shop that sold my Betty dresses, then I hoped to ask them for the coin up front so that Uncle and I could take two sheep home with us. "Sheep?" he said. "Aye, the wool waulking is starting up again and I am the only one without any sheep. So, in preparation for the clipping season, we need them today," I responded. "Where will they shelter then tonight?" he asked. "With the donkey until I get it sorted," I replied.

The ladies in the dress shop were thrilled to get two new dresses as they already had orders fully paid, so the money for the sheep wasn't a problem. We bought bread, butter and honey while we were there with our sheep and with the extra coin, I also bought linen fabric for new men's shirts and fabric for Margaret's Betty dress.

The day had started out rather miserably, but in the dying light on the way home, whilst passing the time, as usual, I asked Uncle Allan for his advice and said I needed to talk to him about Griger Og, who didn't seem to know a lot about his clan's history. I said to Uncle,

"Do you think he's safe when he's on his own up at the oat fields? What if those Campbells still have those black hounds?" "I have an idea love," he replied, "this Irish Hound that keeps following us looks like it could kill one of those blood hounds easily. I'll tie him up at your place tomorrow morning outside the donkey house. You act innocently when they tell you that he's there and give him to Grigor Og. That way, he'll have a good companion and a protector. After all, the owner hasn't shown up and the dog needs a good home anyway," he said. "What a bonny idea," I said. I then had a new reinvigorated plan for all our futures in our lovely Glenmoriston.

Isobel of Glenmoriston

Isobel of Glenmoriston
Isobel's Story
1759, Scotland

The letter read:
To my dear friends, Grigor and Morag,

I hope you don't mind receiving this news in the form of a brief letter instead of in person via Grigor Og, who will be responsible for the farm today. Today I am visiting our lawyer in Inverness with Uncle Allan, who is concerned about the status of our land, should Padruig not return or pass away.

I have, however, received a letter from Bishop Gordon and his wife in London informing me that Padruig is alive but unwell, and convalescing with them for some weeks. It appears he was wounded after all with improper attention resulting in a serious infection.

The parishioners there in the London Episcopalian Church have collected his fare together, as he hopes to return to Scotland as soon as is possible. Just the same, today at the lawyer's office, the land will be transferred into my name should he pass away or vice versa. My Will and Testament will then reflect that Helen Grant and her spouse, as well as Patrick Grant, will inherit Craskie Farm after I die.

I apolgise that their names can't be written as MacGregor yet, due to the proscription laws, so Helen's name will still appear as Grant. I will explain to Mr. David, that as soon as proscription ends, it will read Helen Grant MacGregor and Grigor MacGregor as well as Patrick Grant to inherit from us at this present time.

My sincerest apologies for this formality between friends.

Most affectionately yours,

Isobel of Glenmoriston

Isobel of Glenmoriston
Isobel's Story
1759, Scotland

Craskie Farm,
Glenmoriston
Scotland, 1762

Dear Diary,

I had woken up tired the next day after the lawyer's visit. Even my dreams had felt exhausting. I vaguely remembered that Padruig was calling me, so I woke up. But it was Grigor Og at my door. "Ma, there's a strange big dog tied up outside the donkey house and he won't let me open their door," he said. I knew immediately that it was the Irish Setter. "Does Helen have a spare bone in the kitchen?" I asked. "Aye, Ma," Helen replied. I quickly pulled on my old boots and warm clothes to deal with it and asked if she had already lit the fires. It was a bitterly cold morning. Taking the bone and a bowl of goat's milk, I walked outside to see the offending animal. "Hello you. Come here," I said. He was pleased to see me, wagging his tail and ran up to see what I had for him and I realised it was a bitch. "Eat this and have some milk," I said to the scruffy dog. I was thinking, 'well done Uncle Allan.'

I called for Grigor Og and let him know that there were two sheep also housed with the donkey. "Sheep?" he asked. "Aye, sheep," I responded. "They are for the wool waulking. Don't let them into my garden,"

91

I insisted. Helen came outside curious to see the black-faced sheep. "Och, they're lovely," she said. I must admit, the light was too dim the night before and I hadn't appreciated their beauty. I asked Helen if Henrietta could deal with breakfast while she put a rope on the sheep and walk them around for a while and tell them where they could and couldn't go. "Please introduce them to the goats," I said. At first the sheep weren't bothered by much at all, but the billy goat didn't like the two new farm animals. "Come on billy," I said and patted his head. "Try and be nice." They were all eyeing each other off from the wee horses to the coos and the goats. The chickens were the only disinterested farm family and Patrick led the coos further away.

The dog had finished off her food and joyfully came running up to me like she'd found her new home. "Oh dear," I said, "looks like we're stuck with you." Grigor Og took a fancy to her, thankfully and asked if he could take her up to the oat fields before breakfast. 'God bless Uncle Allan,' I thought again. "Of course, she is yours if you like," I said, "but she might have fleas, so you may have to wash her in

the burn. Don't bring her into the house and remember to show her who's boss," I said. Grigor Og replied, "Are you sure she's a Setter Ma? Aren't they more reddish or red and white? Could she be a mixture of Setter and Irish Wolfhound because of her greyish colour with only a little red here or there?" he asked.

Then it was a debate. Hound or Setter? "I think it's too playful to be a wolfhound. Maybe it is a cross between the two. It is possible that the Irish brought both breeds with them in the '45 and this might be the offspring of what survived," I said. Grigor Og then said, "So, is she ours now Ma? Are we keeping her? Henrietta won't like feeding her out of the kitchen," he said. "She'll have to catch her own food, such as pheasants, there's plenty of them. Can you encourage her to do that?" I responded. I then headed back to the house for breakfast but Helen, God bless her, had already prepared a hot bath for me and made my bed and laid out my clothes. I felt blessed to have such a wonderful daughter and life in the shieling was finally over. It had been hard to keep clean while living on a dirt floor and bathing was in the freezing cold burn rather infrequently.

"What's that beautiful scent?" I asked. "It's the scented soap that Henrietta and I made. We made a lot so we could give our guests a gift of soap each this weekend. We also made scented candles," Helen answered. "God bless you my dearest Helen," I responded. "While you are washing my hair, I have something to tell you. In my Will, this property passes to me if your Father dies or vice versa. But after we are both deceased, it passes jointly to Patrick and you and your spouse. I'll give you a copy of the Will from the lawyer when it comes. However, as you know at this stage, due to proscription, we can't use the name MacGregor in the Will or on the title deeds until they change that law, so your name is reflected as Helen Grant," I explained. Then as she gently washed my hair, she said, "I didn't know that I'd be inheriting anything, Ma. That's truly amazing," she said through teary eyes. "Oh, thank you Ma." Then there were lots of kisses all over my face. "You've worked hard here, like I have. Why shouldn't you be equal to your brother? Just don't tell Patrick yet," I said. I went on to tell Helen that I wanted to talk to her and Grigor after dinner that night.

After a long hard day for all of us, later that night with them both seated at the table looking very serious, I told them to relax while I made us all coffee. "I just want to have a wee chat is all," I assured them. Relaxing, while drinking our coffee, I firstly addressed Grigor Og. "Now lad, if you ever see a big black dog, have your dog set on him and kill it!" He was shocked at my sudden ruthlessness, but asked why in his usual calm and polite way and I went on. "Have you heard of the Campbell's black hound dogs?" I asked and he replied, "No, just the Campbells. I know Da hates them with a vengeance." "Rightly so," I said, "they've taken nearly all the MacGregor lands and tried to have you all wiped off the face of the Earth. Criminals!" I said, then I realised that I was getting angry myself. Trying to calm down, I then told him that they had trained fierce black hound dogs to hunt down and kill the MacGregors in the past, so he had to keep himself safe when he was on his own. In the future, he needed to teach that Irish dog to defend him from one of those hounds if he ever saw one or more. "Not that we've ever seen one in these parts, mind," I said calmly.

Then the thought came to me, Helen and Grigor Og would have bairns one day that would be part MacGregor and part Padruig Dubh Grant, so in addition I said, "When you both have bairns, you'll need to channel their energies, especially if you have a lad. And you must teach him to fight with his written word. Education, especially law, will guide your family", I said. "If we have a lad," Grigor Og responded, "I'd like to name him Aonghus Grigor. Do you think that sounds like a good lawyer's name Ma?" "Aye," I replied, "a very fine name." Helen then added, "I like Isobel-Mairi if it's a girl and if we have two girls, I'd like to name her Morag-Freya." I told her that I thought that was so lovely. "You have honoured both of your Mithers and your Grandmother," I told her.

"Have you heard the old story of the Campbell lassie who fell in love with a MacGregor lad a long time ago?" They shook their heads curiously. "Her name was Marion and your Da might know the very sad Gaelic song about them. It's so sad," I said. "Why?" Grigor Og asked. "I am sure your Da could tell this story better, but the Campbells tracked the two of them down, her with child and another wee bairn and they beheaded Marion's beloved in front of her. The two boys would grow up to be very clever fighters, but after the Battle of Glen Fruin, that they won against the Colquhouns, the King banned the name of MacGregor at the behest of the Campbells. But you probably know that lad," I said. "Aye, I know," he said sadly.

"But never you both mind. As I've already mentioned to Helen, today I saw the lawyer in Inverness about Craskie Farm and Helen and her spouse will inherit this land as well as Patrick. At this stage, I can't put the name MacGregor on the deeds due to proscription, I can only put "her spouse" and that's you Grigor, but when the law is changed, which I am sure it will soon, this land, Craskie Farm will become a Grant-MacGregor enterprise," I explained.

I took the last sip of my coffee and looked at the two of them and said, "Are you interested to hear a sad Gaelic song concerning Clan Gregor?[21] I only know one song that my Mither taught me. I am no songstress, but she loved that Gaelic song about Clan Gregor. Maybe

I could sing a bit for you?" I offered a bit shyly, not having sung it in years. Both Grigor Og and Helen were keen to hear my Mither's song, so I stood and started to sing its sad lament until it came to the chorus when Helen interrupted and asked, "Ma, what does 'obhan obhan obhan iri' mean?" I was about to answer when I heard an unexpected quiet knock at the door of our sleeping house. It was late and it disturbed Da from his slumber enough for him to walk out rubbing his eyes and pouring himself a cup of tea to join us.

I opened the door to Morag and Grigor Mohr and welcomed them both in. Grigor Mohr was carrying the letter that I had left with his son the day before and his face appeared displeased. "Would you like hot soup or tea to warm yourselves up? I hope my letter didn't bring you out into the cold?" I asked. Morag replied that she'd love some hot soup and Grigor Mohr wanted coffee, which Helen hurriedly prepared for her parents in law, whom she greeted respectfully. Morag was very fond of Helen and kissed her cheeks and then hugged her son warmly. "Do you want us to go to bed Ma?" Grigor Og asked me, but it was Grigor Mohr who answered. "Nae. I'd like us all to chat."

His son looked worried, but not more than me. Then Morag, trying to sound light hearted asked, "Dear Isobel, you know that Gaelic song? We could hear you from outside. I didn't know you sang and it was truly lovely. Where did you learn it? I don't know all of the words." I then replied, "It was the only song that my Mither taught me and I don't normally sing, but I can give you a copy of the words." Then, in a serious tone, Grigor Mohr asked, "So, why are you singing it to Helen and Grigor? Do you think I've not taught my lad enough about my Clan? Aren't you a Grant from birth? Why sing a MacGregor song?" he asked accusingly. To this, Da touched my hand and beckoned me to be seated while he answered.

"Aye, she is a Grant. Born a Grant to my second wife. My first wife, Ailsa, died in childbirth. Both Ailsa and our bairn are buried in our cemetery. Ailsa Grant and John Grant Jnr, may God rest their souls. Their graves are next to my second wife, Freya Grant. Isobel is my only child because my second wife was already thirty years old when I married her and childbirth was a risk, so Isobel was a gift from God to us both," he said then kissed me lightly. "Isobel, your Mither adored you. The song you ask about Grigor, now that you know my whole life story almost lad, I will explain, after which I hope you will accept our hospitality and stay the night in the spare room, saving you going out into the cold again. My second wife was a widow when I married her, which I've never told you before, my dear Isobel," he said.

Sitting now uncomfortably in his seat, Grigor Mohr still persisted and said, "But why that song?" and Da went on. "My second wife was the widow MacGregor," he stated plainly. I am not sure who was more shocked in the room, but probably myself and Grigor Mohr, followed by Helen. I think she wanted to leave the room and go to bed and so did I, but Grigor Mohr had something on his mind and Da had the bit between his teeth. Morag decided to take out her knitting to relax herself. 'Good idea,' I thought. "Da," I asked intrepidly, "if Ma was a widow at thirty years of age, did she have other children?" "Aye," Da replied. "A strong wee lad, who tried to lift a sword and hack at my legs when he heard the word marriage between his Mither and I. Och, he was a bonny lad with black hair like ours. I'd carved a wee wooden toy Clydesdale horse for the lad and I gave it to him. I think he liked it, but the MacGregor family were critical of my occupation as a Clydesdale teamster and a farmer. I wasn't their idea of a real man," he said sadly.

With sad reflection in Da's eyes, he continued. "I asked for Freya's hand in marriage and offered her and her son our life here at Craskie Farm where I'd teach him horsemanship and how to be a teamster. I promised to protect Freya and her son with my life. The family all refused any of it at first, but Freya said "aye" to me and wanted to hand-fast right away. She wanted us all to leave that day and come home to Craskie with her son. Grigor was his name. The MacGregors refused to release the child and eventually said that only Freya could go, but they'd raise the lad as a true MacGregor not a Grant. My poor Freya was heartbroken, but to lose me was unthinkable for her and so they decided that I could take Freya, but we could never see the lad again." My poor Father had to stop for a moment to contain his emotions.

"So, I hope you're satisfied now, Grigor, that Freya would lament the loss of not only her first husband, but her son too. She became overly protective of wee Isobel. When I put her onto the Clydesdale's backs, she'd come running and yelling abuse at me and take the bairn back inside," said Da. Then quietly Grigor Mohr reached into his sporran and took out a wee carved wooden Clydesdale that was obviously well loved. "Is this the horse you carved Da?" he quietly asked, almost afraid of the answer. Da took it and looked carefully at it. "Aye lad, see I've left my mark here. It was J for John. Where did you get it?" Da asked.

Helen and Grigor Og both under-stood immediately and looked at each other. Grigor Og said, "Helen, we are cousins. Is that still okay?" "Aye, of course," she replied. "Lots of cousins get married." Then she added, "Ma, we are tired. Can we both go to bed now?" We all agreed and they left us, both hand in hand. "I'd like to go to bed in the guest room too," said Morag. "Goodnight," and she packed up her knitting and walked toward the guest room. "Da, I am so sorry," said Grigor Mohr. "I was worked up over Padruig's ill health in London and then I heard one of our songs and it just came out all wrong. Please forgive me? I wanted you to

be my step father as a wee lad. I cried for so long, I was given a whipping for it and told to 'be a man'. I always wanted to be as good as you were with horses." Then he turned to me and said, teary eyed, "Isobel, you are my sister." Dropping his head, he wept silently and Da took him to bed. Flabbergasted, I was left alone to smoor the fire, put out the candles and more than ever, I felt all alone going to bed with all of that information swirling around in my head and I knew I would not be able to sleep well that night.

Isobel of Glenmoriston

Grioghal Cridhe – Beloved Grigor (Grigor's Lament)

Gaelic –	Moch Maduinn air
	Latha Lunasd'
English –	Early morning on Lammas Day
Gaelic –	mi surgradh mar ri
	m' ghradh
English –	I sported with my love
Gaelic –	Ach mu'n tainig
	meadhon latha
English –	But by midday
Gaelic –	Bha mo chridhe
	Air a chradh
English –	My heart was wounded
Gaelic –	's iomadh oidhche
	fhliuch is thioram
English –	Many a night of wet or dry weather
Gaelic –	side nan seachd sian
English –	Or of all the seven elements (of storm)
Gaelic –	gheibheadh Griogal
	Dhomhsa creagan
English –	Gregor would get me a corner
Gaelic –	ris an gabhainn dian
English –	Where I could shelter safe
Gaelic –	'Obhan 'obhan 'obhan iri '
	obhan iri 'o
	Obhan 'obhan 'obhan iri
	'S mor mo mhulad, 's mor
English –	Great is my sorrow, great
Gaelic –	Nuair bhios mnathan og a' bhaile
English –	While the young wives of the town
Gaelic –	nochd 'nan cadal seimh
English –	serenely sleep tonight
Gaelic –	's ann bhios mise
	air bruaich do lice
English –	I will be at the edge of your gravestone
Gaelic –	bualadh mo dha laimh
English –	beating my two hands
Gaelic –	Obhan 'obhan 'obhan iri '
	obhan iri 'o
	Obhan 'obhan 'obhan iri
	'S mor mo mhulad, 's mor
English –	Great is my sorrow great
Gaelic –	Chan eil 'ubhlan idir agam
English –	I have no apples left
Gaelic –	's ubhlan uil' aig cach
English –	While all the others have
Gaelic –	's ann tha m'ubhal
	cubhraidh caineal
English –	But my apple is fragrant, spicy
Gaelic –	's cul a'chinn ri lar
English –	and lies low on the ground
Gaelic –	Obhan 'obhan 'obhan iri '
	obhan iri 'o
	Obhan 'obhan 'obhan iri
	'S mor mo mhulad, 's mor
English –	Great is my sorrow great
Gaelic –	Obhan 'obhan 'obhan...

Isobel of Glenmoriston
Isobel's Story
1759, Scotland

Craskie Farm,
Glenmoriston
Scotland
March 1762

Dear Diary,

It had been an exhausting but wonderful weekend. All our family, including Alex and his wife Therese, our friends and our neighbours were here to celebrate the completion of our lovely new home. We prayed in each room and asked God to protect and bless our home. All the children joined in and were very happy.

Helen, Henrietta and I had been cooking for two days, despite the colossal family revelations of late. In preparation, Patrick had slaughtered a coo so that everyone ate very well. There was corn, a goose, beef, neeps and kale, and lots of bannocks and bread with butter and goat's cheese. The beef stew was laced with onions and tomatoes and herbs from my garden. I provided goats milk and some of the men brought over whiskey to make it an occasion to remember. They refrained from offering me any because they knew I didn't drink.

Looking at Grigor Mohr in a new and sensitive way, I presented him first then Uncle Allan, Donald Chisholm, Hugh Mohr and Grigor Og with a new shirt wrapped up as a gift thanking them all as I presented it to each man. Da was already wearing his and he had chosen the Prince's style, which looked very fancy. Helen and Henrietta presented everyone with a bar of scented soap with a ribbon tied around it as a gift. I took the opportunity when the noise died down a bit to give a little speech to thank all of them for their assistance to our family.

Then to surprise them, I produced the letter from Padruig saying he was finally coming home. I read it out loud and everyone cheered and then the eulian pipe music and dancing started with bodhrans, fiddles and flutes. It was a wonderful evening and the men loved their shirts and the women loved their soap.

For a moment, I thought I saw Grigor Mohr's face become emotional. Then the Chisholm brothers and he sat together and told old stories and began to laugh. I approached them tentatively and asked Grigor Mohr if I could speak to him in the morning before Padruig returned, if it suited him. Surprisingly, he stood up, put his arm around me and I put my arm around him, which horrified the Chisholms and said to them, "This is my sister." Donald laughed and said, Yeh, yeh, you can't fool us. Get your arm off her or Padruig will have it chopped off." Grigor left his arm there, which was making me shyly happy and waiting for his next words to his friends, he said, "Nae. If I want to put my arm around my sister, I will and what I said is what I mean. A couple of nights ago both of us discovered that we are half brother and sister. That is, we share the same Mither, Freya MacGregor, who married John Grant," he announced boldly. They both looked at each other in disbelief. Hugh Mohr was going red in the face from anger I thought and said something like, "You'd better not be having us on." Donald then looked directly at me, seeing the truth of it in my eyes, as well as knowing me, that I would've withdrawn from any man trying to touch me had he not been a brother and asked me directly, "Isobel, is this true? Are you and Grigor brother and sister without having known all of this time?" "Aye," I responded, "it's true." I once again turned to Grigor and said, "Grigor, can I please speak to you first thing in the morning? There is so much I need to talk to you about and I want to be clear in my mind before Padruig gets here, so that it's easier to explain to everyone else." "Aye," he said. I added, "We might be interrupted around here. Do you mind if I take you into the forest and show you an old stone where I used to play as a bairn and we can talk there? It's quiet and peaceful," I said. "How far?" he asked. "Och, it's not far. It's in the forest that way," I pointed. "Okay," he said, "good idea. Do you mind if I ask you questions about Mither from when you were wee?" he asked. "Nae, ask me anything tomorrow morning after I've fed and milked the goats. Is that okay?" I asked. "Aye," he said. I then left the men to it and got back to the bustling party.

My son Patrick came up to me soon after and kissed me on the cheek unexpectedly and said, "Thank you Ma. Thanks for bringing me home. I've never been happier and Henrietta is now with child!"

So much news was exchanged and gradually most of them departed by midnight and others fell asleep by the fires. There was a mess to clean up, so we didn't get to bed until three o'clock in the morning, working quietly around sleeping people. Therese helped with the cleaning up, which surprised me, but Alex went straight to bed. They were leaving soon in the morning without waiting to see Padruig. I invited Therese to come back if they wanted to and welcome Padruig home, but she seemed reluctant and said there was a lot of work to do on her Father's farm. I wished her all the best with it and didn't pursue the matter. She made an interesting comment though, by asking if Patrick and Henrietta were going to stay at Craskie permanently. "Aye, that's true," I replied and her face showed jealousy of some kind, so I asked her, "Does it bother you that all of the family are here except you and Alex?" She answered candidly, "Yes, it does a bit. I thought we'd all live independently." I responded with, "There's no need to spread out all over, when the house is big enough now for everyone, including you and Alex and the farm can feed us all now." That hopeful remark of mine didn't help her facial expression and she went up to bed. They were both gone before breakfast without saying goodbye which saddened me a lot. I loved and missed my wee Alex, as I had once called my precious youngest son. I wondered if an intervention would work with them and decided against it, but just the same a chat over breakfast was in order.

I asked everyone once they were all settled down with their tea or coffee, what they thought of Alex and Therese leaving so early. "Rude," was Helen's response. "At best, impolite," was Henrietta's. Patrick was reserved, so I asked him directly and he looked sad. "I think it's sad that they can't be happy for all of us, especially with Da coming home. I don't understand them and I feel there's nothing we can do about it". Grigor Og said, "I shouldn't comment Ma on a complex family matter. Breakfast looks great ladies, can I help?" He is forever the optimist and never likes to stir up trouble.

"From where I sit," said Helen, "they might have problems in the future. Good on you Ma for sorting out the Will or I would be worried about it. I'll keep them in my prayers, just the same. Who knows what problems they have over at Therese' parents place. I don't feel like inviting them to our wedding though with their sour faces." Grigor Og indicated to her to tone it down, which made us all smile." It's okay," said Da. "We used to say terrible things to each other when Alex was living at home. It's been peaceful here without him and Padruig Dubh won't stand for any nonsense from either of them, so personally I think it is better they left early," he said. "Thanks, Da but I am still sad that Alex left without giving me a kiss," I said. We all then finished up, cleaned up and went back to work. But, before I opened the door, Patrick said, "What's this about the Will and the land Ma?" "Nothing bad for you son," I called back, "but I have to milk the goats right now. I'll talk later," knowing I had to hurry in order to meet my arrangement with Grigor Mohr and as such, I had to spend less time with my goats.

I called to Helen and passed the bucket of beautiful milk to take into the house to Henrietta and went to look for where Grigor Mohr was. He was observing everything from the edge of the forest where I'd pointed and was quite camouflaged. "Isobel," Grigor Mohr spoke quietly, "here I am." "Brother," I said and embraced him. It was a wonderful feeling although odd to say at first because I had always imagined I had a brother. "It's not too far," I said and started leading the way. "The crofters' bairns didn't want to play with me when I was wee," I explained, "because I was Himself's daughter. When they were playing a hopping game, I'd ask to join in and they'd politely explain how it was played and the rules, but then they'd all find an excuse to leave and return to their crofts. So, that's why I found this place, being so lonely even though I had the best parents. One day, listening to the birds overhead, I was trying to memorise their bird song, so I could repeat it to Mither and I took note of all of the markings on their wings and hoped she'd be able to tell me what type of birds they were. But looking up for so long, I suddenly found myself on the ground having walked straight into a rock. I had a sore ankle and a sore knee and I was lying in a patch of briers covered in prickles. I tried hard not to cry because I didn't want to lose my sense of direction and get lost. When blinking through wet eyes, I saw what it was that I had tripped over. At first, I just thought it was an ordinary stone like you find in the oat fields, but taller, much taller and stuck in the ground. I noted that where I had fallen against it, moss had come off, so I pulled a bit more off and there were these odd-looking markings on the rock; all over the rock actually. So, I made myself a nice place to sit in front of it, pulled all of the prickles out of my dress and leaned up against it and found it to be a very peaceful place. From then on, I told the rock that he was going to be my fairy rock and whenever I was lonely, I would come back and talk to the fairies. It was getting kind of misty all around me. Not a fog, mind, just misty and I thought Mither would be wondering where I was. I brushed off as much of the dirt and briers that I could, tried not to limp and went back home."

"Brother," I said as I looked up into my brother's face, whose eyes were almost identical to my own, "I want to ask you, now that we are brother and sister, did you know when I was born?" "Nae," he said. "I was two when Mither left and nobody told me when she married your Da or if they had children, but later, naturally, I expected that they had," he said. "We could have been playing together all that time when we were wee. It's a bit sad. You also said that Ma was the widow MacGregor because she married your Da. Did you know who her Mither's clan was?" I asked. "I can play with you now Isobel," he said and tickled me and went on, "I was raised by my Grandmother, aunties and uncles, rather harshly, all of whom were MacGregors and didn't know who Mither's family clan were," he said. "So, you never met anyone from the other side of the family?" I asked. "Our family was very insular, so nae and all my Grandmother told me was that she vaguely thought it could've been Clan Chattan," he said. "Clan Chattan?" I replied. "But that's lots of clans," I said. "Aye, I know, but I think because the MacPhersons sought me out for service, that it may have been MacPherson," he said. "MacPherson? Well, they're nice folk and they often pass on news to me about the MacPhersons. That makes sense," I added.

Grigor Mohr then said, "Can I ask you a question about Mither?" "Aye," I responded. "Did she talk about me and tell you that you had a brother?" he asked. "Nae, she didn't brother, I'm sorry. The only thing she taught me of her previous life was that song, which I know made her very sad, but I thought it was to do with her first husband. Upon reflection, it can't have been because she loved my Da so much. What do you want to know?" I asked. "Did she ever ask to leave Craskie Farm to visit anyone?" he asked. "Not that I know of. She was always at home, cooking and sewing and teaching me my letters and my mathematics. Both Da and her wanted me to be clever at school," I responded. "So, did she teach you how to read then?" he asked. "Aye, she did. In Gaelic and then in English and Da had another language that he taught me for the horses later. Old Irish I think. He said Erse was better for the horses. I don't know why, but it was," I answered.

"Can I tell you one story that involves Mither but it's a bit strange?" I asked. "Aye" Grigor said. "One day, when I was wee, after returning back from one of my afternoons in the deep forest beside my fairy stone, I had felt a scary presence near the tree line and was suddenly really afraid. I ran as fast as I could toward the house. Da had the team all standing in front of the house unloading something from the back of the carriage. The stallion, who I called Old Boy, was closest to me and looked at me invitingly, so I ran to be underneath him and clung to his front left leg. He didn't even flinch with me there. What appeared was a Daoine Sith, [28] trying to grab at me angrily but couldn't for a reason unknown to me then. Its face was indescribably evil and terrifying and it persevered to try and get me. He then went in front of the two lead horses when the other lead horse started stomping her hooves and snorted at the evil before her. The Daoine Sith then tried from that side to reach me, but still couldn't and when that horse became noisier, it attracted Mither from inside the house and momentarily also stopped Da from his unloading work.

The Dacine Sith hadn't given up and came back to be closer to where I was still clinging tightly to Old Boy when I heard my Mither screaming at my Father. "John," she screamed, "Isobel's under the horse. She could be killed. How many times have I told you to keep Isobel away from these massive beasts?" She then saw, out of the corner of her eye, the Dacine Sith slithering back into the woods at Ma's appearance. It was considering coming back until Ma said words in another language and it was never seen here again. Ma then said, "Sorry John. It were Dacine Sith." Surprisingly, she then patted Old Boy on the nose and said, "Good boy." I then felt safe enough to come out with the Dacine Sith gone and jumped into Ma's arms saying, "Nothing will take me Ma." Da looked a bit perplexed, but took it in and asked me directly, "Was it Dacine Sith, Isobel, trying to kidnap you?" I then answered, "Aye. I hid under Old Boy so it couldn't get me." Then Ma said, "It's the iron John. The horse's shoes. It formed an impenetrable force because of the iron." "Aye," Da said, "but how would Isobel know that?" Ma had a knowing look on her face, patted the horses again and even kissed Old Boy on his muzzle and we went inside for cake and milk. I was always allowed then to learn teamstering. I later heard Ma asking Da if he had been digging up peat from a different mound to which she had specified that he dig from and he had been. She was angry with him and told him that it was his fault that the Dacine Sith came and to not to dig there again, take back any left-over peat from there and to take a small offering of food and milk there. Da did what she asked, but thought it was all nonsense. She was really strict about where we could dig peat. So, Grigor, are you surprised that our Mither could not only see the Dacine Sith, but also make it go away?" I asked. "Nae, not really. It explains a lot about her deep understanding of nature. Thank you for telling me that story Isobel. I didn't even know that about where you can't dig peat," he said.

"Do you want to know more about her life here on the farm?" I asked. "Aye," he said inquisitively. "When I was about four years old, I had thought that Ma didn't like the Crofters who had lived here, but I came to understand that she was only asserting her authority as 'Himself's' wife who they had to respect, which they did. When she passed by their crofts, the men would always tip their caps and say

Ma'am and the women would be very cautious around her and refer to her as Mistress. They knew that they would need Ma when they were with child as Ma would deliver most of the bairns. When I was old enough to accompany Mither to learn about childbirth and how to deliver bairns, she would enter their croft without knocking nor mentioning them by name. She would just commence the job of first assessing the Mither or enter straight away into delivering the bairn. After she had checked on the health of the newborn, she would also deliver the placenta then tell all of them to clean it all up and without a cup of tea or payment, she would leave as she had arrived. If the weather was unusually warm and sunny, she preferred to deliver the bairn in the burn with my assistance in case the bairn slipped from her hands. She'd have a maid further down the burn in case we both lost hold of it. She told me this way was still preferable because the crofters were not clean people and infection could've been a problem. When delivering in the burn, everything but the bairn is washed away as well as the placenta and clean, she'd say to me. She'd wash the Mither too sometimes. Ma said that they would not always agree with this method due to their superstitions regarding the placenta and wanted it kept and not washed away. Ma told me that they ate it if they didn't have any meat that day."

Grigor was obviously feeling a bit ill at the last story but said, "It means so much to me," Grigor said, "to hear this Isobel. As a child I'd always wonder what she was doing, what she was like and what she did every day and if she had found happiness. She found a life for herself here and her not mentioning me to you while it's heart-breaking to hear, I also understand it because I think I understand her better now. She was a dignified yet very deep and spiritual woman and therefore I believe she kept me very close to her heart and always loved me. Do you agree with that?" he asked. "Oh aye, I know she did and I think Da did also and must've always felt aware of your presence and to be careful not to upset his wife."

Grigor then went on, "You and I both have the same hair." "I've got Da's hair, don't I? Both Ma and Da had jet black hair," I said. "Aye," he said, "but Ma had a curly bit. Not curly all over, just one little bit and you've got that." "Aye, I do," I said, fiddling with my hair. "Can I see your hair because you always wear that big bonnet?"

I asked. He took off his bonnet and I took a look and asked to touch his hair to feel its texture to compare it to my own and found the same curly bit. "Aye, it looks and feels the same," I concluded. "Doesn't it feel strange that we can touch each other after all these years?" I said. "Aye, it does but it feels very natural at the same time." He then went on, "Your Da doesn't have that curly bit, but our Ma did," he said. "Oh, she did too. I just wished I'd noticed," I said reflectively. "I wished I'd known before now," said Grigor. "So, do we all. I know Da really wanted you as his son when you were wee, I saw it on his face the other night. Will you be his son now do you think? He loves you so much and he would've loved to have had a son to help him with the team, especially with the loading and unloading. That was hard for him to do on his own. It's such a shame you weren't here, I guess I always knew that I wasn't good enough at the job. It's all so sad for all of us, but especially you. I am so sorry Grigor," I said. "As I am your brother," he responded, "so too is Da my Father and Isobel, you were good enough at the job." I felt really good about that. "Was I really? Do you think so?" I asked him. "Everyone talked about you as the lass who could drive an eight-horse team of Clydesdales and I remember feeling envious, not knowing that you were my sister," he said.

Sitting in front of the old stone, he said to me, "This is Pecht. You know? The ancient people that used to live all over Scotland." "Where did they go?" I asked. "Not sure, probably Clan Chattan," he replied. "Oh, so you mean they just became clans like everyone else?" I asked. "Aye, I think so," he replied. "Did they look different to other people?" I asked. "All I know is they were a bit shorter, like you," he said smiling. "I'm not too short," I replied. "You're not tall Isobel and neither is Helen. She has it. You can see it," he stated. "Has what?" I asked. "That bit of us that is Pecht," he said. "I don't know what I'm looking for when you say that," I said. "Okay, let me ask you a question," he said. "When you sat here as a bairn and you said there was mist, did you talk to the mist by any chance?" At first, I was too embarrassed to answer, but I did. "On many occasions, I thought it was just my imagination that I would see individual quivering mists appearing in front of me that would make me feel that I had companions and I no longer felt alone. I was able to talk to them through my mind and also out loud. No harm ever came to me, just a sense of peace and strength," I tried to explain. "Well, there you go. Pecht."

"So, Grigor, what do we tell Padruig? When do we tell him and how do we tell him? Should you do it or me or both of us together... or all three of us — Da, you and I?" I asked. "Well," he answered, "Donald, Hugh and I have a surprise for him, which I don't want you to mention. So, I would prefer it if it wasn't today. You'll probably need time together as a family when he gets here. What about tomorrow with Morag, Donald and Eilidh, Hugh Mohr and his dogs? How about we come over for dinner, because you two have a lot to catch up on and you don't know his true state of health yet," Grigor said. "That's true. Okay, then tentatively tomorrow night with Eilidh and Morag, but I am happy for you to tell Morag," I said. "Aye, I already have," Grigor said smiling, "Oh, that's nice. What did she say?" I asked. "She's so happy, for both of us," he answered and then I went on to say, "To be on the safe side, before Padruig is told that you are my brother, it may be better to not hug me or he may accidentally kill my only brother," I said. "Right," he said knowingly. "Once he knows, we'll just be normal brother and sister. Is that okay?" I said. "Sounds bonny lass. I'll hug you so much and kiss you to death," he said, smiling from ear to ear as he kissed me all over my face and hugged me tightly to himself. I was giggling so much from his amorous attentions that he had to remind me to kiss him back and so I kissed him so much and it felt strangely wonderful.

He told me that he remembered being breast fed by his Mither up until she left and said that my breasts had always looked familiar. "You looked at my breasts?" I asked feeling embarrassed. "Aye," he said, "we all did, especially Hugh." "If you and I had grown up and played together, we would have also slept in the same bed" and he laughed raucously. "You are just too cheeky for words," I said. Apart from the shyness that came about from thinking of adult Grigor in that way, he went on to ask if I had ever slept in Ma and Da's bed with them. In answering this question, the guilt of what I had done that day washed over me as if it had been yesterday and so I answered it as best as I remembered. "I don't remember sleeping in their bed before I was three years old, although I might have, but following

an incident that happened, I remember crawling into bed with them."
"What incident?" he asked.

"You remember that Ma said I could be around the Clydesdales after
the Doanne Sidh incident?" "Aye," he said. "So, one day Da was
shoeing two of the horses and he had a particular way of doing things.
He laid the shoes on the ground in order in one long line with the
nails for each one in between each shoe. When Da was on the other
side of the second horse, I began playing with the shoes, not placing any importance to the order that they were in and when I started
playing with the nails, I had an idea, as you do when you are wee.
I thought if I put a few of them in my mouth, maybe five, and swallowed them that I would always be protected from the Doanne Sidh.
So, the nails were poking out of my mouth when Da came to get one of
the shoes. Luckily, he saw me with the nails between my lips, dropped
his tools, ran to me and made me spit them out saying, 'Isobel, you
naughty girl!' I had never been told I was a naughty girl until then,
so it was clearly serious. Then he sat on his stool and took me over
his knee, lifted up my dress in full view of the Crofters' lads, who
were all laughing at me, and began smacking me with his bare hand
at first. I was crying and kicking my legs, which made him even more
angry, so he told me to behave and take my punishment for doing such
a naughty thing." Grigor was giggling at this story and I said to him,
"It wasn't funny."

"Okay, then what happened?" he asked. "He took the wee horse whip,
so I'd take it more seriously and stop complaining," I said. "Aye,
sounds familiar," he said. "He whipped me, which really hurt," I said.
"Ma had come out to see what was going on, but knowing that he'd
never done it before, she didn't stop him. The boys had gathered in
numbers to look at the spectacle, so she shooed them away. When Da
had finished, he told Ma what I'd done. Ma just told me to behave or
I wouldn't be allowed to be around Da's horses. That night, in bed
alone, I was still sobbing. My loneliness had overwhelmed me after
being called naughty. That sounds silly, I know, but I never wanted
the only people who loved me to think so badly of me, so I crept out
of bed and I climbed into their bed. I climbed over Ma and lying
between them, I clung onto Da saying, 'I'm sorry Da, I'm sorry, I'm
so sorry,' as I wept. He woke up and held me close to himself and said,

'It's alright. You're not naughty. You're my wee lass.' And that's the way we stayed sleeping for the whole night. After that incident, I often climbed into their bed for a cuddle and a kiss and I could tell them that I loved them and that I would try to be good and always prayed to be better. It would have been so nice if you'd been there, Grigor, so we could have held each other all night at times, especially during storms or if one of us had been in trouble."

With his hand resting on my knee at times or my head resting on his shoulder, we continued chatting about random things for another half an hour before returning to our chores on the farm. Touching each other was as big a part of our meeting up and exchanging information as we both needed to feel total acceptance of each other. We confided details we never thought either of us needed to know, including the details of Mither's slaying, which horrified him. He had had no prior knowledge of those shocking details and he cried at first into his hands and then in consoling him, we both held each other weeping for our lost Mither and rubbing each other's backs. We both longed for the day when her death would be avenged somehow. I told Grigor that Da did say though that he could hear Ma speaking to him, even though she was deceased. She said that he still had to carry on in order to look after me and the bairns, no matter what and he heard her say, "Run John, run and look after Isobel and the bairns," and so he did.

Isobel of Glenmoriston

Isobel of Glenmoriston
Isobel's Story
1759, Scotland

Craskie Farm,
Glenmoriston
Scotland
March 1762

Dear Diary,

The home was busy, as if we were preparing for the most important occasion of our lives. I'd busily sewn more shirts for the men, including Padruig and Patrick, Grigor Og, my new found brother Grigor Mohr, Hugh Mohr, his brother Donald and my precious Da. I'd also made new dresses for both Helen and Henrietta for the day of Padruig's arrival with two lovely knitted shawls. For the bairns, I'd made warm woollen outfits with knitted beanies and for Beth I made a small shawl. James wanted a woollen vest so, as I was running out of time, I asked Helen to make that.

My goats were brushed and combed, just to look good, but their hair was always saved as Da had always instructed me, and their enclosures were spotless and tidy. Then I saw Grigor Mohr arrive with brothers Hugh and Donald who were looking rather secretive. Grigor Mohr said, "Isobel, do you mind if we make the wee stable a little larger in case Padruig has expansion plans?" Of course, I agreed and I asked him if he was going to give Beth and James their last riding lesson that day. I told him also that there were some wood and stones that I had stored behind the stable for that purpose if he needed them and I had found a large drum that I thought would be good for water, if they needed that. They went to work immediately buzzing away and speaking in low tones. I thought to myself, 'they're up to something', but it would only be good, God bless them.

Grigor Mohr interrupted his building work by giving his last horse-riding lesson to Beth and James. On that occasion, while I was listening in, Grigor Mohr lifted one of the pony's hooves to explain it again to the bairns when he named the soft part underneath a "toad". I turned instinctively and said, "it's not called a toad, it's a frog," then I felt as though my brother had led me into a trap. "Your Granny's right bairns. It's called a frog. Clever Granny." He smiled knowingly at me and I was starting to become aware that I had a very tricky brother. I went inside and decided to watch through the window. Da came up to me while I was still watching and knowingly said, "Beth will be as good a horsewoman as you were one day, my sweet Isobel, but I've got your back. They'll never hear it from me." I responded by just holding his hand and knew then that I needed to talk further to Grigor Mohr before Padruig arrived home.

I approached my brother before he left that day with smoko and asked him if we could talk a wee while again. "Dearest brother," I said, "I am sorry, but I didn't tell you everything this morning, as this is hard for me to talk about. Can we please talk again?" I asked. "You are my brother and can I please ask of you not to speak of me to Padruig in connection to horsemanship at this stage? My husband is a smart man, but he is also a man who can hate deeply and, in his condition, right now especially, it's not the time for him to learn of a terrible untold story. Uncle Allan and Da both know the story and between us three, we have kept a secret from Padruig for seventeen years" I said. "Go on, I'll only agree once I've heard you out," Grigor said. "Horses would have been part of our marriage if it was meant to be, but it wasn't. In the early part of our marriage, Padruig would only visit me at the farm whilst on a wee break from the Highland Company when he would talk incessantly about their achievements and about what Alexander and he were doing very cleverly, militarily speaking, as you would know. He would also show us three all of his weapons, including a very sharp sword — his hilted claymore — and showed Da how it was used. I saw the look on Ma's face at that with her hand over her mouth as she could visualise what he actually had to do with that sword. Ma and I, listening to him over dinner, just didn't want to interrupt him as it made me feel a little sick but he was clearly very proud of being in Lord Lovat's Company and learning those skills that he learned. That included when he was with the other subsequent companies whose names I lost track of," I said. "What's this got to do with horses Isobel?" he asked. "Please hear me out brother. In that time, I was Da's assistant as a teamster and Padruig simply didn't know and he also didn't know that Da gave me my first horse. She was a beautiful yellow mare," I said. "I've seen that spirit horse above your head, so I'm glad you've told me," he said.

"As a young new wife, I didn't dare interrupt him and I hope you understand that from a female perspective. Da didn't appear to worry about the one-sided conversations anyway. So, Padruig didn't learn basic farming such as the crop cycles or the breeding cycles of the animals, let alone anything about the team. I think I assumed that he just knew there was a team anyway, but it was Da's business. Then Padruig would receive a letter calling him back to duty and he'd be gone once again for an unknown period of time and that was our life. I was with child two of these times, the first one being Patrick. He wasn't present for Patrick's birth, but I hadn't expected it. I only needed Ma there. Ma delivered Patrick, Helen and Alex. We were all happy enough and Padruig imparted part of his wages to Da. We would just go back to work after he'd gone and there was no judgement on him. He was a soldier after all and we loved him dearly. Da was proud of him, but he knew that I was still his responsibility just the same and so did Ma."

"As you probably know he was with Lord Lovat's Company for six years, it was just most unfortunate that Lord Lovat lost his Company and then after that it was unclear to us whose regiment Padruig was actually with. When the rising occurred in '45, unfortunately the Laird of Grant took all of our Glenmoriston men to rise for the Prince, and he may have had bad intentions from the start, like Norman MacLeod did."

"When you rode passed the farm escaping from the battle of Culloden in '46 and went to your place of hiding, we had to hide in the shieling soon after, as I told you this morning, then Grigor Og saw us there. Once the soldiers had gone and everything had been burnt down, Ma had been killed, the Clydesdales and coos stolen, my horse killed and set on fire, the crofters ate some of her and left the following day. I didn't think it could get worse than that, but it did. A terrible thing happened and nothing can change it, so please say nothing to Padruig now. It will only serve to make Padruig feel less of a husband with only Uncle Allan and Da knowing the details," I expressed with great difficulty and the look on my brother's face was panic as to what he was about to hear with his imagination running wild as to the many number of atrocities that had occurred. He was holding his hand over his mouth while I continued.

"I was with Uncle's wife, Aunty Margaret, when she passed at the fort. The dragoons said that spies had been looking for Padruig and had seen us here after the crofters' departure, because they wanted our land, but they realised that Uncle Allan, Aunty Margaret, Da and I were all alive and still here and therefore they deduced that Padruig was still alive. They then dropped us back here like sacks of salt, one alive and one dead," I said. "That's not the whole story Isobel. You are my sister now and I'm your older brother don't forget, so I insist that you tell me what happened now," he said. "Aye," I said tearfully. "The dragoons grabbed my three bairns, me and Aunty Margaret. Uncle and Da demanded us back, but the dragoons wouldn't part with either one of us without payment. It cost Uncle Allan forty coos to save the bairns and Aunty Margaret. Suddenly becoming emotional, I said, 'They said they would kill us all and take the coos anyway,' so I told Da I would go and endure it. I couldn't have my bairns harmed. The murderers grabbed Aunty Margaret at the last minute despite the payment and we were galloped off on their horses and restrained. There was nothing either Da or Uncle Allan could do."

"We buried Aunty Margaret the next day. We then took a pact to never reveal what happened. You are now part of that pact. Will you swear to me that you won't repeat what I have told you? So, you see, it was most fortunate that you Glenmoriston Men fought for those sixty coos to be returned to Uncle Allan because forty of them were needed on that fateful day. He swore he would always look out for me, as did Da. Aunty Margaret's life was snuffed out so easily, like Mither's. I see Mither sometimes like a mist, over her grave and where she was killed. She seems like she is guardian of the dead, just waiting for Da and us one day."

"So, Sister," Grigor said looking directly into my eyes, "what made you think that if you couldn't ride or didn't know much about horses,

that Padruig wouldn't put those things together about the Fort? A
lot of our poor women couldn't ride horses that were taken there for
those abominable races, many of whom died, like Aunty Margaret or
took their own lives afterwards. Was concealing being a teamster protecting you from Padruig suspecting that you could have been of those
taken?" Grigor asked. "Aye," I said. "I know what you're implying,
but I feared any slight connection with any horse was going to raise
my husband's intense intuition. Having no connection whatsoever with
horses has been my only defence, tenuous though it is, from my beloved
knowing of what happened at the Fort. If he knew, the consequences
would be unthinkable," I said eyes down remembering that terrible
time. Grigor then said, "It will be hard for me, as Padruig is my
close friend, but I will do what you've asked, although I think these
kinds of secrets are always found out. Look how easy it was for me to
discover how much you knew about horses. Besides which, the horses
themselves give it away when they see you, but he won't hear it from
me. That is what I promise and I am really sorry for it, for your suffering. Sister, I know you haven't told me the whole story, but I want
you to know this. You can always talk to me no matter how hard it is
for you to talk about and I thank God that you survived your ordeal."

Grigor Mohr then went on to say, "When I was in my early twen-
ties, I had been pressed into service with John Campbell, who ten
years later became Lord Louden. I'd tried everything to hide whenever they came around to our place, but eventually Granny MacGregor
gave me up to that Campbell dog. Padruig had been with Lord Lovat's
Company for years due to family connections and was an experienced
fighter by then with Alexander MacDonald, our good friend as you
know, but the Fraser's didn't ask for me, no matter who was in charge
of Lord Lovat's Company at the time. Padruig and Alex were a fighting team, really fierce and in turn and in tune with each other. So,
when I was forced to sign, I had to walk passed Craskie Farm along
the Drover's Road on the way to Fort Augustus, where Campbell was
present on that particular day.

"On the Drover's Road, I saw an awesome sight in front of the Old
School House, which was quiet at that time. What I saw was a magnificent Clydesdale team of eight horses with a thin, silver haired man
on the road giving instructions in Erse to a lass up on the carriage,

who was holding the reins for all of those huge horses. I didn't want to be seen at first, so I hid in the school yard to watch. It must have been your Da, when as a young man his hair was as black as a raven's wing, but on that day was more silver than black and the horses towered over him as Clydesdales do. He spoke to the horses as if in a horse language, to which they responded and so did the lass. It was bewitching. I was confused. Why would this man have a small lass control eight Clydesdales? Surely that is not possible, I thought. But he spoke quiet instructions to the lass and to them as to what to do, gently and beautifully as if in a song. You must have been carrying something very heavy in that carriage to have needed eight horses and then it began to rain heavily. Not for a moment did I imagine that it was you, Isobel and oddly, your hair was like mine - black with that annoying curly bit, I saw before you quickly covered it with a plaid so as not to get wet yourself. I couldn't take my eyes off the scene in front of me and then I decided I would ask for a ride to the fort. Do you remember that day?" asked Grigor Mohr.

"There was a day," I responded, "when we were really busy and needed to get to Badenoch by nightfall with a heavy load. We had to go around Loch Ness you see. Were you the lad that came out of the rain and asked for a ride to the fort, soaking wet?" I asked. "Aye," he said, "and I told you I had been called to serve with the Campbells. Your Da had said, 'Well son, you could always desert. That's the important thing.' And you said to climb up and sit with the two of you. Sitting up there and looking over those magnificent horses was truly amazing, but more amazing was observing a lass having all of those reins in her tiny hands."

"You then told me to give you plenty of time in which to rein in the horses before arriving at the fort, as the horses had started to gain speed. Calm as could be, you started to slowly rein them in, talking to them in Erse, which they understood with their big ears listening and you dropped me out in front. That was you, wasn't it Isobel?" he asked. I told him, "Aye, it was. The fort had been a good customer of Craskie Farm, while we still had crops, we would sell our oats to them for their bread and our teams would carry the oats down there. That's how they knew where to find Da's Clydesdales on the day of the burnings. The two front horses were two horses that Da had bred himself,

116

they were like his babies and you just can't get those bloodlines back once they're gone."

"Da won't show you his bloodlines book, but both of us hope that Beth will start her own breeding stock in preserving the bloodlines of at least the Highland Ponies. We have to preserve our Scottish bloodlines. You can tell Da and I if you think Beth will do that better than James." Then Grigor Mohr said, "In my opinion, you are both right about Beth, but just the same I wouldn't ignore James' capabilities and at some stage when he is old enough, you will need to send him to university or college of some kind because I think business is going to be his future," he replied. "Thank you dear Grigor, I am deeply indebted to you, for what I've told you and what you've told me. Now we just have the waiting game for Padruig's return." Grigor's eyes expressed great sorrow for the story that I had revealed to him as well as admiration that I had indeed been that teamster lass that he had seen all those years ago, right up until when our horses were stolen.

When I returned to the house, I asked Helen if the dog was with Grigor Og, as I hadn't seen him. "Aye," she replied "he seems to connect with that scruffy dog. He's named him 'Dilleachdan.'" she said with a cute smile for her husband's way with names. The oat field was to be finished today and ready for planting, so I was praying that

117

the seeds were coming with Padruig. "Helen, have you cleaned out the chicken pen thoroughly?" I asked her. "Of course," she said, "We've also been given a rooster and four more little hens last weekend, which is a God send with Da coming home and loving eggs, so much." she said. "Our wee herd of coos had increased again too thank goodness, with the birthing of two more calves and Patrick handles them beautifully," I said. "The black faced sheep follow him around too, while the donkey seems to just keep a look out for any intruders," she said. "I think I'm nervous as the time fast approaches," I said to Helen. "I am too," she said. "It's been so long. I've knitted Da a scarf and Henrietta is going to make him his favourite cake when he arrives. Do you want your hot bath now Ma? You've been so busy," she asked. "What a wonderful idea," I thought. "I'll take a bath and then lie down for a while," I said. "Dinner is prepared already and freshly roasted coffee is brewing for anyone who wants it," Helen said. "We both baked two loaves of bread and it's really nice and we've tried it already with honey," she added. "Okay," I said, "I'll have a coffee and bread with honey while you prepare the bath with your special soap and shampoo." I was worried if Padruig came early what he would think of me now, with a few silver hairs and wrinkles about my eyes. I planned to smell and dress as attractively as I could. The coffee was delicious and so was the bread. Our lovely home felt so warm and cosy and I was grateful for it all over again. "Helen, don't worry if you see Grigor Mohr and the Chisholm brothers building onto the stable. They're adding more stalls I think," I said.

I relaxed into my beautiful bath with Helen washing my hair and scrubbing my nails. "Each day you put out a new outfit Ma. Is it just in case Da comes today?" she asked. "Aye," I said a little shyly as I'd made myself new night clothes as well as day clothes, thinking of my first night with Padruig back home. After the luxurious bath, Helen helped me dress. She lifted up one of the dresses I'd made and said, "I like this one the best. With your big shawl, you'll look more beautiful than ever," Helen said smiling. I decided to lie down and rest awhile as the farm busily worked around me and I slipped into a dream. In the dream I imagined my Padruig was home and I reached out for him. To my shock, in my half sleep, my hand touched a face. Then I awoke.

"Oh my God, Padruig. Is it truly you? My darling man," was all I could say to my husband who had been absent for more than three long agonising years. I then descended into tears and held onto him so tightly and felt his shoulders, his arms, his face. I even kissed his hands. "Please God, never let this man be gone from me again." The emotions that I'd held in for those years, finally flowed freely and his tears flowed also into mine as we both sat on the bed weeping. 'Forgive me', he kept saying and when I tried to speak, my throat closed over. Eventually, when I could see him clearly, he was beautiful. Margaret Gordon had painted an ugly picture of his illness, but all I could see now was the pure beauty of the Highlands. A man who had been robbed of his freedom, his family and forced into battle, knowing he had to come back to me alive.

Finally, I could ask him, "How's your leg?" "Och, it's fine now. I need to change the dressings each day and exercise those muscles. Lie with me just a wee while," he said. We lay in each other's arms and fell asleep. At some point, Helen put a warm blanket over us and closed the door quietly. No one disturbed us. That time with Padruig was precious as if our souls floated together as one and hovered over the bed. We didn't feel hungry or thirsty or the need to talk to anyone else. Everything else could wait and what was important was Isobel and Padruig of Glenmoriston were once again reunited in the most beautiful of ways.

It was nearly dark when one of us stirred to the room becoming colder and more voices could be heard from the kitchen and sounding excited. We kissed ever so fondly and he caressed my face. "Do you think we should go and see what that's all about?" he asked. I smiled a happy smile and reluctantly agreed. "At least I don't have to brush your long black hair for a while anyway," I teased, feeling the short hair on his lovely head. "Are you well Padruig? Can you eat dinner?" I asked. "Of course, I am, and aye, I am starving. I can't wait to eat normal food", he said. I knew my man was well and truly back home. "Come on Dar'Thula," he smiled broadly and we climbed off the bed to eat dinner, we thought.

When we opened up the bedroom door, it felt like every eye in the room was on us and I felt thirteen again, as if I had been caught kissing my boyfriend behind the stables where no one could see. Then an almighty

119

roar filled the room with clapping and cheering from Da, Grigor Og, Grigor Mohr, Donald and Hugh Chisholm, Patrick, Helen, Henrietta and the two bairns Beth and James. The bairns then ran to Padruig and held his legs, "Grandda, Grandda, will you please stay home forever now?" they cried. Tears rolled down Padruig's face again and Grigor Mohr came over to him and held his old friend in his arms with such love and then he also embraced Donald and Hugh Chisholm.

"Do you want to eat before we give you our little surprise or do you want to take a look at the gift from your old friends before you eat?" Donald said. Naturally, he was so curious about what they had for him, so he replied, "I'd be honoured to receive a gift from you all and I have some wee things for you as well." "Look at ours first," Donald said. "Okay," Padruig said excitedly. "Come outside and take a peak. It'll only take a wee while," said Donald. Padruig followed them outside while my daughter put on more coffee. He walked out through the front door and out onto the porch then stepped where there was a big black stallion just standing there. Thinking it must belong to Grigor Mohr, he just waited to be shown his present. "He's yours," Grigor Mohr said and handed the stallion's reins to Padruig. "This beauty? How could I accept such a beautiful gift?" asked Padruig, whilst already patting and caressing the stallion's neck. "What price is friendship?" they replied and repeated. "This horse is from us to you for all of our years of friendship, love and loyalty, one to the other. If you accept our gift, it will take a load off our souls for all you have done for us over the years and for your recent suffering. Incidentally," Grigor Mohr said, "his stable has already been built fresh today and I think Isobel caught on." I smiled at them all and was so happy for them in that moment when they were four of the Seven Glenmoriston Men again, standing proud and defiant. We all watched the four of them take the magnificent black stallion to his stable for the night and waited while they fed him. As our friends left the stable, they all waved knowingly to me and said they'd be back tomorrow night. I watched the three of them walking off into the cold misty darkness as my husband came back to the house with a slight limp.

Over dinner, Padruig told us all about what had happened to him in the Americas and on the ships. The wolves in New York were particularly scary. We were all eager to know everything, especially how it all came to be in the first place, but I didn't want him to get tired. Young Patrick took him outside with a hand-held lantern to locate all four privies and when they came back in, I thought he looked pale so I wound up the dinner and asked Helen to prepare him a bath in our room and stoke the fire. Padruig went to his large travel chest first and pulled out a small silver time piece for Da and gave it to him, embracing him fondly. Da was thrilled to have Padruig home and really loved his wee clock from New York. Padruig then called the bairns over to him. The leather boots he bought in New France were the right sizes for them both and they looked beautiful. "Okay you two, it is bedtime now," I said to them. "We're all tired, but you can wear them in the morning." He had already given me my beautiful fur lined leather socks, so my feet felt warm for the first time in ages.

Padruig called Grigor Og over and handed him a large bag of oat seeds and his face could have lit the whole room. "This is wonderful," he exclaimed. "We can start spring planting tomorrow." Padruig gave him another large gift, but he concealed it so I couldn't see what it was, then he wanted a word with him about the wedding by the fire. We all cleaned up after a wonderful meal and I asked Henrietta what they needed for tomorrow's meals, while Helen readied the bath with her special scented soap. We all said goodnight to Da and left Henrietta to smoor the fire when she was done in the kitchen.

Helen was both proud and relieved to see her beloved Father again. Padruig had always loved his wee lass, but now he was proud of the woman who stood before him. Grigor Og was in awe of his father-in-law, God bless him. Patrick had come back home and taken on responsibility and wanted to live up to his Father's expectations. Henrietta did make Padruig his favourite cake and he applauded her cake making skills, so she'd make him another one no doubt. Padruig even congratulated the two of them on their pregnancy. Da was so relieved to see Padruig again that it made him look years younger and he didn't complain once about his pain over dinner. Our son Alex was Padruig's only disappointment, but it had always been hard between Padruig and Alex. In my prayers that night, I visited each room of our home in my mind and thanked God for this miracle. When I lay beside him and felt the heat from his body, I was home. Padruig was my home.

Padruig and I were alone again while I bathed him and washed his short hair, keeping his bandaged foot out. "Do you have new dressings with you?" I asked, "so I can change it for you?" "Aye," he said. His body was leaner than it had been, but I knew we would feed him up and he'd put the weight back on. While bathing him, he asked about Alex, so I filled him in and he said he'd ride his new horse, named Blaze, over to their farm with Alex's gift after breakfast, give him his gift and then come back and help Grigor Og with the seeding, God willing. It all sounded perfect. I dressed him in his new bed clothes that I'd made and he showed me the underwear from London. I couldn't help but laugh, but they were sensible enough if the weather was cold. He wore one pair to bed under the night shirt I had made him, then I changed into my new nightdress, smoored the fire and we both slept peacefully, knowing the bairns were asleep with happy hearts that their grandfather was home.

Isobel of Glenmoriston

Isobel of Glenmoriston
Isobel's Story
1759, Scotland

Craskie Farm,
Glenmoriston
Scotland
March 1762

Dear Diary,

The morning after Padruig's return was a little more chaotic than expected. I'd milked and fed the goats and let them out and had my usual chat with them and took note of the new stable with the new horse's head poking out and neighing hungrily. The wee ponies had been fed and let out by Grigor Og, as usual, but no one had fed Blaze or let him out into the pony's enclosure. I thought I'd better ask Padruig before I let him out, but I did give him feed and checked his water. Grigor Og must have already started the seeding early, so he was due back soon for breakfast. The coos and the sheep were with Patrick as usual and all the eggs had been collected by Helen and the lovely chickens were pecking away at their feed. I had considered some kind of chores chart on the wall, so that Padruig would know what went on each day.

We all descended on the breakfast table like hungry wolves. "Shoes!" yelled Henrietta as we entered the house. "No mud in the house please," was yelled at anyone coming in through the door. God bless her, she kept everything so clean but it could be jarring to hear her yell so early in the day. No-one spoke loudly in the mornings except Henrietta. Padruig came sleepily to the table dressed, but not really prepared for a day's work. Grigor Og came bursting through the door. "Ma, someone has marked five of our big trees in the east field opposite my oat field," he said. No one baulked at the "my" oat field, except Padruig, but he said nothing. "That was me," said Da. "You're doing the spring planting for oats, which will take eleven months to ripen. We need two fields, so that means a winter planting as well. I've measured the field opposite yours, so it's the same size, but it requires the felling of at least five or six big trees and some wee ones. So, I was waiting for Padruig to return to do that job. What we don't use here in the house for Isobel's furniture, we'll use for any external outbuildings that Padruig has in mind. Then, we can sell what is leftover, which will bring a pretty penny for you Isobel. How does that sound family?" said Da confidently. Grigor Og said he was thrilled and after the seeding of this crop he said he would start work immediately on the soil in the other field. Grigor Og had a passion for soil. Patrick added that he was also available for the seeding and the tree felling with his Father, as it was a big job. Da had put himself back to work and for that alone, I was happy.

"Getting off the subject of the field for a moment Padruig, all the animals are fed before we are, so I've fed your horse, but he is still in his stable. Did you want to let him out to stretch his legs a little bit?" I asked. "Nae!" was his sharp response as he didn't want the horse to take off. "After breakfast I'm dropping off Alex's gift to him, so he'll have enough exercise, but he will need his own yard separate to the ponies, or he might bite them. He is a stallion." Padruig said with attitude. "The donkey might bite him right back," said Grigor Og. Grigor hadn't liked the way Padruig had spoken to me. "That trunk over there looks ideal for manure Padruig," said Da trying to change the subject. "Can I have it once it's emptied, so Isobel has something to put the manure into? I don't imagine you'll need it on a ship anytime soon," he smiled wryly.

Padruig was catching onto the morning routine, but went across to the chest and fetched out Da's other gift from New France. "Sorry I didn't give it to you last night Da. I got tired suddenly." Padruig produced the most beautifully embroidered leather vest and said, "Da, I hope this keeps off the chill in the cold mornings." Da was very happy with his second gift and he patted Padruig warmly on the shoulder. "You're a good lad. I love this." He put it on and we all admired it. "Patrick, lad," Padruig said, "this is a very sharp knife made by the Algonquian tribe. I have another the same for your brother Alex and I'd better get going now to see him. Thank you, ladies, for my eggs, they were delicious," he said. As he was about to leave, Henrietta said, "Da, don't leave those saddles on the floor. Can you please put them in the horse stable?" Unaccustomed still to everyone's expectations of him, he just agreed and took the three bridles as well.

"Do I get a kiss my love?" I said. He gave me a warm kiss and we were all smiles again. "Bye my darling and give my love to Alex and Therese," I said. But Da said, "But no need for them to move in here too. We're a full house." That made Padruig laugh and he quickly left with his saddlery and intended to gallop off on his big new stallion. Then he poked his head back through the door and said, "Da, I'll empty the trunk tonight if I have time. Then you can have it." "Thanks son," Da said, who was beaming. "Ya know what I predict now Isobel? Now that he has horse giganticus?" he asked. "What Da?" I said. "He'll want a hitching rail, right out front of the house and his horse will make a smelly mess. So, that's my new job once he's built it. How much?" he said offering a wager. I wasn't going to gamble, because he'd be right. Neither did Henrietta, but Helen said "I'll cook your favourite desert for a week if you're right and if you're wrong, you make the coffee for everyone for a week." "All right," said Da, "you're on."

Padruig must have galloped very fast to Therese's family farm because he was back in no time despite his leg wound. This time, he did let Blaze out to roam wearing a halter. I'd been on my way to the oat field with coffee for Grigor Og when he galloped back in. I hadn't seen anyone gallop into the farm since the day the dragoons came, so it was unsettling. Nothing looked amiss on his face though and he had clearly enjoyed the ride. "Nice ride?" I asked. "Oh aye, he's a beauty. You won't mind if I gate the front entrance of the farm will you, in case he wanders off or worse still, someone takes a mind to stealing my new prize?" he said looking proud of his horse. "I won't mind nor will Grigor Og either, I think that's a good idea. I have dreams of building in the whole perimeter of the farm in stone. Is Blaze a

125

particular breed of horse darling?" I asked. "I mean, does he have a thoroughbred or anything? He looks valuable," I said. Padruig said he agreed that he looked valuable but he would have to ask Grigor Mohr if he was a thoroughbred, but probably not. "How was wee Alex?" I asked cautiously. "Don't really know," was his strange reply. "There was a maid there, so I asked her to get Alex, which she did. He came out looking rather shocked at the sight. Like he'd seen a ghost. So, I just said that I had a wee gift for him from New France. I tossed him his sheathed knife, which he caught and reminded him that it was very sharp, then turned and came back home," he said. Poor wee Alex, I thought. They would never understand each other. Padruig had been raised by a tough family, I had always thought, who sent him to train to be even tougher than them. The first time I ever saw his Father and all his Grant family Uncles, I took off and ran as fast as my little legs could take me into the forest to hide in fear.

"Alright," I said, "so are you building the gate or are you seeding the oat field with Grigor Og and Patrick now?" He replied that he'd be building the gate now with Grigor Mohr and added that he'd also have to build a larger palisaded enclosure near the ponies, as well as a tackle and feed room added to the existing stable in time. "Also," he said, "would you mind if I built a hitching rail in front of the house?" Smiling to myself at Da's win, I told him exactly how I wanted the hitching rails and exactly how far from the house. There had to be two, one each side of the path, so that the path wasn't blocked and one side would be for individual horses and the other for wagons and carts. The manure had to be cleaned up immediately, but Da had that covered. Then the manure would be put into his sea chest, located near my garden, covered over so as not to encourage midges. I realised then that my reply was long and too detailed for him when I saw him smile condescendingly.

"My dearest Isobel, you have run this place like clockwork, with intricate details and I am ashamed that I didn't appreciate just how hard you and everyone else have worked. I hope I can rise up to your standards. Do you want the French silks now or later?" he asked trying to take my mind off work. "Later," I replied, "when we're all back in. I am in the potato fields today if you need me. They all need picking, storing or being given to the kitchen. Then I'll be collecting corn for storage as well and for our dinner. Be careful your horse stays out of the garden and the crops. Does he have a rope in case I need to walk him away from where he shouldn't be?" I asked. "Aye, I'll get it for you. I think when Grigor Mohr comes I'll ask him to help build that enclosure," he said. "The Chisholms might be quicker," I opined. The horse looked energetic and ran off once his saddle was removed kicking up his hind legs. Then I asked, "Will you be able to catch Blaze later?" "Positive," he replied.

Grigor Og had already seeded four rows when I arrived with his coffee and bread. "Smoko," I called, then the two men came over. I then worked almost all day in the potato field delivering some to the kitchen and the rest to the storage room. It was looking depleted in stock, so I was pleased with the additions. After picking what I thought was all of the rows of potatoes, I went along each row with a hoe digging deep and turning over the soil. This exercise found another ten really healthy potatoes, which went straight to the kitchen.

The fisher lads, Hamish and Hugh Og, had dropped off four lovely big fresh fish and left the buckets of seaweed too that I had asked for. "Did you pay the lads Da?" I asked. "Nae," he replied. "They were looking for you to be paid," he said. So, I fetched coin from my housekeeping tin and went looking for them. "Fisher lads," I yelled. One came out of a privy and the other one was patting Blaze down the field, much to my surprise. Blaze towered over the lad, but seemed to like him. "Here's your coin lads and I'll need five fish from now on. 'Himself' is back home and that's his horse," I said. Both lads were amazed by the big black horse. The second lad came down and said, "Whose horse Misses?" "It's Himself's horse," I repeated. "Does he need a groom and someone to muck out the stables, maybe clean the saddlery?" he asked. "Maybe he does," I said. "How much do you charge for that lad?" "I won't charge if I get to ride him," Hugh Og said. "Not a chance of that," I retorted, "but you can lead him around on a rope, make sure he stays out of all of the gardens and the crops and doesn't escape through the front while there isn't a gate there. That would still include brushing him every day and all the other stuff you said, like an apprentice groomsman, but you need to ask your parents first and I need to ask my husband. Come back tomorrow with more seaweed and we'll exchange answers." Both lads left gleeful. "Misses," said the first fisher lad whose name was Hamish, "did you want that extra fish tomorrow too?" "Aye", I said. "Make sure it's a big one or two smaller ones. Himself likes fish." Both lads were impressed that 'Himself' was back after being away for years and were very excited with the additional order and possible job for at least one of them. "There might be more work for you too Hamish, when we start work on another field lifting rocks and clearing the land with Grigor Og and my son Patrick. I won't pay much, understand?" Then Hamish said, "Do you think it might be a shilling a day Misses?" "Nae, that's too expensive," I said smiling. They tried me and I don't blame them. "Is a penny each enough?" I asked. "Oh, aye misses," they both said. "Then I'll tell Himself and see what he says" and they left.

Back to work. I was running out of time with the seaweed on the potato patch. I had to collect the fresh corn for the dinner or the lasses would be looking for something to cook. We had the Chisholms, Grigor and their wives to dinner tonight and the light was fading. Hurriedly, I took the corn to the kitchen. "Ma," said Helen, "you're filthy and we're expecting guests and you haven't eaten all day and your bath is ready." "Okay love, I have to put the corn in the storage room and then I'm finished. The goats are in. Are your chickens in love?" I asked and she said, "Aye Ma. Grigor Mohr's already here and the ponies are in and fed too." "Okay, give me five minutes," I said. I stocked up the storage room and closed its door securely. Then it was time for a bath.

As I ran back to the house, the four men were strolling happily towards the house carrying the gifts that Padruig had brought them back from New France and they were looking very pleased with them. I assumed that Morag and Eiladh were coming together a bit later. Taking off my boots, I dashed inside. "Okay Helen, I'm in. Can you get my clothes ready? The men are coming." "Okay Ma, you're never this late or this dirty. I'll need to scrub your hands," Helen said. I still enjoyed the hot bath and Helen washed my hair too. "These clothes will all have to go straight out to the laundry. Henrietta and I are doing a big load of washing tomorrow. Da's clothes will need washing too. What were they doing?" she asked. "Building a front gate so the horse can't escape that way," I said. "The horse won't escape if he remembers to stable and feed it," Helen said. I noted the critical remark, but ignored it. "Your dress looks lovely Helen. Thank you for working so hard," I replied. "You're the one who has worked too hard and Grigor too, my poor husband. Da was supposed to help him with the seeding," she said critically. "Give him time," I replied. "He's still adjusting after four years of army life and then illness must take its toll. If we're patient, it'll all work out fine. In the meantime, we will have to see that the horse hasn't been left out and ensure that he has been fed. Okay love? Please don't upset your Da. This is him trying," I said.

Despite its difficult start, the dinner was very successful and I noted that Da was helping Henrietta in the kitchen, but she was looking a bit pale. Her pregnancy was taking it out of her on top of all the activity. Over dinner, I thanked Grigor Og and Patrick for their seeding efforts and asked if it was finished. "Not quite", said Grigor Og, "just a bit to go," he replied. "Can I ask you to put in a hedge-row when you finish on this side to keep the horse out and on Uncle Allan's side of the other field to keep his coos out?" I asked. "Aye Ma, be a privilege. I saw Uncle Allan today over his side, just look-ing at what we were doing," he said. "It's okay Grigor, he's waiting to be invited over here to see Padruig, so he is next to join us for dinner. Ladies, when would it suit you to have Uncle Allan over?" Henrietta grouchily said, "I'd like a break tomorrow, so after that is fine" and Helen agreed to keep the peace with Henrietta. "Just us tomorrow then," I said feeling a bit disappointed. I missed my fre-quent visits with Uncle Allan and Henrietta was starting to annoy me. Grigor Mohr and I then looked at each other as a signal to tell Padruig that we were brother and sister, so I called Da over and asked him to join us. "Padruig," I said with a rapidly beating heart, "there's been a revelation that none of us saw coming, but it's good news, actu-ally the most wonderful news you could imagine. Unknown to myself, my Mither Freya had a wee bairn before she married Da because she was the widow MacGregor. The lad was raised by his Father's family and as it turns out the lad is none other than your best friend, Grigor Mohr. Grigor is my brother."

Both Eilidh and Morag had obviously already been told by their respective spouses, Donald and Grigor Mohr and were both look-ing excited to see Padruig's response. Smiling at him, as most of us were, the pressure must have felt quite intense for a joyful response. Calmly, his facial expression changed only from the tension that he'd been carrying to a look of momentary relief. Unsure then, however, how to respond, he looked to his friend first, Grigor Mohr and embraced him genuinely. It was confusing to know what he was thinking, but his love for his friend was obvious. He then reiterated what he'd heard. "Grigor, am I right in believing that you are my brother-in-law?" Then looking toward Da said, "and Grigor is your stepson Da?" "Aye," said Grigor Mohr. "Aye," said Da. Grigor Mohr was unable to show Padruig the carved wooden horse because of the promise he had made to me.

The next few hours were spent going over the night Grigor Mohr heard me singing "Grioghal Cridhe" [21] and how many times that we'd seen each other since childhood without ever knowing of our relationship, that we shared the same Mither. Not many things shocked Padruig Dubh, but that night's news did and he simply blew the candles out and fell asleep. I wondered if he'd felt like me the night I'd found out that Grigor and I were brother and sister. There had been a mixture of feelings of isolation and loss as well as the new comfortable emotions attributed to family. Was he thinking of the time he and I first met at the Glenmoriston School? He was playing futball with Grigor and kicked the ball further than Grigor could and was a bit taller than Grigor. When I rolled over to sleep, there was a discomfiture in wondering what his thoughts could have been. We then slept without words of love that night, but I missed the lack of expected intimacy from Padruig after all those years apart. I had expected he wouldn't wear his English underwear all night long and that he would have an insatiable appetite for intimacy, but I was sadly mistaken. He certainly didn't need me to take off my night gown and I had never worn underwear anyway, which he didn't take advantage of. He didn't even seem to need to be loved, cuddled or kissed. I needed the love that I'd been starved of, even if it was just kind words but it wasn't there. I just hoped we could rekindle the flame once he was well again but I'd never had to work at getting his attention even if it was a bit clumsy at times, God bless him. I was worried and a little needy.

Why couldn't he make love to me? I asked myself who I could ask for advice on such a sensitive topic. Could I ask Uncle Allan and risk it getting back to Padruig? Could I ask Morag, who herself was ravished and couldn't think about desire the same way as I. Grigor Og might be embarrassed if I asked him, Da would only say I was expecting too much of a man just returned from the theatre of war, I wouldn't ask my daughter for obvious reasons. I wished Ma was alive, she would understand and know what to do. I wept silently into my pillow missing my Mither. 'Oh Padruig, where have you gone?'

Isobel of Glenmoriston

Isobel of Glenmoriston
Isobel's Story
1759, Scotland

Craskie Farm,
Glenmoriston
Scotland
April 1762

Dear Diary,

Since Padruig's return, life had altered at Craskie and we'd all made adjustments, including Padruig, whose leg still pained him occasionally. Sometimes he just sat by the fireside in the evening and read a book on Erse poetry or caught up on the news. A big horse and rider came earlier today with news from my lawyer with the copy of the Will and land deeds. His horse was tired and I offered the rider a bed for the night for which he was most grateful. He was chatty, but a pleasant enough fellow with a lot of news from Inverness and the Islands. Malcolm MacLeod of the Isle of Raasay had passed away[14] virtually unnoticed, which was very sad. He was one of those like my husband, who had helped the Prince too and lost everything as a result. John MacKinnon passed away also at the young age of forty-eight years, in hospital in Bath, England. Poor soul had suffered to the end after the terrible torture he'd endured carried out by the English when in search of the Prince. The rider showed us his epitaph in the Scots Magazine and it reads:

> Epitaph of John MacKinnon published in The Scots and Edinburgh Magazines for May 1762[14]

> Afflicted with an obstinate lameness,
> By the best advice
> He struggled to Bath,

133

Where some generous souls,
Enamoured with virtue under a cloud
And merit in distress,
Generously insisted to support him
In every article of expense.

But his goodness of heart,
inflexibly the same,
As generously refused,
And chose
To go into the Hospital,
Rather than be burdensome to friends,
Where he remain'd till his death.

The tender care and assiduous attention
So feelingly given him are past all description.

Virtue, attractive of veneration,
has honourably deposited his remains
In the burying place of a gentleman,
By order
And at the sight
Of the generous proprietor,
With a monumental inscription
Descriptive of his character,
for the instruction of posterity.

Regarded in life;
Revered when dead.

We were losing count of how many had died who had helped the Prince
and these two men were brothers-in-law. May God rest their souls.
Grateful that my husband was still alive, I hurried to make Margaret
Gordon's dress and get it sent to her as soon as possible. Padruig had
finally given me the lovely French silk and I was overwhelmed by its
beauty. Now I'd be able to make a beautiful wedding dress for Helen

and a Maid of Honour dress also for myself. Henrietta didn't want anything more made until after she'd had the baby. So, I presented her with some new baby clothes that I had made and a white baptismal gown that I made out of white French silk. Both her and Patrick became busy with baby preparations and explaining things to Beth and James. He'd built a beautiful cradle for the baby.

I'd planned to buy more sheep with the coin from the Betty dresses, as well as an ox for Grigor Og, so that meant lots of sewing for me. The decision for the fisher lads was made by myself out of necessity for a 1d per day each for both of them. Hugh Og would work with the horses and Hamish would work with Grigor Og on the new oat field. Grigor Og was very pleased at getting some help and it all seemed very simple.

Uncle Allan's fish dinner initially went well and he was really pleased to be reunited with Padruig. I had missed Uncle so much. He asked Padruig if he had met up with Paul Chisholm over in New France or on one of the ships, but he was reluctant to answer that question, so Uncle Allan persisted and asked if the money was all paid back to him that was owed. Padruig wasn't pleased by that intrusive question at all and stood up to get Uncle Allan's money that he had owed him for Alexander MacDonald's debt. None of us were supposed to know about the debts or Paul Chisholm. Henrietta was relegated to a comfortable chair by the fire with her feet up while the rest of us cleaned up as they talked. Afterwards, I changed Padruig's dressing and I thought his wound looked healed, so I asked if it needed another dressing. "Tomorrow," he responded. "How's the pain then?" I asked and he said it was getting better. I was just pleased to see him gaining weight.

I told Padruig about the wool waulking that was coming up and the plan to get two more young sheep with my coin from the Betty dresses and he looked thoughtful. Beth and James asked him if he was going to give them their riding lessons and he said he would once the new pasture was cleared but said "Why don't you ask your Da?" and he added, "Grigor Mohr is busy now at his own farm." I took this opportunity to tell him that I'd hired an apprentice groomsman, who was one of the fisher lads named Hugh Og for 1d a day and a farmhand for Grigor Og and Patrick for the same, but instead of being pleased, his face went dark and he was clearly angry with me. "A groomsman?

For my horse?" he exclaimed. "Aye, he's just a lad who loved Blaze and the extra hand is needed. I did try to ask you, but you were always busy with Grigor Mohr and the Chisholm brothers. The lad's Father is dead," I said, "and their Mither would appreciate the little coin and the two jobs for her sons. I'll feed them both lunch as well. Just bread, cheese and a piece of cold meat." Then he shouted violently at me, "It's not the money or the food or their family's circumstances, Isobel! How dare you employ someone without my permission."

By then, the whole room had gone silent and Da was worried that this could turn really ugly. He came over and stood by me and said, "Settle down lad. Isobel is just trying to help everyone like she always does, even your big horse, that you forget to feed. This way, it is guaranteed that the horse is always catered for and that you are not overworked. I can go guarantor for the fisher lads. Give the lads a chance, eh?" Grigor Og had also strategically placed himself between Padruig and I and then I saw Helen and Henrietta both moving all the break-ables. Then I was so embarrassed, I am not sure what happened next, so with my eyes cast down, unable to look at my family directly, I took myself off to my bedroom and lay on the bed and cried my eyes out. My husband had shouted at me.

When Helen came in, she lay next to me and gave me a handkerchief. "It's okay Ma," she said softly, "like you said, Da is not yet well or adjusted to life on the farm. He forgets to feed his own horse. You did the right thing. Hugh Og will be here early to feed him, then brush him down and that's nice. All our animals are loved like that," Helen said. After I stopped crying, I said that I'd still apologise to Padruig for any offence and if he didn't want Hugh Og here, then I'd find him another job on another farm. I had never been yelled at by Padruig in all our years of marriage. "What did Uncle Allan say?" I asked Helen. "He said nothing Ma, he just looked so sad. He knows how much effort we have all put in to saving this farm, building it up little by little, with his help. I feel unappreciated too and I know Grigor does by Da, not you," she said. It then worried me what had happened to him over there in New France that he wasn't telling us. It'd taken him days to empty that sea chest and give those belts to his friends that he'd bought from the Indians and he'd forgotten to buy

Uncle Allan anything. I decided then, that it was time we visited the Reverend John Stewart in Inverness for help. "Helen darling, can you get your precious Grigor Og to ask Uncle Allan when he is going to town next?" I asked.

Isobel of Glenmoriston

Isobel of Glenmoriston
Isobel's Story
1759, Scotland

Craskie Farm,
Glenmoriston
Scotland
April 1762

Dear Diary,

We went to Inverness with Uncle Allan the next morning. He had sent down a message with his farmhand that he was picking us up very early, so we could get home before it was too dark.

I was dressed and ready with Margaret's Betty dress to post off to London, with two more dresses that I hoped to sell in order to buy three young sheep and two pairs of clippers, so I'd have a total of five black faced sheep. I'd drawn up plans for a wool waulking room on the side of the house, but I knew that was a long way off and I daren't ask Padruig to build it in his mood. I wondered if Patrick could? Helen gave me a nice parcel of food with coffee for us all to eat and drink on the way to Inverness. She kissed me lovingly on the cheek and wished me good luck in seeing the Reverend. Last we knew of the Reverend, he'd wanted to talk about Os 'Iain, John MacDonald, whom I knew was in poverty because he'd come to the shieling once, hoping for a handout which I didn't have.

Padruig and I were still distant since the altercation, even though I'd apologised and offered not to have Hugh Og at the farm, but he allowed the lad to come and, in my opinion, both lads were doing an excellent job. I'd asked Hugh Og to brush the ponies and the donkey as well and muck out their stables and told him where to put the manure for my garden. The saddlery was beautifully cared for now and the stalls were spotless. Padruig knew it had been the right decision until he decided to take some responsibility for his own horse. All he'd done was cut down two trees up at the new field, which had exhausted him. He never apologised for yelling like that to me in front of everyone, but it was clear to everyone that his intentions were to appear to be the one in charge and I had threatened that role even though it had suited him for the near four years that he was gone.

While we waited for Uncle Allan, I asked Padruig who it was that had forced him onto that ship in Leith and he wouldn't answer me. I was extremely frustrated that my husband was protecting the identity of the anonymous person who had turned all our lives upside down for the last near four years. I persisted and asked him if it was Simon Fraser, the Master of Lovat or Donald Fraser as the Reverend had suggested, but still there was no response. "You're not going to give up, are you?" he said.

"The MacPhersons told me that one of their own was a recruiter for the British forces and used a dirty trick for recruiting a lot of men.

They told me that he used a shilling with King George's face on it, naturally, and would put it in an unsuspecting man's drink in an alehouse. Then he'd say, 'You've accepted the King's shilling, so you have to appear the following morning for service or be arrested for desertion.' Did that happen to you in Leith Padruig? Did you stop in an alehouse after seeing Rev. Forbes? Did you meet one of the MacPhersons there? Or did you meet up with Paul Chisholm in Leith, chasing the money you owed him?" I asked him directly.

Then we were interrupted as Uncle arrived. He scanned our faces with full knowledge of what had happened the night before. "So, what's with you two then?" he asked. "None of your business," Padruig answered rudely. "Well," said Uncle, "that's where young Alex gets his bad manners. So, Isobel what are your needs today love?" he asked. I told him first we needed to post a Betty dress, then visit the Reverend Stewart, then take the other two dresses to sell in order to buy three more young sheep, two pairs of clippers and hopefully an ox. He then said, "Well love, I doubt we'll fit an ox on this cart, but we can do the wee sheep," jested Uncle Allan. I almost fell for it and was sure for a moment that the ox had to stand up in the cart. At least it got a smile out of Padruig. "Uncle Allan," I levelled my speech, "I am sure an ox would really enjoy a ride all the way from Inverness to Craskie Farm, he might even want a wee lie down, but as you say, there's nae room, so he can be tied to the back of the cart and run all the way," I said. "Any objections to an ox tied to the cart?" I asked.

Smiling broadly as he always did, God bless him, he just went on to talk about my sheep. "So, you like your wee woolly black faced sheep, do ye Isobel?" "Oh aye," I replied, "so does young Patrick. They are so intelligent. They follow him around like pets." Uncle Allan then said, "I've never had sheep myself. I am told they eat grass right down to the roots if you have too many and then there's nae enough pasture for any other beasts to eat." "That's right!" Padruig piped up wanting to have his say about sheep. "Can't keep too many sheep, Isobel." he said. "When you receive your woollen jumpers or your first new plaids, you won't be complaining about sheep," I retorted sarcastically. "That's true," Uncle Allan said, "so you'll make me a new plaid, when they overturn the law Isobel?" he said. "Of course, I will Uncle. Your plaid will be the first because you've helped me with my sheep, then Patrick, my son, second," I replied. "Thank you, Isobel. See Padruig? It pays to keep in good with the ladies that make these things," he said knowing it was going to be a rough journey up to Inverness through the Great Glen. "Padruig," I said, "are you going to answer me about the shilling and if you were tricked into service with the threat of arrest? Why won't you answer me?" I asked. "Nae, Isobel, I wasn't tricked by a MacPherson in an alehouse but your imagination is alive and well," he said. "Then what? How did it happen? Why can't you explain it?" I said. Then sitting uncomfortably in between us, Uncle Allan said, "Now you two. If this continues, one of you is going to have to walk to Inverness, so please be quiet. I am too old for bickering," he said. We then stopped. "I'm sorry Uncle Allan," I said.

Whoever my husband was covering up for must indeed have been close and I might have known him. Did he owe someone a favour from long ago maybe? Was it another Grant? My mind wouldn't stop. I dreaded that it may well have been Paul Chisholm, Hugh and Donald's Father who hadn't yet returned from New France. It was a relief to post off Margaret Gordon's dress to London and I wrote and thanked her once again for caring for Padruig. In the parcel I also included a wee note requesting that the Bishop write to Padruig in a support-ive way and informed them that we were seeing Reverend Stewart. I thought there was a deeper problem needing to be addressed and was worried about his mental state.

At the Manse, Reverend Stewart's housekeeper greeted us warmly and took us to his study and gave us milky tea and I complemented her once again on her beautiful roses and she told me that she would give me my own pots of wee rose bushes to take home and plant on the farm. The Reverend came in after his prayers, I thought, and greeted us with true happiness. "How lovely to see you both," he said, "and Padruig, you'd be on the Chelsea Pension now?" he asked. Padruig said it had been applied for, but he did not know where to get it. "Should be wait-ing for you at the Post Office," was the Reverend's reply, "or they can forward it to the farm. I can do that for you Padruig. Now, I wanted to talk to you about Os 'Iain John. I suppose you know he is in pov-erty? Money's short, I understand that, but I was hoping you could drop around and see him and take him some meat. His family is strug-gling," he said. Padruig replied. "Aye, I can kill him a hart one day and drop the whole beast to him." "That's wonderful, thank you Padruig. How's the farm coming along now Isobel?" Directing the question to me, I feared it would start something again, so I candidly spoke about Padruig's condition and how our marriage was suffering, we weren't even making love and I asked him for help.

I told the Reverend that I thought there was something deep within Padruig that he was holding back. Maybe about New France? So then, before too long with the soft direct stare of the Reverend, he said to Padruig, "It must have been hard for you to have to kill an innocent Indian, with whom you'd had no quarrel or even the French, whom you'd never considered were your enemies, Padruig. Does it bother you?" Tears then began to flow down Padruig's face and I held his big hand. "Aye, it bothered me a lot, having to fight under the British flag and kill people to stay alive. When I was stuck in New York in a tent, I'd wished I had died there instead of carrying the burden. But here I am. I promised Isobel that I would return to her and I know I've been a bad husband. I have yelled at her and I really wanted to hit her." Then looking at me, he said, "Please forgive me Isobel? I think I always misunderstand what's going on. I've never been a farmer and I feel so inadequate compared to everyone else." He kept weeping for a while with the Reverend by the fireside, so while they were busy, I quietly left the room and asked the housekeeper about the roses. She had six potted plants ready for me and Padruig to take with us. I hugged her farewell and thanked her for the roses and she promised me lavender next visit. It was exciting to think where I was going to plant them. Then Padruig came out and we left to complete our other tasks. I was able to sell the two Betty dresses and bought my three beautiful yearling sheep, the clippers and I paid for the ox to pick up later. We ate Helen's food and drank the coffee as we looked for Uncle Allan to go back home. My husband carried my yearlings and put them in the cart, kissed me on the forehead and said, "Crafty move, but thank you. We best not forget the ox when we leave to go home."

Isobel of Glenmoriston
Isobel's Story
1759, Scotland

Craskie Farm,
Glenmoriston
Scotland
April 1762

Dear Diary,

Once we finally arrived back home last night, Uncle Allan advised me to move the donkey to the spare horse stall to keep an eye on Blaze and where Hugh Og could easily tend him also. That way it was all equine business in the one area. Then there was room for the three new lambs in the donkey house, which we'd have to rename "The Lamb House". "What's the donkey's name?" Uncle asked. "I didn't give him one," was my answer. "I had a male donkey named Frederick once. He looks like a Frederick," Uncle said and smiled and I agreed on his name as he moved Frederick to his new stall, while Padruig still lay asleep in the cart with the yearlings. 'So, he does like sheep,' I thought, that's good. Because I knew there was money in the future to be made with these sheep and the wool waulking. Uncle Allan picked up the lambs gently and placed them carefully inside the lamb house with the other two sheep friends and made sure they had feed and water and closed them all in.

"It's going to be cold tonight Isobel. Better get him to bed, but I must prepare you for what's ahead. You will need a grain storage shed and the whole family will have to work on the crops when its harvest time. Start giving Beth and James more chores, you'll need them. This winter is going to be colder than usual and so later on this year you'll have to think about preserving beef and goat's meat into storage barrels to see you through the winter. I've a few barrels that you can have, but you'll need to buy a few more as well as a couple of scythes for the harvesting and string for the harvest. My cart here is available to you during harvest time to cart it to wherever you build the shed and I emphasise that you'll need salt. Do you have any?" I was so surprised at all the advice, but said I only had one bag of salt. "Margaret, my late wife used to make all our salt and she sold it as well and it's a big job, however the equipment is still there. Do you know anyone who could revive the salt making?" he asked. I had an idea. "I'll ask the fisher lads if their Mither has a job. She's the widow Chisholm," I said. "Okay, send her up to me and I'll ask if she can do it and we can revive the salt production and then there should be enough for all of us and possibly an income as well," he said. Padruig started to wake up, so Uncle Allan wished me well and reminded me to build that grain storage shed, preferably with dry stone. "Before I go, can you get Grigor Og to untie your ox and take the braw fellow over to be housed overnight with your Highland coos? But let him out early in the morning in case they don't get on," he said.

I called out to the quiet house that hadn't even acknowledged our arrival yet to my son-in-law "Grigor, lad? I have something for you, but it is too big for me to handle," I said. Grigor Og gingerly put his head out the front door, "Aye Ma? What can I do for ya?" I replied, "It's your precious ox and she has trotted all the way from Inverness behind Uncle's cart." If he'd been a lad prone to crying he would have in that moment, as his eyes fell lovingly first on the ox, then me, then Uncle fetching Padruig out of the back of the cart, then to the sorry wee cart pony. "Oh Ma, Uncle. God bless you both. Uncle, can I help the wee tired pony too and put him with ours to be fed and watered? I can unhitch him, if you like while you and Ma eat dinner?" Grigor Og suggested. The lad then untied the ox first, patting her lovingly on her head and he welcomed the braw beast to Craskie. "He's a good lad Isobel," Uncle said. "A really good lad and I could do with dinner. It's cold up at my place with no fires lit and no prepared food. Thank you, Isobel, a night with the family would be lovely." The wee pony was so tired and Grigor Og took tender care of him. It was dark, but not too late, so all four of us entered the house at the same time with Uncle still helping the tired and staggering Padruig.

"Hello family. How is everyone?" I asked, as I went inside. Helen was looking anxiously from face to face, but her eyes relaxed once she saw that her husband was clearly very happy then Padruig went over and hugged her, much to her surprise and thanked her for the lunch.

"I hope there's lots of dinner left" he said and smiled, "we're all famished." The tension left the room, but Da sidled up to me and asked if I was really alright. "Aye, Da," I said and kissed him on the cheek.

"Well, it was lucky I had saved plenty of dinner for you as it turned out," he said as he led Uncle over to the fireplace. "Allan, take a seat by the fire old friend and share a dram wi' me." From out of nowhere he produced a bottle of whiskey and the two of them sat by the fire, ate their dinner on their laps and drank their whiskey. Any awkwardness that had been there in the room was addressed by Padruig who finally said out loud to the whole family, "You can all relax. Your Mither dragged me off to see the Reverend Stewart. Now we're all good and Grigor Og has even got himself an ox thanks to your Ma's coins and Uncle Allan's kindness. God bless you Uncle," Padruig said. "Thank you and sorry for my earlier rudeness."

I was ravenous. It had been a long and emotionally exhausting day. "Ma," said Helen quietly. "Is it really okay?" I kissed her darling forehead and reassured her that it was. "I'll put water on to boil for your bath then for after you've had your dinner," she said. "Coffee first would be nice," I said. "I asked Henrietta about her feet and ankles and suggested she put her feet in hot water and elevate her legs to stop the swelling. "Where's Patrick?" I asked. "Upstairs finishing off the nursery, he'll be down soon," she replied unenthusiastically. I addressed sweet Grigor Og and let him know that the donkey, now named Frederick, was no longer in the donkey house and that Uncle Allan had moved him to the spare stall with the horses, so the sheep could all be together. "That's a bonny idea," he replied. "Do you still want me to feed the donkey?" he asked. "Aye, just for tomorrow morning, but if you see Hugh Og, tell him that Frederick is now his job to feed and he can let him out also. Grigor, there's a spare bridle in the tackle room. Why don't you ride Frederick up to your field? It'll save some energy and time. We should use him more," I suggested. His response was positively gleeful at such a small gesture, so I suppose that was aye. "He can graze up there on the new field on a rope to be there with you. Padruig, are you tree felling tomorrow?" I asked. "Aye, another two I thought," he replied. "Okay, just make sure they don't land on the donkey, or move him first. I am off now for a bath," I said. "It's ready Ma," Helen called.

"Incidentally everyone," I called back before I reached my bedroom, "we are going to be building a grain storage shed just beyond the pony stables, out of dry stone. I'll draw up the plans first, but Padruig we'll need a lot of that stone and some of the wood from your trees. And ladies, apparently after this summer, we are going to be heading into a really bad winter, so we have to start saving up salt and barrels now, so when the time comes we can preserve the meat, fruit and medicinals from my herbs. Goodnight to you all," then I kissed Da and went into my room to finally relax. Helen then said "I think you've sorted it out Ma. Da didn't object to any of that, not even the grain storage shed. Well done!" "He just needed to talk to someone who'd understand," I said. "My hair had better stay dry tonight Helen. It's very cold. Can you put a bigger log on the fire too?" I asked. "Did you like the dinner Ma?" Helen asked. "Oh aye. The corn was especially delicious, I thought?" I responded. "I cooked it", she said. "You are a wonderful cook my darling," I said.

"Are you available tomorrow to try on the wedding dress that I've made you?" I asked. "Oh Ma," she said through wet kisses. "You're not crying are you love?" I asked. "Well, I thought Da had forgotten our wedding?" she said, sobbing. "Nae, how could we forget your wedding, my dearest? We made the date at the Kirk today. Tell your beloved Grigor that it is May 15th and I'll make him a new shirt in the Prince's style with a waistcoat. He'll have to wear those English style pants for the wedding though and not a kilt. I am sorry love, but he can wear it before we leave for Inverness," I said. Helen then said, "I am happy just so long as we are legally married in the Kirk, so we can have bairns like Henrietta. I want to be pregnant Ma." I must have been smiling broadly at this as it cheered her up again. "Can I ask you to deal with the smoko tomorrow morning darling for the three men and the fisher lads? I can continue sewing if you do that for me. By the way, the donkey's name is now "Frederick." She laughed while she helped me into my night dress. After brushing my hair, we said goodnight.

Before I fell asleep I had an idea as a compromise to the wool waulking room now that we were getting a grain storage shed. At the rear side of the house near Helen's room, was an inadequate laundry and the ladies in town were putting in fires in their laundries, one that had a small pipe like chimney and the fire was under a huge copper bowl. The idea was to boil your clothes and bed linen after you washed them. The second wood fire wasn't large, but that was for keeping the irons hot and as yet we didn't even own an iron. It would mean a new structure was to be built out of stone and would be added on to the burn side of the house with a door into the wool waulking room that led into the house. It would mean having to buy a few more things for the laundry from Inverness the next time I went, as well as ask who could build the two rooms and get us a wool waulking table. I thought I'd leave it with God as always and slept.

Isobel of Glenmoriston

Isobel of Glenmoriston
Isobel's Story
1759, Scotland

Craskie Farm,
Glenmoriston
Scotland, 1763

Dear Diary,

A shy looking middle-aged lady came to my front door today and introduced herself as Mary Chisholm. "Aye," I had said, "What can I do for you?" She had expected me to know who that was, but I didn't and so she then apologised and explained that she was the fisher lads' Mither. Then I was embarrassed and invited her in for coffee. "Coffee," she said, "what a treat." "Aye," I replied. "I bought it in Inverness when I was there last week. Is there a problem with Hamish and Hugh Og? I really hope not because they are doing a marvelous job and they fit in here like family," I asked "Oh nae," she exclaimed. "On the contrary, I wanted to thank you Mistress for giving them the jobs and myself also. I've just been to Master MacDonald's house about the salt making job and my Mither used to do that, so I am familiar with the process. I have accepted the offer of the job up there at his farm," she said. At the back of my mind, I wondered if Uncle Allan was thinking of more than salt.

"Himself is wanting me to move in there rent free wi' my twa lads, but he needs your permission," she said, "seeing as how the lads work here," she said. I took this information in and said that I approved, so long as she was sleeping in a separate part of the house so that people wouldn't talk. Not that there were many people here these days. The Glens were getting quieter and quieter as families were forcibly taken off their land and sent to the colonies or emigrated by choice. Most all of my friends were either dead or gone now and it made for a lonelier existence.

Fortunately for us all, Padruig, God bless his soul, did complete the work on both the laundry and the wool waulking room despite my misgivings given the timing of Henrietta's baby's due date. He followed all of the drawings I gave him and with the coin I received from the next sale, I purchased the big copper for boiling the clothes as well as a dolly, clothes washing barrels, barrels for the salting of the meat and scythes for the crops, come time and the string for the bundles of oats as Uncle had instructed. I made a note to myself concerning having to buy two irons. Henrietta's baby was due soon. I just hoped that she wouldn't mind us noisy wool waulkers once it all started up again because she took no interest in the wool waulking and she always appeared agitated nowadays. Padruig and Patrick then both worked on the grain storage shed with both Hamish and Hugh Og, alternating with their other tasks.

Patrick was then teaching Beth and James mathematics, reading and writing by himself in both English and Gaelic and found it enjoyable. At least that was one less job that I had. After their lessons, the bairns had to go to the fields and help in the clearing with their Father and the other adults, as Uncle had recommended. Alterations had been made to the plough based on the improved design features that Padruig had seen in the Colony of New York, so after hitching up the ox, Grigor Og started ploughing slowly at first and then gained momentum with his new deep plough and became much better quite quickly. His ox would need resting however, as she tired easily, unlike what I knew of our Clydesdales. Grigor was often seen patting his precious ox. I felt like applauding, but I contained myself. It was such a sight and I knew Helen was a proud wife — she had no ordinary husband and I was really happy for them both as well as confident that one day Craskie would be managed capably by the two of them.

Finances were not great, but I concluded that I would need to make more dresses and men's shirts to sell. Some shirts would be in the Prince's style with waistcoats, which followed the European styles. Up until then, it had just been us ladies that wore waistcoats in these parts, but with our stays of course. Padruig also said he could sell some of the wood to inject money into the farm, so with his pension, we were getting by.

April 15th was approaching quickly for Helen and Grigor's wedding, so their wedding clothes were completed first, followed by the rest of the family and the invitations went out to attend their official Kirk wedding. Grigor Og had made his preferences known about a few things concerning the wedding dress. It was not to be low cut, the lace had to come up to Helen's neck for modesty purposes, the sleeves had to be full length and the dress was not to reveal her ankles. Helen was happy with all of his expectations and that was the key to their marriage. The dress was made of the purest French silk and the lace that Padruig had brought over from New France and I had embroidered the bodice with all of our native flowers.

I'd had some coin put aside in a tin that I had hidden under the bed since the year Padruig was taken away and when possible, I would just add a few coins to it from the goats or from a shirt or dress here or there. I counted it and there was enough for brand new, matching slippers and my daughter would be the most elegant and beautifully dressed bride in all of Inverness shire. Both Henrietta and I did her hair in big bangs and as a gift to her from Padruig and myself, I gave her my own Mither's hair comb, so that it would sit in her hair and sparkle. Mither had worn it at her own wedding to Da which had miraculously survived the burnings, found amidst the ashes. Of course, the weather would be cold, so I'd made a special arisaid for Helen to wrap herself in going in to the Kirk and then leaving again. Underneath the beautiful dress, also for warmth, I'd added two petticoats.

I didn't ask Helen or Grigor Og about a wedding ring because Padruig had never given me one and so it wasn't expected and I left it to them. Padruig had given me a big brooch that held my arisaid together and kept it from blowing off, so that I could work in the fields whilst wearing it. It was beautifully decorated with thistles in solid silver and of course it was circular like a wedding ring. So, to me the brooch was like my wedding ring.

During Helen's fitting, her dress needed only one tiny alteration and my teary-eyed daughter was so happy with the end result. I asked for her opinion and approval concerning Grigor Og's shirt, waistcoat, stockings and new breeches that I'd made that he'd be wearing upon departing our property. I hung the bride and groom outfits side by side and asked her honest opinion if there was anything that either of the outfits needed any alteration or an addition. In response, she said, "Aye Ma, Grigor doesn't have a nice coat". I remembered that beautiful coat that Padruig came home in from London, which he had never worn again and said to her, "Do you think Grigor Og would wear that woollen coat of your Father's, your Da never wears it?" Of course, she loved the idea and I told her to just leave her Da to me. That's when I took the new slippers out from under the bed and presented them to her. "What about these darling?" I said, "Would you like these for your wedding? They are from me," I said. Overwhelmed and overjoyed, Helen said, "Of course, oh Ma. They are beautiful. I have never seen anything like them." With that final touch to the wedding outfits, they were ready.

An emotional Padruig stood and recited the poem that was on the back of the invitations and a Papist Priest had travelled up from Edinburgh as our old Kirk in Dornie was not only a long way away, but in severe disrepair. And so, the wedding was to take place in an Episcopalian Kirk in Inverness. The wedding feast, organised by the Reverend John Stewart's wife and housekeeper, was held in the Manse in Inverness. I saw both Padruig and Grigor Mohr standing shoulder to shoulder and I had never seen Fathers prouder than on that day. Two of the Glenmoriston Men, tall, handsome and braw, witnessing their children marrying and joining our families until the Day of Judgment. It wasn't long before Donald and Hugh Mohr Chisholm wandered up beside them to congratulate the two Fathers. What a grand sight they all were.

To Gregor and Helen,
May love flow through and from you.
Into each other
Receive God's gift, unlike any other
One that calms on a windy night
One that warms on a chilly day
One that protects the heart
And cannot be dejected
When the wolves are at the door
May your children be strong as you are
And carry this your love

Into each other and into every
generation
So, safety is in your company
Comfort is in knowing you
Let this be your legacy, we pray.
From both your Mothers
and Fathers.

There were white table cloths on
the tables, pretty candles, flowers,
nice china and pretty glasses for the
beautiful wedding feast followed by
traditional music and men performing Highland dancing. Laughter
and Gaelic songs filled the air and
there was a great sense of celebration with friends of old and new,
neighbors and family from both the Grants and the MacGregors. We
then all stayed overnight in a boarding house in Inverness and returned
to Craskie the next day carrying more plants from the Reverend's
housekeeper. This time, she gave me twenty lavender plants. I was
overjoyed that Helen finally had what she wanted and prayed that she
would fall pregnant that night as was her heart-felt wish. Her Father
had also left his special gift of the polar bear fur on their bed back
at home. We both prayed for more grandchildren. Thankfully, she did
decide to invite her brother Alex and his wife Therese, who brought a
wee wedding gift along with them. My old Da was just so pleased the
next day that we were on our way back home. He was tired, which was
understandable, considering he was nearly eighty years old but I felt
he was missing his beloved wife.

Back at the farm, it felt different because a milestone had been reached
and I looked around at our achievements over the past years. We sent
our blessings to those people who had died, those who had had to leave,
were forced to leave and the few that had stayed. There was still such a
thing as a Highlander, though the English had tried to wipe us all out
one way or another. I saw it on Padruig's face as we passed through
the Great Glen where friends once played or men once worked and
women laboured. It had been a good life until Charles Edward Stuart

had arrived on our shores in 1745, but we survived and despite this, Padruig loved him still, I knew that and so I kept my opinion of the Prince to myself. The braes of Glenmoriston were quiet now and there was just the sound of the clip clop of our horse's hooves all the way home.

Our first oat crop was truly a sight to behold thanks largely to Grigor Og. The stone building we had built, in which to store the grain, stood strong and proud. The winter crop was planted and for a while things were running smoothly until Mother Nature hit us hard with one of the worst storms in living memory. The snow piled high around the house and Padruig shoveled us out each day despite the front verandah. Sadly, for me, the snowy winter lasted longer than our prepared meat could feed us. Despite all of our efforts, our entire herd of goats, except a breeding pair, had to be slaughtered to keep us all with enough food. I was too sad to replace my precious goats for a time, so I bought sheep and expanded the wool waulking and we had both Beth and James knitting jumpers each night at one time. Our sheep flock came to be thirty and their home at night became the expanded goat house. Disillusioned about buying any more goats, I kept the remaining two in the donkey house, where Beth, James and Sarah could learn how to milk the nanny. Fortunately, everybody loved lamb stew, lamb roast, lamb sandwiches and any other creative way of cooking lamb that we could come up with.

Hamish and Hugh Og tried to bring some levity to our situation with such a bad winter season and considering that Craskie Burn had frozen over, they began to teach Patrick, Henrietta, Grigor Og and Helen how to play a sport they called 'curling'. One morning I went into my kitchen and found that all of our brooms were missing. I found the six young people with my brooms in their hands doing what strangely seemed like sweeping the frozen icy surface of the burn and much to my surprise, these very large rounded Caledonian granite stones started moving toward them all by themselves. It looked like magic and using one of Padruig's words, creepy.

I was worried about the weight of the granite stones on the ice, given that we were coming to the end of winter and the ice was no longer as thick as it had been. I was also not happy about my brooms being destroyed. "Make your own brooms for tomorrow thanks lads," I yelled to Hugh Og and Hamish from the porch. At the suggestion of Beth and James joining in, I could imagine my grandchildren sinking beneath the ice and being carried at a very rapid rate all the way to Loch Craskie, never to be found again and said, "Stop! That ice might break. At least half of you and one of those stones need to get off the ice now!" Stifling a giggle, Helen jumped

off. "Sorry Ma," she said, "we were just having some innocent fun." "Helen, you can't even swim and I would never have thought that you would combine housework with competitive sport?" I said. "Ma," she said, "we'll fix the brooms and I am sorry for worrying you." I didn't feel like a spoil sport at all, I just couldn't bear the thought of losing someone to a game. I had never developed an appreciation for sport for fun because of the continuous rejection I'd experienced from our croft- ers' bairns who wouldn't allow me to join in with their games because I was Himself's daughter. Ultimately, I would take refuge in the forest or go back home to Mither and read.

Helen stepped onto the snowy edges of our burn and was followed by Henrietta who was carrying one of their heavy stones. I heard the sounds of heavy crunching footsteps in the snow and looked up to see Padruig and Grigor Mohr taking in the sight with smirks on their faces. They waved in an attempt to placate me, I suppose. "It's my fault Isobel," said Padruig. "All my idea," he added. "We taught the Indians in New France how to play this game and I thought it might cheer everyone up and use up their energy," he said. With my hands on my hips and a frown on my forehead, I said in disbelief, "This was all your idea, to put heavy rocks on thin ice with six to eight young adults enthusiastically sweeping the ice? This has to be the most irresponsible idea you've ever had. I could've lost my daughter, my granddaughter, my grandson..." He stopped me at those three and then, to my surprise, asked why I thought that? Grigor Mohr had half turned away in case I saw that he was almost laughing. "The ice," I said. "This part of the burn never usually freezes over, for a start, so if it was going to be used for recreation, surely it had to be observed over time first before usage. Have you seen how thin that ice is today? I guarantee by tomorrow morning that there will be water and ice flowing in this burn," I said adamantly. "On top of that, Padruig Dubh, none of our children can swim," I added. Grigor Mohr, then turning around, asked me, "Thin, is it?" then he looked very worried. "Aye," I said. "Grigor!" he yelled. "Get off the ice!" Then Hugh Og came over to Padruig and apologised and waited for what else was to transpire. Everyone and the stones then came off the burn.

"Okay," I said. "Both you and Grigor Og come here tomorrow morning after sun up and if I'm wrong, I'll apologise and give you all of my brooms. Does that sound fair?" I said. "Aye," Padruig responded, still smirking. "But if I'm right, this summer, when it suits you all, I propose that we plan a picnic at Loch Craskie to learn how to swim. You first Padruig, with the two Hughs and Hamish as the teachers seeing as they're so good at teaching. What do you think?" I said. Grigor Mohr then added, "We can go fishing too Padruig, it sounds bonny to me." With that, Padruig reluctantly agreed to the idea and inspected the burn the following morning with Grigor Og. To his surprise and a little horror at the reality that his Helen could have actually fallen through the ice just as I had said, what they witnessed was a burn flowing with a combination of ice and icy water. As more ice was melting, the burn widened and ordinarily one would admire its beauty, but the two men sighed, went back inside the warm house with all eyes on them, waiting upon their observation. "Looks like I am learning how to swim this summer, Isobel," he quipped and sat down for an enormous breakfast.

Henrietta had never hugged her father in law before, but on that morning, she came to him and hugged him from behind and thanked him anyway for his kind thought and added that we'd like a picnic at the loch, provided we all took our midge nets. I couldn't help but detect a sinister undertone that Henrietta was looking forward to her Mother in law looking the fool. I hadn't thought of the midges, so we tried swimming lessons just the once as a family. Hugh Og tried hard to teach Padruig how to float first but he kept panicking thinking he would drown. Hugh Og then tried a method of holding him up from under his back until he was confident enough to be in the water before trying to get him to swim while being instructed to kick his feet and paddle with his arms only to swallow half of the loch. Choking on the loch water, he'd had enough and wanted to go fishing instead with Grigor Mohr.

Hugh Mohr then said it was my turn. I wasn't laughing then as I contemplated trying to learn how to swim. Helen and I were wearing our white cotton petticoats and tops in which to swim. I didn't think of what that would look like wet but co-operatively walked into the cold water and was immediately regretting my idea of learning how to swim. Being much shorter than Hugh Mohr, I was trying to reach him out in the loch for the lesson, where he stood tall. The loch hadn't looked deep, but then my feet weren't touching the sand and like Padruig, I too panicked. I called to Hugh who looked a bit amused, but he supported me as Hugh Og had done with Padruig, but his hand was on my stomach being supported face down. He calmly told me to kick my legs and lift up my arms to paddle, but all that happened was swallowing water too and I began to choke, not to mention worried about that hand as it moved about. As I exited the loch in dripping wet clothes, Padruig dropped his fishing stick and came running over with a plaid to cover me. "Isobel, you can see through your clothes when wet. You had better change," he said like a typical panicked husband protecting his wife's dignity. I didn't dare tell him about that hand, after all it had been harmless, I thought. Helen did better than us both with Hamish, but this time I took a plaid to her as soon as she got out. Swimming was an embarrassing sport unless you're wee, I concluded. It had been a fun day, but I had to wear a midge protector across my face for the rest of the day, as Grigor Mohr tried to relax fishing and swatting the midges with poor Morag by his side. I didn't think my idea had been much better than Padruig's.

We laughed about our silliness in bed that night whilst scratching here and there. "God knew what He was doing when he created the Highland Coo with an inbuilt midge protection over their eyes," Padruig sighed and after a very full day of only achieving how to float, my poor darling just wanted to sleep without putting any demands on me, but I had other ideas. My hands ran up his broad back, sensually finding his long black and silver hair. I ran my fingers through his hair and along his broad shoulders. He rolled over and his kisses were softer and warmer than ever and as he brushed my thick hair out of my face, he said, "I am lucky to have a wife like you." "And me you Padruig Dubh," I said. When caressing my hands above my head slowly he said, "This is beauty. There is no flower, no mountain view, no glen nor waterfall, no new born bairns that could ever be more beautiful than you in these moments." We enjoyed a lovely sensual night, not knowing what to expect next as I had not experienced this side of my husband since his departure to Quebec. Finally, the spark had returned, even if it had been at the expense of our dignity.

The morning after the abortive attempts at learning how to swim, Hugh Mohr came on in through the front door at breakfast time saying, "Good morning family, how are you all today after our day out at the loch? Can I join you for breakfast?" Hugh had an enormous breakfast, as usual and as nobody had yet responded to him about the loch, he asked again. Grigor left for his oat fields, Helen got up to clean up but Padruig answered, "You can count me out of swimming lessons ever again Hugh, but we had a great day, a bit itchy scratchy from the midges, but I'm glad we did it. Good for a laugh and a fireside story. Did you enjoy yourself?" he asked. "Oh aye, best day in weeks. Wouldn't mind doing it again meself. I can still teach Isobel with your permission," he said. "Aye, you can, of course but Isobel you'd have to wear something better next time. Not white maybe, then you can go with Hugh if you've finished all your work," Padruig said. I was aware that I had to reply to this offer without seeming suspicious of Hugh's intentions. "Don't you have work to do Hugh?" I asked. "Nae, all done and I'll leave me dogs here if they're needed to round up your sheep. How 'bout it? We could try again. On your back today so you don't choke at first eh Padruig?" he said. Hugh was grinning and very enthusiastic, so I agreed to go. Helen made us both a flask of coffee and as we left I saw that the cart and pony were already standing there ready, waiting and hitched up. Hugh hadn't prepared for no as an answer. Taking the reins on the wee cart, he made excited chatter the whole way there, which was unlike him.

When we arrived at the loch, it looked very pleasant and there were no fishermen or other swimmers there. There didn't appear to be any swarms of midges either. The weather was nice and we were completely alone. I had my long hair tied back into a bonnet and like grease lightning, he was at my side of the cart to help me down. Tying up the pony, he shed what seemed to be a lot of layers of clothing, leaving only his shirt and his small kilt, not a plaid. He did leave a plaid on the beach for warmth afterwards, I thought. "Right," he said, "time to swim Isobel. Come on in and get wet," he said very cheerfully. He beckoned me down to the water, his big blue eyes seeming even bigger and bluer today and I was immediately regretting this decision, but I had to make the most of it. I'd had no choice. He seemed taller and I felt even smaller against his frame. "Take my hand so you won't panic," he said. Reluctantly, I took his big warm hand walking into the cold water and he immediately threw off his kilt onto the beach, so it wouldn't get wet. "Oh my God Hugh, you're naked, put it back on please," I said. "Of course," he said and strode confidently back to the beach. Realising then that I would see his nakedness, I quickly turned my head away. "Is that better?" he said, then told me to lie on my back this time to learn how to float. My hands had to keep moving so I wouldn't sink. "Put your head back," he instructed me, but then my cap fell off and my hair floated about everywhere with the movement of the water. Momentarily, he appeared mesmerised by the sight and said, "Isobel, your hair is so beautiful and so long." I thought it was inappropriate for him to say that, but I excused it. "Now you're confident floating, turn over, paddle and kick and I'll hold you," he said. I couldn't turn myself over and I felt panicky again. "It's okay, I've got you," then taking me by my waist, he turned me over as I clung to him and he told me to keep my head up. This time he placed one hand under my chin and the other was on my stomach again. "Now try and kick," he said. "Lift up your rear end and kick from here," he said as his hand fell on my wet buttocks and I thought he moved it back and forth, then his other hand was coming further down my chest away from my chin. I knew he was surveying my whole body shape, skinny as I was, I didn't feel attractive, just embarrassed and I hoped he couldn't see the scars on my bottom. Then his hand was across my breasts saying it was better for buoyancy and he touched each leg up and down and told me to kick. I then swallowed a lot of water and choked at his touching my breasts. "Hugh, don't." He then lifted me up into his big arms, "Are you okay?" he asked. "Aye," I said. "Try again then," as he lay me back on my stomach, but this time his hands were fondling my breasts, his other hand was suddenly inside of me. "Hugh, stop!" I exclaimed, realising then that he had lost his self control and he wouldn't stop. Pulling up his kilt, he was suddenly inside me and I gasped in shock. He then carried me to the beach and out of the water to lay me down on his plaid. I was in disbelief as his full manhood then thrusted and thrusted as I was unable to escape his grip holding onto the back of my neck and shoulders. As his lips met mine, he kissed my mouth and my eyes and he was unable to stop himself, no matter how many times I asked him to. 'Oh my God,' I was thinking, 'I am married and my vows are now broken'. He was truly beautiful, I admit and my own needs started to emerge as we were both engaged in an overwhelming need that our bodies had been starved of for years.

"You want me now Isobel. I'm going to marry you one day, you'll see. Isobel, you're mine, I love you," he said with passion. "Hugh, you can't love me, its pointless. I can't give more bairns. Please stop," I said. Then I found myself weeping for a lost love, my loyalty to my husband was always part of my faith and what would I do now? "I know that you can't give me bairns and that suits me, but what are these scars from?" He ran his hand over my buttocks as I flinched from his touch. "Don't flinch Isobel, show me them and tell what they're from," he demanded. "Uncle Allan's coos", I lied. "I know a bayonet scar when I see one" he responded. "Why are you lying to me? Allan told me himself how it happened." My mood wasn't one of lust, I just descended into grief and I clung to him sobbing, relieved that someone else knew. He ran his hands gently over each scar, even the very deep one. He told me that I had the sexiest bottom he had ever imagined on his woman. Caressing me gently, he still wanted more, holding back my legs he wanted to see me in the full light of the day fingering each part of me before he entered again repeatedly and moaned when he came. His heart was racing and so was mine, but for different reasons. "Does Padruig know the truth?" he asked. "Nae, please don't tell him the truth about the scars or what happened here today or one or both of us will die for sure," I said, panicking at the thought. I knew I would not survive a beating or whipping from Padruig Dubh if this incident was known to him. Packing up to leave wasn't an amorous affair for me, it was a serious, almost grave matter that we both faced and would have to be very careful, but Hugh wouldn't stop touching me and feeling and kissed my lips holding my face still to face him. He ordered me to kiss him too and I did what he asked and then I finally felt the pleasure of it and kissed him all over his face and held his manhood in my hands, but the lingering thought was how would I face the family now or even could I face them without giving away this truth, this mistake or could I even call this a mistake? Grigor Og could always see what was on my mind, I was worried he would see it immediately. Helen found grass in my hair that night. Over dinner, Hugh told them how much I had improved in my swimming, but Grigor Og looked suspiciously at us both and I prayed he wouldn't tell my brother or a beating from him would also come.

Nova Scotia

There's no doubt that there were many things about New France that were kept private between the Reverend Stewart in Inverness and Padruig. I knew well of his ability to keep secrets, but not in a malicious way, like the Prince who stayed with him in his cave whilst seeking the assistance of the Seven Glenmoriston Men. It was more than a year after the Prince's eventual escape to France that Padruig told me about that chapter in his life, which I understood. What I wasn't expecting was another secret about New France, which only became known when my younger son Alex, Therese and their four bairns came to visit and announced to us that they had decided to move to Virginia in the colonies where land was on offer. They had intended booking their fares once everyone had been told.

That's when it happened. Padruig stood up from our dining table, all 6'7" of himself and as big and broad as ever with his long black hair flowing down over his shoulders, with streaks of silver here and there and said, "A toast to you both on a grand decision." Just as we were all about to stand too, which all seemed rather ceremonial and unusual, he continued, "But why not go to Nova Scotia, which is a British held colony and not likely to fall to the Americans or the French? You can all live on the land there that I was given as a grant by the government after the Quebec campaign of 1759." I was astonished. "Land in New France or is it Nova Scotia?" I demanded. "But you said that you had forfeited the land in order to come home," I said.

Padruig went on to say, "That's true, but I was able to do both. I just didn't want you to think that I would take us all to that frozen landscape of New France. So, if Alex wants it, it's there and it makes sense to sign it over to one of my family before I die," he said.

What could I say? If Alex was happy to accept the unconditional offer, then so long as he forfeited all his claims on Craskie or any other Scottish inheritance in writing, that would be fine, which he did. In addition, I said to Padruig that he would need to take young Alex to the lawyer's office in Inverness to make it all legal. "So, Alex, are you happy with that?" I asked him to his face. He said "Aye" and accepted Padruig's offer very happily and they joined the many Scots who had gone to carve out an entirely new life there and Padruig gave him a lot of names to look up who would help him develop the uncleared land, where it was possible Indians still lived.

Sadly, Alex lost his youngest daughter, Elizabeth, to small pox on the horrific sea voyage across and another daughter, Therese, to a black bear soon after their arrival. They kept working hard despite these tragedies and continued on to have two more bairns, Alexander and Jean. Alex sometimes writes to us. They had avoided the American disruption and were grateful to Padruig's gift of land and a swathe of new friends and companions, a lot of whom were Frasers. For once, Alex respected his Father which meant so much to him. They had been two bulls in a paddock here, so they had to part and go their own ways. Wee Alex had been a damaged child. I had often seen him holding his hands over his ears, just as he had done on that fateful day trying to not hear the screams of ravished women, most especially his Aunty Morag.

Alex wrote a personal letter to me, quite secretively and said that living there in Nova Scotia, even with the frosty winds that blew and the wild life threats, he no longer heard the screams of the ladies from the day that the dragoons came to Craskie in '46. As a traumatised little bairn, he had carried that with him all those years and he disclosed to me that sometimes he yelled at his Father just so that it would be louder than the screams in his head. I replied telling him that I still heard them, right up until Grigor Mohr's wife, Morag passed away and I asked Grigor Mohr if she could be buried in our small cemetery. I had promised to grow flowers on her grave and water them every day if needed. I knew her soul would be at peace away from where it had happened. Although he was both surprised and puzzled, he agreed so long as he could visit her as often as he liked. Morag was finally at peace after the rose bush was planted there and I talked to her as if she was just a friend who was still alive and told her that I had known of her pain all along. She had known of mine and it was kept a secret, but she didn't know that I had also known of her secret agony. The screams in my head, especially at night, were simply silenced. This was something that Alex and I then shared but we didn't talk of it.

The women here in Glenmoriston and beyond, that were faced with that problem, had all dealt with it in their own individual ways. Some husbands were there at the time of the ravishings. Some were told much later. Some never knew, but if a woman had become diseased and died from it or become pregnant, there was an understanding between the women to help her lose the unborn by whatever means. My religion couldn't have allowed that and so I was just relieved all over again that it hadn't happened to my dear wee Helen. I think of the women as the quiet heroines in our stories and decided to dedicate our other white rose bushes to those women who had died at the hands of the English or whose grief finally killed them. Mither was one of those who was decapitated as she ran to follow Da into the woods that fateful day. I asked Hugh Og to carve their names on wooden plaques. Morag was the first, with that rose bush on her grave. Then my Mither, Freya, Mairi, Abigail, Sienna, Ailsa and Lilidh. May their souls be at peace. Then of course, there was what happened to me and Aunty Margaret.

Uncle Allan had gone on to marry the shy looking lady, the widow Chisholm and they were all content up there for a time and I didn't get to enjoy his company as much anymore and I missed him so much. She would occasionally wave to me from a distance. Her sons, Hugh Og and Hamish, built some kind of sporting field that they called gowf. They kept the grass clipped and had a small hole that a bat was supposed to hit a wee ball into. I had my own opinions about that sport. Padruig told me Uncle Allan was leaving him his entire farm and coos in his Will and after this, I saw Padruig glancing up that way at the rise behind Uncle's house. Then he'd say, "Isobel, that would be a magnificent spot for a fine stone country manor one day" and I'd reply, "You have big dreams my love, from living in a cave to a country house on a hill. You must have slept in more strange places that anyone that I know. But I pray that your dream comes true."

Isobel of Glenmoriston

Isobel of Glenmoriston
Isobel's Story
1759, Scotland

Craskie Farm,
Glenmoriston
Scotland, 1763

Dear Diary,

Entering Craskie on their lovely horses, Padruig, Grigor Mohr, Donald and Hugh Chisholm had that facial expression that I was very accustomed to by now, where they'd been up to something. Most often I'd let it slide, but as they tied their horses to the hitching rail, I asked them what they'd been doing. It wasn't that I objected to them being gone for a long time, just curious, very curious. Hugh Mohr, shadowed by his two collie dogs, wasn't going to say a word and kept his eyes down. Grigor Mohr, being my half-brother, was torn between his loyalties. So, I said openly, "You have a secret Padruig. Why don't you just say it?" "Well, there's nothing much to tell," he said. "It's just that as Grigor, Donald, Hugh and I were trotting our horses' home as we always do when we passed the old School House with its teacher's cottage at the rear, all very overgrown. We would never normally stop, but on this occasion, we did and I asked Grigor, Donald and Hugh if they knew who owned the property these days. They didn't know. The old wooden sign still said Glenmoriston School with CLOSED atop the sign, swinging in the wind hanging from one nail. It has been that way since 1747. The building wasn't damaged during the burnings, due to it belonging to the government and it wasn't vandalized, just overgrown. I wanted to look inside at its condition, so the four of us did just that," Padruig said. "No one was in a particular hurry today and our curiosity was peaked," he said.

"When we were there Grigor said, 'I have only bad memories of this place. The teacher made me wear a sign about me neck each time I spoke the Gaelic. I couldn't speak English, so I had no idea what he was saying. Apparently, the sign said, "English only." I'd find any excuse to not travel down the mountain to that school or I'd just hide in the heather. That teacher had it in for the MacGregors in my opinion." Padruig had gone on to tell me more. "After we went into the School House, Hugh Mohr said that the flooring was solid oak and in really good condition. The walls were double stone and the fire-place was good, apart from needing a good clean. The windows were all good and not one was broken. The back door was warped, but Donald said he'd be able to salvage a door from an abandoned house, so he was going to replace it, if I was interested. Hugh Mohr then said, 'let's take a wee keek at the teacher's house.' It was really overgrown outside the door, but the trusty key was under the potted plant, as most people used to do. The house was more cottage than a house, with an open fireplace, wood stove, two separate bedrooms complete with furniture and very mouldy mattresses and curtains. The occupants had just left without taking anything," he said. "Even school texts filled the shelves of the book cases, but not one on the Gaelic or Erse, let alone, Erse poetry," said Padruig.

Padruig had said that the property was adjacent to Craskie Farm. "Is this the border that Craskie shares with the School House?" Grigor Mohr had indicated at a pile of rocks and no fence. "Aye," said Padruig, "that's our border." I had then said to them all, "Come on in and we'll chat over coffee."

As they talked, I made them a coffee and got them their cakes that I'd already prepared. The curious Hugh Mohr then said, "There's a path back there behind that teacher's house that led to a wee shieling." "Aye," said Padruig. "We then followed Hugh down the rocky path, around low scrub branches and through patches of overgrown grasses. We looked around passed Hugh's broad back and caught a glimpse, of what could have, at one time, been called a bothy or a shieling, but our trained eyes knew what we were looking at but an outsider could have walked right passed what looked like overgrowth. Hugh Mohr pulled back the unhinged broken door to look inside, only to find signs of habitation. Some broken clay baked goblets lay on the dirt floor, surrounded by scattered ashes, some woolen stockings and what looked like a potty corner". At this, all four men looked down in shame and went on to say some young lads and lasses had been there with their Da's whiskey and they'd have to pray that their identities remained a mystery or there'd be hell to pay.

Our trusty path finder, Hugh Mohr and his dogs, followed the path that led away from the evidence of today's decaying youth, which led to the neighbouring property belonging to James Grant. He was at that moment walking toward his stables and Padruig called out "James" and the man was astonished to see four men climbing through the under-growth onto his property. "Sorry to disturb you James. We've just been taking a wee peak at the old School House and its teacher cot-tage. What can you tell us about it?" "Well," James replied, "it's nice to see you Padruig, Grigor, Donald, Hugh. As far as I know, that property is still owned by the government. They tried to get me to buy it for chips, but I wasna interested. Your lawyer should have the deeds registered in Inverness and he could write to the owners for ye," he said. "Thanks James and by the way," Padruig added, "there'd be an old bothy back there in the scrub that's being used for purposes that your Granny might faint over. Who might be up to no good there, or shall we leave it up to you?" In reply James Grant said, "Leave it to me Padruig," as he felt for his belt. "Best burn down that old bothy I reckon," Padruig added. "Are you missing any whiskey?" and at that James' face paled and he quickly thanked the men and called out to his lads.

"You don't have the money to buy that old School House, do you Padruig?" asked Grigor Mohr, who had found the day's revelations all a bit much. "I got back pay from the military that I've never used. That lawyer wrote to London and asked for back pay and a certificate of valour, which I received and I never show anyone. It's a cause for shame and I didn't want the money to touch your soul Isobel, you being so devout in the eyes of God. I thought it would harm you in some way," Padruig explained. Both Hugh Mohr and I looked at each other when he said that with guilt re-surfacing. "So, if it's the right price, why is it okay now to spend it on the School House?" Grigor asked. "I thought Helen could use it as an art gallery business while leaving a quarter of it as a school if a teacher and students came together one day. Donald, if I could buy it, with Isobel's blessing, do you think young Hamish Chisholm would take a security guard course in Inverness and live in that teacher's house one day?" "But first things first," I said to them. "We can go see the lawyer, find out who owns it, how much it would cost to buy and renovate, but more importantly if Helen would be interested in it being an art gallery one day." Grigor Mohr then said, "Every time I look at her paintings or her drawings, she gets shy, but I must admit that that very large painting on Drumossie Moor of Fraser of Inverallochy being shot is an amazing painting, unfinished as it is. There are a few technical details in there Padruig, that you'll have to tell her, like the positioning on the field that day, although I've got to say she's got the colours down perfectly. She really is a great artist," Grigor Mohr concluded. He then added, "and the poem Isobel wrote to accompany it really helps to get the emotion captured within it. I saw it on the desk there." Padruig asked what poem he was talking about and he said that he could recite it for him.

Who will remember Fraser of Inverallochy?
Buried in the English telling of Drumossie Moor
Buried in time to be forgotten
Fraser of Inverallochy bravely led his clansmen
Into a clash of metal against metal
Still alive while all around his men fell
His death was a murder ordered by the Black Prince
No, I'll not commit murder Wolfe said,
So, another emptied his gun into his heroic and defiant heart,
Into Fraser of Inverallochy

"When would it suit us to go into town then?" I asked, thinking of all the other tasks around the farm. Hugh Mohr said he'd rather leave it to us, so that he could work with Donald on their current house project and we all agreed, then Grigor Mohr said, "The plan has my support theoretically if there's enough money to pay for it. I suggest you offer them the lowest possible price, because no one else wants it. You heard James Grant, they want it sold for chips." Grigor Mohr then left on his lovely bay gelding. "You'd all best put away your horses now as the temperature is dropping fast," I said. "I'll rally Henrietta and light a few more fires in the house and would you remind Hugh Og that it is still his job to put the Highland Ponies away and feed them please Padruig?"

It was at that moment when Da came out of his room from his nap and Helen came into the kitchen. "Looks like I came too late to an interesting conversation," she said. I looked directly at her and asked her if she thought that wealthy folk would pay for her artwork. "Pay?" she exclaimed. "I never thought of my hobby like that." I replied by saying, "I know darling, but if you had a lot of artwork, over time, do you think it possible? Like my Betty dresses?" "Oh." Helen became thoughtful then. "Well, there's two lines of thought there. What does one charge for art and do I want to part with it?" At the last remark, I smiled and understood, I thought. "Sweetheart," I said, "if you had a dedicated place just for you and your art to be displayed and sold, do you think that would be something you'd like to do in the future? Obviously not now, while you're having bairns, but later? And in answer to the second part, if you had an attachment to a particular painting, could you not paint two, sell one and keep one?" I asked. Helen beamed, but I am not sure what she was thinking. She replied, "That's an idea Ma, but which one would be the original? Like that big one Da's helping me with of Culloden, I wouldn't want to do two of that because it is exhausting doing one," she said. "Is it?" I asked, "I didn't realise that". She explained that heart and soul went into it, so it was particularly draining, especially when she was with child. "Oh, sweet Helen. Sit down. I'll make you a tea or coffee," I said. "Don't fuss Ma. You still have the sheep to bring in," Helen said. Then the front door opened and Hugh Mohr was there again and I couldn't help but smile at his re-appearance. "Just letting you know Isobel, that me dogs have already rounded up your sheep and they are aways for the night with their feed," he said. "God bless you Hugh," I said and made Helen a coffee with her feet up.

As Henrietta cooked a beef and tomato stew, laced with onions, potatoes and cabbage from my garden, the home had warmed up nicely and we all sat down to a lovely family dinner and everyone's stories from the day were exchanged. The old Irish setter still worked with Grigor Og up at the oat fields and was taking particular notice of the presence

171

of the Collies whenever they came onto the property, that seemed to have preferential treatment. The bitch was expecting a litter of Collie puppies. Hugh Mohr's usual plan was to sell a few and keep two to train up before the others were too old to work. I got the distinct impression that Grigor Og might have been a bit jealous that Hugh Mohr had a breeding pair and I felt for my son in law who would have to part with his old dog eventually.

Then the old School House came up in conversation and Padruig told everyone that he and I would find a suitable day to take Uncle Allan's cart up to Inverness for the day to visit the lawyer and begin the inquiries. "No pressure Helen", he said, "it is just an inquiry love and no obligation on you at this stage. It can sit there for as long as we like until someone needs it," said Padruig. "Out of interest love," I asked, "if you had ten years to paint in between raising your bairns and your work here, how many pieces of artwork do you think you could paint?" I asked. "Ten years?" she said. "We are long term thinkers, aren't we? To be honest with you, I have no idea. It depends on what I am painting and what else we have to do, like the wool waulking orders," she said. "Okay, but could it be like one every six months or one a month?" I asked. "Ma, it doesn't work like that with art. I have to feel the inspiration. For example, I have a piece in mind where the men are washing the sheep down in the burn in their plaids. It is a beautiful scene. The fleeces are lying out on the purple heather to dry, but I have to wait for clipping season first, and then have the time, the feeling and the materials," Helen explained. "I think I get it," I said, "but you would have ten at least at the end of the ten years as well as all those that you have out the back, wouldn't you?" I asked. "Ma, would you want to part with our life story?" Helen asked. I just smiled and was a bit conflicted about that for a wee moment and then I answered. "If it meant that the World would learn what happened here, then aye."

The visit at the lawyer's office proved to be very interesting. The old gentleman, still wearing his wig, also had a flair for accountancy as it turned out and was holding Padruig's money in trust and was familiar with the Glenmoriston School's history. He informed us that it had been built in the late 1600s by the Papists under the name of St. Michaels and a Kirk was intended to be built next to the school also, but only the foundations had been completed before they were "made unwelcome". "So, the building stopped on the Kirk and the Priest, who had lived with the teacher in the cottage, was recalled to Rome. At the time when the two Papist men were running things at the school, the Gaelic was not only spoken, but it was the language in which the lessons were taught. Then the government-based policy group, I think they were Presbyterian, took over and replaced the teacher with the intention of "discouraging" Gaelic and to only speak and teach in English. The school then lost its numbers and its popularity – you might remember that Padruig? Very few students stayed on, until its complete closure in 1747. So, if they could sell it, they would be very pleased," he said.

When asked the price, he looked at the balance of Padruig's payment and said, "Well," as he tapped his fingers on the desk, "I wouldn't give them all of your payment lad. Maybe a quarter of this amount for both the school building and the wee cottage, as well as the land up to the border, being James Grant's property currently and all the way back to your Uncle Allan MacDonald's property. If a part of the building was still dedicated to schooling, there'd be no tax on it, so it could go into Helen's name now, if you like, and she'd still not be paying any money out for the time that it is empty," he explained. "What you could do, Padruig, is look up this Papist entity in Italy, or I could write to them and ask them if they are still interested in building a Kirk, but stipulate a time in the future when Papacy would be more accepted, like ten- or twenty-years' time. All that land behind it would be yours too, in line with Craskie and James Grant's property. It says here that the Papists had intended to farm as well, in order to be self-sufficient, meaning a Monastery was probably intended to be built. That wouldn't be a popular decision, so I suggest you take over the land behind the school yourselves as part of Craskie and I can submit that land division for you if you're prepared to pay tax on it. You could divide that land into two in the names of Helen Grant MacGregor at the front and Craskie Farm at the back or as another farm entirely. For taxation purposes, you could name it Grant Farm for instance."

"So, are you both interested in expanding your farm Padruig and Isobel?" he asked. "Aye," we both said. "The coos need extra grazing and we could do with extra crops." Directing his attention then to me, the lawyer said, "Bigger farming would need a lot of planning and a team of Clydesdales. Probably two horses to start. Aye, two Clydesdales and all the gear that goes with them and the deep plough. And didn't you say you saw all of that over in New York Padruig? So, you know what I'm talking about." "Aye," Padruig nodded, trying to take it all in. "They have a lot of fandangle equipment over there in New York," he added. "Even a machine that you can pour the seed into and stand on while you're holding the reins of the Clydesdales, so that you don't have to do it by hand," he said.

"First things first," I said. "How about we put in an offer to these people for the whole lot and then sort out the rest when we've had time to go over it? Maybe buy a book on Clydesdales?" I said. The lawyer, Mr. David said, "Very wise, very wise Isobel." But with a frown on his face, he then said, "When I was a younger man, your Da had Clydesdales, Isobel. He was the best Clydesdale teamster in the whole of Inverness-shire. You'd be able to operate that thing yourself if you could stand on it. Do you remember your Clydesdales Isobel?" he asked. I didn't feel that I could talk about the loss of Da's precious Clydesdales with Padruig's curiosity peaked and so I just said, "Respectfully, we'll still need the book Mr. David," and I wanted to leave.

"So, the offer should be a quarter of this I suggest," Mr. David concluded, referring to Padruig's backpay. The offer went in and we just waited. Padruig said, "You've been a great help Mr. David. We look forward to hearing from you." The lawyer said he'd just write to us when he found out and submit the land division application that we had decided on. Before we left to begin the long journey home, we decided to buy the book on the Scottish Clydesdales and a few items that we needed as well as a present and some new baby clothes for Helen's first bairn.

Padruig and I decided to treat ourselves to a hot cup of tea in a tea house in Inverness to go over the day's business. "I can't believe it was a Papist school first," said Padruig. "Me neither," I responded. "I am so disappointed it didn't stay that way, because unlike you, I had to keep going to school. Mither and Da wanted me to have English, even if I hated it, so that I could read and write in both languages. Then there was the mathematics, which I really loved. So, I stayed on some days when I was older, to learn book keeping." I then said to him over the cup of tea, "Padruig, do you remember when I first met you when I was six and you must have been seven?" "Aye," he said. "It was at that school and I loved you from that very moment and I thought you were the most handsome creature on God's earth and I still think it. You were taller than all the other lads, you were smarter and you could kick a ball further than any of them. I was in love with you when I was six." He looked directly at me and responded, "Well, I was showing off just to impress you and it obviously worked. I would've killed for you Isobel. Plus, you were the bonniest lassie I could ever have imagined, with your jet black flowing locks and I couldn't have any other lad getting you. I really hated that school and the only reason I kept going was to see you. But when Alexander and Grigor didn't want to go anymore because of the English, we all stopped going. But not before I found out where you lived," he said smiling. "That's when I got me Da to act on it for me when I was away. I knew him and me mean Uncles could secure you," he said remembering his relatives. I wasn't smiling.

"It seemed like forever before I spoke to you again when one day I was herding some coos up the mountain to fatten. The weather was lovely and the wildflowers were blossoming and suddenly there you were and so much taller. You came up the mountain side and sat on a rock to talk to me. You must have been thirteen by then. Were you?" I asked. "I was fourteen and I wanted you to know that you were mine," Padruig said. "My Da," he continued, "said he wanted me to train with the Frasers because of the Rising and I was going to be away for a while and I wanted you to wait for me." I then said, "So you told me nice things. I remember." We were like children again over our cup of tea remembering that time. "I love you Padruig," I said. "I love you too Isobel, but what's this about your Da being a Clydesdales teamster?" he asked. "It's true. He was," I said.

On our journey home down through the magnificent Great Glen, I rested my head on my beautiful man's big shoulder and I was happy to be alive. I had everything I ever needed and wanted.

Isobel of Glenmoriston

Book 3

Years in the Earth

Chapters: 177

Isobel of Glenmoriston
Isobel's Story
1759, Scotland

Introduction

Craskie Farm,
Glenmoriston
Scotland, 1788

Dear Diary,

My fingers are very sore now as I try to write my first diary entry in what must be more than twenty years. My dearest Padruig is more than a year in the earth and now I am struggling to climb the stairs or see too far without my glasses, but Hugh still talked me into marrying him as I had promised. My hair is still very long, but it is all silver now, the wrinkles around my eyes are too many to count as well as a few on my forehead.

I thank the Almighty God that my dear Helen still cooks for me, Grigor and Hugh. Helen still helps me with my bath and getting dressed, which is harder these days. The privy is too far for me at night, so Grigor Og invented a chair with a chamber pot in it at sitting height. I had also hired a laundry lady, Mary, who came on Mondays and Tuesdays. She was a diligent middle-aged woman, who even ironed the bedsheets. She always went home at 4pm before our house was busy with dinner and baths. Mary could be relied upon for many things, but she kept to herself especially after her husband Joe had died. He left her comfortable in a nice cottage not far from us, so she never slept over in our house. She'd say it was to feed the cat, but I think she went home to feel the presence of her beloved husband.

Reading our collection of letters with Padruig's old glasses on my nose from that terrible time apart, brought back so many memories. This diary was my way of staying strong and close to my beloved Padruig. Life became extremely busy once he returned from Quebec, praise God, and my fingers were made busy tending crops and sewing, rather than finding any time, or need, to write in this diary.

Recently, my grandson James' wife wanted a wee break from her husband and her work at the Manor House and needed the use of one of my rooms, so I put her in the attic. I had buried under decades of belongings, this precious book and the hand-written letters between Padruig and myself and also one from Bishop Gordon. What tumultuous times those were.

Despite my new beloved husband, I feel quite alone now sometimes without my dearest old Da, Grigor Mohr and Uncle Allan with all his advices and Padruig. We wouldn't have been prepared for the drought in 1763 if it hadn't been for Uncle Allan's advice concerning the urgent preparation for grain storage. Our oat crops, as well as our potatoes, saw us through. It meant droving the coos along our ancient droving roads higher up into the mountains for the pasture and Patrick slept there in a shieling. They all returned fattened and safe. It was the last time we would be able to do that.

The Hart of the Highlands Manor House

Uncle Allan did as he promised and left his entire property to Padruig and all eighty of his beautiful Highland coos. He kindly left me all of Aunty Margaret's antique china. Uncle Allan had remarried the widow Chisholm who stayed on after his death, with her two unmarried sons Hugh Og and Hamish, until she passed. The two lads worked for Padruig extending the golfing field much further because he had big plans for golf. The country manor on

the hill became a reality with two floors and a lovely roof purchased from Fraser's Trading Post. It was most beautifully built in his spare time with the lads help and it had the best laundry in all of Inverness-shire. Before my darling Padruig passed, he named it "The Hart of the Highlands Manor House." His plan had been to attract English tourists up to Scotland and pay a lot of money to stay in a Highland manor, play golf and hunt deer. He felt his best revenge was their hip pocket and he lived to see his dream fulfilled through his son as he passed it onto Patrick who completed the interior and started running it as a business. Padruig chose to stay at our house at Craskie and watched on from a distance.

With Henrietta's help, Patrick finished off the interior with Italian fixtures. A trip to Rome had brought beautiful floor tiles, crystal lighting fixtures, elaborate drapes and furnishings in every room, complete with Turkish rugs. The inheritance from Uncle Allan paid for it all as well as our new slate roof on Craskie. In addition, my husband paid for Mary's daughter Cora to be a servant for me, who was later replaced by Agnes and then Meredith.

My plans with the existing labour, two of whom were new and relatively unknown to us, hadn't changed so I went about securing the full length of the frontage of Craskie Farm. The droving trail ran along the frontage, so the first job was to fell all the trees along the full length that belonged to us and then build a 5' stone wall with the stones we'd taken off the additional oat fields. With the donkey and cart, Hugh Og and the men took loads of stones to where Padruig had built a gate to keep Blaze in. Then I was happy to see that Craskie would become impenetrable and inaccessible from the front. There was word circulating that thieves and land buyers from the south were taking up our lands and they were not getting Craskie or Grant Farms or the Hart of the Highlands Manor House.

Where I'd had the trees felled, we planted apple trees on both sides of our entrance and I have been told it will only take about five years for them to grow apples, so we will be able to have plenty for everyone on the farm, but hopefully also to sell some at the weekly market. We were able to sell some of the felled trees and kept some, keeping a little of the money for a long-term project I had in mind, which was the family Chapel I had built before Padruig's passing. We had already built state of the art stables for our Clydesdales on Grant Farm.

We hung a big sign over the front gate saying, "Craskie Farm". Another one lower down said, "Do not enter unless invited" and "This property is under surveillance, keep out!" in both English and Gaelic. It took a while to build the rock wall and a few of our friends thought I was extreme, especially when I got Padruig's old guns prepared from the attic aimed directly at the entrance with ammunition, until those nosy English land thieves did come, but decided against trying to enter our properties. Our intention then was to fully fence the farms and the school on all sides. We had no choice, so the young men just kept on building.

Padruig had already moved as many of Uncle Allan's coos onto Craskie Farm as we could accommodate and the rest were sold for a wonderfully high price. He had also divided up the land, giving more to Craskie Farm because the Manor House would have no need for it as he only wished to expand the golf course. Across Grant and Craskie Farms, there were eight fields for oats, with two always remaining fallow and what a sight they were. Praise God Chisholm House had already been built for Hugh Mohr to live in as a permanent resident free of charge. It was right near the border and he was able to rent out his other rooms to farm hands at his discretion.

Diversifying for the Future

I had already had lengthy conversations with all of my family to focus on the future and plan in a business like manner and to diversify if necessary. I did, however, press both Helen and Grigor to educate at least one of their children to become a lawyer for the future, as we would all need that protection and knowledge of the law with the laws changing constantly. Helen and Grigor and their three lovely adult children, Isobel-Mairi, Aonghus Grigor and Morag-Freya, still reside on Craskie Farm, but Aonghus is away most of the year at university in Edinburgh, studying law.

It was decided that the two homes, Craskie and the Manor House were to be run as two businesses, with Grant farm being a part of Craskie. The two homes were separated with Patrick and Henrietta taking over the Manor House after its completion and Helen and Grigor taking over Craskie and Grant Farms. My will reflected Helen and Grigor as the new owners of Craskie and Grant Farms now that proscription of the MacGregor clan name had ended. [34]

All my sewing was moved to Da's old room downstairs opposite mine and the maid was put in the wee downstairs servants' room. The whole family used Padruig's old office upstairs with its poetry books, bibles and folk lore stories, as well as books on farming. I had always done the farms' books downstairs as it seemed easier to be available when needed as well. Padruig had never been a big reader, but Grigor Og is and he ordered so many books that took his interest. He is an avid reader and had always taught his bairns more about the world and there were even books on English, Gaelic, Latin and French, so his bairns could speak all four languages fluently. The office had become the family school room until the school re-opened. He had been interested in sending his bairns to Italy to be educated initially, but didn't want any of them becoming Priests or Nuns after he was told one of Helen's nephews, Archangel, had entered the Church in Nova Scotia. They weren't interested in entering the Church anyway and his son Aonghus had chosen to study in Edinburgh because he didn't want to leave Scotland and wanted to be able to come home during harvest seasons.

France had itself in the news a lot these days and it looked like a civil war was approaching there and I advised him not to send any of his children there or even to travel through there if they could avoid it. I just hoped we'd have the money left over from the MacDonald inheritance for their university fees in one of those countries or indeed here in Scotland. Although, I had observed Isobel-Mairi to be disinclined to even leave Craskie Farm. She was a bit like me. Morag-Freya, however, was interested in being educated, but also didn't want to leave Scotland. Patrick wanted his son James to work with him up at the Manor House because he would ultimately take over that business from his Father.

John Fraser of Stratherick

About fifteen years ago, while doing my books one day as the farm worked hard, there was a loud knock at my door. Not expecting a visitor, I called out "Aye? Who is it?" I was so engrossed in numbers and balances and didn't want to be disturbed. It was a man's voice who politely asked to speak to the Master and Mistress of the house. Straight away, I knew it wasn't a local, so I reluctantly left my head of numbers and opened the door to a handsome but ruddy complexioned gentleman, who was about fifty years old and unknown to me. Well dressed and standing as straight as an arrow, I figured him to be a trained soldier and well bred. "Mrs. Grant, may I introduce myself," as he tipped his hat. "My name is Fraser, John Fraser of Stratherick. Your good husband may remember me from the first Quebec Campaign, the Plains of Abraham." I nodded suspiciously, noting his shiny shoes and hoping he wasn't there to get Padruig involved in the military in any way again. I was totally over the military. "Is it possible to speak with yourself and your husband concerning a family matter?" he asked. I relaxed a wee bit then at the mention of family and called for young Agnus to fetch Himself, as she always called him, and invited Mr. Fraser in for tea or coffee. Surprisingly, he said he'd enjoy a cup of coffee if it wasn't any trouble.

Seating him at our dining table, I became aware that he wasn't an ordinary fellow and some of his facial features and pale blue eyes were truly of Fraser stock, so I began to pry before Padruig arrived. "You said a family matter? My name is Isobel. Can I call you John?" I said and he responded, "I'm pleased to meet you Isobel. My lands," he went on, "have all been restored to me finally and in getting all my papers in order, as well as my Will, it had occurred to me that Simon, my oldest son, was to inherit after me and would need not only a good wife of impeccable reputation, but with family connections too. My wife, Anna enthusiastically said that Isobel of Glenmoriston had a bonny granddaughter, Elizabeth Grant and I'd need to hasten to secure such a beauty the like of her grandmother. My wife, Anna, also told me that Elizabeth was already widely known for her horse-womanship and was not yet betrothed. In her explaining who you were, I realised that I was already acquainted with your husband. I apologise if this sounds too personal, Isobel. I knew your husband as my superior officer in New France and was astounded that at his age, he was able to scale that cliff the way he did. It is indeed an honour to meet his wife, whose letters he guarded with his life," he said.

At that moment, Padruig burst through the door. His sweaty face displeased at the disruption to his labour, until he saw who was seated at the table. "John," he said, while washing his face and hands, "you're a ways from home. No more action for you then? I see you've met my wife?" To my surprise, John had stood up in response to Padruig's entrance into the room. Anytime now, I had expected a salute, but his ruddy complexion had changed to bright red which crept down his neck. "Sir," he said, "please forgive my intrusion into your busy schedule and hopefully, I will not keep you and your good wife for too long as it is a matter that is personal between us older folk and the younger generation. Like I just explained to your good wife, my lands have all been restored to me in Stratherick," he said proudly. "So," said Padruig, "you didn't take up the offer of land in New France then?" he asked. "Och, I did acquire land in Nova Scotia, as did many others, but returned to Scotland with my son Simon when things looked like they were going to kick off again in Quebec. The Fraser lands were before the courts here and so I returned to fight for it. Since the Clearances, there appears to be more land than I remembered and so it has been an enormous job. But I am taking up too much of your time with all those details," he said. I was thinking that this man could talk a lot.

"I was long married at the time that I met you, Sir, on board the ship and my oldest son, Simon, was not yet ten years old. The family joined me in Nova Scotia to establish a trading post, which I've left in the capable hands of my youngest. Like I said to your good wife, Simon stands to inherit all of the lands here in Scotland when I pass and he is now twenty-three years old and ready for marriage," he said. At that moment, Padruig asked me for a coffee with eyebrows raised predicting that this conversation would take some time before Fraser would make his point. Happily, I gave one to him as well as one for myself.

"So, what do you need from me?" asked Padruig. Once again, looking red faced, the nervous John Fraser said that his wife had mentioned our granddaughter Elizabeth to him and had recommended her to him. "Hmm..." Padruig made a noise. "Go on..." his eyes looking at John sideways. With a burst of confidence, John then replied, "I am here to ask for you and your wife's permission for Simon and Elizabeth to be introduced with the view of courtship should Elizabeth like my son and if successful, betrothal and God willing, marriage between the Grants of Glenmoriston and the Frasers of Stratherick. Of course, her Mither and Father would also be present, as well as my wife, Anna. Should they be compatible and the families all agree with a written contract in place, we can discuss wedding plans if we are all that blessed. My country house is not yet completed, but it will be within the year with internal plumbing and half of the house is set aside for the new couple," he blurted.

I think Padruig was a bit shocked at this announcement, so I took over and said we'd both be pleased to meet Simon and would get the required blessings from both her parents and permission of Elizabeth herself. I took out my trusty calendar and wrote down the date for the meeting to be held at our home and reminded him of her age being just nineteen years and that the duration of the courtship could be about a year approximately, all going well, given that the house was not yet ready and her conditions in the contract were not yet known. I did know, however, that she wanted her own stables in which to breed Scottish Highland Ponies so that she would have an independent income, to which he wholeheartedly agreed.

"Trading post you say?" Padruig said to Fraser thoughtfully. "I've got a patch of land to be leased next to a school I've purchased down the ways and am looking for someone like yourself, to set up a small trading post of goods selling things folks need like seed and animal feed and the like, tools, ploughs. Flexibility would be needed for Saturdays as a Market Day, so folks around here could buy and sell excess produce, if you're interested. A Papist Kirk was going to be built there in the 1690s, so there's footings in the undergrowth. Whoever is interested has to build it themselves. I'll show it to you one day." With that suggestion, 'Fraser's Trading Post' was a reality within the year next door to Glenmoriston School and Helen Grant MacGregor Art Studio. Helen also earned an independent income from the lease of Fraser's Trading Post to maintain the school, the art studio and the houses.

The poor man left having accomplished his weighty task, but secretly I was pleased. There weren't many good suitors left and a Fraser to boot. I'd sleep well that night, but Padruig wouldn't.

It is lovely remembering these times from before Padruig passed and how he worked so hard to establish our family. It took quite a while to fine tune the marriage contract between Simon Fraser and Beth Grant because Patrick, her Father, was in no hurry to part with his daughter. It is lovely to know now that she is a horse breeder on her own patch of land and stables in her name. On the day of their wedding I was so happy, but realised that Beth's bairns may not have our trademark black hair, the Frasers all being ruddy or pale brown. Once they were married, I encouraged my grandson in law Simon to enter into politics in order to protect our families on several fronts and influence the Council's decisions on matters such as the widening of the Drovers Road into a proper road and a dedicated Glenmoriston Post Office built in our area.

Beth moved away to Stratherick with Simon Fraser once they were married and it was expected that James, with all of his accountancy education, would stay on with Patrick to help run The Hart of the Highlands Manor House that Patrick had inherited from Padruig as an early inheritance. He then would have no claim on Craskie Farm, Grant Farm or any other purchases made by Craskie Farm. Patrick and Henrietta were very engrossed in their new business venture, which suited them. James was set to inherit it when his Father passed away. James married a local lass, Susan, who seemed to get along well with Henrietta, which was fortunate because not everybody did. We never saw his sister Sarah, Henrietta's third child, because when she was young she was always in a boarding college of some snobby kind or another, but that changed.

Alex, my younger lad, who was well established in Nova Scotia on his Father's land, successfully became involved with Fraser's Trading Post there and sent Indian furs across and traded other items directly to the Trading Post in Glenmoriston. These items included the latest in ploughs and seeders, saddles, bridles and metal cooking pots of all shapes and sizes, and supplies of whale oil and the latest in torches. I was proud of my youngest son, who had finally found his place in Nova Scotia, but the second death of one of his children marked not only the end of their marriage, but the eventual end of his life there. Grigor and Helen were the bedrock of Craskie and Grant Farms and Helen was also busy establishing her art gallery and maintaining the wool waulking business.

Grigor MacGregor's Funeral

Tragically, thirteen years ago, my dear friend Morag died after suffering ill health for some time and was followed soon after by her husband Grigor Mohr. My sorrow was enormous at the loss of a brother found late in life at Grigor Mohr's passing. Although healthy, he died of a broken heart, so his death weighed heavily on us all, especially his son Grigor Og and his friends Padruig, Donald Chisholm and Hugh Mohr. I invited his MacGregor relatives to Grigor Mohr's simple funeral at our growing cemetery where he wanted to be buried beside his beloved Morag. Grigor Mohr's death was probably the first and only death I felt that I may never recover from. I knew my Mither was dead the day we were hiding in the shieling from the dragoons when I saw the look on Da's face, but it was a choice to be strong for the bairns and therefore I had to recover very quickly. Giving in to the emotion of it could have had us all killed. We were no longer in those times and so when Grigor Mohr died, it had become safer to feel.

Donald Chisholm recited this at the graveside for Grigor Mohr and it was called Grigor of the Mist.

It's true to say that Grigor, son of Grigor
Could recite the names of all the Scottish Sith.
His Grandmother taught him no English
Important only was the knowledge of the unseen.

Escaping as a deserter
Joining with the Seven Glenmoriston Men to live in a cave
Needed was he with that knowledge, through the mist
But of his sister, he knew naught.

Captured by the Redcoats imprisoned was he,
Not short of friends to break him out
Yearning always for his lost Mither
And the sister of whom he knew naught.

Taking a ride on a teamster with a lass at the reins
Her face, her voice he still knew naught
Married to his best friend, black hair like his Mither's
No recognition as the sister of whom he knew naught.

The song of Grioghal Chride broke the night air
His heart pierced as an arrow of the Mither long gone
His sporran held the key all along, a carved wooden Clydesdale,
Of a team driven by the sister, Isobel of the mist, brought to light.
By Donald Chisholm

Many people came to farewell one of the famous Seven Glenmoriston Men, including a very elderly MacGregor woman accompanied by six others of Clan Gregor. Padruig's eulian pipes rang out across the

189

mourners at the graveside with a sad lament to his dear friend. Cora then sang a beautiful Gaelic lament to the mourners. It was hard for her to continue in her own sadness, so others joined her. We had pre-prepared food for all of the mourners down at the house afterwards.

At the graveside as my brother entered the earth, my loss felt too great, but it was then that the very old MacGregor woman approached me. Her hands were crippled with arthritis and her face was so wrinkled, it was hard to believe she could've lived this long. She spoke openly however and said, "So, you'd be Isobel then? My Grandson's sister?" "Aye. Grigor was my half brother," I replied. She then took out a very large brooch and said, "This brooch was to go to your Mither. No doubt you know that story. There's only you left in that branch of the MacGregors, so it is yours now. It reads S Rioghal mo dhream 'Royal is my Race'." I responded, "But, I am not a MacGregor, Mistress MacGregor. I am Clan Grant." "Aye," she said slowly, "you are on your Father's side, that's true. Your Mither, Freya MacGregor married my son, Grigor MacGregor. They were both MacGregors of different branches you see, so I've held this in trust. It's an antique heirloom that neither the Campbells nor the government could find. It were buried with all our antiques. You invited me to this funeral and you could only do that if you were a MacGregor. The family are all in agreement that you have it and pass it on when you die. Protect it as I have and remember 'Royal is my Race'" and with that the intense little old lady put the brooch in my hand and nodded a kind of approval. I thanked her very much and said, "Please join us inside for refreshments."

At that time, I noticed Padruig was departing the graveside taking long strides towards the house. He had lost his best friend and like me, had to deal with the grief somehow. James and Beth followed after their tall grandfather, leaving their spouses behind, but Padruig didn't appear as if he wanted them to follow him, so they came back a little bemused, collected their spouses and then went to the house together with them.

Simon Fraser looked very confused momentarily, then stood at the foot of the grave and saluted our Grigor Mohr. 'Must be a Fraser thing,' I thought. James' wife went with him, Henrietta and Patrick, to make sure that everyone had food and drink. Just before Helen and Grigor Og left, I ushered them over to introduce them to their MacGregor relatives. Mistress MacGregor looked wide eyed and with a crooked, toothless smile, said to Grigor Og, "What a handsome MacGregor you are lad." This really did not impress him, but he was calm and polite as always and gave his greetings and condolences to her before following the others to the house.

Hugh Mohr was left behind and asked if I needed his help. "Maybe," I said, "can you please assist Mistress MacGregor to the house?" Reluctantly, he said, "Aye." "Mistress MacGregor, do you need Hugh to carry you on his back?" I asked. "Oh, aye," she replied and willingly climbed on board. Hugh Mohr hadn't been prepared to have to carry the old lady, but she could barely walk. He sat her down gently at the fireside in the house, where Beth and James had been talking as brothers and sisters do when they are gossiping. I left the old lady with them to look after, while I searched for Padruig. He wasn't in any of the rooms of the house, so I thought he might have been in the privy. He was using it more frequently these days, so I went to get coffee myself. I was tired, but I had to see through the last of the remaining guests lamenting Grigor's loss and regaling his talents as a horseman.

Cora and Hamish came to me saying that they had put on another big pot of stew and brewed more tea and coffee to save me any trouble. Agnes was run off her feet cleaning plates, glasses and cups and keeping the floor as clean as possible with the mud being trampled into the house. Cora then said they'd be on their way, as they hadn't yet cooked anything for themselves at home. I told them to take one third of the huge pot that they had already cooked and they happily left.

About that time, Donald Chisholm came to me and said that his wife Eilidh had a wee cold and he would also take his leave whilst espousing his sincerest sympathies. "I am so sorry Isobel," he said. "You both meant so much to each other, he was a different man for having you in his heart. If you ever need anything at all and Padruig is not around, you can always rely on us Chisholms." Overcome with emotion, I hugged the big Highlander after many years of never touching him and through tears I thanked him. He patted me gently on my back and went out into the pouring rain. "Wait Donald. You said Eilidh's got a cold, can I give you some of Cora's stew?" I offered. "Oh nae, I don't like Cora's cooking," he replied. "I can fix it," I said. "It'll just need tomatoes, salt, and other tasty things that I add." "Well, alright," he said. After a few taste tests he said, "Aye, that's it!" I bucketed more of the stew into a lidded pot and also gave him some dried herbs for Eilidh to steep into a tea for her cold. "God bless you Isobel," he said. "And you dear Donald," I replied. He departed much happier.

Hugh Mohr came up to me quietly and said, "Where's Padruig?" "I don't know. I've looked in all the rooms. Maybe the privy?" I answered. "Oh," he replied, then said with his back to the MacGregor woman by the fire, "When's the old crohn leaving?" I almost laughed, because she did look like an old crohn. "It is best that she leaves soon," Hugh Mohr said. I agreed and picked up all of the MacGregors' plates, bowls, cups and glasses and thanked them all for coming. "Am I getting a ride to me cart on that lad?" she said pointing to Hugh Mohr with a crooked pointer finger. "He's busy now Mistress. Maybe one of your clansmen?" I suggested. I gave Mistress MacGregor an old plaid of mine to protect her from the rain. Hugh Mohr was so relieved at this and subsequently a reluctant family member put her on his back, grunting unhappily and they all filed out of our house, like a cold wind to the cart that had brought them. Grigor Og came up beside me and said, "Can't say I am fond of the MacGregor relatives." "Och," I said, "funerals and sometimes weddings too, can be dangerous places to be." Hearing their sad old pony trot off into the rain carrying all seven of them, I was relieved, but it had all been for the living to farewell our beloved Grigor Mohr.

Their departure was the signal for everyone else to leave and Agnes was still cleaning furiously as the house vacated. "I can't believe people walked in all that mud without taking off their boots and leaving them outside on the verandah or scraping off the mud," she said in the most judgmental tone I'd ever heard come from such a quiet lass. Then my Helen put a big pot of water on to boil for my bath over my bedroom fire and stoked it. "Ma, eat something please," Helen said. "You haven't eaten." So, I ate some of the amended stew and it tasted alright. I washed it down with coffee sitting beside a busily eating Hugh Mohr at the dining table. I was just about to go to my room for that beautiful, relaxing, scented hot bath, when a drunk Padruig entered the house through the back door. He must have been by the burn in the rain waiting for everyone to leave. "Hello my sweetheart," I said. "I wondered where you were. Would you like some of Cora's stew?" I said. "Aye," he said. And Agnes quickly put down a bowl of stew in front of him with a coffee and said, "Would 'Himself' like anything else? A glass of milk maybe?" "No Agnes, this is bonny. Thank you," he replied.

"I am just off for a bath Padruig to wash off the day then take a wee rest," I said. Gently touching his arm, he suddenly pulled me to himself, for a rough embrace in front of Hugh Mohr, Agnes as well as Grigor and Helen and the rest of the family. They all knew that he was drunk, but it was extremely rare to see him like this.

Then he said, "I saw you, Isobel, hugging Donald by the door. Is this what it felt like?" Kissing me roughly on the lips, I thanked the God Almighty that the family then had quickly left the room except for Hugh Mohr. I was so acutely embarrassed. His hands  began to grope when Hugh Mohr bellowed, "Enough, you'll not embarrass Isobel like that". Padruig then pushed me away and out of the corner of my eye, I saw Helen frantically ushering me into my room for that bath. I quickly scampered to my room and closed the door behind me. "The men can deal with him Ma. You relax," Helen said. It was impossible to relax, wondering how much of Aunty Margaret's china could be broken by morning. But I went to bed with the stramash entering into its second phase when Grigor Og entered the foray, then Patrick, but Simon just watched on apparently, trying to save anything of value, he claimed. Helen scuttled passed them all to her room and all we women literally left them to it with our doors closed.

Sometime during the night, I awoke to hear snoring on the floor by the fire, so he was still alive, the sounds of broken china and glass being swept up could be heard and I left it with God, as I always did.

I awoke the next morning after Grigor Mohr's funeral and Padruig had already arisen. The day was dreich, so I dressed in something very warm and pulled on some boots. While doing so, I noticed a bruise on my chest and the memory of the previous day's insult flooded back into my brain. How could my husband suggest such a thing of sweet Donald Chisholm and I? And with him leaving me so often. I tried not to appear any different to other mornings, but I knew it would be hard seeing that Aunty Margaret's china was gone and maybe even our old pottery that I'd made by hand in our kiln.

Taking a deep breath, I opened my bedroom door to Simon Fraser's blue eyes staring straight at me with Beth calmly eating her breakfast. "Good morning Granny," he said, trying to be positive I suppose. "Good morning Simon. How are you both this morning? Not too disturbed by the stramash I hope?" I said, directly addressing the obvious. "I'm fine Granny," Simon replied. "I managed to save you a bowl of Aunty Margaret's," he said, proudly passing it to me. "Only one bowl?" I said disappointedly and I walked over to where it ought to be and all of the shelves were empty. "Glasses too?" I asked. "Aye," he said. "Just one of the antiques remains, but there's wooden bowls in the kitchen. And Grandda's outside mending the chairs too," he said.

"So, you're both back to Stratherick then?" I asked. "Aye," Beth replied. "The horses are expected back at Loch Ness and my ponies need tending. Simon's Da is minding them while I am gone, but I don't want to over burden him," she said. I then spoke to Simon directly and asked him if he was going to tell his Father about the stramash and he said that his Da would expect the full story. "Fair enough, like most military men, I expect he'll think it's funny and laugh. I've never understood that about military men," I confessed. "Surely not Granny. It's not funny, but most Scots do seem to make light of serious things," he said. "Is that so?" I replied. "I'll just go tend the sheep son. Say goodbye before you leave then and send my regards to your parents."

Kissing both Beth and Simon, I went outside and saw that Padruig was hammering at what was once a chair and just kept walking. I couldn't even bring myself to greet him. I was harboring painful contempt that felt unfamiliar to me. I'd always been a forgiving person, but this was different. I had loved that china, that's true. I'd spent hours making our own plates and bowls and paid for the dining suite out of my own coin. Padruig had never bought a stick of the furniture for the new home, despite having the Chelsea Pension.

My blessed black faced sheep, now thirty in number, were all impatiently hungry and noisily waiting to be let out of their confines. I noticed as I walked passed the chickens, that they'd already been fed and let out, but Helen was nowhere around or in the house. Hugh Og had already been to feed the wee ponies and muck out their stables and they were all busy eating. My only two remaining goats always sidled up to me for love and I patted them like pets, fed them and milked nanny, God bless her. She still gave us a little milk. The sheep meandered peacefully here and there and I directed them to some greener grass with my trusty shepherd's crook.

Curious about Helen and Grigor, I wandered up to the oat fields to see them both working hard together. They waved and smiled as if nothing had happened. Hugh Og and Hugh Mohr were deep in conversation no doubt discussing the stramash as I approached them uneasily. Feeling a degree of shame, I said, "Good morning," hoping that both men would still be the same people today as they were yesterday. "Good morning Isobel," they both said and came directly to me. "Are you alright?" they both inquired. Relieved, I then said, "I have a wee bruise, but I think you have more, Hugh," pointing at his eye and his lip. "Have you dressed your lip Hugh?" I asked, "it looks painful." "Aye and aye. It is painful. Thank you," he replied. Holding back emotion I was relieved that they hadn't judged me somehow. I then said lightly, "There's no china left so you'll have to bring your own cup for coffee or tea and Padruig is fixing the chairs, but we'll get by. Funerals can be dangerous places to be."

My Clydesdales and the Missing Coos

In the weeks that passed, Simon had spoken to his Father, John, who did laugh as I'd predicted, but justified it to his son and asked for a piece of the china to inspect. "It's Turkish," he said. "Our contacts for Turkey are here in Scotland." Unexpectedly, my grandson-in-law Simon and his wife Beth returned after the stramash just a few weeks later, following behind a delivery carriage led by two beautiful matured Clydesdales, who I recognised immediately.

Da had bred his 'babies,' as he called them, from our Sire and Dame and when both foals were born, they each had a white spot on their right front legs just beneath the knee in exactly the same place. I was aware that both Simon and Beth were trying to say something to me, but I was oblivious to their excited chatter as I inspected the harness and reins on the Clydesdales. Noting Da's mark "*I*" on the leather, it was confirmed that the gear had been made with my Father's own hands. I patted down the horses faces and necks and spoke to them gently in the way Da taught me, softly in Erse and they knickered and rubbed their faces on me. They remembered me and they wanted affection. How I had loved these babies. "Agnus," I called, "run like the wind and get Hugh Mohr and Hugh Og, Donald, Grigor and Patrick for me with saddled horses and an extra saddle and bridle, then go inside and fetch pen and paper as quick as you can." I then told the chatty Simon to close the gate.

The teamster was an aging, fat, red-faced, sweaty and dirty looking fellow of some kind of English extraction. "Been here long in Scotland?" I asked. "Oh yes, since the '45 and never left," he responded. He looked like a cruel man. My heart was pounding so fast, it was hard to control. How was I going to get my horses back legally? Thank God Padruig had picked up on the serious difference in my demeanor and knew something was afoot and went inside and fetched two pistols and his long rifle. He was permitted to carry arms, due to having served in the 78th Fraser Regiment. He passed me a pistol to hide in my apron. He held his loaded long rifle over his shoulder, as casual as can be and stood beside me.

"Allow me to introduce my husband, Padruig Dubh," I said to the teamster, who was then alighting the carriage. Much shorter than Padruig, the fat dirty man went pale. "Padruig Dubh you say?" he asked with an obvious quiver in his voice recognising the name. Playing on his fear of course, Padruig said, "Aye, that's me and this is me wife, Isobel Grant, daughter of teamster, the late John Grant." Looking directly at me, the teamster then said, "so, you'd be that lady teamster?" "Aye," I said. "Familiar with this property are you Mr.... ah, um, what did you say your name was?" I asked. "Me name's Fred Jones, Missus, formerly a Corporal of His Majesty's Army at Fort Augustus in 1745 and 1746. I wasn't sure if I'd been here before Mrs. Grant."

"Now that you look around you at your location," I said to him, "in relation to the fort, do you remember coming here to Craskie Farm on May 4th 1746 with other dragoons, in search of the Prince? If so, you either killed or were in company of those dragoons who killed several innocent people including my Mither, raping two women, burning down my home and all of the crofter's homes, stole forty of our coos and our Clydesdale team of eight horses, as well as the gear and the carriage made by my Father's own hands?" I pressed on, feeling the importance of details. He clearly remembered as his dirty face paled as much as it could and his shifty eyes moved from side to side assessing an escape route I guessed. He wasn't going to confess to murder or rapine but he might confess to stealing. I was determined to get my babies back. Agnus had begun to write down his name, the date I had mentioned, all of the details as well and the eight Clydesdales.

Hugh Mohr, Hugh Og, Donald, Grigor and Patrick had arrived with their saddled horses, looking like a cattle rustling party and tied them all to the hitching rail and I went on. Hugh Mohr was looking worried sick and itching to do someone harm. "Mr. Jones, these two Clydesdale horses and the gear, but not that carriage, belong to me as I was to inherit the team of Clydesdales and the bloodlines from my Father, Mr. John Grant, who has since passed away." "Well, Mrs.," he said, "you must have them mixed up. They all look alike. I'll unload your goods for ya and that'll make ya day," he said. "Go ahead, unload it and put it all over there," I said pointing at a dry spot on the verandah, then I told Simon to move it into the house with the assistance of a rather curious fence builder who had come to watch. It appeared to be very large boxes of new china from Turkey and a beautiful mahogany dining room suite complete with twelve padded chairs and two velvet upholstered carvers.

"It is indeed a lovely delivery Mr. Jones. Getting back to what I was saying sir. You were here on May 4th 1746, were you not? And I should add, that while I am known to be patient and forgiving, my husband and his good friends, Donald and Hugh Chisholm, are not. You have heard of the Seven Glenmoriston Men I presume? You were looking for the Prince and my husband while you were working for the Duke of Cumberland. Isn't that so?" I demanded.

At that, Padruig pointed his rifle at the despicable man's head and growled, "Answer my wife or there's no tomorrow for you and I can kill you legally, being that I've served with the 78th," Padruig bluffed, with spine chilling effect. The man wet his pants and fell to his knees, feeling the intensity of the threat and his own guilt, with both Padruig, Donald and Hugh standing over him, all three men being over 6'6" tall. Beth came and stood at my left and I told her quietly to keep her horses saddled. Simon looked terrified and came and stood behind me.

"Simon," I said, "you go inside lad and unpack this beautiful china and place it decoratively, as I know only you can do and Agnus can fetch water from the burn and wash it all for you then wait here, while we all take care of some business. You'll have to put the chickens away as well and round up the sheep if we are late, okay?" Simon nodded, without asking questions. "Give me that piece of paper Agnus, and a few spares in a satchel and put dinner on for all of us later, but don't forget the tomatoes and if you need a man, Hamish is up at the MacDonald farm." I instructed the young lad, who was now helping us as an assistant groom, Bruce MacKay, to make more room for more horses and then continued with Mr. Jones.

"Mr. Jones, this paper is your confession that you stole from us, the Grants of Craskie Farm, eight Clydesdales on the 4th May 1746 and wish to make reparations. And so, the thing you'll do is sign the confession concerning the horses commencing with these two that are here today declaring that you are willingly parting with them," which he did. "Then you will tell me if the other horses are still alive and if so, where they are and if the Sire and Dame have had offspring and how many and where they are." It's amazing what a gun to the head will do. He signed, confessed and told me where my aged Sire and Dame were, miraculously still alive, but very old with only six offspring of various ages, at a farm further down the Great Glen, closer to the loch on a property owned by a member of Clan Cameron. They had concocted charges against that family in order to take the property and they were subsequently transported to Nova Scotia.

Currently, a former soldier lived on the farm alone, reaping the benefits of the lovely property that he had stolen, as well as being an accomplice to the crime of Clydesdale and property theft. My blood was boiling and I couldn't help wonder if this was the soldier who had killed my Mither as well. But as I didn't see that man's face on that day, it could only be a niggling question at the back of my mind. "Did you by chance also take our forty coos to that same property or were they taken to a different location?" I demanded to know. "Yes Missus. Forty there on that day and forty on that other day when that lady broke her neck. A total of eighty," he blubbered. "So, you'll take us all to that property, Mr. Jones and remain in my husband's custody," I demanded.

"How much did you charge my grandson-in-law to deliver the goods here today?" I asked. "£100 Missus", he said. "So, you'll need a donkey to take your cart back later to wherever you come from as well?" Miserably, he answered, "Yes." "Give my granddaughter, Beth, the £100 and we will rent you and provide you with a receipt for our donkey, Frederick, as well as a farm hand with which to remove your cart later. But, firstly, you will lead us riding that donkey to that farm." Very reluctantly, he parted with the money, choosing life over death and agreed to the terms by signing.

Everybody was keen to know what their role was to be in this excursion that I was concocting. I was silently praying to God constantly knowing also that Padruig was learning things for the first time. First, I instructed Grigor to hold a rope leading the donkey, to prevent any escape effort on the way to that farm where we were all to follow, being myself on one of my precious Clydesdales, Padruig on Blaze, Patrick on his grey mare, Donald riding his chestnut gelding, Hugh Mohr on his bay gelding shadowed by his Collies, Hugh Og on Simon's horse and Beth on hers. In total, we were nine people, accompanied by the two fence workers who had volunteered and rode the highland ponies and carried all the gear needed if we found the carriage.

Approaching the farm, everybody was testy and Padruig wasn't leaving my side, which was something I had never experienced on horseback with my husband. Grigor was out the front of us all, leading with the little donkey, they went into the property and I immediately saw our Clydesdales in the paddock off to the west side. I instructed my son Patrick that his job was to search for the carriage on this property. Grigor was to keep control of Mr. Jones, while Beth and I and two of the fence workers opened up the gate and went in to rope up the horses. There were six Clydesdale offspring and how lovely they were, as well as the poor old Dame and Sire, who recognised me immediately. Speaking to them in erse, quietly and gently, they followed me and all of their babies followed them. I could feel the men's anxiety, but it wasn't hard.

Backbred

It went very smoothly until we had them out of the paddock, when in readiness, Padruig had his rifle trained on the front door of the farmhouse, but without warning, the occupant within went to fire directly at me. His gun miraculously misfired and he fell through the doorway onto the porch, bleeding heavily. Rather ruthlessly, I went up onto that porch to the bloody individual and asked him directly, "Did you kill my Mither, Freya Grant, at Craskie Farm on 4ᵗʰ May 1746, by first cutting off her arm and then her head?" With raspy breathing, he replied, "Yes, so what if I did? Scot scum!" I continued calmly, "I believe your name is 'Fred Bowls. Is that true?" "Yes, what if it is?" he retorted. "Do you confess to murdering Freya Grant on the 4ᵗʰ May 1746 and being complicit in stealing Clydesdale horses belonging to John Grant and forty coos on that day? Remember sir, that you are dying. There's nothing I can do to save you because your own gun has killed you. Is this your confession before God?" I asked. "I'm not Papist, but yes, so what? And another forty on that other day when that woman broke her neck. I should've broken yours as well." "Sign here please sir," I continued in a monotone voice, "that these are the crimes that you confess to," I said as I held the paper and Padruig held the gun, again.

"Now, we'll be taking the horses and the coos today. Are you in agreement with that?" "I asked. "What difference does it make?" he barked. "Before God, it will make a difference," I said. "Do you agree? Yes or no?" I reiterated. "Yes, take the bloody things. I am going to die anyway," he gurgled semi incomprehensibly. "One other matter sir," I continued. "Does this property legally belong to the Camerons?" I asked. "Yes, it does," he reluctantly said whilst grabbing at his side. "Did you concoct charges against them to send them to the colonies? Because there is a witness here by the name of Mr.

Fred Jones, formerly a Corporal from your regiment who has said that you concocted false accusations against them to have them sent to the colonies in order to take their land," I stated. "Yes," he said. "And if I report that at Fort Augustus, can they have that family returned?" I asked. "Yes," he mumbled. "Thank you for your cooperation sir. If you are able to sit up and write, repeat after me, 'Before these nine witnesses, I am willingly returning the living bloodlines and Clydesdales belonging to the family of John Grant of Craskie Farm, being now Isobel Grant and the equivalent number of cows that I stole on the 4th May 1746 and wish to make reparations for that theft'. Sign it please sir and date it today." As he signed the document, he asked, "Now, are you going to get me to a doctor?" he demanded. "Och, of course, sir. We'll get you some medical attention as soon as we get the horses and the coos back home," I responded. "What? I need medical attention now," he gurgled. "The horses and the coos come first sir. Okay, let's start rounding up the coos and moving them down the road. Grigor, help me with the team. Beth on horseback, help Hugh Mohr and the Collie dogs move the coos."

By a miracle of God, Patrick found the carriage in an outbuilding and we attached it to the team in perfect condition as it appeared to have never been used. With the assistance of the unusually helpful volunteer men, I harnessed up the old Sire and Dame and four of the horses. The other two looked untrained and I asked Donald if he could lead them home from on horseback. "Our lawyer will send you a letter sir," I said to the man. "What about a doctor?" he cried, through bloody lips, holding his side. "Once we get these animals home and out of this dreich weather, we will hopefully send medical attention." I replied.

It felt as if the image was all in slow motion as miraculously, we moved the eighty coos up the Glen taking their time, as highland coos do, and still with Frederick the donkey and our prisoner at the fore. The team was jittery having lived through the same trauma as we had. We were not going to be able to fit an additional eighty coos on Craskie Farm, so I had asked Padruig if we could put them all on his newly inherited property from Uncle Allan at MacDonald Farm until we could sort them out. We'd move them up the old drover's path onto the golf field, which Padruig was a bit sad about at the time, but we knew we could fix that. The important thing is that they had food and there was plenty of grazing land still on MacDonald Farm. The younger Clydesdales were able to be stabled with the Highland ponies. All of the others were able to go onto Grant Farm, where the new stables were to be built, in temporary accommodation which the young groomsman, Bruce MacKay, had pre-prepared to the best of his ability on such short notice.

The day had started out dreich, but the rain came down hard as we all were all finishing up our tasks. A place by a warm fire and a meal felt like it would never come.

Helen and her daughters had been out visiting for the day with one of the lassies' friends who was getting married and were attending the pre-wedding party and therefore weren't expected home until nightfall. Her son, Aonghus, was still at university and I thanked God that they had all missed the action of the day. The oddly curious volunteers were paid and told to go home except Alasdair who insisted on accompanying the donkey and Mr. Jones to a location that he chose outside an alehouse in Invergarry and he returned a tired but happy looking Frederick back home. The donkey had done a really good job and he had enjoyed his day out, but was very happy to be stabled nice and warm and out of the cold and wet at the end of the day, except he would have to be washed the followed day as he had been soiled on by the prisoner, Fred Jones.

I was going to have to face a barrage of questions that night, but I just held that off until everybody was fed, dry, satisfied, paid, animals all fed, safe and contained. The only loose end was the bleeding farmer on his front porch. We sent word to the local doctor that there may be an ailing farmer on his front porch due to a misfiring weapon at that Cameron property. Fort Augustus and the Cameron issue would have to wait for another day. I had concluded that Padruig was going to have to make that decision and speak to the current Lochiel, given that he is a distant relative of the Camerons.

Hugh Mohr's Collies were lounging by the fire eating their meal and being towel dried by their loving master, Hugh Mohr but I was now not feeling so brave in the safety of our home and felt a need to be held by the handsome Hugh Mohr. He hadn't made any further attempts at gaining my affections and I had concurred his brother may have put a stop to it. There was no sign of any animosity between the Chisholms and Padruig however, for which I was grateful. We had all worked well as a team and I was proud of us, no matter what I had to answer to that night.

I asked Beth when she was due back at Stratherick. She replied, "tomorrow Granny. We'll leave in the morning." I then said to her, "Can you engage the assistance of your father-in-law, John Fraser in case this blows up in our faces." And of course, we all ate off the beautiful new Turkish china, but it wasn't the same. I sent my gratitude back to John just the same, by way of a letter and a block of mild sheep cheese for him to try as well as new shirts for both him and Simon.

Simon was very proud of himself for the arrangement of the china over dinner and was expecting praise. 'Funny lad,' I thought, but well intentioned. They were first to take themselves off to a hot bath and bed that night, followed by Helen and her girls, who'd had a really big day, they said. We all looked at her when she said she'd had a 'big day.' Padruig couldn't help himself, "You've had a big day, have you love?" he asked. The emphasis being on 'you'. "Aye, Da. A really big day," she responded, "Well, I'm glad of it love" and the girls went to have their baths and go to bed, but not before saying, "Ma, I've put your water on to boil. Can you do the rest yourself?" she asked. "Aye, love." I responded. "I can help you mo chride," Padruig said. And then Patrick thought out loud, "Oh my God, I have forgotten all about Henrietta!" "Patrick, where is Henrietta?" I asked. "She went out to visit her Mither," he answered. "Were you meant to pick her up?" I asked. "Aye, but with all the excitement, I forgot," he said. "She'll forgive you son. Leave it till the morning now," I said, hoping that I was right and told him to go to bed.

Donald piped up and said, "Well, I've got to say Isobel, Hugh, Padruig, Grigor, that I really enjoyed the action. I felt young again, but most importantly, for you Isobel, you've nailed the killer.

We could have been the Seven and a Half Glenmoriston People," he said and laughed at his own joke. Grigor didn't laugh I noticed. "Seriously, I have to say congratulations, that was good work. I know it's hard, but I am glad we know who the killer is, so let him suffer and I hope that the Camerons get their property back. Padruig, are you going to go see Lochiel tomorrow?" "I should, aye. I'll take these notes that Isobel has and show him," he said. "Ah, no," I interjected, "you're not taking the notes. I'm going in to see the lawyer in Inverness, first thing. You can copy what it says, but I need the originals. I need to go up in the morning in case this situation back fires on us and I expected that you'd come with me," I said. "You mean, in case that fellow dies?" Padruig said. "Oh, he is going to die, nothing surer. That doctor wasn't going to be able to get there till tomorrow morning. He'll freeze to death if nothing else. I wanted confirmation from the doctor though. Padruig, what's the priority for you first thing tomorrow? Because I need you to come with me to the lawyer. Do you want to see Lochiel after that?" I asked. "I'll go with you and sort it with the lawyer then," Padruig said knowing it would cost us a bit. "Alright. Bring me home after the lawyer then depending on the legal advice, it'll be clearer what we are to do and you may not even need to see Lochiel," I said.

I asked Grigor how he was, because he had done such a great job with that prisoner. "I'm still wound Ma. I feel a bit uncomfortable that the Englishman is a loose end. For the first time in my life, I actually wanted to finish him and I only thought that other MacGregors felt like that, or Da and that I'd just be a farmer and never feel that. But, och did I feel it. I wanted to kill him." At those words, I think all of us raised our eyebrows. Our sweet Grigor had lost his innocence during that raiding party, but we were also aware that it was the maturing of a man who would one day soon run Craskie and Grant Farms.

"Isobel, do you mind me asking something?" said Hugh Mohr. "No Hugh. Ask me anything," I said. "Och, it was a long time ago now, before the '45. Grigor Mohr told me that he had seen a team of Clydesdales on the Drover's Road and there was a wee lassie controlling the reins of eight horses. I didn't know that that was you, but it was, wasn't it?" he asked. "Aye, it was," I answered. "He said that it had started to rain, so he had asked for a ride to the fort and you'd put your plaid up over your head, so he couldn't be sure who you were if he ever saw you again. He didn't recognize you when you married Padruig. He was stunned that a wee lass could be a teamster and he went on and on about it and said he'd always wished that he'd been a teamster of that many horses or even more. And he could've been, as it turned out, now that we know that he was your brother all along. That is a sad story," he said with real feeling. "Aye, it is, but God kept putting us together? Through yourself, through Padruig, through situations like that day? He was even playing fussball with Padruig when we first met. I was just six years old at the school when he was kicking the ball further than Grigor Mohr. You were taller than him Padruig and I only had eyes for you," I said as Padruig had entered our conversation. Padruig held my hand jealously possessive. "Isobel, whatever reason you had for not disclosing the business you had with your Da and being a teamster, I accept it. You had your reasons. But I have to say, riding beside you today, I've never felt prouder of you as me wife." I squeezed his hand back as Hugh was left disappointed that our conversation had ended.

"Hugh Og," I said to Hugh Og, who was staring into the fire, "are you off to MacDonald Farm to your Mither soon? It is surrounded by all those coos and you might want to keep an eye and your Mither might feel a bit disturbed about it all." He looked up and said, "Good point, she's a bit scared of coos." He then took his leave, followed soon after by Donald and Hugh Mohr, after we'd thanked them profusely once again. Fortunately, I had also made spare shirts for those two and gave them a shirt each. "Just one thing," Hugh Mohr said just before leaving, "I think you're going to need more permanent workers here on the property to help with all of the horses." "Aye, we will Isobel," Padruig added. "There's a lot more work now. I agree. Are you available Hugh?" I said. "Aye, we can discuss it then when I come over next," he said Padruig offered a coo each for Donald and Hugh to slaughter in the morning. As he was leaving, Donald said, "If you need the coos to be moved to the markets, we'll help you drove them in." Smiling cheekily, he said, "It'll only cost ya a little bit." "Aye, Isobel," said Padruig, "we can't keep all of them up there, we don't have enough grazing land for them." "We could move them further up the mountain," I replied. "Aye, Patrick could do that. He's done it before and then we can decide how many are going to go in to market," Padruig said. "Well, market day is coming up," said Donald. "Consider that and let us know if we are needed!" We all said our weary goodnights and the brothers went out into the misty damp air followed by the dogs. Agnes was cleaning up and I asked her if I could leave smooring the fires and putting out all of the candles to her, while Padruig and I went to bed where we could have a quiet discussion during our baths. Padruig was more affectionate than ever with no questions and it was truly a beautiful night.

Justice at Last

The following day's tasks felt horribly taxing. Over breakfast, the bright Simon asked if we needed anything from his Father's Trading Post and I subsequently ordered a tub of whale oil and two large metal

free standing torch lights to be situated either side of our entrance. I wanted to see anything or anyone coming, even in the dark. Overnight, it was obvious that Helen had heard the whole story from Grigor. I wanted two whale oil street lamps in front of the School House as well. Surprisingly, the results of the day were more successful than I had expected. Our aging, but determined lawyer, had only wanted a portrait of himself as payment and said that he'd deal with it all. Enclosed is a copy of our lawyer's letter.

He was very satisfied that Mither's killer had been identified and that I had it all in writing from a legal perspective. "The Duke of Cumberland basically made it legal to do what they did, but in these letters that you have written, the wording says that the men wanted to make reparations for their crimes that they had committed and therefore, in taking back your Clydesdale horses and your Highland coos, it was legal for you do so. However, Isobel, that man's attempt initially to kill you, is still attempted murder. So even though his own gun killed him, you are entitled to further compensation, which I will apply for you on your behalf. The doctor has confirmed, by the way, that the occupant of the Cameron Farm, Mr. Fred Bowls, formerly of Fort Augustus, is dead, very dead. I will be writing to a number of powers to be, including that damn fort that I want closed. They will have to return the land and its titles to the Cameron family, but I'll also deal with that. I'll also write to Lochiel, Padruig, so no need for you to go there today, as you both must be feeling exhausted." He paused, then looked directly at me and said, "Isobel, I don't know if your Mither's death can be compensated for, but I am going to try through London, given her innocence and your great losses," he said.

"The horses born to your Da's Scottish Clydesdale horses, Dame and Sire, are proven to be yours by the bloodline books, which you have provided to me. As you have inherited them from your Father, the late Mr. John Grant, any horses born of that Dame and Sire in this district are also legally yours. If I find any more, they will have to be paid for to yourself and I can do all of that digging and put the bloodlines now in your name, Isobel Grant, with Helen and Grigor MacGregor to inherit when you pass away. Do you have any questions Isobel?" I shook my head in the negative. "Were you considering registering a separate business name for the Clydesdale team when you get it up and running?" he asked. "First things first, we will need to build the stables, but I had wanted to keep the team in Da's name, being John Grant Teamster," I replied. "Thankyou Isobel dear, now Padruig, you need to do what you have to do with the coos and given you'll need huge stables for the Clydesdales, I'd suggest selling half of the coos right away and then there'll be enough money to pay for the labour and the materials to do that. All of your witnesses, as well as yourselves will be sent letters, absolving you all of any blame in Mr. Bowls' death. The cause of death being a misfiring weapon, which can be confirmed by Dr. Jones. You'll also both receive written confirmation concerning the ownership of all of the horses and coos retrieved from that property. I might need to line a few pockets. Do you have any cash on you?" he asked. "Aye," said Padruig. "How much?" "£200 will do it. The fort is not getting any, don't worry," he said.

"Now the matter concerning Mrs. Margaret MacDonald, the wife of your late Uncle Allan MacDonald, will have to be investigated and that will involve you too Isobel, as Mr. Bowles had said in his dying statement that you were present and wishing that he'd broken your neck too. Can you explain that?" he asked. "Aye, I can but it is of some delicacy you understand?" I replied quietly as my husband looked at me quizzically. "Am I right in saying, dear Isobel, that Padruig has not yet been told of you witnessing this event?" he asked. I felt my heart would crumble with hearing those words coming from the lawyer. All those years of hiding any association to that day at Fort Augustus had gone up in smoke with my Da hiding it from Padruig with Uncle Allan and more recently my brother, Grigor Mohr. Would he ever forgive me if I was to relate all of that which I wish I didn't know, I asked myself?

"Can I write it down in full for the benefit of the legalities on the matter, with your secretary in another room please Sir?" I said trying to gain better control of my emotions. "Suffice it to say here and now, that myself and Aunty Margaret were snatched by dragoons on that day, but they had initially wanted my children. Uncle Allan paid them forty coos in exchange for my childrens' safety as well as his wife's. They were going to take at least one of us and my hands were tied behind my back. Can I please be excused to make my statement with your secretary?" I asked. "Certainly, Isobel dear. May I confirm before you do so however, that you were an eye witness to the events that caused Mrs MacDonald's neck to be broken?" he persisted as I was about to stand. Then recalling the sound of the crack in Aunty Margaret's neck from the horse that I was on, knowing that she was then lifeless, made me too dizzy to stand.

"Isobel," I heard like in the far distance. "Isobel." I heard my name over and over until I finally spoke. "Aye?" I said. It was the kindly housekeeper and the secretary, pen in hand to take the rest of the story down in another room lying down on a rather uncomfortable couch. Then Mr. David came in to ask of my well being and said, "Do I have your permission to go ahead, as you are a witness to her death?" "Aye," I replied, "so long as they don't come on to our property. You are welcome, but they are not," I said. "Aye, fine. Also, with your permission, I'll have the newspaper print a sad story about both Freya and Margaret's tragic deaths. Do you agree?" he said. "Aye, Sir," I responded, "I'll get Helen to do your portrait Sir. It could

take a wee while." Adjusting his wig, he said, "Och, that'd be lovely."
"For an aging man who had never married, vanity was surprising,'
I thought. Re-entering his office to my sad, silent but reflective hus-
band, Mr. David said, "Now I have to ask, are there any loose ends?"
"Grigor was worried," Padruig said, "about the teamster driver, Fred
Jones. We didn't harm him and he was left outside an ale house in
Invergarry. He works for a delivery business outside of Stirling called
Clop 'n Drop." The lawyer then surprisingly said, "I'll have him
arrested. You two both go home and rest. You look like you need it."
No wonder this man never had a wife, I thought.

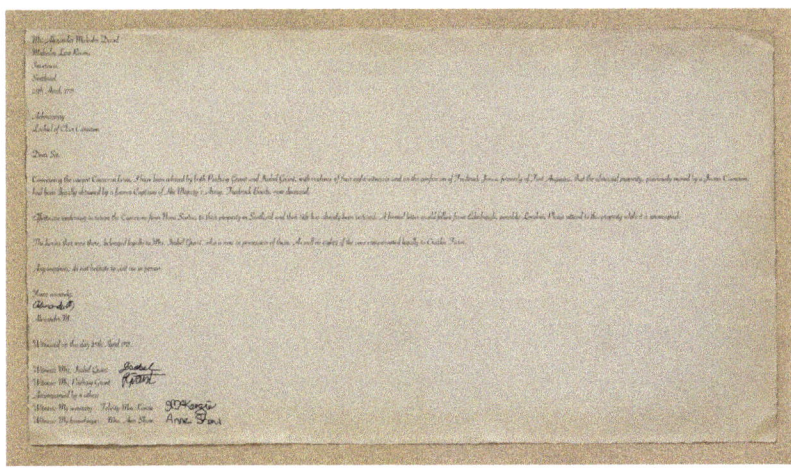

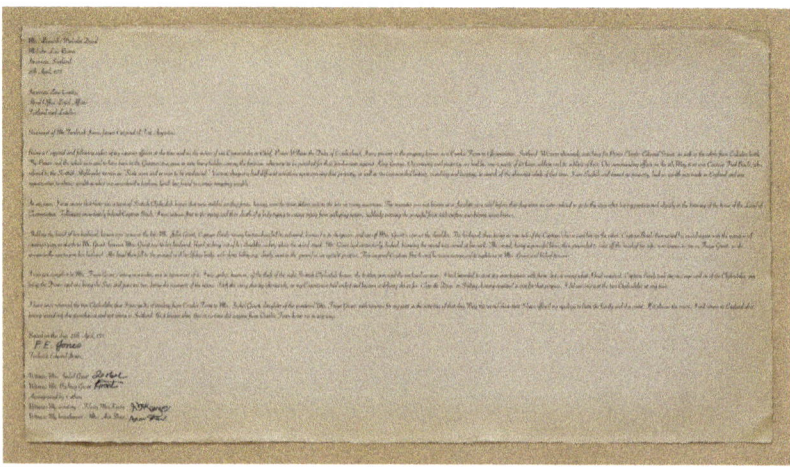

Both Padruig and I were relieved that we could go home and just tend to our farm and rest, despite the long journey through the Great Glen. There were so many details my dear husband had never known and his quietness on that journey home I attributed to the many emotive issues he'd had to deal with over the last week whilst still missing his dear friend, Grigor Mohr. "Who's the horse for?" he asked, breaking his silence. "I bought her for you as a sort of apology and because Blaze is getting old. She's 16hh and four years old, well broken and a good-natured mare," I responded. "Please forgive me, Padruig, I just couldn't bare you looking at me differently. I still wanted to be your beloved despite what had happened to me. Do you forgive me?" I asked.

"Was it only Da and Uncle Allan who knew of what happened at Fort Augustus?" he asked. "No, Grigor Mohr had guessed and so he knew some of the story as did Morag but not all and due to your circumstances, I begged him not to tell you, Hugh guessed also. Donald doesn't know anything. Women around here witnessed each other there, so there was a pact, although silent, that it would never be spoken of. Now most of those women are dead or have been transported due to the clearances. We didn't want each other's husbands to put themselves in danger or worse still be rejected by our spouses. Padruig, you haven't said if you forgive me yet for purposefully keeping it all from you, there was just so much to deal with and if there was even the slightest chance of losing you, I would not have been able to live," I responded with a fearful heart. "My dearest Isobel, nothing could ever change

210

how I feel about you, so aye I forgive you, but I understand, so you don't need to ask as it was not you who perpetrated that terrible crime against yourself and Aunty Margaret. I am really sorry about her china. Please continue working with your Clydesdales as a teamster from now on if you want to," he said. "The horses are not to blame, poor things. They were victims too of the violence against all of you. I am so sorry Isobel. You know I adore you more than life itself, don't you? I will love you until my grave and beyond," he said lovingly. Then brushing his hair from his eyes as the wind came up I pulled his bonnet further down and I said, "I know too how you felt after Grigor's funeral. Maybe stay away from Da's whiskey, eh?" I attempted a smile and we enjoyed our ride home, watching the dying light.

Lochiel of the Camerons

The next day brought new challenges as a lovely bay stallion pranced into our property with its owner having opened the gate confidently. The handsome gentleman sat tall in his saddle and his face was familiar, so I called Padruig to come and see. "Och, you need glasses Isobel. That's Lochiel from the Camerons." Then hitching his lovely horse to the railing, Lochiel strode up to the door confidently to be greeted by Padruig. "Lochiel, good to see you in these parts," he said. "Good morning Padruig, good morning Isobel. I hear from this hastily delivered letter that you've both been busy." Stomping the mud from his boots, he entered our home on our invitation with Agnes glaring at how dirty his boots still were. The lass could imagine washing the floor yet again. I had to ask her for a fresh pot of coffee for our esteemed guest, Lochiel of the Camerons. Upon hearing 'Lochiel of the Camerons', she quickly made coffee and commenced baking a cake. I was starting to wonder about the changes in this girl.

"So, we had to peel a body off the porch of that farm house mentioned here in this letter by your efficient lawyer. How much do you pay him?" he asked. "A portrait," I replied without even yet asking Helen. "I'm here to thank you both for restoring a Cameron land and having the family returned to us. I am in your debt," he went on. "There's also a matter of coos. I'd like to buy forty or fifty from you, at a good price mind, as I hear you've quite a few." 'Cheeky fella, this Lochiel' I thought, but I liked him and I needed a stable. So, I replied, "so long as its split 50/50 between Padruig and I, Lochiel." "I can see why you married Isobel all those years ago, Padruig. Very smart move Padruig. How about I put the money on the table and you two split it? I'm not game to get between the two of you," he said. "Okay, put £4000 on the table if you have it Lochiel, for forty coos," Padruig said. The men both agreed and I quickly took my half, much to their surprise. "Well, I am building a very big stable," I said, "for the Clydesdales," I clarified. "I've drawn up the building plans already." I said. "Then you are as organised as I am Isobel. My Camerons are outside your gate. Can they come in and drove the coos home?" he asked. "Aye, bring them in," said Padruig.

Quickly writing a letter for Patrick to release forty coos and be reassured that it was not a raiding party of Camerons, I handed Lochiel the letter to take up the mountain to Patrick and told him to keep them off my oat fields. I also gave Agnes a letter for Grigor with the same information and told the lass to run it up to him as quickly as possible before all twenty Camerons burst onto his precious oat fields, which she did and all was well as the lovely coos meandered back on down slowly avoiding any crops. Grigor was standing there like Moses with a shepherd's crook, moving them on, as was Patrick.

Now we just needed my stable builders, I thought. "Do you have today's paper?" Lochiel asked as they were all walking passed. "Nae, we don't," I said. "Why?" "You're in it," he said. "Just one correction though Isobel. Your Mither wasn't a MacPherson, or any of the Clans Chattan to our understanding. Your Mither was Freya MacGregor, God rest her soul, who was married previously to Grigor MacGregor who passed away two years into their marriage before she then married your father John Grant. Is that right?" he asked "Aye," I then answered. "Good to have all the details right and I've taken the initiative and sent word to who I think will know your Mither's Clan name accurately. A well-respected man by the name of Gillcrest MacNachten, sometimes spelled MacNaghten and I've also seen it spelled MacKnight. Originally Pecht, they did have a castle called Castle Dunderave in the heart of Campbell country, who succeeded in taking it from them. With the Clearances as well, I only know one elderly gentleman of that name now who lives in Loch Insh and I hope he can help you. I've written to him, he has your name and address and has read the newspaper. Failing that, there is one other person who may be able to help, he is a font of knowledge and a scientist. He is a young man whose name is Gillcrest MacLachlan and he works at the Inverness Hospital. He has all of the knowledge of those who have historically been recorded as having lands in Argyle, which would include the MacNachtens who were granted land there. Hope that helps. I am sorry for your loss Isobel," said Lochiel. I thanked him and we waved them off.

Then glancing at the newspaper, I understood why Lochiel left us a copy. The whole district would be buzzing now. "Padruig, I thought Mr. David was just putting a wee sad story on one of the back pages and it's front-page news," I said. He put his arms around me and kissed me, which was nice and I looked into his big blue eyes questioningly. Then he kissed my lips softly as the Camerons closed the gate. "Glad to see someone remembers to close gates around here," he said. I held my husband tightly around his middle and asked, "Do you think I'm short?" He replied, "What an odd question Isobel, but I'll answer it like this. I've seen Highlander men, even taller and broader than me, standing over you, speaking in meek tones to ask permission to do this or that. All 4'11" of you gives them permission or not and quietly even, gives out a dozen instructions to all and sundry, to which they obey without shame concerning your height or your gender. If you'd been in the military, you'd have commanded entire armies I am sure. You are not tall, it is true my love, but that is part of what I love about you," he replied.

Fragmented conversations that I had had with Grigor Mohr about the Pecht people, the ancient people of Scotland, would swim around in my mind and I wondered why Mither had never taught me about her ancestry. While I understood her previous name was MacGregor, I had assumed it was due to her first husband's name of MacGregor. What I didn't know were details of my Mither's parents and their Clans. When the teacher at The Glenmoriston School asked us all to write down our clans on both our parents' sides, I had to leave empty spaces for Mither's parents' Clans and was told to do my homework and bring it back the next day with the spaces filled in. I felt like

I was in trouble with the teacher and embarrassed because everyone else was able to fill in their family tree. Taking my homework home to Da resulted in him visiting the school. I don't know what was said, as I was told to wait outside, but I was never asked to complete that homework again and the teacher was replaced within the month. "You're a Grant," Da would just say. So, here I was getting old and wanting to know, especially since Lochiel's visit.

After Grigor Mohr's funeral, I could see the ghost of my half-brother sitting opposite me at the dining table, sometimes just standing by the fireside, sometimes walking across the yard to the horses. This had never happened to me before and I put it down to our shared Pecht blood as a possible explanation. I didn't mention it to anyone and my brother seemed pleased that I was making enquiries concerning our shared and quite unique ancestry, although if my brother had known more about the Pecht people I deduced he would have told me who they were.

Having a lot more to deal with than ancestry, I had to focus on getting the farm to settle down again after the events of the previous week and make plans to build a very 'state of the art stable'. With forty coos sold to Lochiel, I could now afford to do it. Padruig also distributed twenty coos to his close friends that had helped us and we managed to absorb the remaining carefully selected coos amongst our usual herd. Selected by colour, weight, height and gender, we had to ensure there had been no interbreeding with other coos like the Angus.

Nanny, my old goat, had her first kid in ages, so she had become my main concern on this particular day, when once again our front gate was being opened, but slowly this time. I couldn't see anyone over the top of the gate. I put that down to my poor eyesight and decided to get those glasses that Padruig had suggested. My poor love was hard at work again on his country manor house and had enlisted the help of the three fence builders, who had nearly finished the perimeter of the farms. Both Hugh Og and Hamish were up there too on MacDonald Farm, either helping Padruig or repairing their precious golf field. The second story of the huge house was nearly complete. With the widow MacDonald's ailing health in the old farm house, it was clear that it wasn't going to be long before Hugh Og and Hamish would need alternative accommodation.

For a Scottish day in the Highlands it was surprisingly warm and for once the clouds had gone and there was actual blue sky. It was so beautiful. I noticed the blue of the sky was the same as my Mither's eyes and Grigor Mohr's and my own. Padruig's blue was a deeper blue, like the loch on a summer day. I was briefly annoyed at whoever it was at the gate. Our family was only just recovering from a multitude of issues and there was a lot of work to be done. I really wanted Hugh to work here as soon as possible. Combing down my new wee kid, I was aware that Grigor Og in the oat fields, wasn't taking his eyes off me or the gate. He hadn't come to terms with the reality that I could've been shot by that same man who had killed his grandmother-in-law. He was more protective of me now than ever, even though I thought I'd been strong and confident enough on that awful day, besides which, I didn't actually see the man aiming for me. I had just heard the gun go off. It was awfully loud and Padruig first rushed to me and then we both went to see what had happened. Poor Grigor had seen the whole thing play out in slow motion and had felt helpless, being unarmed as he was.

Mither's Clan

A wee old Highland Pony came through the gate with a shortish, aging man carefully closing the gate behind him, so I started to walk slowly towards the house to greet this new visitor. He led his pony in and waved a little to me and I gestured for him to tie him up where there was fresh water. "Good morning Misses," he said with a slight lilt in his accent. I responded and asked what I could do for him. He produced a letter from his pocket. He was barely 5'5" tall, with silver hair, wearing brownish old woolen attire with a similar cap. His shoes were like mine had been for years, they barely existed and I wasn't sure if they even had soles, for which I didn't judge. "My name is MacNachten, you can call me Gillcrest if you like. You must be Mrs. Isobel Grant?" he asked while also taking out a satchel from his pony's saddle bag and continued to say, "It's a bit isolated here Mrs. Grant. How do you manage without a village nearby?" he asked. A curious man, I'd thought but I answered anyway and said, "We make all our own clothes, grow all our own food, make our own bread and cheese and if we have a need, we go into Inverness." Well, I have to say Mrs. Grant, it's a beautiful part of the country with its many

215

streams and rivers and the wee loch nearby," he had observed. "What's the name of the wee loch?" he asked. "Loch Craskie. Walking distance for fishing and the horses like a summer swim and it's not that far from Loch Ness," I replied.

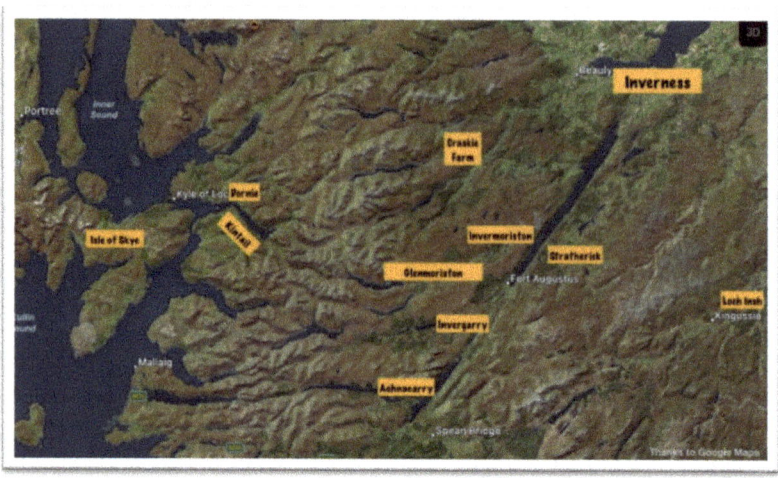

"I've come from Loch Insh, where I have a small croft and a wee business. My old pony hasn't enjoyed the long journey much because it is much further than I'd realised," he said. I offered stabling and feed for the pony but he declined saying he didn't want to take up much of my time, understanding the work of a farm. Behind me, I heard the familiar sound of our beloved Grigor's footsteps. "This is my son-in-law Grigor MacGregor," I said. I noted that Grigor was suspicious of Mr. MacNachten, so I explained to Grigor that Lochiel of the Camerons had written to him, to which I had gathered he was responding. Looking at the kindly old gentleman, I offered both Grigor and Mr MacNachten tea or coffee. "Now I haven't had coffee in a while, so that would be nice," he replied, finally relaxing but Grigor declined.

I asked if he would like to sit on the verandah in the rare sunshine on this lovely day. Padruig's efforts at repairing the old dining suite had given us four rickety chairs outside with a half table. Helen had overheard everything and had already made the coffee for four people and we sat outside at least while we had sun. "I'm Helen," she said joyously to Gillcrest. He responded, "It's very nice to meet you all. I've read the newspapers and the first one mentioned your late Mither, Isobel, Freya MacGregor, your grandmother Helen and that is why I'm here. I've collected some Parish papers that have previously been in the old Papist church and are now just sitting around in boxes. I rummaged through it all and I have a copy of the marriages of Freya to Grigor MacGregor and Freya to John Grant that you might like to keep. In addition, I have copies of both births of Grigor MacGregor, born to Freya with Mr. Grigor MacGregor and yourself, Isobel Grant, born to Freya MacGregor and Mr. John Grant. Freya is not a common name, so it wasn't too hard," he made all of those statements so casually that we were all shocked. Why hadn't we thought of the Parish papers?

Both Grigor and Helen stood up and went around to read the papers that he had. Gillcrest asked me if that was alright and I nodded. "Ma," Grigor exclaimed, "it says here that your Ma, Freya MacGregor, when marrying Grigor MacGregor, had witnesses with the same name as Mr. MacNachten." Then still standing very tall, said, "So, where is this Clan MacNachten? I've never heard of them," he asked. "Show me son and relax," I said very curious. "Agnes, bring out some short bread biscuits will you please?" I requested. "As I started reading through all of the old documents, especially that one, Helen said, "Da's coming". "Why are there MacNachten witnesses on here, Gillcrest?" I asked. He only had time to say that we'd be related somehow but wasn't yet sure of the relationship.

All the men were then meandering down like coos for their morning tea, so I changed the short bread biscuit order and said, "Let's all go inside together with my husband, Hamish and Hugh Og while we all have a bite to eat." At first, Padruig frowned at the man, but upon hearing the name, he understood and liked the suggestion of taking the conversation inside to a larger table and a meal. Mr. MacNachten and the hungry workers were all ravenous. Hugh Og suggested moving the wee pony into a stable to have a feed too and this time the offer was accepted.

It sounded like progress on the manor house was excellent and Hugh Og was relieved that at least some of his precious golf field had been repaired. "I am happy for you Padruig," I had said. Unexpectedly, Padruig then directly addressed Gillcrest and asked, "So, is my wife part Pecht or Druid or some such?" Someone sniggered, but Grigor shut them up. "Aye," he replied, "probably both, but there is no way of finding these people on Freya's original marriage to MacGregor, as I am aware that they are either dead or have been transported. There's only me that I know of now and I think our families are related through Freya to Isobel albeit distantly, I'll have to go through my own paperwork to be exact," he replied.

Padruig then asked, "Do you live near the Chapel of the Swans in Badenoch?" "Aye, I do," he responded, "in a small croft nearer the loch. I've seen you before," he went on, "but you were not with the other six of you. You were with Prince Charles Edward Stuart and money passed hands from Cluny MacPherson to yourself and then you hastily left. I remember you clearly because no one else was as tall as you, especially Cluny. Naturally, I minded my own business. However, it didn't stop government dragoons from destroying the lovely old Kirk," Gillcrest added. Ignoring much of the man's astonishing revelation, Padruig continued his questions. "Is it true about the Bell of Insh possessing magical properties and flying through the air from Insh to Scone?" [29] Padruig asked. "Nae," Gillcrest answered, "Christian nonsense to convert the pagan Pechts," he said.

With some people looking reflective then, while others were positively uncomfortable, Helen then said, "Excuse me Mr. MacNachten, are we not going to find anyone else that are related to us?" He shook his head and she was so disappointed.  "Mr. MacNachten, if you are one of few people, can I please paint your portrait before you go?" she asked. "Nae, nae," he replied. "We never really disappear, do we Isobel? You've seen your brother since his death, I'll wager?" he said. "Aye, I have seen him in many places in the house and on the farm. I didn't tell you that I had a brother." I said. "He'd be this lad's Father, Grigor, am I right?" he said. "Aye, he is" I said then thought it a good time to show him my fairy rock as discomfort was setting in.

Some people weren't ready to hear about ghosts sitting across the table or misty ancestors keeping you company and so I said, "Mr. MacNachten, I have something to show you," realising I had met a kindred spirit. "Would you mind coming with me?" I asked. We left the buzzing table and trusting me completely, we both walked deep into the forest on our farm where I showed Gillcrest the Pecht stone. "It is Pecht," he said very joyously, "you are so fortunate to have this here Isobel, but I can only guess at the language of the symbols. I can tell you what it doesn't represent. It is neither a gravesite nor a battle site, but this stone does go much deeper into the ground and that indicates just how old it would be and the likelihood that there are other stones and they may be buried near here possibly in a circle. These are called stone circles. At a guess only, it is probably where a group of the tribal leaders or chiefs met to discuss any manner of things, even marriages between the different branches of the tribes, mostly youngsters but not exclusively. It's a really wonderful stone to have here on your property. Don't tell a museum, Isobel or that will be the end of it and they'll dig it up and claim it and what they don't understand is that its location is of vital importance to understanding its purpose, such as the direction the stone is facing thus indicating the rising and setting of both the sun and the moon. Even be selective with whom you impart the existence of this stone to within your own family. You will come to understand the signs of those within your own who have inherited the Sight. You are relatively close here to the MacMartins or Marthains, who were also an ancient people thought to be Pecht or Pict whose main area was Letterfinlay on Loch Lochy. Bear in mind that the Pecht or Pict peoples never called themselves that. Those words were attributed to them by the Romans and others. The Welsh have an entirely different word, as do the Irish, but we don't know what they called themselves. After Culloden the MacMartins suffered a heavy depletion in their numbers and are now a Sept of Clan Cameron. They are a fiercely loyal people who fought alongside Lochiel at Culloden and maybe the current Lochiel would have those records. Did your Mither ever mention Loch Insh, Loch Lochy, Loch Fyne, the MacMartins or the MacNachtens because some folk say that we are one and the same, but all originating from the Great Glen as indigenous people?" "My Mither told me nothing of my ancestory, partly to please my Da, I think," I answered.

"Isobel," he then said looking disturbingly into my eyes, "you will lose another close friend soon and I am sorry for it. Prepare your husband for the loss. He is weary despite his bravado. I am going to leave the papers with you to pass on to your children, but your efforts need now to be in the present, not the past. My pony and I are now going to take our leave as it a ways to Loch Insh, but I truly thank you for this wonderful opportunity to have met you and your family and for your trust in sharing this with me. It truly is very special. Thank you. These ancestors here will take care of you and yours but you have always felt that. Another matter, the man who loves you, will wait for you and you need not feel any shame or guilt for his love."

We walked together through our beautiful forest to the stables to collect his dear old pony and then he departed, closing the gate behind him and I felt a sadness at his leaving, but concern also for who it was that may be going to die soon. I hadn't expected that news and decided to bring the sheep in early. The weather had already changed, the sunshine was no longer. As dark grey clouds then rolled over the mountains, I decided that Padruig should stop working due to the sudden weather change too and I even put the chickens back inside. When Grigor Og came out to see the dark grey day, he saw that the visitor had gone and I was finishing up. "Storm coming?" he asked. "Maybe. Can you please ask Hugh Og to put away the horses and make sure everything is closed up when you come back? Bring a lot of corn back with you too please and double check the front gate," I said. He just did what I asked and Padruig came outside. "You're knocking off darling," I said sweetly. "It's too dangerous to work on the house now with this weather coming. Can you get the lads to put it all away for tomorrow?" He was surprised and knew better now than to argue and reluctantly, he agreed and what a storm it was. I hoped the old man had made it to the nearest town.

When Grigor Og had gone to secure the front gate, he had found an unusual parcel left there, wrapped in cloth. He gave it to me saying where he had found it and unwrapping the old cloth, there was a note around an object. The object was a truly beautiful brooch, but not like the old brooches with the battle cries or any kind of language on it. The note read, "My dear Isobel, in my old age I am forgetting things, for which I apologise. This brooch is for you to keep in your family.

It is Pecht and very old, made from silver and glass, I am told. The stories of the Pechts always being naked are false, although they may have fought naked to prevent infection. There is a storm coming, so my old pony wants to  go home, but we might only get as far as Invermoriston. Affectionately, Gillcrest MacNachten."

Showing Padruig, I told him I'd been given another brooch. He thought that the MacGregor one I had been given should be given to Helen now rather than wait, as she didn't have one, then I could choose which brooch I wore. His or the Pecht one. So, the Pecht brooch was carefully hidden in my tin under my bed, to which Padruig was very pleased. It was too valuable to wear, but nice to know that we had a link to the past. My Grant brooch meant the world to me, because it had always been my wedding ring. I felt relieved also that 'the man who loved me', being Hugh Mohr, needn't feel guilt any more and a weight was lifted off my heart.

The widow MacDonald, in Uncle's old house, died the night of that terrible storm and we buried her next to Uncle Allan and Aunty Margaret. It was a small funeral, but her sons were devastated. They had adored their Mither, naturally, but it is always upsetting seeing grown Highland men cry.

I asked Padruig if we could have an additional home built on Craskie Farm beyond the cemetery, but before the borders of both farms for Hugh Mohr to become the permanent farm hand. His dear brother, Donald, had a nice place, but upon his death the lease would end and I wanted to secure Hugh Mohr and his Collie dogs on our place, as it was getting harder to round up thirty sheep, especially if I was alone. Their previous differences had vanished, and I thanked God for it. He agreed and asked it to be a lease, whereby Hugh would pay no rent, due to all of the work that he had done on our house. But, if his nephews moved in, they would have to pay rent to Hugh Mohr. Hugh had loved me for so long now and the feelings were finally reciprocated although neither one of us wished to hurt Padruig, so we would wait. The nephews were still in the old MacDonald farmhouse, not paying rent because they were either fixing or building the golf field and helping Padruig build the manor house. I was glad we already had that agreement, because I could relax incase "the friend" was Donald.

Padruig's Paternal Ancestry

As Padruig and I lay in bed one of those nights, he had his glasses perched on the end of his nose as usual and was reading a well-thumbed old Bible while I was still trying to finish reading the encyclopedia on Clydesdales, when I asked him if his Da had ever told him about his ancestry. "Of course," was his response, "but I got bored listening. Silkies would be a more interesting story, don't you think?" he quipped. "So, I don't remember much of it except one bit, which I think was a lie anyways," he said. "I'm curious. What did he say?" I asked.

"Well, apparently there was a group of folk who were unpopular in Ireland a long time ago because their hair wasna red or blonde and they didna have freckles on their faces," he joked. "So, I suppose their hair was as black as a raven's wing like ours?" I said sarcastically. "Aye, blue eyes and black hair, so the Irish said to those folks, 'This willna be your home anymore, coz you look like the Silkies' who they said we resembled!" Padruig went on. "Tall, handsome, broad shouldered and braw men packed up their belongings with their equally gorgeous wives and took to the wild seas and made their way up the coast, through the islands until they reached a nice wee spot to land in Scotland, where they were welcomed. Some people in Scotland still thought they were Silkies, but most folk were just jealous of their handsome looks and their broad shoulders and tall frames, with their long black flowing locks, even generations later when some of them got shorter," he smiled and then he laughed.

"Oh Padruig, it was all just a tall story," I said. "Aye," he smiled cheekily. "But we Scots are a mix of this and that, so it's at least entertaining, not like wee ghosties at the dining table. What was that all about, Isobel?" he asked. Reluctantly, I answered. "I see Grigor Mohr sometimes and that old gentleman who visited us, Mr. MacNachten, didn't even know that Grigor had passed away, let alone that I'd seen him," I replied. "That's creepy Isobel. You're just missing him and imagining it is all," Padruig replied. So, I just went along with his theory and asked about those Irish. "So, which bit of you is the most Irish then?" Poking him I asked, "this bit," poking him again "or that bit?" and tickling him we both exploded into laughter. It had been a long time since we'd laughed. "This bit," he said and the night was lovely once again.

I did take Gillcrest's advice with Padruig and let him sleep longer and cooked him breakfast myself the next day with the eggs that he loves and my home grown tomatoes, with grilled bread on the side. Helen came in and asked, "Ma, your sheep are bleating. Do you want me to do anything about it?" I responded to her. "Can you please let them out and feed them darling? Your Father and I are enjoying some time together." Helen then said, "Aye. I heard you both awake late last night." Walking in and overhearing, Grigor Og added, "I hope Helen is happy to 'stay up late' when she is your age." Helen kicked him and Padruig said to him, "It's naught to do with age lad, it's love. Isn't it precious?" as he kissed me with eggy lips. "Aye, my darling, it's love. Pure love," I replied. Helen then said, "I'll let your sheep out for you and milk the goats and feed them." Grigor turned to help his wife agreeably.

Hugh Mohr unexpectedly arrived and walked on in as usual. "Good morning family, do you need help with the house Padruig?" We invited him in for breakfast first, on the nice plates, which he accepted and told him of our plan for the home to be built for him passed the cemetery. A nice stone home of his design, if he could build it, without ever paying rent and for him to then be our permanent resident and farm overseer. He queried my reasoning and wanted to know more and asked why because he already had a place to live with Donald. I tried to cover up Gillcrest's premonition of an upcoming death soon by saying that we needed an overseer on top of which we also loved his Collies and needed them more if Donald could spare them. He knew it wasn't the reason, so he asked if Padruig was sick, then I just told him to think on it and that he could have his nephews live with him if he liked. Padruig piped up and said, "I'm nae sick. This is Isobel's big plan," he said. "You're not telling me something Isobel," he said, munching on his bread. "It's a wee detail," I said. Then Padruig asked, "What is?" I answered it carefully by saying, "Do you remember when Uncle Allan told us to prepare a storage shed for that drought we had?" They both nodded. "It's like that," I said. "Being prepared is all." I decided that my breakfast was over and left the two men to mull over possible plans for a comfortable new stone home on the property bordering the MacDonald Farm.

Chisholm House

Upon entering my bedroom, my maid Agnes was already in there changing my bed sheets and making up the bed with ironed sheets. It had been such a luxury having both a laundry lady and a house helper. I touched Agnes gently on her skinny shoulder and thanked her and asked if she could make our room especially nice today with a scented candle for later. As she was cleaning out the ashes from my fireplace, she turned, smiled and said, "Aye Mistress and can I talk to you when you're not too busy?" "Talk now," I said. "It's about Alasdair MacInnes, Mistress," she said. "Who?" I asked. "He is one of the fence builders. He's the one took the horse thief to the alehouse," she said. "Aye? Go on. I hope he's well," I said. "Aye Mistress, he's verra well, we're all verra well," and standing up, she touched her stomach. "Are you with child lass?" I asked, closing the door. "Aye Mistress, we're hand fast till we can find time to go an Episcopalian Church," Agnes said. "Protestant are you lass? Congratulations. When's the bairn due?" I asked. "August Mistress, plenty of time. I've no morning sickness at all, but Alasdair said you should know, seeing as my parents are both in the ground and both of his parents were transported to the colony of South Carolina in the Americas," she explained. "So, where does he live?" I asked. "With his old grandparents in a small croft up by Loch Carn ne Toiteil," she added. "So, I suppose you'll be moving out then. Thank you for the notice. I shall start looking for your replacement straight away." By the look on Agnus' face, she hadn't expected that response, so quickly finished up making my bed and left the room.

When I told Padruig of Agnes' relationship with one of the fence workers, he was disappointed. It turned out that Alasdair had been

Padruig's preferred worker out of the three young men. Alasdair would have to care for his new wife at his Grandparent's house up near the wee loch. "Is he an honest person, Padruig? You're not missing tools or some such?" I asked. "Nae," he said looking worried. Thankfully Padruig said to leave it with him and he'd prefer to continue discussing the new house plans with Hugh Mohr who had considerably warmed to the idea, provided there was enough land as well on which to grow food and keep chickens.

Hugh Mohr, owning the lease on Chisholm House, as they called it, went on to live with his nephew Hugh Og and they seemed happy enough for a time, with Hugh Mohr's Collie dogs in their new stone house that they had built. It was a four bedroom stone home with a piece of land behind it that would be perfect for growing potatoes and kale and was located on one side next to our small cemetery and on the other was the border between Craskie and MacDonald Farms. "So, Hugh," I said, "it will be your life long home and you'll be in charge of collecting any wee rent you get from your nephew." I drew up a contract so the lease was in Hugh Mohr's name and I think he then had the face of a contented man. Hugh Mohr was a wonderful help with his Collies. In addition, I asked him to ensure that none of the English tourists from The Manor House ventured onto Craskie Farm and to maintain security along that border as one of his roles.

Padruig had demolished Uncle Allan's old farmhouse after the widow died, so once the paying guests would leave the Manor House, Hugh Og would stay in Chisholm House with Hugh Mohr. I encouraged Hugh Og to marry. "One day," he kept saying, "but where are the women then? I refuse to take an English wife like sae many are doing now." I believed that God would give him a wife one day, even if he was old and that he would marry possibly one of the younger wool waulking girls. I had noticed Cora looking at Hamish for a long while before they had gotten married and his face had gone bright red every time. She had obviously admired him for some time, despite him being a bit older. Age differences didn't seem to matter as much any more but I thought it was still better to keep our marriages within the clan and we had some lovely girls in the wool waulking.

Shortly after that stone home was completed, Hamish had married Cora and they moved across to the old School House after they had both gained qualifications as a security guard and teacher respectively, once Cora's Mither had passed away. He earned a small wage from us for acting as security for all three properties and Cora earned from the families of the children she taught. Helen had plans for him there to build three new privies. It felt good to know that Hamish and Cora were well set up in the teacher's cottage adorned now with Cora's flowers.

Hugh Mohr sidled up to me one day and said, "Now, Isobel, I should explain something to you about my nephews," he said to me. "Aye?" I responded. "Do you mean Hugh Og and Hamish?" I asked. "Isobel, you do know that they're not really my nephews, don't you?" he asked. "Nae," I said. "I thought they were. They call you Uncle Hugh," I said. "Aye and Beth called Grigor Mohr, Uncle Grigor, before she knew you were actually related, out of respect. The lads are Chisholms and so there's respect on their part toward me and a degree of responsibility from me to them, especially after their Father died, but I don't actually have a real nephew. My brother Alexander died before fathering children, to my knowledge and Donald's wife, Eilidh, couldn't have bairns. He knew that when he married her, but still wanted to marry Eilidh to take care of her after what had happened. She was ravished, like many others and badly damaged internally like, and was lucky to live with all the blood loss. They had been friends as bairns, like Padruig and yourself and he still wanted to care for her until her passing, which he did. God bless him," Hugh Mohr explained. "I'll plant another rosebush for Eilidh then. I am very sorry Hugh, I didn't know." I felt sad at the many times I had seen Eilidh poorly and wished I had done more.

"Can you tell me how the lads' Father died then, if it's not a private matter?" I asked. "Isobel, you can ask me anything and aye, I can tell you what I know of their story. You've met their late Mither?" he asked. "Aye, just the once. Uncle Allan sent her to me to get permission first from me to ask if they could live at his farmhouse and if I had advice. I only saw Mary from a distance after that. She kept to herself once she moved onto MacDonald Farm and then married Uncle, to my surprise," I responded. "Well, Mary and her first husband, David Chisholm, lived closer to Loch Craskie and had just the two living boys after having had two miscarriages. She was always quiet when I met her. Her husband was the opposite, very loud and drank a bit, but he taught the lads how to fish, even fly fishing. They'd fish Craskie Burn, Loch Craskie, River Cannich, River Glass, River Beauly, Beauly Firth, Rosemarkie Bay and the Moray Firth as well as Loch Ness and all the way to the east coast. They'd bring back seaweed on a wee cart to sell sometimes to the farmers as well. He'd fish pike, salmon when in season and brown trout with a long stick and line attached. I've never seen someone catch so many fish as their Father did without a boat. He'd know where they were, instinctively, so the young lads had a good teacher. David could swim too and he taught them to swim in the warmer months," he said with a cheeky grin, which I chose to ignore.

"He'd take his catch to any alehouse or farm to sell them. His wife didn't see much of the coin or the fish, I am told. One day, however, when fishing alone, his line was caught on rocks at the bottom of Loch Craskie. Being strong and confident as he was, he dived straight in to free it up and while doing that, must have run out of breath. It's a deep loch, as you know now, so when he decided against persevering any further, his foot must have become tangled up in the reeds and he drowned that day."

"The only evidence of his ever being by the loch were his worn-out shoes and his stash of fish, which had begun to stink. Someone went to his wife and asked where he was and naturally she answered that he was fishing by Loch Craskie. Then the lads came home and they were asked if they'd seen him and they all decided to go together where his shoes had been left beside the loch." Hugh Mohr then stopped speaking, as if deciding whether he'd tell me what happened next. "You don't have to tell me Hugh. He is in the Earth now and Mary went on to marry Uncle Allan," I said, touching his hand, which felt somehow enticing." It's okay. They went and asked if somebody could dive deep into the loch and take a look around and search for his body, which was found. So, at least she could bury him and become a respectable widow."

"The lads had a skill and that's how they met you, the wee rascals, selling fish to the farmers," Hugh Mohr said. "Aye, they were characters that pair and never complained. A bit mischievous at times," I said. "I've never regretted hiring them Hugh. They're family now. I hope they don't ever dive into that loch. I'd hate to lose them. I used to swim the horses there without Mither knowing. They'd love a swim on a warm day. Were you close with David?" I asked. "Nae, not my kind of fella really, but I bought fish from him. He was unfaithful to his wife, you see, so I am glad she found happiness in later life too." With that, our gloomy conversation ended and we both got back to work, but I couldn't help but feel so drawn to the handsome man, perfectly designed by the Almighty. Hugh Mohr was shadowed by his beautiful Collies.

Our dear friend and Hugh's dear brother, Donald Chisholm did pass away only one month later. Hugh Mohr was obviously broken hearted and I wanted to hold him and wipe away his tears. His funeral was a very large one and I was glad of Gillcrest's premonition. I had been feeding up my husband and he was as well as a man of that age could be. Instead of marching off to get drunk like he did after Grigor Mohr's funeral, he turned to me and remarked that his new horse that I had bought him, was looking fat. "She's pregnant too," I said. "Blaze had a mighty exhausting time with the four year old mare, but hopefully they'd have a foal." Narrowing his eyes, he asked, "Who else is pregnant?" "Agnes, darling. She will be moving her things out of her room today," I said. Frowning, he let me know that Hugh Mohr and himself had to go up to Inverness to collect necessities for the Manor House the following day. Then he whispered quietly to me that it was more of an exercise to support poor Hugh Mohr who had lost his only remaining family, his Father also having died a few months ago in Chisholm country. Padruig then went on to say, "We are all going to miss Donald and he wrote that beautiful poem at Grigor Mohr's funeral about Grigor and you. It just broke my heart listening to it. Donald had a sensitivity to him underneath that tough Highlander outlook," he said. "Aye," I replied, "he was a real sweety, like all of the Chisholms that I've met."

The Cameron Family Returns

Early the following morning, just after Padruig and Hugh Mohr had left, Lochiel came to introduce the Cameron family recently arrived from Nova Scotia with their three daughters, the oldest girl, Lilias, being fifteen. Looking poor, I gave them bread, meat, butter, cheese, flour and tea to make a start, but was surprised when Lochiel asked if I knew anyone who could employ Lilias as house help. "Can she cook?" I asked. I was given a full list of what she could cook, including fried chicken, cakes and biscuits of many varieties. "How much per week, if it includes room and food?" I asked. They wanted too much at first, but 2s 6d per week was agreed on with every second weekend off provided she was happy to wash the floors more than once a day because of the mud. I added, "Her parents also would need to pick her up every second weekend for Kirk and family time." I explained that although Agnes had been a wonderful house helper and very clean, she had fallen pregnant to a labourer and as such would need to know if Lilias did her prayers and wouldn't keep secrets like that. The parents were naturally horrified at that story and they agreed she'd do her prayers and would tell me instantly if she had an interest in a lad on the property or vice versa and then it would follow the proper channels through her parents.

Helen had been part of that conversation also because she would have to train yet another home helper and show her how we liked our stews and asked her, "Do you know what a tomato is?" Thankfully, having lived in the colonies, she regularly ate tomatoes and was educated in English, French and Gaelic. She was an overweight, homely looking girl with thin brown hair, but quiet in the presence of her parents. I explained that Padruig would need to be consulted first before a position could be confirmed. The family agreed to spend that night with her at their own home and left with Lochiel to give me time to consult with Padruig when he came home. Their plan then was to bring the lass back the next day, for our decision. I felt under pressure to accept the girl.

I had asked Agnes to leave her room spotless as a new occupant was expected and for the first time, she looked sorry to leave the warmth and comfort of our home. I gave her a small note of proof of work in case she worked again in the future and I waved her off at the verandah with her few possessions in a sack entering into the world of marriage. Helen came up beside me and said, "It's is a shame she didn't tell us anything about Alasdair, let alone hand fasting, then pregnancy." "It's what happens when the Kirks are few and the parents are even fewer," I responded. "Poor lass. She is not prepared and we know little of Alasdair other than his laboring skills," I said. "Will you miss her cooking, Ma?" Helen asked. "Can't say I will my darling and I am not confident about Lilias," I added. Helen then asked, "What do you want me to focus on first in training her Ma, if Da agrees?" "Cleanliness, the privies, all the fireplaces, showing her where everything is and correcting any bad language you hear or nearness to the men." I added, "Once she has the beds, the floors, dust and privies in perfect order, then move on to the food, but only after she has tasted your cooking. You know how fussy our men are."

Late in the evening, Padruig arrived home after having stopped in at Fraser's Trading Post. "Family?" he said upon entering. "My love," I responded. "Before I forget, I have glasses for you Dar Thula, for both distance and reading, so you'll look even more beautiful and you won't lose your sheep. Also, there was a wee message for us at Fraser's Trading Post, letting us know that John, Anna, Simon and Beth are all coming over for dinner tomorrow with some news," he said. "Let's get you fed and dry darling," I said. "Helen, please put bath water on for your Father and lay out dry clothes." I was admiring my new glasses as he was eating and after an obviously successful but big day, I chose my time to tell him that we didn't have a cook yet, except Helen and I, but hopefully we would get by with the Frasers and it would be delicious.

Preparing for the Frasers

Surprisingly, Padruig took Blaze's death well. The poor old fella slipped in his stall one day and broke his hip and his leg and had to be put down. I couldn't bear to see how his beautiful old body had been disposed of, so other than pointing in the general direction where an enormous hole could be dug, I stayed away and unlike me, I didn't interfere. That particular land was part of Grant Farm and general grazing land and Padruig asked Grigor, Helen and I if we were happy for his Manor House to have its entry up there using the Drover's Road that existed between the late James Grant's farm and the next property. I had told him that on no account could his tourists enter Craskie or Grant Farms for any reason because of the many diseases from southern farms. Grigor Og was in complete agreement and saw his oat fields as a boundary with Hugh Mohr also agreeing to keep out anyone, other than family, from entering. He had kept his long rifle and would use it if necessary, along with his guard dogs.

Patrick and Henrietta had spent a long time in Rome buying what was needed for the Manor House because they were going to move into it once it was completed. They didn't seem to be in any hurry to come back and they also saw it as a pilgrimage. They had spoken to leaders of the Church in Rome and to those who had previously owned the School House again and asked if they would take over the ancient Parish of Glenmoriston by rebuilding it closer to us. Where it was presently was closer to Skye not Glenmoriston. I thought it was a stretch and held out no expectations at all.

The Frasers coming to dinner had started out very congenial and more successful than I had expected without home help and I quite enjoyed cooking up a storm with Helen and we sang along as we cooked. She mentioned a wool waulking lass named Meredith who had heard of Agnes' departure and had asked for her job. Poor Helen hadn't known what to say, other than that I had a Cameron lass under consideration and if that didn't work out, we'd definitely ask her next. She was a really nice girl, already twenty, pretty and very talented in harp playing, singing, cooking, cleaning and had parents who were Catholic like us, but had wanted her to find a life for herself.

When the Cameron family came with Lilias the next day, as agreed upon, Padruig had wanted to meet them, hoping Lochiel would be there, but he hadn't come on this occasion. Padruig agreed to the lass having a two week trial period on condition that she could keep the floors clean. I reiterated that she'd need to learn the basics of cleaning before cooking if she were to take the job and the room, to which she agreed and her parents departed.

"It's verra nice Mistress," she said. "Much nicer than our old farmhouse that's in an awful state and smells something terrible." I didn't tell her about the dead body that had been on the front porch and suspected that this was the cause of the awful smell. "I am glad you like it lass," I replied, "but keep it very clean, just like all the other rooms." I had made her a uniform looking housedress with an apron and a cap because her clothing was old and ill fitting. She was overweight and ate too much, I thought. "This is what you'll wear to start and I'll make you another if it is the right fit. Now get to work straight away because we have some guests coming and Helen will give you a list of your tasks for the day and for the next two weeks. You have a fireplace of your own, but you must smoor it every night, if you're going to light it at all. There is peat in the donkey house," I added. Then leaving her I'd gone to the garden to select some fresh vegetables in preparation for the evening's meal.

We lit the new lights we had bought from Fraser's Trading Post on both sides of the front gate. Helen and Lilias were raking and sweeping all the way to the door. Then Lilias was on her hands and knees scrubbing the porch until it was spotless. Helen was becoming a hard task master and I hoped her husband wouldn't soon muddy his boots on that porch, which of course he did and she scrubbed it again. "You'll get used to the mud," I just said. She didn't look too impressed with her new job and I'd wondered what her life had been like in North Carolina and so I asked her, "Slaves would do this job Mistress, not us." She'd answered with the emphasis on 'us.' "Who were the slaves then?" I asked. "Black folk, of course," she replied. I'd known of our own Scottish men sent into slavery in '46 and '47 beyond and I took an instant dislike to this girl and made plans to move her on right away.

Beth and her husband Simon loved coming home to visit and seeing her old ponies and offered to help out with the harvesting season. They would stay overnight or longer, because it was quite a journey from Stratherick, but Simon enjoyed getting a wee boat to cross Loch Ness, then take pre-arranged horses from a friend on the other side and ride together to our place in Glenmoriston. Their horses were stabled happily with the ponies and they were always sad to leave. Simon also checked out his Father's business, Fraser's Trading Post run by a manager and reported back to his Father.

Beth's Baby Foal

Over dinner, Beth and Simon and her parents-in-law looked like proud parents to be as they were about to make their announcement. The goose we had cooked was an enormous bird and the flavours were just perfect, laced with neeps, potatoes, tomatoes, carrots grown in my glasshouse, onions and selected spices with an additional kale and carrot salad. After the usual praise over the food and our praise over the wonderful dinner plates that John had given us, he raised a glass. "Do you mind Isobel?" he asked. "Just the one dram to celebrate?" I'd agreed for them but not myself as I had never been a drinker. Surprisingly, I saw Padruig put his hand over his glass and he asked for some milk. "It doesn't agree with me anymore John. Milk for me ladies. Goats milk or the Highland coo milk for me is delicious," he said. John Fraser, sitting straight as an arrow as always said, "That won't matter, so long as we celebrate Beth's good news." Smiling, almost clown like with sheer joy, he said, "We're all going to have our first properly bred Highland Pony foal. To Beth's success everyone," as he raised his glass, joined only by Simon. Not expecting the news to be a foal, but seriously happy for Beth, I realised that I had been holding my breath awaiting the news and allowed myself to breathe again. "Och, Beth," and I went around to my pretty Granddaughter and congratulated her. "To the first of many to come my darling," I said. There were claps and 'here, here's' to celebrate. Helen and Grigor, expecting different news, appeared confused too and were slow to congratulate her. I didn't like to spoil the achievement by telling her that Padruig's chestnut mare had already birthed her lovely wee foal with a long white blaze down her face and two of my Clydesdales were expecting also with my old Sire, which had almost killed the poor old fella.

Our new stables were a sight to behold. Comprised of two rectangular shaped buildings, the full width of that land being Grant Farm. On one side were the mature horses in large stalls that were tall for their sizes and with plenty of room to move in each one, which included a feeding box. The opposing building had two slightly smaller stalls and an enormous tackle room with a door leading into the room containing both the carriage and the cart. The last room contained feed, such as hay and oats as well as medicinals.

I'd wanted a roof of some kind stretching from one building to the other due to the mud, as well as the bitter cold and snow. In consultation with a very clever builder, we came up with a very high arched roof, so snow could slide off it. Realising then, however, that it would be too dark inside, he created four windows in the roof that could be opened on a warm day, but more importantly, they would let light in.

In addition, we kept an external pair of wall mounted torches if we needed to go and help them birth a foal at night. The ground between the two buildings was heavily dug up because of the horses' enormous hooves, and so, that same builder chose hard wood sleepers the full length and then river stones to be placed atop them to make a cobble stone avenue from one end to the other. All stones were held in place with a product, whose name I cannot recall.

In the centre of the 'avenue', as we called that section, was a newly invented fire made of steel. It had a front door, in which to put peat or wood and it wasn't flush with the floor. It sat on another steel pole and the chimney from the fire was also metal, extending all the way to the roof top to take away any smoke. It was a popular place for workers to stand rubbing their hands together for warmth. It also had two circular plates on its square surface that one could open with a wee instrument too. A kettle could sit atop it and smoko was easier with that invention, but it had cost me every penny of what I had received from Lochiel, so Padruig's inheritance had to help me a bit. But he didn't mind if the horses were all kept happy, safe and contained. The heavy stable doors at either end had heavy locks and bolts. Beth, however, on that same night of the dinner, asked me about how the new stables were going and wanted a tour before cake.

Something's Amiss

I agreed that we'd take a stroll with Beth, Padruig, John and Simon, with Helen and Grigor not too far behind. Anna had decided to help Lilias clean up between dinner and desert. I'd always kept the stable locked and bolted and that was the first clue that something was amiss.

The fire shouldn't have still been lit, but it was with two strange men dressed in black standing beside it when Alasdair came from out of one of my Clydesdale's stalls. "What are you doing in here?" was my instant reaction. "Who are these men Alasdair and why are you in my stables? Horses are not your business." Then I am not sure what came first, but Padruig and John came up beside me as two more men appeared from out of the stalls. "Grigor," I said, "check all the stalls please. I want to know how many people exactly there are in here," which he did, producing another. There were four Irish and two

Lowlanders, scruffy, very thin and shifty and aged between twenty and twenty seven, I thought.

Alasdair's face had changed from the one trying to please his employers to an angry face, possibly dangerous looking man and I caught on, but saw that we were outnumbered. We were three women and three men with no weapons of any kind and they were six wily and fit men who were possibly armed. "Again," I asked, "Alasdair, who are these strangers and why are you in my stables?" "Now, don't go getting all worked up Misses," Alasdair said with an Irish accent. "It's cold outside. Me friends just in from Dublin, needed to crash the night," he responded. Feeling for my skein dubh, I walked towards them and heard one of them cackling, "Alasdair? Heh, heh, heh." "Is your name actually Alasdair MacInnes?" I asked.

Padruig and John Fraser stood on each side of me and my husband said, "You've already lost my trust lad, so that's your job on both the fence and the house, so you might as well answer my wife." One of them, who was probably the oldest, said, "I'm Mihael O'Sullivan. These two are me brothers and his name is Rory O'Rourke when he's in Dublin. This pair are brothers, Edward and John Murray, all coming to these parts for work, but no luck except for Rory here and the two Murrays. So, he said he could put us up."

"Put out the fire please," I said. "It's not to be lit at night," wondering what to do next. I thought they were all a gang of thieves, but didn't want to die proving it. I asked Grigor to check every corner again and thank God there were no more of them. I heard John ask Padruig what we were going to do with them in Scots Gaelic. Padruig had said, "Somehow John, we have to get them all tied up and taken to Fort Augustus as our prisoners." Then suddenly a flurried, very pregnant looking Agnes rushed in through the huge stable door, blurting out, "I am so sorry Mistress, so sorry, please forgive me? They were cold, is all. Please believe me?" she said. "How long have you known that his name is Rory and that he's Irish?" I asked the shaking girl. "About a week Mistress," she said. Then surprisingly, it could be heard, "You lying treacherous bitch. I told you my name when I met you and told you not to tell them," Rory said.

I went on pointing to two of them, "So you Lowlander brothers are the fence builders?" I asked. "It's a shame, you were doing a good job on the fence and now you have trespassed and broken in to our property at night and that is an offence in the law." Those two brothers did look remorseful and pointed to the older Irish one and Rory, alias Alasdair, and said, "It were their idea to light the fire and sleep in here and he said we could do it every night Misses coz you wouldn't know that we was here," he said. "You do know that he's not the owner of the property, don't you?" I asked. "Aye Mistress," they both said. "We are sorry. We'll leave now." "Not yet," I said. "Are you a gang of thieves? Because that is what you look like," I asked. The lowlanders both went pale and looked to their Irish leaders. "Are you accusing us of thieving Misses?" the older one said. "Turn out your pockets, all of you and I'll decide," I responded.

Then it was Agnes who broke down, "Aye Mistress, they are. They was planning to rob ye and all the other farms round here and stash it in that croft near that other wee loch. He doesna really have grandparents here. It's just an old croft full of stuff they've stolen," she said. Then Rory picked up an iron object and threw it at her. Luckily, Grigor caught it midair and the fight was on, the Irish had  decided. Instinctively I grabbed Helen and Beth and pulled them both aside when suddenly the far end of the stable opened, cold air came rushing in and a tall, armed, silhouetted figure accompanied by growling dogs on either side of him, said, "Stop! Or you Irish are all dead!" while aiming his long rifle at their leader.

Padruig then had Rory in a neck hold and tied him up and John had the leader hog tied. The two Lowlander brothers, who were sitting on the floor, began to whimper. The other two put their hands in the air to Hugh Mohr's rifle and were subsequently tied up with the Lowlanders.

Fort Augustus

We took them all like that with Agnes to Fort Augustus, leaving both Beth and Helen at home with Hugh Og. Hugh Mohr, Padruig, Grigor and John stood guard over our captives while I drove my team of Clydesdales with them in the carriage, right through the fort's front gate up to the door. This was not a place I had ever expected to be again. A lot transpired over the next two hours. The commander of the fort, being a Captain, upon being informed of our situation, had them all arrested and locked up while sending a group of soldiers to that croft beside Loch Carn na Toitail to search it for the alleged stolen goods.

The Captain then introduced himself as of English stock, by the name of Stanley Johnson. He ordered cups of tea for us five and went on to say, "Well Mr. and Mrs. Grant, Craskie Farm is it? It is most fortunate that we both have some time to kill and business to complete, as I have been meaning to write to you both." It sounded sinister. "Are you happy for private business to be discussed in front of Mr. Fraser Mr. Chisholm and Mr. MacGregor?" he asked, rather insincerely I thought. "Aye," Padruig said. "Good. I have received all of the documents relating to the investigations from your lawyer that appeared in all the newspapers. The first one concerns you, Mrs. Grant, about your Mother, Freya Grant in the year 1746," he said. "Go on," I said. "The decision made by the courts has been that the soldier was under orders by his superior officers and had no premeditated intent to take the life of Mrs. Freya Grant. That having been said, this has no precedent in law and you have been awarded compensation of £250, which is in my safe and I can give it to you tonight to save us all time if you agree to this amount and sign for it," he said. I couldn't see any point arguing and it would buy Mither one of those nice headstones that Fraser's sold, I thought. "I agree," I said and signed "on condition that I can count the money." It was all in order, but I felt sad for Da and Grigor Mohr. Had I let them down?

The Captain went on, "The second point of business concerns you Mr. Grant about the death of Mrs. Margaret MacDonald in the year 1746 with you as heir, with Mr. MacDonald already having passed away. This complaint had different consideration as it was for

237

recreational purposes and they had also broken their word to her husband. The British armed forces, have in this case, broken their honour and disgraced the Service as well as themselves. Your compensation, thanks to your very good lawyer, is £1500. Do you accept this amount or do you wish to contest this decision?" he asked to a sad Padruig, while Hugh, John and Grigor looked on very shocked. Padruig responded, "I accept if I can also count it first." My poor Padruig looked worn out as he signed and I put all of the aforesaid moneys into my satchel.

The Captain went on to say, "The third part of business is quite serious concerning the attempted murder of your wife, Mr. Grant, which luckily for you all, resulted in his own death with a backfiring old pistol. The compensation could have been his property, had he legally owned it, but as you well know, the lands have been restored to the Cameron family, now residing on it." "Aye," said Padruig, "and so?" He went on, "According to the witness, Mr. Frederick Jones, the former soldier from this fort, Fred Bowles, had a stash of personal goods and stolen goods under the front porch of said property to which you are entitled if the Cameron family allow you to enter the farm, lift the boards and uptake what is there. Conditional on repairing the porch.

There is a proviso, however, that if some of the goods obviously belong to a living person, you would be required to return it to them if they can be found in Scotland. Do you agree to this compensation on these provisos?" the Captain asked. Padruig said that he would be in agreement if the fort would write a letter first to the family informing them of the situation, as well as Lochiel of the Camerons and our lawyer, Mr. David before entering the property and pulling their porch apart. A condition he also added would have to be that Lochiel of the Camerons was present while obtaining the goods and then every effort on our part would be made to return the goods to their rightful owners, if found. What was left, Padruig said he would be pleased to accept for the threat to his wife's life. Padruig also added that all of the business of this present night of all the parties be written down and sent to the lawyer. To this we all agreed and signed. Both Hugh Mohr and John signed the document as witnesses.

Then there was a commotion outside his office door and the Captain concluded all of that business and handed us the paperwork and said,

"Well that deals with all of that. Now let's see what all that commotion is about. Can you all please wait here while I see what the soldiers have come up with?" he asked. There was considerable noise outside his office, with the sounds of large objects having been placed on the floor as well as excited conversation. Eventually, the Captain calmed the men down outside and was obviously organising what they had with them and moving it around.

We all looked at each other questioningly when the officer came in and said, "Well, it seems you were right. Apparently, it was a veritable Aladdin's cave, without the diamonds of course. And so, what we'll do from here first is ask you Mr. and Mrs. Grant, if any of the stolen belongings outside in the room opposite, belong to you and if so, it can be signed for tonight and you can take it home with you," he said. I hadn't noticed anything missing so I wasn't expecting to find anything as we all filed into that area, when Padruig said, "That's my wee saddle from New France made by the Algonquian people and the bridle too. How did that go missing without Hugh Og noticing?" I replied that maybe it had recently been taken before Hugh Og was due to clean the tackle. Horrified at the potential loss and handing the saddle to me, Padruig began to rummage through everything amongst a mountain of goods of all kinds, including jewelry.

The Captain found a gold wedding band and upon seeing that I wasn't wearing one, he asked if I was missing my wedding ring. "Nice of you to ask," I said. "Nae, I don't wear rings. They get in the way of farm work. My wedding ring is this," I had said, pointing to my Grant brooch. I think he was trying to tempt me to take it and so I put my hand up once again and said, "No thank you Sir, but I am sure someone is missing their ring and I hope that you find her."

A gasp came from Padruig then. "Isobel, Grigor. The polar bear rug that I bought back for Helen and Grigor is here." Naturally, we instantly took that precious item into our possession, when the Captain asked Padruig, "Were you in the Quebec campaign against the French?" "Aye," said Padruig then pointing at John he said, "We both were and he can vouch for this here rug and they're mine." The Captain's demeanor changed completely and he said, "Oh, I've never had the honor of speaking to an actual veteran of that campaign under General Wolfe. I was too young for the first one anyway, but the second one, umm, well, my parents wouldn't allow me to go. So, I'm in awe at what you did. What you both did," he said. He was really starting to annoy both John and Padruig with his complete switch from the heartless manner in which he handed over our meagre compensation money to then suddenly wanting to be our friend. Typical English I thought, but the darkness that crossed Padruig's face worried me and I thought he might punch the man.

Then out of the corner of my eye, I recognised Grigor Og's wedding gift of the weapons from New France and automatically gasped at the sight of them. "Padruig," I said with urgency, tugging at his shirt and as I was about to say, Grigor's weapons, I stopped myself because of the law against carrying weapons and corrected myself. "Aye?" he said. "It's your set of weapons here from New France that were well secured in our house and now they are here". Grigor Og was standing by, waiting on Padruig's lead. Both of us looking at Grigor's wedding gift and the need to conceal who owned them, were grateful when John came over, eyes wide also and said, "They've managed to find Padruig's weapons that I saw him being given at the Plains of Abraham. I was, after all, his junior Officer and he was greatly revered for his fierce fighting skills amongst the 78th Fighting Frasers."

All of us were aware that we could all be arrested for possessing the weapons outside of service and nervousness set in momentarily. The Captain came over and asked, "What do we have here exactly? We have a targe, a dirk, a long rifle, a pistol. That's not English," he noticed. Padruig replied, "Nae, it's French. The English pistols were known to backfire." "Ah. What's the small knife there called again?" he asked, making us even more nervous than before. Calmly and convincingly Padruig explained, "That's a skein dubh. It makes up the minimum kit."

I piped up and said, "How could they have found these in the house?" "It must have been Agnes going through our closed cupboards," Padruig said, hoping to convince the soldiers all around us. "Well, they have been well locked up since you came back from New France via London. You were still sick if you remember and after coming home, you haven't accessed them since," I said "That's right," Padruig said, "I had to recuperate in London with Bishop Gordon for weeks." Still trying to convince his audience drawing ever closer, he went on,

"Our lawyer, with whom you are familiar, Captain, had to assist us then." "Didn't he write to the authorities for you?" I asked, Padruig, feigning ignorance of the answer. "Aye, I got one of those certificates of valor thingys then and backpay on my Chelsea Pension, thanks to that lawyer. He has the certificate in his office," Padruig said.

The Captain's mood altered completely and he said admiringly, "So, Mr. Grant, or should I call you Captain? Am I to understand that these weapons were from the Quebec Campaign?" "Aye," Padruig replied, "they were replacements. Scaling the one hundred and eighty foot cliff face, hauling up Englishman with their armoury, I lost my own long rifle and pistols and was unable to retrieve them for obvious reasons. But after fierce fighting that resulted in even my broadsword and targe snapping in two over the head of a Frenchman, and as we were still expecting fighting at the mouth of River St Lawrence where the French were waiting, I needed replacements. I got the whole lot replaced at His Majesty's expense. I later had to use the long rifle to fend off hungry wolves in the colony of New York," he concluded valiantly, being the master of bluff that he was.

"Captain Grant, was it?" he asked. "Yes," Padruig answered. "You can take your weapons Sir. Be sure to secure them better this time, especially the two fire arms and any ammunition, at least until the law changes." Then admiring the pistol once again, he said, "So this one's French?" "Aye," said Padruig. "We took their weapons and their colony," he stated trying to have bravado in his voice. It worked on the impressed listeners who gave him back his weapons. "A receipt for them please," I heard John say, "authorising the carrying of them between here and Craskie Farm." "Of course," said the Captain still admiring the French pistol and in awe of both Padruig and John.

Then John asked the Captain, "Are you one of our clients? The Fraser's Trading post, I mean?" "No," he replied. "Why not? Come in and open an account, seven day's payment of course," and the Captain said, "Are you able to obtain fire arms for our troops?" John replied, "Only if you get the necessary permits and permissions for us to do so." The Captain went on and said, "The Americans have a lot of weaponry. All right," the Captain said, "I'll do that paperwork and send it to you with an accompanying order. How does that sound?" Triumphantly, John said, "We are in business, so long as you pay your bill in seven days. The two men went on discussing business while Padruig, Hugh Mohr, Grigor and I searched through the last of the stolen goods.

One of the junior officers was then heard saying in a cockney accent, "Who'd steal coffins and 'eadstones?" That drew John's attention away to look at those items and they were all from Fraser's Trading Post, being four coffins, four headstones, clocks of all shapes and sizes as well as tools from his shop. He was outraged and his face went bright red all the way down his neck and he had trouble controlling his anger. Padruig then calmed him down. "It's okay John, luckily Isobel brought the carriage, so we can take it all back to your shop tonight." Then taking a few breaths, the poor man said, "Thank you Isobel. It should all fit, but are the headstones too heavy for your lovely Clydesdales?" he asked. "Nae, nae," I said hopefully. "It should be okay for this short distance." It was truly fortunate that I had brought four horses with us from the stables, I was only worried about how slippery the forts' entry road was with that weight.

The Captain had already started writing down what belonged to John, which took more time as some of it was small hardware items like nails, latches and door knobs. John then spoke to the junior officers and thanked them for retrieving his belongings, while the business-man in him advertised the shop at the same time. He gave them a wee clock each as a gift with the commanding officer's approval. I wasn't giving them anything, still feeling the pain of my Mither's value of just £250. Then John, God bless him, added, "Now dear Isobel, I'd like to give you a headstone for your Mither if I may." "Thank you, my friend. I accept and can I buy one for Da too, to match?" I'd responded. Then Hugh Mohr surprisingly put his arm around my shoulders and offered to engrave their names on them and with a side-ways glance from Padruig, he took his innocently gestured arm off me. I could have done with the reassurance that all would be well. The night had been scary as well as shocking and with Mither's tiny com-pensation I still needed to get the goods home.

The officer asked us to look once more through the belongings because he had to write to all of the local farmers to ask them if they were missing anything and it was only then that I saw a painting that belonged to us painted by Helen of the White Roses. "Oh Padruig, it's Helen's paintng of the vase of White Roses," I'd said. Padruig made a guttural sound. "I could ring the necks of those men." "But darling," I said, "The men couldn't have been in Helen's room, I am sure. But Agnes was. Do you think that she took it out and gave it to Rory?" It was then that John replied, "I think so. Look what's here too. One of the Turkish china boxes Isobel, thats she was meant to clean and unpack and put inside your cupboards. So, it wasn't noticed by Simon," he said. "How we trusted Agnes. I felt so silly. I never imagined she'd do such a thing".

The Captain was then listening in with serious contemplation. "What will happen to her?" I asked him. "Firstly, she will be charged here and then taken to the home for unmarried mothers until the baby is born and in my opinion the court will take the baby from her for adoption but that's their decision. After that, the charges, being as serious as they are, most likely she'll be transported," he replied "and as the America's become less and less of an option, it will most probably be to New Holland, possibly Nova Scotia. Most convicts are being sent to New Holland now. Putting my hand over my mouth, I whispered to Padruig, "I trusted her so much Padruig," and he wrapped his arms around me. "I am sorry that I misjudged her. Please forgive me?" I said wanting to cry. All in unison, at least three men said that with dealing with dishonest people, there had absolutely been no fault on my part. The Captain actually had a surprisingly empathetic demeanor just imagining that girl was sleeping just one room away from us and said, "Mrs. Grant, whoever you hire next, may I suggest you obtain references from a previous employer," he said seriously as I thought of the Cameron lass who I already didn't like. "Aye, good idea," I responded. "Thank you, Captain."

The Carriage Ride of Recovered Goods

There was quite a lot of the Frasers' belongings compared to ours, but it was all loaded into our carriage that Da built. Luckily it was strong enough for headstones, but just the same, negotiating the exit from the fort onto the Drover's Road on a slippery surface, was tricky. I asked John and Grigor to jump down and go to the rear and hold the handles either side of the carriage door to prevent too much forward movement.

A soldier standing idly by was also asked to help by placing foliage under each carriage wheel and another with a fiery torch was asked to stop waving it around and to go down to the Drover's Road and halt any traffic, so we could come out and turn wider than we would usually turn and be on our way. I thanked them both and continued talking to my horses in Erse to calm their hearts and they followed my instructions ever so carefully. They did such a good job.

Hugh Mohr sat with me to my left and Padruig was in the carriage falling asleep amongst the coffins. I hoped it wasn't a sign, being so comfortable between the two coffins, but it was usual for Padruig to fall asleep in carriages and carts. He found the sound of the horses' hooves to be restful. Hugh Mohr had stopped offering to take the reins, so he sat there confidentaly and produced his long rifle from out of nowhere. He wasn't trusting anyone this dark night until we got ourselves, our goods and our horses safely home. I had the satchel with the paperwork and both our moneys securely strapped across me, where it couldn't interfere with the reins, initially but asked Hugh to carry it for me after which he kissed me on my neck. I was concentrating hard on the task at hand while also speaking to my babies, as Da always called them and praying we would all get home safely. I felt the warmth from Hugh's body in that cold night air and it was somehow reassuring. He must have read my mind and his hand ran up my thighs and then up my dress to settle on me just as he did that day in the loch. Never wearing underwear, it was distracting, knowing I couldn't say anything. Both of us silently wanting each other desperately. John and Grigor had jumped back on, once we were on Drover's Road, but rode on the back until we approached 'Fraser's Trading Post oblivious to where Hugh's hand was, as he grew even more frantic in his explorations. It was a particularly dark night, as well as wet and cold with only the Craskie Farm entrance well lit as we were approaching, so I slowed my babies down in preparation to stop soon and Hugh removed his busy hand reluctantly. I focused on the horses, who I'd loved so much and had missed all those years of the challenging work of teamstering. The worse part by far was having to deny that I had ever worked with Da as a teamster. It was heartbreaking losing our horses, but doubly heartbreaking hiding it from Padruig. So now, I felt that God had given me back not only the Clydesdales, but my identity too and being allowed to feel comfortable being loved by the man who sat beside me. Mr MacNachten had called him 'the man who loves you.'

As we approached the Trading Post, I felt John and Grigor jump off the back and call out "nearly there" and I slowed my babies right down then halted them calmly. John ran up to his dark shop's front door, unlocked it and lit internal and external lamps. "John," I said, "I think it would be better if you had front lights run on whale oil like ours, it would help a lot when it's so dark like tonight and it might deter criminals," I said. "You're right, Isobel', he called, "I didn't realise just how dark it was out here. It is too easy for these criminals," he said. "What about a high perimeter fence too, like ours, only higher? I've seen them in Edinburgh with bits of broken glass on the top as well, to deter anyone climbing over the wall," I added. "What about a guard dog too?" added Hugh Mohr. "Not my type of dog mind. They are too docile. Maybe one of those Dutch ones," he said. John replied that he was a bit too tired to make those decisions, but the three of them unloaded the coffins and head stones and other things from my carriage to go back into his shop. He gave Hugh Mohr a gift of a nice grandfather clock for his home and gave me two enormous wall clocks with huge numbers on it for the stables, one for each end. Puzzled, I asked, "What's this John? Another gift for me? You've already given me one for Mither and I'm buying one for Da." Then John said, "Isobel, because you're the teamster you deserve payment too," he replied. "Nae, I don't. You're family John. This happened to all of us" I said and I tried to give them back." John insisted on my gifts and furthermore, gave Padruig and Grigor a beautiful gold fob watch each that attaches to their vests.

"What a night," I said. "Anna must be worried sick about you John. You'll be glad to get back to Stratherick tomorrow, I suppose?" I asked. "Only for the wee foal, aye," John responded, "but everything happens out here." It was then that I pointed to the side Drover's Road that Padruig wanted widened for his entrance to the Hart of the Highland Manor House and to get Simon onto the Council for him to achieve those widenings. I mentioned also the wee bridge that we thought should cover the burn flowing over the Drover's Road also and

John said he'd be sure to get Simon to action it and the new planned Post Office, no matter how long it took.

Hugh Mohr climbed back up and so did John this time, so I guessed Hugh's hand would have stay on his rifle. I asked Hugh to ring the bell on our carriage. It was really loud and Hugh Og heard it from inside the house and came running to the gate and opened it for us, God bless Him. I told him we had to stop in front of the house first to drop off Padruig and a large box of our china, to his horror, the lovely polar bear skin rug, Helen's painting, the wee saddle and bridle and some other items as well as John. Hugh Og, Hugh Mohr and Grigor offered to help me unhitch the horses, rub them down, feed and water them and put away the carriage, which was too heavy for me. Dramas, like this evening, took its toll on me but feeling Hugh had definetly alleviated my earlier stress.

Grigor Og and I said our sincere thank yous to Hugh Mohr for storming the stables as he did to save us from potential disaster. He was greeted by his beloved dogs and was modest about his role in the evening's affair, but I would never forget it. His actions that night were truly heroic and the image of his silhouette wielding his long rifle in the stable doorway will forever be burned in my memory. Hugh Og waved from their house and Grigor and I slowly walked home in the freezing cold night air, while they watched on and I missed him but it was more than that. I needed him too and it was hard to part. I was thankful that I had worn warm, fur lined leather boots. My feet didn't much like the cold. "Is Da alright?" Grigor enquired. "Aye, I hope so, but he is exhausted, so he can go straight to bed, son," I added. "He is in bed Ma. I helped him undress and put those long English under-wear thingys on him to keep him warm. Helen had already lit your fire and put a bed warmer in your bed, so your room is comfortable and warm. She thought you'd still want a bath, as usual, so she's put water on too in case you do," Grigor said.

"Is there any cake left? I didn't get around to serving up the cake," I asked "Aye, John just had a piece and went to bed. Anna was already asleep. There's a big piece of cake and cream left for our pre-cious Ma," he smiled. " God bless you Grigor," I said and I kissed both his cheeks. "By the way son, please tell Helen that I'll be need-ing Meredith, but I have to talk to Cora first and ask if she needs a

French and English teacher at the school and whether Lilias could live there with them in the teacher's house. Don't say it yet in front of Lilias, but she has to go," I said. "Good. I don't like her, she has funny ideas. She's not one of us for sure," Grigor said. I was ravenous and thrilled to see my darling Helen. "Your painting Helen," I said. "Thank God we got it back and your polar bear blanket." She threw her arms around me and cried her eyes out. "You could have been hurt again Ma," she said while she wept. "And you too, and Beth," I added. We both sobbed, hugging each other. "Did you and Grigor want to change rooms, given that Agnes was rifling through your possessions? Do you want Da's old room?" Helen shook her head and said, "Nae. Nae. Grigor really loves it up there, but we'll give it a really good clean and make sure nothing else is missing. I am just grateful to God that my MacGregor brooch was not stolen. It means a lot to me and to Grigor. Just like yours does." "Is Beth asleep?" I asked. "Aye, Simon took her to bed early, so they could go home to their new wee foal in the morning. I'll get your bath ready Ma," she said. That bath was pure luxury, so relaxing, while Padruig snored peacefully. It was hard to believe that we had all nearly come to grief and I thanked God for saving us once again. I then drifted off into a fantasy land, where Hugh was making love to me, but Padruig's snoring broke me out of it.

The day arrived when the necessary letters and legal formalities had been sent and responded to concerning the Cameron farm as our farm worked on as hard as usual. Foals were born, lambs too, as well as calves, and finally some more kids, so our family was relieved at having our goods returned and things normalizing. Agnes had been taken to a hospital to have her baby and she was going to be transported to the Colonies. The leader of that group that night, along with Rory O'Rourke and the Irish were sent to New Holland and the two Lowlander Scots were being sent to Barbados. I felt for the Murray family and hoped that they would see their sons again.

Fortunately, there were still labourers in Glenmoriston available, whom we vetted better this time, asking for references. Cora needed another teacher at the school, as her numbers were growing and needed both English and French languages taught at the school, so after a two-week course, Lilias worked there and lived in the teacher house with Cora and Hamish. We just prayed they would all get along, if not she'd have to go back to her parents farm to live. Thankfully, Meredith started work as home help and was a very conscientious worker and cook. She often gave Helen a break and didn't mind scrubbing our front step and she frequently washed the floors. I'd hear her occasionally playing her wee harp, so thank God that chapter was over. We just had to deal with whatever was under the Cameron's front porch.

What's Under the Porch?

Padruig and I rode our horses and waited outside the farm that day, while the Cameron family on the farm were readying themselves for us to enter as pre-arranged. Hugh Mohr drove our horse and cart in case we had to bring a lot of things back home. Armed with our letter of permission to enter, surprisingly the Captain from the fort rode up on his horse to join us. "Good morning, Grant family. I thought I'd better oversee this to ensure Mrs. Grant isn't fired at again," he said. "That's not likely to happen," replied Padruig dryly. "Lochiel's down there with them and when they open their gate, we'll go on down, but thanks for the thought," Padruig said, wishing the annoying man wasn't there. "Thank you for your kind thoughts Captain," I said trying to keep the hard-earned peace.

Lochiel waved then to us indicating to come through the gate and we both went down, side by side, leaving the Captain overseeing us all from the hilltop. Hugh Mohr followed with the cart that also contained tools and wooden planks in case we broke a few. Closing the gate behind us, Lochiel asked what the Captain was doing there watching on. Padruig said, "The Captain claimed he was making sure that Isobel wasn't shot at today" and they all laughed.

The family went about their farm work, while Hugh and Padruig started the business of clawing up each board. Lochiel looked on and remarked, "To think he died on top of his stash." "If there is one," replied Padruig. "There's only one man's word on it. Could be a waste of everyone's time. Sorry Lochiel," he said. "Not a problem Padruig, and thanks for sorting out young Lilias in the teaching job. You were right Isobel, much better suited to teaching than scrubbing floors," he said. "Hope it works out for them all," I replied.

As the boards were lifted, it was obvious that we needed some light, so four candles were brought out for us. There were a lot of small belongings, mostly jewelry and coin, silverware, silver candelabras, silver cutlery, silver candlesticks and antique kitchenware, all blackened with age. Frayed sacks of things, which were falling apart were put straight into the cart. "Most of this would have belonged to women," Padruig said a bit sadly. "Do you recognise anything Lochiel, I mean from your family?" "Nae," he said. "But it's all so tarnished being left under here." "Aye, we'll do our best to clean them up individually and maybe if there are expensive jewelry items, we can ask folk what they had had stolen from them in '46 and if it matches up, return it," he said. "Do you think it is from that long ago?" he asked. "I do," was his answer. "Look at this brooch," he said. "It's silver, but so blackened. It will take a lot of cleaning to discover which clan it belongs to." Lochiel then asked to hold it and feel its weight and rubbed off some of the dirt and tarnish. "I think I know," he said. "Could be Clan MacKenzie, what do you think Padruig?" Padruig said that he couldn't tell. "You've got a big job to do here. I don't envy you." Once the boards were replaced, we went on our way thanking the family and leaving it all in good condition. "Looks like a lot of rubbish to me," said Hugh Mohr before we drove off. His dogs jumped up beside him, licking his face and we left them in peace. The soldier had long gone.

Helen did drawings of each piece and we considered having a meeting in the art gallery where people could look at them all, but our lawyer seriously advised us against it, saying "There were too may liars and thieves." Then I suggested the newspaper that could publish one item at a time and a volunteer could sit at a desk in their office and wait to see the response and take their details. "And then?" enquired my sweet sarcastic husband. "And then, if someone from that time period could tell a truthful story of the item or items, then we give it back," I said. Both the lawyer and Padruig looked at me as if I was as naive as ever. "Sweetheart," I said, "we can't harden our hearts. These items might really mean something to someone. Personally, even cleaned up, a lot of it is really ugly and I couldn't have ever worn it, but sentiment overrides good taste, doesn't it?" I said.

"Then who's the volunteer?" they both asked. "I can ride into their office on one of my horses and stable her for the time and hopefully the paper will give me a desk to sit at." Our aging lawyer looked to Padruig for his go-ahead, then asked Helen for her first sketch that she had already done. It was an enormous ruby brooch with yellow gold filigree edges. Not knowing the value of such things anyway, we all agreed that the ruby brooch would go first and the lawyer would have his editor friend from The Inverness Morning News put it on the front page in order to locate its owner with a nasty addition saying something like, "Do not consider claiming this if it is not yours!" or something like that. In addition, more letters went out to those who were knowingly looted in Inverness-shire in '46, who still lived here. They would have to prove somehow that it belonged to them, if claiming an item, and would have to describe the item or items being claimed for. I listened to both men chat to one another outside a while and then our bewigged old lawyer left on his cart with his jobs in hand.

Padruig said to myself and Helen, while we were scrubbing away at the items, that the coin was ours and he was getting back to work as we had wasted too much time already as it was. He wanted to attend to his new foal, who was delightful, but an awkward wee foal. I thought I would need to check in on her later. He was thrilled that she had a white blaze down her face, but was not Blaze's colour. She was pure chestnut like her Mither and he named her Blaze also. As Padruig was getting older, I think he was softening his heart to all our wee animals, especially our new borns. At one time, I had feared that he would never become a farmer with his earlier life focus constantly being militarily involved. So now I was watching on, waiting for him to employ trustworthy men on the farm and waiting for him to finish both the fence and the big manor house, including the roof, before Patrick and Henrietta returned, he had said, but work had been slowed down. "Ma," said Helen. "Are you really going to ride to Inverness all alone and sit in a newspaper's office and wait for some random person to come through the door to claim this ruby brooch?" she asked. "Aye, but maybe I'll just do it once."

Mary, Joe and the Laundry

I was about to tend to my sheep who were outside bleating in the pouring rain waiting for me, when our laundry lady, Mary, who never stops to talk, asked if she could speak to me. I had very negative thoughts in that moment, hoping I wasn't losing my laundry lady too, so I said to her, "You're not leaving too, are you Mary?" "Ah, nae Mistress," she said. "Then please sit down," and Meredith gave both of us a cup of coffee. I was surprised at Meredith's efficiency. "Thank you Merry," I said. "It's Meredith," she responded with a broad smile. "Lovely girl, that Meredith," said Mary. "So, Mistress. It's about the big house being built up there by your husband," she said. "Aye?" I responded with curiosity. "My husband, Joe and I were talking about it and we both agreed that if I was asked to do laundry for a house that big with tourists 'n all, then I'd have to say nae, especially if I was given a wee pay rise here Misses," she said. "How much do I pay you?" I remembered saying and we agreed on 6d a week more, which made her very happy. "Remind me on payday Mary," I added thinking the conversation was over, but she remained seated.

"Concerning the big house, as you call it, that's not a problem. I'll tell my husband," I said. She went on to justify her reasons unnecessarily, like how many table cloths there would be to wash, boil and starch and how many sheets there'd be to wash, boil and iron, as well as the family's washing. She said that, at her age, it was too big a job but she could recommend a Mither and daughter who were young enough, strong enough and experienced for that work. She gave me their names and I asked if they'd be able to furnish references, because there may be valuable items lying around in guests' rooms and as such, their honesty would be paramount. "Aye, Mistress. That's why I am recommending them, they've already worked in big houses for wealthy folk and could get references," she said.

The other matter she mentioned was in the building of the big house and that "Himself" would need a very large laundry and I don't think that Padruig had even thought of a laundry and so I asked her if she could give advice to Padruig where it should be located on the site, the size and its access to water. You ask him first Mistress if you can do that and then I'd be willing to go up there to give Himself advice if he'll listen? Also, will 'Himself' be plumbing it internally like Master Fraser?" she asked. "If the Manor House is internally plumbed, I wouldn't mind my house having that as well, but its unlikely with the cost of the pipes," I said. We finished up our coffees and I thanked her for her work and the advice as well as the two ladies' names that did turn out later to be gold. I'd never even thought of such details, and yet Mary and her husband seemed to have a complete understanding as to what would be needed. My mind turned to her husband then and as she was leaving, I asked if she would bring her husband with her when she was to talk to Padruig. There'd be other wee jobs I suppose and he might need a little one, given his age and inside knowledge. She agreed and my sheep were complaining. "My babies!" I called and they happily came running. They had become so affectionate like my goats, but I still missed my goats. "Come inside now, my beauties," I said to them all who now didn't seem to need the dogs anymore. However, Hugh Mohr watched over me from his house smiling and waved and I waved back. I could never forget what had happened at the beach but it didn't look like it would ever happen again and I wasn't expecting him to visit me in the lamb house.

The One-Eyed Man

As each of my beauties were wiped down, fussed over with their feed, especially the wee ones, sucking away, Hugh Mohr unexpectedly came to the door and called out "Isobel," he said. "What's this about you riding into Inverness alone tomorrow, on horseback, just for someone's brooch?" He was getting more and more protective these days, but that was his character, which I liked about him. What I hadn't expected was as our eyes met both of our hearts softened to each other. I don't know if he was remembering the beach, but I was because I could count the number of times Padruig had made love to me since coming home from Quebec after a near four year absence. I had to concentrate then on the answer to his question and said, "That's right, it is going into the paper to see if we can locate the owner. It is an odd looking thing, but it would have cost a lot in its day," I replied. "That's not the point," he quipped. "You always used to go into Inverness with Uncle Allan when he was alive. Don't you think I should accompany you now?" he asked. "I could take you on the cart and get a few goats and geese while we're there," he added, as he came close enough to me that I could feel his body heat. I was worried that I was falling in love with this handsome man at my age and I think he knew it, so I agreed. Then I was surprised when he gently caressed my face. "You are so lovely, I've missed you," he said. He lay me carefully on a hay bale and he held both of my legs back and lifted up my dress. "I want to know you better", he said. The glory of it took me to another dimension until he was fully inside of me and thrusting with my legs wrapped around him, my fingernails digging deep into the skin on his back, until in synchrony reaching the peak of joy, while he was trying to muffle the sound of his pleasure. "Donald told me I'd be too big for you. You being so tiny," he said looking into my eyes. "Am I?" he asked. The sound of footsteps outside stopped us and we both stood up with his big hand still clutching at me, as I stood behind him where I could lift his plaid to feel his beautiful buttocks and felt all of his manhood. "It's not too big Hugh." He spun around and was inside me again from a standing position. Luckily, my sheep bleated as my groans were unable to be suppressed. No-one came in, but he said that he'd better slaughter a sheep for dinner tonight to have at my house so no-one got suspicious. "With the new lambs you've got thirty six sheep now," he said. I wasn't wearing my glasses and hadn't counted them all. "You should wear your glasses or you'll lose your sheep," he added. He didn't want me to be parted from him, so turning towards me again he lifted my dress while his hand kept moving back and forward and told me to look him in the eyes, while he asked me any questions. Is that enjoyable? Is that better? Is that when you want me to enter? I'd answer each question with great difficulty looking at him so directly, then entering again the last time was more aggressive, more lustful for us both, then sucking my mouth with his tongue exploring inside it and around before kissing me all over my face and eyes. I couldn't break away from him, but knew we had to, even though his hands were both squeezing my breasts. Naked by then, he was a man needing all of me and I had never felt so needed and it was arousing. "I'll nae give you back your clothes until you say you love me Isobel," he said and it was easy to answer. "I love you Hugh." I smiled at this beautiful man and knew that it would be easier now to deal with my new found love. Hearing people outside again, I quickly dressed and said, "It's a grand idea for the dinner, so long as you do the slaughtering and all that and wait for me to leave before you do it." He was coming with me to Inverness and with that he was very pleased. "What if Padruig objects to you coming into Inverness or if he needs you here?" I asked. "If he needs me, then I'll stay for sure," he said. "Perhaps Hugh Og should come to dinner as well now that you have lost your cook," I added. "Aye, he can come and he'll do what I tell him to do anyway." With that, the big braw man helped me with the last of the feed and the water but never missed an opportunity to rub my bottom or between my legs. We both locked up the sheep as Padruig was walking down passed the oat fields, waving to Grigor Og as he went. Hugh Mohr squeezed my breasts again saying, "Go my Isobel and I'll do the killin'." Always had a way with words, did my Hugh and I said, "Thanks Hugh."

Going on to my horses, I checked on each one carefully. "My poor babies," I spoke in Erse. "Do you want to go for a ride tomorrow?" kissing their soft muzzles. I hadn't heard that Padruig had followed me into the stables and he asked what ride I was talking to the horses about. "Hello my darling," I said as I reached up to kiss him. "That brooch is in the paper tomorrow and I have to sit looking silly, waiting for its owner I hope. So, I'm going to Inverness tomorrow on big Bessy here," I replied. "What about the cart?" Padruig asked. "It's faster on big Bessy, that's all, but Hugh Mohr said the same thing and advised getting more goats too while there. He said we needed a lot more geese as well as another donkey. Frederick is old love. What do you think about getting another donkey? I'll follow your decision dear." "What were you doing talking longer to the old washer woman about?" he asked. "You don't miss much," I said. "Just cause I'm up there, doesn't mean I don't know what's going on down here," he added. That remark made me a bit nervous.

"I've got a bird's eye view of Craskie Farm," he smiled. "And what was Hugh Mohr doing in the lamb house?" he persisted. "That's two questions darling. Which one do you want me to answer first and do you mind if I keep checking the horses?" I responded. "The washer woman. What was she saying?" said a worried Padruig. "Don't worry love. She's not leaving, but she did want a wee pay rise," I answered. "What?!" he exclaimed. "They think we are suddenly rich because of someone else's bawbees?" he demanded. "No darling, just 6d per week extra to stay on in my house, so long as she didn't have to work in the big house," I said. Then suddenly looking guilty that his 'big house' was the cause of the pay rise and not the 'bawbees', he quickly moved on to the next topic. "Hugh Mohr in the lamb house?" he said next. "He's slaughtering dinner for us all. I can't do it," I answered, "it makes me cry. I can't even choose the animal, so he is doing it for all our dinners. Both Hughs are coming up to join us. Do you mind?" I replied. "Of course not, that's a bonny idea. Now they've no cook, they can come every night," he was quick to reply. "Are you finished here now? I'll walk you to the house," he said. "Aye, I've finished." I held his arm and we walked together, my lovely man and I. I had explained what Mary had said about the laundry for the big house and he was grateful for the input and he was looking forward to talking to both Mary and Joe. "Are you installing internal plumbing?" I asked, feeling a little envious. "Must be nice for the kitchen at least, to save on trips to the burn". I never got my internal plumbing.

Dinner with Both Hughs

Our home was back to its usual self, with the exception of the bawbees, when both Hugh Mohr and Hugh Og came to dinner. Hugh Og had dropped the lamb off earlier for both Meredith and Helen to cook with the assistance of both Helen's daughters, Isobel-Mairi and Morag-Freya. What we hadn't been furnished with was the chemistry between Meredith and Hugh Og. It was quite the feast as the whole table was filled with delicious food from our own farm. I thanked God always for providing for us as it wasn't long ago that I was almost starving. Helen's son, Aonghus had arrived late on a wee bus from the university on a three day leave weekend, wanting to know everything that had happened. That was an exhausting conversation that we left Helen and Grigor to relate. Young Aonghus told us he needed to work with a lawyer unpaid, apparently as part of his university program called an Internship to gain practical experience and asked us to recommend someone. Naturally, we recommended our own lawyer, Mr. David, from Malcolm Law Office and because I was going in to Inverness the following morning, I could drop him to the lawyer's office, while I went on to the newspaper.

Both Hugh Mohr and Padruig looked at each other thinking the same thing and I asked Aonghus, "Horseback or cart lad?" but I wasn't as clever as I thought when his response was, "Cart please Granny," as his horse-riding was a bit rusty and so cart it was. It pleased Hugh Mohr, who reminded us both then to remember to buy at least four new nanny goats. I interrupted and said, "I can't get geese Hugh. They'll fly off." Hugh Mohr just wouldn't let up about geese, going on and on about how good they were as guard birds to scare off intruders. He really was taking liberties with me. I started to

feel outnumbered when thankfully I remembered we had a cage, hopefully big enough for geese. I told Aonghus to be ready very early the following morning and I'd give him an introductory letter to Mr. David to accompany the one that he already had from the university. Helen then asked her son how he was going to get home every day if he was accepted into a job in Inverness, considering he didn't want to ride a horse. He said that he would ride one of the Highland Ponies and stable it, if I didn't mind, but he wanted to practice first over the weekend and so his sisters offered their assistance. So, I had company on the way in to Inverness and company on the way back from Inverness, which pleased everybody especially, if I came back with nanny goats and geese. "Padruig," I added, "are you paying for the nannies, the geese and the donkey this time?" I asked. To which he reluctantly handed over a small pouch of coin. "Thank you dear," I said sweetly. "I'll make you a new shirt this weekend," I promised.

It was lovely to have Aonghus back home again and hopefully to stay a while whilst completing his course. He had become such a tall and handsome young man, taller than Grigor, with the chiseled features of his Father and grandfather, but the straight black hair of my Padruig, only much shorter. Life at university in Edinburgh had however made him physically unfit and he did need to work the farm with Grigor, I had thought, in order to become fitter. I imagined the lassies in Inverness would turn their heads at this handsome young and intelligent man that he was becoming, with speech that sometimes eluded me. I hadn't understood all of the English that he now used and looking across to Padruig listening to his grandson, he too hadn't understood much of the comprehensive language Aonghus had now adopted in his new profession to be. So, I was pleased that Padruig asked him in Gaelic if he was keeping up his Gaelic and if he still recited Erse poetry in his spare time. He did love his Erse poetry, which was pleasing to Padruig, but admitted to not using Gaelic at all when at university and only used it at home. "Gaelic's not used at university," was his simple response. "In fact," he went on, "it's discouraged."

Hugh Mohr had moved to sit by the fire and had been joined by Padruig to drink their last cups of coffee at night, contemplating when Hugh said once more, "I think I still should go with the two of them, if you agree Padruig, just to make sure they both get home safe," he said. It was during this time that neither Hugh Mohr nor I, nor Padruig had noticed Meredith admiring Hugh Og. "Afterall, these bawbees have been advertised in the paper. We should all be vigilant and lock up that stuff into the Priest hole," which they did. Hugh Mohr was up very early with Aonghus as we prepared the cart for our journey, taking a packed lunch, which Helen had prepared, God bless her. So, in total we were supposed to come home with a young donkey, three or four nanny goats and three or more geese, if they could fit in our cage. After all of the chatter about the beasts, at least it had totally taken my mind off what I was to expect at the newspaper office.

I dropped off my beautiful grandson Aonghus to the Malcolm Law Office, peaking my head in to introduce him quickly, then stabled my pony and cart for the day, carrying our food and the huge red ruby brooch, leaving Hugh to buy the beasts and he stole a kiss on the cheek as we parted. Walking into the newspaper office, a few eyes looked up, but no one knew who I was, so upon introduction, they gave me a desk in front of their front door and embarrassingly, I just waited for a response to the newspaper's article that had pictured the brooch. Hours went by and I had to use their rather unclean facilities and wash my hands. I drank only Helen's coffee upon return when I heard the squeaky office door open, not expecting it to be in response to the newspaper's front-page picture by then. A really old man with only one eye, the other simply being a stitched-up socket, entered gingerly with a severe limp. He sported facial deformations from very old wounds and he had an amputated arm on his right side. It must have been very painful for him to move at all, I thought. His one eye was bright blue and it darted around, wondering who to talk to, so I asked him if I could help him. "Och aye Misses," he said very quietly. He then asked "Do ye speak the Gaelic?" and I responded that "Aye I did" and then our conversation was only in Gaelic. He had said, in the paper today was his Mither's old brooch and "I got the shock of me life when I saw it. Her body was dug up by dragoons, you see, after Culloden and being buried with her tartan and her brooch, the soldiers had taken both, leaving her body uncovered and threatened anyone with death if they tried to rebury her." [12]

He had watched on in horror at the time in hiding in a tiny goat shed where he was suffering from his wounds from the battle on Drumossie Moor and could do nothing. Bleeding profusely and with his eye hanging out, he had wept for his Mither who had loved the brooch and had wanted to be buried with it. He hadn't seen it since that horrible day until it was on the front page of the morning paper. He pointed at it with his own copy of the day's paper, looked at me and asked, "Are you Mrs. Grant? Can you tell me who has it?" he asked emotively. "Aye," I said. He was completely believable and the sight of him took me back to those days. I took the brooch out of my satchel and asked him, "Is this your Mither's brooch?" Tears flowed from his one eye and worrying if he would faint, I asked him to please sit down. "Aye, it is. Where did you get it?" he asked. I retold the story, including the death of my own Mither by the same soldier and he held it in his hand, reliving the moment his Mither was dug up. People in the office had begun to watch on and listen in sadness. "Would you like it back then Sir?" I asked, without even having yet asked his name. "Aye, Misses, and my name is Donald Shaw. Are you Padruig Dubh's wife?" he asked, "Aye," I said, he then went on to say, "Mrs. Grant, thank you from the bottom of my heart. Mither can rest now." He stood up awkwardly and departed, carrying his precious item. I gulped back my own tears at the many tragedies of 1746, but grateful to Bishop Forbes for taking down all of the eye witness accounts, so it would be forever known what was done to the Scottish Highland people under King George the second.

So, it looked like, due to the success of the first bawbee, that it would be repeated in the next days paper, but I asked them to wait until my grandson was back at university, so we could all spend more time together, to which they all agreed and asked for sketchy details of the success without revealing his name and description to protect him from theft. They wanted to sell more papers. Given that they were doing it for free as a Community Service and given that today alone, their papers had sold-out all-over town, the wee story was to read (without our names):

The Wee Story

"Due to this newspaper's publication of a ruby brooch stolen in 1746, found only recently by Glenmoriston farmers, the ruby and gold brooch was returned to its owner's son. An item of immense sentimental value to the gentleman's Mither at her passing. She had been buried only for it to be stolen by dragoons who heartlessly dug up her grave and stole the sentimental brooch and her tartan in 1746. Many thanks go out to the family restoring as many items to their owners as possible. There will be another item advertised in next week's edition of the Inverness Morning News, where only genuine people need apply, believing the advertised item to belong to their family, stolen either after the events following Drumossie Moor by HM soldiers in 1746 thereabouts. Some of the items, understandably, may be in poor condition and tarnished. This newspaper sends our condolences to the family involved today with the ruby and gold brooch and look forward to the next item to be advertised free of charge as a community service."

Mr. Kenneth Menzies, The Editor, Inverness Morning News.

Note: The local constabulary have warned that false claims against any item will be punishable by law. Our well-known lawyer, Mr. Malcolm David of Malcolm Law Rooms have represented the party involved with the restoration and has similarly cautioned against false claims. Today Mr. David is quoted as having said, "It is a very great honour to return stolen items of value of that terrible time in our history and I thank Inverness News and the volunteers assisting for their efforts in the reclaiming of this part of Scottish history."

That wee story was on the front page of the following day's paper, with a drawing of Mr. David, accompanied by none other than our Aonghus MacGregor, described as currently Mr. David's intern from Edinburgh University, completing his law degree in this city hailing from the distinguished local farming family of Mr. and Mrs. Padruig Grant and the son of Mr. and Mrs. Grigor MacGregor.

Aonghus

Hugh Mohr, Aonghus and I returned late from Inverness that night, with our lawyer reluctant to part with our grandson at first, but he had informed me that he had employed him for the full year of his internship and therefore didn't need to go back to Edinburgh unless his Professors asked him to. He was very excited to have an assistant and obviously really liked Aonghus and Aonghus liked and respected him. "Thank you, Grandma," he had said with one of those wet kisses like Helen gave me. We had time to pick up the vocal donkey that Hugh Mohr had organized, the reluctant geese were inside our cage and four sweet nannies sat happily in the back of the cart. This time Padruig and Grigor had shared in their cost as my sewing days had slowed down a lot. I sat between the two men and the donkey was happy to trot behind our cart, as I handed Aonghus and Hugh their sandwiches that Helen had made, which they ate ravenously, washed down by the last of the coffee. Hugh Mohr, happily driving the cart, seemed to have had a nice and productive day, choosing all the beasts and the journey home was pleasant and chatty, sharing in all our experiences. Hugh's thigh was more over my side than necessary and holding it up against me, it kept me warm, so I didn't mind. My hand might have wandered too underneath my arisaid across to him under his kilt. I wondered what we would be doing if Aonghus hadn't been there, so much so, that my grandson had to repeat himself a few times. Aonghus warned me of the following day's newspaper article and what it would say with his actual name, he very proudly said, was to be printed Aonghus MacGregor. Without realising it, my grandson was launched into the Highlands with its many admiring lassies.

Everyone was relieved to see all three of us arrive home safe of course with our tall and braw protector, obviously proud of his purchases,

Hugh Mohr and put the new donkey into her enclosure, the geese with the other geese and the nannies into the goathouse, now sometimes called the lamb house. He called the new donkey Betty. My Padruig congratulated me on actually finding the owner of the bawbee, as he called it and hoped I wasn't leaving again the following day, which I wasn't. I wanted to spend time with my family, especially him. I was so pleased to see his lovely face and even happier when he held me in his arms and told me he'd missed me. I'd missed him too, so much. I hated being apart from my family.

The family had prepared a gorgeous meal for the three of us as well as for Hugh Og, Hamish and Cora. They'd left Lilias at home and I thanked God for small mercies. Having already eaten, they had prepared a musical night. Grigor played his wee flute, Meredith played her wee harp, Padruig his uillean pipes and Hugh Mohr played the large bodhran enthusiastically after he'd eaten. They asked me to play Da's fiddle after I'd eaten, even though I didn't play as well as Da but because Isobel-Mairi and Morag-Freya were trying their skills on lute and the smaller bodhran, I agreed. It was quite an oddly matched band to start with, but as we flowed into the Gaelic music and the rhythm, it took on a life of its own. There were amusing songs about goats, others about rabbits, lost lovers at sea, but then Grigor asked me to sing his favourite MacGregor song. My Mither's song. Griogal Cridhe.

Uncertain that it may bring Grigor Mohr's ghost into the room, at first, I declined, but Helen was insistent because I had not finished singing it that first time. So, with the accompaniment of the harp, Padruig's pipes and Grigor's flute, I began to sing it with my dear Mither in my mind as well as my old Da and my brother Grigor Mohr, whose ghostly self did walk in and looked at me with great sadness at first. I had to force myself to finish that Gaelic song, as it requires such a depth of emotion that one has to dig deep into your own soul without breaking down to weep. Then I saw the approval of Grigor Mohr's apparition as he slowly vanished. I saw my husband look to where I was looking and I think it was at that moment that he did finally believe that his old friend could appear at times. There wasn't a dry eye in the room when I finished. Helen saw that I was exhausted and thanked me, but said after all, I was half MacGregor.

261

Not everyone knew that and it added another dimension of respect, which I hadn't expected. I really needed to bathe and be with my sweet husband. I felt fragile after seeing the one-eyed damaged man in the morning and then with all of the combinations of emotions of my beautiful family and friends, as well as my brother Grigor Mohr, who I couldn't stop missing every day.

Helen prepared my bath, but Padruig took over and we said our good-nights. Padruig was gentle and sweet and loving and apologized for not believing me about Grigor Mohr. I held him tightly and we both wept for him as we slipped into a gentle lovely night. I had told Padruig about Mr. Donald Shaw whose brooch it was and how damaged his body was, obviously from Culloden from all those many years ago. He had never shared his horror stories of that day, just that the Laird of Grant had betrayed the Glenmoriston fighters who had all been sent to their eventual deaths after the battle.

That being the reason for the hasty creation of the Seven Glenmoriston Men who left together that day, including the young 17-year old Hugh Chisholm. They had all arrived on their horses at the front of Craskie Farm, where I was holding young Alex in my arms. On horseback, Padruig told me it had been a terrible loss and they had to flee together or face hanging and for me to take care of the children, or something like that. As the seven of them galloped off like the devil was at their heals, only one of them looked back, Hugh, the seventeen year old. I waved then, in what felt like slow motion. I then understood why Hugh Mohr, to this day still looks out for me. He had been a brokenhearted young man, strengthened by the leadership of Padruig Dubh and Alexander MacDonald. Then guided by Grigor MacGregor and loved and protected by his brothers, Donald and Alexander Chisholm.

I was always glad of Padruig's choice. I couldn't have lived on if he had been executed by the Duke of Cumberland and life would not exist as it had become, with grandchildren if he had died. Padruig Dubh indeed made a hard decision that day and I am grateful for it. In bed that night, he told me graphic details of the Battle of Culloden and the murders of injured soldiers afterwards, like Charles Fraser of Inverallochy, but had always harboured doubt about the sincerity of the Master of Lovat, Simon Fraser, who had conveniently arrived late to assist in the battle. With heads blown off, bodies blown apart and blood running like water, his decision was the bravest option he had at the time and Padruig and his men even went on to save Bonny Prince Charlie when he was in need.

Will the MacKenzies Approve?

Isobel-Mairi and Morag-Freya burst into our room just like their Da used to. "Granny, Aonghus is in the paper with that old lawyer who wears a wig," they said. We both tried blinking ourselves awake at our energetic grandchildren, as well as taking in what they'd said. Padruig took the paper off them and there they were, Mr. David and Aonghus MacGregor. "Oh dear," I said. "I forgot to tell Grigor that Aonghus was in the newspaper."

We both prepared for the day, first dealing with our animals. The goats had settled in beautifully but wouldn't give milk until they'd had kids, so it was only old nanny who I milked. Wearing my glasses, as Hugh Mohr suggested, I then counted the sheep being thirty five in number now after the big lamb dinner. Letting them out, they wandered up to graze where it was nice and green. The day had looked pleasant to start, but big grey clouds told another story. The greenish tinge in the clouds suggested a storm, so at first I was just hoping the sheep wouldn't wander too far, but Hugh Mohr waved from his house look-ing up at the same things and said, "Storm coming. Best put the sheep back and give them dry feed," he said. I took his advice and with my trusty hook, I went up to call them back, but they were unwilling to return after just having been let out. "I'll send the dogs Isobel," I heard Hugh say and in no time, they were thankfully rounded up and herded back inside and fed. "My poor babies," I said to them, as we prepared to batter down for a big one. The wind came up before I even had the chance to leave the goats and lambs secured. Thank God the horses had been safe and were all locked in their stables. Hugh Mohr appeared at the goat house door and said, "Come on Isobel. I'll get you to the house but it'll cost you a kiss." I was expecting a peck on the cheek, but what I got was a long passionate kiss. Then clinging to him tightly, we made it to the house with the ferocious wind blowing us sideways. Reluctantly letting him go, I went to make coffees for us all not looking Hugh in the eyes, but touching my lips where Hugh had kissed me.

Meredith was busy closing up the shutters and out of earshot when Hugh Mohr asked if he could talk about a private matter. Naturally, I asked Padruig to join in our conversation by the warm fire, when Hugh Mohr looked decidedly embarrassed. "Well then?" asked Padruig. "What's so important?" I was quietly waiting, as it was clearly important. "It's about Hugh Og," he said. "Is he well?" I asked. "Oh aye, verra well, thank ye Isobel. He wanted me to talk to you both though," he'd said. "We're listening," said Padruig accustomed to these requests by now, so he relaxed into his chair. "He fancies Meredith is all," Hugh Mohr blurted out. "He what?" said an astounded Padruig. I put my hand on his knee, as I had wanted Hugh Og to find a lass, but hadn't expected it to be my new house-keeper and said, "That's wonderful news Hugh." Much to Padruig's horror. "What about our cooking and cleaning?" asked Padruig. "Oh darling, if she fancies Hugh Og too and one day they marry, she can still work here. Can't she Hugh?" I said. "Oh aye," Hugh Mohr said. "So, unfamiliar with this process, I was wondering if we can introduce them, like properly, with you two and I and ask if they'd like to be betrothed?" asked Hugh Mohr. Still shocked at the news, my poor man agreed. "It's understandable," I added. "Both of them are similar ages and fine-looking young people," I said. Hugh Mohr wanted to know Meredith's clan and if she had parents still living or other family. I told him that she was from Clan MacKenzie and her parents were both alive. "Do you want them here too?" I asked. He nervously wanted a meeting with us all and so my trusty calendar came out again and so in writing to Mr. and Mrs. MacKenzie, I had it confirmed that the arrangement was for the following Wednesday if Meredith fancied Hugh Og, which she did and so it happened. Her parents lived in Kinlochewe to the North West. "He may be a fisher-man, but please ask him yourself," I said. "Do lassies have dowries these days?" Hugh asked. "Some do and some don't is my best answer, depending on their financial status," I replied. "Maximum £1000 Scots if they have made those plans. In our case, we included Grigor's name on the land deeds as an inheritor," I said. "Oh, I see. What about inheritance?" he then asked. "Well, once again, you'd have to ask her parents. How will you convince her parents that Hugh Og is suitable?" I asked. "What a question. Of course he is. He is a Chisholm and a kind hearted soul," he said. "He is," I said, "but I recommend that you send Hugh Og down to me to get a new shirt for the meeting and when they come, I'll give you a bunch of my white roses to give to her Mither."

As the day approached, it was obvious that both Meredith and Hugh Og "fancied" each other and it made me smile, but the MacKenzies were an unknown quantity. Coming from the North-West on a dreich day through mountainous terrain, both parents arrived on Highland Ponies, wet, cold and cranky. It wasn't a good start to a negotiation over such a serious matter. Her Father had typical MacKenzie features with a beard and her Mither looked equally as tough and a little over-weight for a Highland Pony. I felt sorry for their horses and stabled them before we started. My granddaughters were listening in at the top of the stairs out of sight while Grigor still worked hard outside. Helen had made cake and biscuits, coffee and tea and then excused herself.

I offered Mrs. MacKenzie dry clothes, but she declined and defiantly stood by the fire instead, so the rest of us sat around the fire. Padruig took the floor and introduced himself and commended them for rais-ing such a lovely girl and then handed it over to me. I introduced the subject and Hugh Og Chisholm, as well as his Uncle Hugh Mohr Chisholm, representing him. Hugh Og then gave the flowers to Mrs. MacKenzie, who just stood there looking at them for a moment and then put them down. "What's this about?" asked Mr. Alexander MacKenzie. "Meredith," he said, "please explain," he demanded. Both Hughs and Meredith then stood and asked permission from both parents to be betrothed. Hugh Mohr, representing Hughs Og's parents, vouched for the young man who was shaking and a bit greyish and Padruig vouched for him as his employer, as did I. But their faces looked unconvinced. "Why should we give our only daughter to you, Hugh Chisholm? I take it you don't own land," Mr. MacKenzie said. Padruig interjected at that moment and asked Mr. MacKenzie, "What had you in mind for Meredith as far as betrothal was concerned? Did you have someone already intended for her?" he asked. Taken aback by the Padruig Dubh style question, he hesitantly admitted that he had not managed to arrange anyone for her. Hugh Mohr then stepped in and stood up to his full height of 6'7' and as broad as he is and listed all of Hugh Og's skills, qualities and the dignity he carries in being a man of Clan Chisholm. He finished by stating that Meredith couldn't do any better than the outstanding fellow standing before them. "As I represent his interests, I must know from you, Mr. MacKenzie, what dowry do you have with your daughter, Meredith MacKenzie?" I glanced at Meredith, who by her face that she knew there was no dowry and was very afraid of losing her chance of marriage at twenty five years of age. She then unexpectedly stood up and in a burst of emotion saying, "Ma, Ma, Ma, please? Da, Da, Da, please. I love him. Please let us marry? I don't think he minds if I don't have a dowry. Do you Hugh?" she asked turning to Hugh Og. "Don't I still need their permission Meredith, with or without the dowry?" he answered, with the saddest face I had ever seen on one of our fisher lads, as he once was.

I couldn't stand it. It was my turn to add to this complicated situation. "If they marry, I will absorb all costs at Craskie Farm, with no costs to yourselves and they already have a house to share with Hugh Mohr here on the property. Do you give your blessings to this young couple?" I asked. With that, MacKenzie simply stood up and they both walked out, making grumpy sounds, slamming the door behind themselves. The groom quickly had to help them get back their horses. She hadn't even taken the roses she'd been given, so I gave them to Meredith. "Both of us, being Padruig and I as Merredith's surrogate parents, give our blessings to you both and wish you both a happy future," Padruig responded, congratulating the pair too, leaving Hugh Mohr a little confused. I quietly spoke to him apologetically and touched his arm and said, "You would've been a really great Father Hugh and you did very well. Who knows what their problem was. I'll arrange the wedding with you Hugh. Is that okay?" to which he nodded in sad agreement and just slumped into a chair by the fire.

Meredith was sobbing and Hugh Og was consoling her and she said whilst sobbing, "Will you still marry me without my parents' permission?" she sobbed. "Aye, I've already a Chisholm brooch for you," he responded tenderly. Then my two granddaughters came running down the stairs noisily with red eyes, hugging the two of them as did Helen. Grigor, the late arrival and ignorant of all the proceedings, just smiled as he entered and asked how it had all gone in his usual positive manner. "Don't ask," grumbled Padruig. I overheard Hugh Mohr saying to Padruig, "I could kill that pair of MacKenzies," and I think he meant it. Padruig calmly said, "It's a long way on slippery mountainous surfaces back to where they're from. Anything could happen. They've cursed themselves Hugh."

Thoughtfully, we ate the cake and drank the coffee while Helen informed her husband of all that had gone down. The red eyed young couple weren't quite ready for his positivity, but accepted his congratulations just the same. Isobel-Mairi came to me confused and said, "So, are they betrothed or not, Grandma?" "Aye, they are. She is twenty five and she can make her own decisions," I answered. Married within the month, Meredith moved to Chisholm House, but continued working as my maid in ours. We had the best of both worlds.

Charlotte the Ox

After the restoration of my Clydesdale team of working horses, it was possible to achieve a lot more in the fields, for which Grigor was pleased on the one hand but sad too because he missed his ox who he'd relied on so much previously. It was lucky that Da had made the yolk designed specifically for his Clydesdales enabling them to not only pull heavy weights, but deep ploughs too without tiring the way an ox would. One morning when Grigor was feeding her, I just happened to be walking past and overheard an affectionate conversation between himself and his precious ox. "Good morning Charlotte," he said, "how's my beauty today?" Up to that point I didn't even know that the ox had a name, so I excused myself at the stall door. "Och, Grigor," I said, "who'd be Charlotte then?" I asked. "Och, Ma," he replied truly embarrassed, "it's the name of the King's wife. Big, German and black hearted, but my Charlotte is a goody!" he said with glee.

Hugh Mohr would tease the lad by sharpening his knives out the front of Chisholm House. "Mighty healthy beast you have there Grigor. Tasty for dinner. I slaughtered one of these for the Prince and it fed a lot of folk that night. Just wandering round by itself it was, like your Charlotte does. She's not needed in the fields anymore, but sure looks tasty," Hugh had teasingly said. Apparently, Grigor had stopped in his tracks and said that if his ox went missing then so would one of

Hugh's Collies. "If anything happens to Charlotte – the Collie gets it!" Grigor retorted. Hugh had responded, "You don't have it in ya lad, my Collies are safe." Grigor then glared menacingly at one of the dogs, which yelped and ran inside Hugh's house. "Or maybe you do? Just kidding lad," Hugh said whilst still sharpening his knives. The ox was never dinner and lived to a ripe old age, being fussed over by her Master.

Rude to Granny

Aonghus had settled in to his internship at the law office and I had noticed slight changes in him. Call it politeness maybe, but it was diminishing respect and I wondered if it was because Padruig and I were both old and didn't have the schooling he had. As it was developing one night over dinner, his questions directed to me came out of nowhere. "Granny," he said. "You've Pictish in your blood, don't you? What can you tell me about the Picts?" Then, without even waiting for my answer, said, "I've joined a club at the university for students interested in the Picts and I told them that you were part Pictish, or some such and that I'd ask you." Padruig was furious at the lad's rudeness, as Grigor looked at me apologetically and said to Aonghus, "Your Granny isn't a subject of study at your university. So, it's none of their business." "That's right," said Padruig. "Where're your manners lad? You can't divulge family secrets at a university."

That should've been the end of it, but ignoring his elders, he asked again, "Well Granny, are you part Pict?" "Lad, you are forgetting your manners and it's Pecht not Pict," I responded. Remembering the beautiful moments when Grigor Mohr and I had sat near my fairy stone, I could never imagine telling my grandson where it was. I felt threatened and disrespected. "My families are from Clan Grant and Clan Gregor. You and your rude friends will learn nothing if you approach learning in this manner. Please leave the table and go upstairs, I don't want to be in your company right now," I said. Looking shocked at not getting what he wanted, he left quietly and went upstairs. Helen apologised for her son and so did Grigor, but Padruig said, "Maybe he should stay in Inverness and board there, while he is working at the law office. He can come home on weekends only if he's polite to his Grandmother." Padruig's decision was final.

And so, it was decided that Aonghus would board in Inverness, while he was learning his manners. His sisters were disappointed, but promised to be polite and then, thank goodness, Hugh Mohr came to visit bringing his Collies. "Hello family. I thought I'd give the love birds a break. How is everyone?" Isobel-Mairi answered and said, "Aonghus was rude to Granny." "Was he now?" asked Hugh Mohr, judgmentally. "How long is he staying here then? I can take him back to Inverness, find a place there for him. Room and board, that kind of thing or he could stay with the lawyer," Hugh said. Padruig said he'd take Hugh Mohr up on the offer and so the following day Aonghus went to Inverness to stay overnight for four nights and then come home weekends, if he promised to be polite to me. Then poor wee Morag-Freya came to me later and asked, "Granny? Is it bad to be that word that Aonghus said?" "Nae love, just private," I answered. "Private," she repeated. "Okay."

That same day I was later told by Mr. David that Aonghus had helped himself to private documents and files in the law room that he was not supposed to have access to. He had the MacNachten name by then and its various spellings and found the address of old Mr. MacNachten, who had visited me and given me the beautiful brooch of the Pecht people. He could've been failed by the lawyer in his internship and sent back to Edinburgh university, but in talking with Aonghus, he chose not to fail him and give him the day off, while Mr. David came to us to tell us where he'd gone. He'd gone to Loch Insh.

It was obvious that Aonghus was quite obsessed with the topic and while we accepted the apology of our lawyer, we also thanked him for keeping him on and accommodating him. As he was leaving he said, "He has a lot of MacGregor in him and what occurred to me was that his grandparents shared the same Mither from Loch Insh, being your Mither Isobel, Freya MacGregor Grant. You won't put out this fire by talking of manners, in my opinion. What he did at the university was wrong, what he did at my office was wrong, but the lad needs guidance and that's obvious. He is living in two worlds now and trying to navigate between them. I can forgive him, Isobel and Padruig, if you can." I hugged the old man nearly knocking off his wig and asked him to please stay with us, as it was getting late, cold and wet. We could stable his pony, he could eat dinner with us and sleep in the guest room, which he did happily. Everyone over dinner was much calmer, but not clearer about the way forward with Aonghus.

His Father, Grigor, was the most disappointed and embarrassed about his son, but Padruig had a word with him about his own poor relations with our youngest son Alex and how he wished it had been different. He missed him, but more than anything he knew that I loved him still as much today as the day he was born and felt guilty that I had lost my wee Alex to Nova Scotia. He advised Grigor not to make the same mistakes that he had made with Alex. We would all need to work this one through. I had to confess my intolerance to the poor manners of the younger generation and that particular topic of my genealogy was too close to my heart to share with disrespectful students who wouldn't understand.

When Aonghus returned that Friday, he disclosed all that he had done because he had made promises both to the lawyer and an old man by Loch Insh, while feeding wild swans. "Wild swans, you say?" I asked. "How did you feed them? Were they tamed by Mr. MacNachten?" "Nae," he said and he explained that they ate from his hand, but at first he had been sent away by the old man because I hadn't been with him and wasn't aware that he was there and he didn't have a letter of introduction. He told us the story that upon being sent away, as he walked to his pony a large flight of swans lifted off the loch making loud noises, which took his attention and so he stopped. Then as he prepared his horse, the swans turned around and came back, flying low over his head and landed nearby. It was then that he heard Mr. MacNachten say, "Just a minute lad. Sit there a while." They both sat side by side feeding the swans and the old man had simply asked him what he thought about the swans and Aonghus had just replied, "They are really hungry." Then he was informed by the old gentlemen that only once before in his entire life had he ever seen swans behave in this way.

Apparently, Mr. MacNachten had said something like, "You will never learn about the Pecht in the way that you were trying to, especially at the university" and went on to say what a huge hole both Padruig and I would leave on our passing. He advised Aonghus to value every precious minute that he could with both myself, whom he described as 'no ordinary person' and the only way he could learn was first to go back home to us and ask forgiveness, write to the Pict Club at the university and resign, join the bird club instead and never disclose family business or relations that could compromise dignity, safety or security. He promised that over time he would tell him what he knew about the Pecht if he did that, if he could return with either myself or with a letter of introduction requesting knowledge. Mr. MacNachten then added, "The Auld ones will show you signs, but you don't know yet that the swans were a sign. One day, you will though."

He was a different lad after talking to both our lawyer, but especially the gentle old Mr. MacNachten. The whole family, including both Hughs and Meredith, were there as the family negotiated a better way to communicate and my approval for him to see Mr. MacNachten again, so long as all our family matters stayed within the family. He apologised profusely to both Padruig and I, then once again said a typical Aonghus thing, "I didn't know you were well known Granny, as 'Isobel of Glenmoriston' and Grandda, that you were Padruig Dubh of the 'Seven Glenmoriston Men'. I thought that was just a folk tale about those men."

Hugh Mohr and Padruig gave up at that point and went and sat by the fire. Helen put her face in her hands and said, "Haven't you seen my paintings?" Aonghus then replied, "Aye, but I don't think I believed it. Bonnie Prince Charlie and all that." I got up too then and joined the men with our coffees and cake and Hugh Og joined us. Hugh Og quietly asked, "Is it a generational thing or is it all that education?" I replied that the lawyer told us it was difficult for him to live in both worlds and we needed to be forgiving. With raised eyebrows, poor Hugh Og just continued to look bemused.

While Meredith and Helen cleaned up all the dishes, Helen's daughters took away all of the plates as they were trained to do. I asked them to help Helen because it would be their job soon. Then Aonghus offered to assist, so Meredith said, "Aye, please sweep the floor. There's mud over there," pointing to near the door. She enjoyed her moment of being a bit bossy and I smiled. There were similarities between Aonghus and Simon Fraser, Beth's husband and so I asked Padruig whether he thought the two should get together the next time Beth visited. His response was amusing, "Simon's not likely to have much input, but it might take the burden away from us at our ages and his parents, who are taking it hard." Grigor was regretting sending him to university at all and I don't blame him.

Trying to be positive, I'd told Grigor that one day he'd be proud of his son. Not just for passing his exams, but maybe he would help us all change the tartan law ban one day, for example. Testing this theory, Grigor decided to ask Aonghus how the changes to the Tartan Proscription Law[22] were coming along, given that that was our cultural dress. Sadly, once again Aonghus replied to disappoint his Father by saying, "No one wears tartan anymore Da. That's old fashioned. I'll always wear breeches and stockings, or even those longer breeks coming into style now. Makes sense in our cold Scottish weather." So, Grigor asked him, "What about us, who all grew up wearing tartan and your Mither and grandmother who made the tartan for the big plaids that Grandda wore all the time until it was outlawed and even afterwards secretly. And he wore it all the time when he was living in the cave as the Seven Glenmoriston Men. Then there's the tartan long dresses for the ladies that both your Grandma and your Ma always wore. Very warm for the Scottish weather and weather proof too." Without Aonghus having time to answer Grigor, both of his sisters said almost in unison, "Aye, Aonghus, we are both learning wool waulking with Ma now and Meredith and Cora, the songstress and a group of other women who bring their own sheep here for clipping after they've been washed in the burn. Uncle Hugh and Uncle Hugh both do the washing and clipping while teaching two young handsome local lads their craft. It's a whole of community thing that we all love and Ma can do the books too now for the orders on what we earn. Grandma taught Ma how to keep the books and I'm learning that too," said Isobel-Mairi. Morag-Freya then asked him if he liked the vests that she'd knitted for him from our own home grown wool. She'd posted them, along with socks, to the university and was then worried that he didn't like any of our home-grown wool. Seeing his youngest sister about to cry at the thought that he didn't wear them and thought that they too were old fashioned, he knew that he was in one of those holes that he so frequently dug for himself.

Unsure then who to address first, realising that he was from a tartan devoted family, he chose to say, "Actually, no matter what our individual tastes are in dress, my intention in doing this law degree is to continuously raise awareness for the reintroduction of the wearing of Highland dress, specificially, tartan. Then, when I get married, I can be like you Da, when you married Ma and proudly wear the MacGregor kilt or plaid if you show me how it's done please Da." In true lawyer style, he had saved himself this time and we were pleased that there'd be action on the reintroduction of Highland dress and so I said, "That's wonderful news Aonghus. Then your heroic grandfather here can wear it proudly again before he dies." Which he did and my beloved Padruig was buried with his plaid, but had wanted his Grant brooch that he had always worn, to go to Aonghus if he helped that law go through and if not, it would go to his youngest son Alex in Nova Scotia. At the time he told me about the Grant brooch, I told him not to rely on my memory and to write it down, sign it and date it even if it never gets as far as Mr. David's office, which God bless him, he did.

Padruig's handwriting was awkward, I had always thought but I had blamed the Glenmoriston school for those early changes leaving a lot of young Scots in the Highlands illiterate in the English language, but fluent in their own native tongue, Gaelic. I commented that he should wear his reading glasses when writing, so it would be more legible, but I wish I hadn't despite his constant joking about how blind that I was becoming the older I got. However, all things are not always equal and even as mature as we both were, there were still wee things that we'd unexpectedly unearth about our lives, whilst apart. As I made the remark, I knew immediately, due to the tension in his body, that I'd hit a raw nerve. In my attempt to retrieve the situation, I said, "This is just fine darling," but that wasn't going to smooth it over. He avoided my eyes and wanted to go to bed, but not before telling me that Beth, Simon, John and Anna were coming over the next afternoon and staying overnight if I could have Meredith prepare their rooms.

He worked too hard the following day on his precious Manor House, but the enormous laundry was now completed and he had the two large coppers purchased from John Fraser, as well as all the other many bits and pieces for it, including four irons. The fires and their chimneys were built and the laundry had a roof already, unlike the actual house. He was waiting for suitable labour to help him to achieve that.

He was running out of energy and enthusiasm. Being in his 80s, the difficult labour was wearing him out on top of the family dramas, not to mention the last of the 'bawbees' yet to go in to the paper. I'd suggested one last advertisement of all that remained, which were mainly silver candle sticks of various shapes and sizes, one huge candelabra and silver kitchenware of many types like fruit bowls and sugar bowls. He had been glad of that suggestion, so none of us would need to do that frequent journey again.

I had to take the pony and cart in for the last advertised 'bawbee' day, which coincided with returning Aonghus to his boss in Inverness. Aonghus helped me unload it all going in through the back door of the newspaper. The office girls were all very pleased to see Aonghus and were all vying for his attention. They loaned us a desk on which to display it all and we both left through the rear door again in order to drop him off and then stable our trustworthy Highland pony who had thrown a shoe. I instructed the farrier there to replace that shoe and to check all of the others in case they all needed replacing.

As I walked casually back to the street, approaching the newspaper's front door, I stopped dead in my tracks and gasped at the sight before me. There was an enormously long queue at the front of the newspaper office waiting to claim one of the advertised candlesticks. I turned and went straight back to Mr. David's office where I found Mr. David and Aonghus deep in pleasant conversation. "Mr. David," I said. "Excuse me, I think I might need some help at the newspaper office. There's an enormously long queue out the front of the newspaper." Without any encouragement, the short, bewigged old gentleman had a spring in his step in feeling needed and he said, "Right, Isobel. Time for me to sort out the goodies from the baddies. Aonghus lad, get your quill, ink and pad and come with me. Your Grandmither needs us. Isobel, you follow behind us strong men," he said in a commanding voice. On our way there he told young Aonghus to put on his scariest 'MacGregor' facial expression, without smiling. It made me remember the look his Grandfather could give me until he knew that I was his sister. It positively gave me the shivers at times.

When we arrived, Mr. David then put on his most threatening lawyer voice and addressed the crowd, "Presuming you are all here in response to the advertisement, my assistant Mr. MacGregor here will take your full names, addresses and what it is you are claiming for today, with its description and when it went missing!" All of them looked suitably terrified and as Aonghus approached the first man at the rear of the queue, putting on his most commanding voice also, saying, "Name! Address!" before he could finish, that wide eyed man bolted as fast as his legs could carry him. Many others followed his lead and simply ran away not wanting their identity known. In total, we were left with only five people. One for her Granny's candelabra, but if it wasn't hers she didn't want it. The other four were women who had various candlesticks or bowls to claim for, but weren't sure that they were actually on the desk until they inspected them to be certain. The younger woman claimed the candelabra for her Grandmother and we all agreed that she was genuine and we advised her to leave via the rear door. In total, all that was left for us to keep, as per the agreement, were six candlesticks. We gave one to Meredith and Hugh Og as a late wedding present. The rest I gave to Helen to sort out, but not to give any to Patrick when he came home or Hamish, Cora or Lilias. So, I got one to help me to do the books, so did Helen, Grigor, Padruig and one for Helen's art gallery. Hugh Mohr missed out on a candlestick, but there was an iron cleaver left in the priest hole and he wanted that. "Bonny," he had said. "Once it's sharpened, be an easier way to chop up the bigger beasts like the coos or even bones on the sheep," he said. Alone in the Priest hole he hugged me warmly, accidentaly touching my breast, while saying his thankyous and gave me a lingering passionate kiss this time, then off he went with his dangerous looking item that we had excluded from the table of goods. Unable to tell anyone of my encounter, it remained unspoken.

I was just glad the 'bawbee business' was all over, but Padruig then told me it wasn't really over. "Oh why?" I asked. Then I needed to sit down with a coffee and relax a bit, touching my breast. He proceeded to tell me that the dirty old coins he had taken, were French. Naively, I just responded that the bank can surely exchange French money. "Not with King Louis XV's face on it saying 24 carats meaning they were gold coins from that era," he explained. "Can we melt them down then, with that 24 bit still on it somewhere?" I asked. "Bonny idea, melting them. So, we'd have small gold bars do you mean?" he asked. "Aye, isn't that currency too?" I said. "I think so, but we'd have to go out of our area to spend it, don't you think," he asked. Then I thought of John Fraser and the Trading Post. "Or we could just sell them at the current price of gold that's in the newspaper to John or pay for the roofing materials that you need to get from him anyway, so long as you only deal with him. It couldn't be known outside of our small group or it will attract the treasure hunters for the rest of it," I said. "Sounds like a plan, Isobel. I'll chat to him tonight then," he said. "How many gold bars would they make?" I asked. "Only four maybe," he replied. "Would that be enough for your roof darling?" I asked. Smiling, then my sweet man said, "Aye." Now, he hopefully had a lovely big roof for the huge place and my man had an unexpected newfound respect for me. "My clever wife," he said. That night, he wasn't interested in reading his Bible and I felt loved again and much respected by my big Highlander. There wasn't the youthful exploration experienced with my lover, nor the euphoric climactic peaks, but a familiar tenderness that was beautiful and irreplaceable for a marriage that had lasted this long in the most dangerous of life's circumstances.

That day Aonghus had visited Loch Insh and had all of the information he seemed to need and in looking over birth and wedding certificates, it proved that my Mither's roots were indeed from Loch Insh. Mr. MacNachten was pleased to have a visitor and to be of assistance and as I'd sent him some of my honey, that I'd finally succeeded with and he sent me wild flowers that grew there. They were beautiful. Over dinner, Simon and Aonghus were seated next to each other at the dining table, so that the two of them might befriend one another better and not just be his cousin's husband, who he'd describe as a "typical Fraser", a phrase frequently heard and it wasn't particularly respectful. During the evening, I asked the two of them if they could do the security checks for me on all of the gates, doors, stable doors, and so on, and they chatted as they walked, both unaccustomed to having responsibility of that kind and each other's company. Aonghus told Simon all about his law degree and how he wanted to pursue the Tartan Proscription Laws and upon seeing Simon being supportive, Aonghus became invigorated in his support of tartan wearing. He'd even taken to looking in on the wool waulking group, when that was in progress, to see exactly how it all worked until the girls had to pee in a bucket and kicked him out naturally. He was then seen asking Hugh Og how to clip a sheep and holding the clippers in his hands for a second, decided against using them on a poor unsuspecting sheep.

John Slips up at Dinner

It was that night when all became revealed about Padruig's curious handwriting. I can't even remember how the topic of Gaelic verses English came up, but when John slipped up saying something like, "Ah Padruig. That was tough with only a Bible in English to teach you with." Realising a terrible error, he put his hand over his mouth, his face and neck went that bright red, while looking at my husband, who was looking back very angrily at John. John's response was, "I am so sorry Padruig. I slipped up. I am so sorry."

Feeling another family issue coming up, all of the grandchildren, including Beth, went upstairs. Hugh Og went home, while Grigor helped Helen and Meredith hurry up with the dishes. Anna just sat there looking confused, but joined the three of us who'd gone to sit by the fire. John was looking at Padruig, waiting for what to say next. Padruig started first by saying that he had never learned English to speak, read or write until late adulthood. When Padruig and I were together, we only spoke Gaelic, so the topic of speaking in English didn't come up. When he received letters from Lord Lovat, before the Independent Company was taken from him, it was all in Gaelic. So, in Padruig's world of the military back then, his family and his friends all only spoke Gaelic. I was one of the few who stayed on at the Glenmoriston School when they switched from Gaelic to English, but he didn't imagine that I would write to him in English when he was at sea.

Padruig began to explain that when he had first heard his name called out for a letter onboard the ship taking him to New France, he had been totally ecstatic until he saw that I'd written it in English. He'd gone down each paragraph, trying to pick out a word here and there that he might understand, but became so disheartened at his inability to read that language for the first time in his life. He hadn't noticed a Sergeant watching on, who hadn't received a letter that day, but couldn't miss the very tall Highlander stride confidently to pick up his letter, only then to descend into frustration and sadness. It was obvious that Padruig couldn't read it, so that Sergeant came over to him with his old Bible and said, "I don't have any textbooks. I've only got this old Bible in English if you ever need any help with your letters anytime, it would be an honour to help out and it would be an absolute secret until the day I die. Apparently Padruig had said something very rude to him in Gaelic at first and dismissed John's suggestion, but after days of trying to read it, he eventually gave in and went to his junior officer threatening severe consequences if he ever spoke of it. Being on board a ship with a lot of uncouth men didn't help when it was known if there was a letter from a girlfriend or a wife. The Murrays were the worst. Foul mouthed lot they were, according to Padruig.

Until then, I'd quietly listened trying to make sense of the explanation but then said, "So John, did you read my letters?" Anna's mouth dropped at how I'd feel about another man reading intimate messages. "Oh John. You didn't?" she said. In reply, realising he was in a bit of trouble with both of us women, he answered. "It wasn't exactly reading Anna, it was translating it into Gaelic so that Padruig could know what his wife had said to him. I don't see the crime in that, but I am sorry Isobel. There was no choice and I was the best person to translate it because he was my superior officer and I was fluent in both languages as well as French and Latin too. It was going to restore Padruig's happiness. He was so miserable having been forced onto that ship and then his only love from home writes to him and he can't read it. Can you imagine how he felt?" he asked. That little speech won Anna over, but not me yet. "Padruig, why didn't you tell me that you still couldn't read English? I didn't know," I asked, "Why would I need English until that moment on the ship and why didn't you write in Gaelic?" he retorted. "The Reverend Stewart told me that the Post Office was still opening all of our letters, so he advised me not to write in Gaelic and so I didn't. The Reverend Forbes said the same thing," I answered. "Why?" asked Anna. "It was like wearing tartan, it was outlawed. It would attract negative attention and persecution with the risk possibly of non-delivery of the letter to the ship, said the Reverend. So, it was up to me still, but thinking that you could read the basics of English, I chose not to risk the letter going missing or a soldier at my door. I am sorry Padruig, but even Da and Uncle

Allan could read English. Da just advised that I include the occasional drawing so that it would minimise misunderstandings.

"It's our own faults though, not even conveying basic information to each other. This is not John's fault. I am very sorry John. It was very kind of you. Did you teach Padruig then, because his letters in English were in the same hand when he was in London?" I said. "Aye, I taught as best as I could, Isobel, not being a trained teacher and only having an old Bible," John said. Padruig then interjected and asked if I'd forgiven them both and I said I did, of course. "It was a terrible heart-breaking time for us both and we don't have to turn it into something that it wasn't now, do we? Afterall, my dearest love, not only did you gain a skill, you gained a good friend who is now family." I squeezed my husband's hand and leaned over to kiss him and was grateful that he received my love. "So long as you came back to me was the important thing and you did," I said. We then changed the subject in order for our home to return to owning its peaceful atmosphere, not saying there wasn't a level of embarrassment that John knew so much detail about our inner lives, not to mention the heartache and lack of transparency. John turned to me and said, "You can trust me Isobel." He must have known that I'd been suicidal, but I knew that I could trust John Fraser of Stratherick, God bless him.

The Roofing

Then the men wanted to talk of gold bars and roofing for the Manor House. Padruig wanted a very high pitched roof so the snow could slide off easily. The Manor House was closer to the mountains and there was more snow there than on Craskie. It would be colder too in his guest rooms, so a larger supply of peat would be needed. I personally wouldn't like to sleep that close to the mountain, but it is what you're used to.

Padruig just had to wait then for the enormous roofing to arrive, which gave us some lovely time together. Some mornings, he even joined me to milk my goats and one day, they even loved it as much as he did. He helped round up the sheep instead of relying on Hugh's dogs, but he suggested we ask Hugh Mohr for a puppy from the next litter. It had occurred to me that the discussion of the division of the farmlands began with a comment that Hugh Mohr had made. A while back when he had been patrolling that border between the two properties at my request, Hugh had said that he had never seen Hamish once on his patrols, despite it being his job as security. He had also told Padruig that in glancing up every night to the Manor House in every stage of it being built, he had never seen Hamish there either. Inadvertently he had called the old MacDonald's farm, "Padruig's place" and Craskie "Isobel's place", to which Padruig had reacted and asked him, "so who do you think owns Craskie?" He'd responded, "Isobel and the youngens" meaning Helen and Grigor Og. Then realising his mistake about the ownership of all the properties, he had corrected it by saying that he knew that Padruig actually owned all of the properties. That embarrassing conversation resulted in deep thought on Padruig's part and the decision was made to leave Hart of the Highland Manor House to Patrick, his son as an early inheritance and therefore Henrietta, Beth and James could live and work there while working the business together and not have any claim on Craskie when we died nor anything owned or purchased by Craskie. Poor James was packed off to an accountancy course, fortunately held in the vicinity. He didn't want to go to Edinburgh, but he came back awfully good at bookkeeping. Naturally, I was proud of him, he turned out to be quite the business man and gentleman. He had never taken to farming although he always liked horses thanks to Grigor Mohr.

Craskie would remain in our names passing it onto Helen and Grigor at the time of my choosing or death after Padruig's death. Helen would own the school and art gallery, as well as its teacher houses and neighbouring land, upon which was later built, Fraser's Trading Post. The land division was then drawn up so that the majority of the top two thirds of that land behind the art gallery, formed 'Grant Farm' and was owned by 'Craskie Farm', upon which now stood my enormous stables and Grigor's additional oat fields which he was thrilled with. Helen would receive the lease income from her tenant, being John Fraser, to run both the art gallery, the school and its needs as well as the upkeep of the two teacher houses. Padruig gave land from MacDonald farm to both Grant and Craskie farms, so these new land divisions were drawn up before Padruig passed away and the coos were moved onto Craskie to deal with.

Tartan Proscription Law

The law against wearing tartan was finally repealed in 1782 and our young Aonghus was very proactive in having it repealed. He even organised rallies in Edinburgh with placards on human rights made up by his university friends in rallies demanding a return to the wearing of the cultural dress of tartan to the Highlands. More surprising was the inclusion in his placards of saving the Gaelic language for Scotland as well as the bagpipes and weapons needed for hunting to feed families. Surprisingly, his university was supportive and it caught on as people talked of it more and articles appeared in our newspaper. My dear Padruig was becoming excited before the law was repealed and Helen and her wool waulking group had dedicated that entire clipping season to the creation of new tartans. For once she needed me to advise her on how to achieve the colours. I only asked for the first plaid to be for Padruig, as silently I knew his health was failing him in every way it does as we age. Whether it's our eyesight, our hearing or our poor old bones. He had overcome so much in his life, as had I, and I had devoted myself to him in his failing years whilst he enjoyed wearing his plaid once again.

When he stood side by side with Hugh Mohr sometimes, I would only need to close my eyes briefly as if to invite a vision and I could see "them" all in a group of seven in a very close-knit circle. They would all appear serious and of one mind. On one occasion I "saw" them in my way that Grigor Mohr would say was Pecht. On that occasion, I was an onlooker and they were the ages that they were post Culloden in 1746 and two of them turned to look at me, who I recognised as Padruig and Alexander MacDonald. When these visions occurred, someone would have to break me out of that world, and on that particular day, I saw that Padruig had looked first at me as if to say, someone's talking about us, 'who is that?' with a curious expression before recognition and then he recognised me and his face changed completely from the hawk looking out for his group of men to pure happiness and love.

Helen had woken me back into reality, asking questions about dyes and how to achieve them and so on. The young ladies didn't like the idea of using their own urine to colour fast the fabric, but God bless them, they got over it and we put up a privacy screen and urinated into a bucket. Looking back now, I knew my vision was a sign that Padruig would join the other Glenmoriston Men soon, but Hugh Mohr's figure had faded before Helen spoke. Glad of some warning, I revealed it to Hugh Mohr about what I saw. Surprisingly, he had seen his brothers, Alex and Donald as well, only recently, but was too afraid to mention it in case I thought he was strange. "Oh no, my dearest Hugh," I had replied, "you are by no means strange but I think we should prepare for my husband's passing. I don't believe my vision meant that it was you," I concluded. "I agree," he replied. "I think Alex and Donald are waiting for Padruig." Our love as those days progressed had become more tender and understanding of each other and of Padruig approaching his end, but he still wanted his needs fulfilled as did I. He would always remind me that what-ever age I was at that time, he would still be my husband for however short that time may be. This would bring tears to his eyes knowing how much he had lost.

Patrick and Henrietta Return

The house was very busy with Patrick and Henrietta's return, but I could see that Padruig just wanted to take Patrick aside with James to explain the new land division and explain how the Wills were written. Patrick was surprised but happy to receive the Hart of the Highlands Manor House as an early inheritance which came with its manicured gowf field and the best laundry in the Highlands with the two laundresses already arranged to work there. Even more pleased, the roof was paid for and on its way from the America's via John's shop. Grigor joined the conversation to understand the land division for the oat crops and his future ownership with Helen of Craskie and Grant Farms which he would eventually be in charge of. I had created a set of books for each working part of the farms, which I then entered into a larger set for taxation purposes. It was also a good way to know which part of the farm was doing well and vice versa and this was also explained but it would no longer include the MacDonald Farm on my books which James would have to take over for them as soon as Padruig indicated the exact date.

Isobel-Mairi had long decided not to leave Craskie like I had done when I was young and I had been teaching her about Clydesdales. It took some time before I actually gave her the reins, with all of her acquired knowledge to that point. The first time she was to take the reins with my guidance from the ground was on Drover's Road, speaking gently in Erse to her and the horses. She had learned the language of the horse, as Da called it. As they started to walk on her instruction, I climbed up beside her feeling it way more difficult than it used to be and she handled the four-horse team beautifully without a load as a practice. We went a distance and turned the team carefully up the Drover's Road and passed Fraser's Trading Post and turned right. They were then walking uphill but effortlessly. There was enough room to turn the team on the grazing land, which she did well. The horses, knowing she was a learner teamster, were patient. Then getting their movement up again, the team went down the Drover's Road to turn left to go back to Craskie Farm passing Fraser's Trading Post. There was a bit of an audience by then in front of John's shop. I just put my hand up to indicate no noise or clapping in case it spooked one of the horses, so they stood silently as we then turned back into Craskie. I had great hopes for her to be our new teamster and I felt a pride in her and prayed her teamster days would be profitable and long, although I had some niggling difficulty in being unable to see myself in her. With the gate wide open waiting for us, her father Grigor was so proud that he cried and he and Helen held each other. It was a beautiful sight. What an achievement.

Morag-Freya

Morag-Freya decided to go into nursing even though I thought veterinary science would be better and was able to work and stay in Inverness. Of course, she was a star pupil with her main interest being infection, inspired by Padruig's leg infection that could have killed him so she wanted to work on a cure for infection. I didn't think Inverness would have that school of scientific thought and asked if she wanted to go to Edinburgh, but she declined. The old lawyer who had employed

Aonghus the year before, was in need of a cook and offered her free board if she cooked him dinner. And so, she boarded with the old man and kept him company over the dinner that she cooked him. He was grateful for the company and the food. She was always keen to come home on the weekends if all her study was completed, to help around the farm. She missed us all, as we missed her. Her conversation was interesting as she repeated some of the gossip around the district. I even had to ask her if she was allowed to repeat all of that gossip and she said that Mr. David never told her that it was a secret and so on she'd chatter.

Reflecting over all Padruig and I had achieved together and apart, it was wonderful to see the new generation bringing what they had to offer into our Highlands. She wanted to work eventually in a hospital nearby. Maybe the smaller one at Invergary? She had also met a young man who she wasn't chatty about and so I asked her to bring him next time she came to meet her parents. Her face was flustered at that suggestion and her eyes cast down, as both of her parents then looked at her. Grigor was not pleased and asked with a very MacGregor looking stare that his Father used to give me at times before he knew I was his sister. "What's his name?" he asked her. "And what's his occupation and age?" "He is a student too Da," she calmly replied. "One year ahead of me, so he is about twenty-two I think, but I haven't asked him," she replied. "Student of what?" Grigor asked. "It's like nursing, but its more the science side of nursing. He's very smart," she said. "So, what are your feelings toward the lad and what's his name?" I asked. "Och, his name is Gillcrest Grandma, and I like him," she answered rather boldly I thought. "What's his clan?" asked Helen. "He's Catholic. His full name is Gillcrest Lachlan MacLachlan from, Loch Fyne, Argyle. That's all I know, but we've been to Kirk together and he's met the lawyer and he stayed for dinner one night. Mr. David told me he wanted to check him out, even his family because he didn't want me to get involved with a MacLachlan unless he was a goody," she said." I'll need to go in with you when you return to Inverness and talk to Mr. David about him and arrange to meet with this lad," said Grigor then very seriously. "Me too," said Helen.

"Just a minute Helen. Firstly, we can't spare both of you for the day, can we Padruig? There's so much work to do. Besides which, secondly,

I am pretty sure that Lochiel mentioned that name to us before in relation to the research on my family tree, had we not been able to find answers from Mr. MacNachten. He spoke highly of him as a knowledgeable Scientist or student scientist, as you say. May I suggest that Morag-Freya returns to Inverness on her own, tells Mr. David that we'd like to invite him for dinner with Gillcrest Lachlan MacLachlan from Loch Fyne and herself and then the farm is not affected?" I suggested. "That's a better idea," said Padruig. "What if you blow your top Grigor? She's your youngest. I can understand how you would feel, but we can't have you getting arrested for punching the lad." "What if I go?" asked Hugh Mohr. "We need you too," I said. "Then Hamish could go and spy on him after what happened with the MacKenzies, we want to know more about them," Hugh Mohr said apologizing to Meredith.

Remembering the MacKenzie incident, Morag-Freya was embarrassed and said that we didn't need to be so serious. "He's a bit like Simon Fraser, a bit of a dill sometimes and forgets things." "You mean like losing an entire box of china?" chimed in Isobel-Mairi. That wasn't his fault were the defensive voices from all corners. "Does he dress nicely or is he like Aonghus with his stupid breeches?" Isobel-Mairi asked. "He has to wear a white overcoat for work," Morag-Freya answered. "When he came to the lawyer's house he wore a nice vest over a shirt and a brown woollen jacket with matching brown breeks and stockings, but I could get him to wear his kilt Da. Would that help?" she said imploringly. "Aye. Wear his kilt here riding a horse, see what sort of man he is," Grigor answered. "Oh Da, please don't make him ride a horse. He can't ride," she said. The room burst out with laughter at a Highlander being unable to ride a horse. "What about Mr. David's cart with Mr. David and Gillcrest wearing a kilt? Okay?" she asked. "He has to bring flowers for both your Mither and your Grandmither," answered Grigor, making Helen very happy. "Incidentally, his family were loyal Jacobites in the '45, and unrelated to the Duke of Argyle," she added.

When the two of them finally came over, with Gillcrest Og MacLachlan wearing a kilt as was expected, Mr. David was driving the cart and we stabled the wee pony for him. Gillcrest Og was to stay in Chisholm House for a wee cost and Mr. David was to stay in ours.

Gillcrest was introduced very formally by Mr. David as Mr. Gillcrest Lachlan MacLachlan, Grandson of the Laird of MacLachlan who died on Drumossie Moor at the Battle of Culloden. Grigor had expected to tear strips off this young man who came with flowers for both Helen and I and was faced with a martyr's Grandson and knew that Padruig would adore him. He called me Mrs. Grant and Helen was Mrs. MacGregor. I knew he had been well schooled by the lawyer to impress and it was working. I quite liked the colours in his kilt and the matching brown jacket. The socks were awful, but we could work on that.

"Welcome to our home," announced Padruig. "A grandson of a martyr to The Cause is always welcome in our home. I was there when your Grandfather was killed. You can be proud of such a brave man, who led his two hundred men into battle. I believe you also didn't lose your ancestoral lands after Culloden. Is that right?" asked Padruig. "Aye, Mr. Grant. That's right, but the English still destroyed Castle Lachlan, so we had to move out. I was born in a humble home built nearby on the lands. Actually, Campbell neighbours helped my Mither when Da died," he added. "You were friends with the Campbells?" asked Grigor. I suppose the lawyer hadn't mentioned the MacGregor Campbell bit in meeting Morag-Freya's family. "Aye, as Ma explained, they were our neighbours and best to keep good relations with them, especially if they were being helpful," he explained. "Did they have big black hound dogs?" asked Grigor. "Aye, they did, but Da bred Irish Wolf Hounds mixed with Irish Setters which could kill them if they attacked us," he answered matter of factly. "I still breed them now, in Inverness actually," rather proud of his achievement. "Da had lost one some years back and had seen a sign in Inverness mentioning a lost dog and chickens, so we figured, as she never came back home, that someone must have killed her worrying about their chickens." Grigor and I looked at each other and decided not to mention our old dog, who had died peacefully just a few years ago having kept Grigor safe all that time.

Helen and Henrietta and the young ladies had shared in the cooking chores and when we sat to eat, Gillcrest Og admired the china. This is indeed beautiful china, Mrs. Grant. Can't say I've ever seen china this pretty before," he said. "It's from our cousin's husband and her father-in-law and the 'Frasers of Stratherick," said Morag-Freya. "They own the Trading Post next door to Ma's art gallery, which is not yet up and running, is it Ma?" said Morag-Freya. "I do admire Morag-Freya's name, Mrs. MacGregor. Such a pretty name combination," he said. I was thinking there was too much flattery, but Helen answered just the same, "Morag is Mr. MacGregor's Mither's name, God rest her soul and Freya is Ma's Mither's name, also a MacGregor at birth, God rest her soul."

It was then that Morag-Freya's older sister, Isobel-Mairi piped in and asked him why he couldn't ride a horse adding that, "I am learning to be a teamster myself. Grandma is teaching me," she said. We weren't expecting a very strange answer, but he went on to say, "When I was wee, Ma wanted me to know all about my ancestors, their graves at Kilmorie Chapel by Loch Fyne and the ruined castle or fort if you like. So, she took me first to the graves and explained the whole Irish connection way back to the Kings of Ireland and it was a peaceful Chapel. Then when we approached the ruined old castle, which I'd always thought was a strange shape, I heard the whinnying of a horse. Thinking it was a real horse, I looked first toward Loch Fyne and then to the castle. I heard it again, but I couldn't see a horse anywhere. I said to Mither, "where's the horse Mither? I can hear it whinnying." Then her face changed completely and she asked me when I had heard it and so on. 'Can't you hear it Ma?' I had asked. Holding her hand, as you do when you're wee, she said 'Nae, I can't hear it lad.' There is no horse here,' but there was after your Grandda died. His horse fled away from the battlefield of Culloden where his Master was killed, then swam all the way across Loch Fyne and stayed here at the castle whinnying for him until the poor horse died. Some people can still hear the horse to this day, like you son. It's a sad tale for sure,' she answered. 'What do you mean Ma,' I had asked. 'Do you mean it is a ghost horse?' 'Aye,' she had said. 'The castle is haunted with the blue-lady too.' I let go of her hand [11] and ran like the wind back home where I couldn't hear the horse and I have avoided horses ever since. I am afraid I'll be scared of them the moment they whinny, like the ghost horse," Gillcrest said.

"You need to toughen up lad," said Padruig. "That horse had a story to tell. All our beasts experience our lives alongside us and that shouldn't be anything to be afraid of. Face your fears is my advice. Grigor could go with you to Castle Lachlan and help you overcome your fears. Is your Mither alive son?" "Aye," he answered. "Then is it possible for you to introduce Mr. MacGregor here to your Mither?" "Aye," he answered. "I could get two weeks off school for family reasons. The school won't like it mind," said Gillcrest. "If you take our two Highland ponies, you'll be back in two weeks easily," I said. "Helen darling, could you do a lovely drawing of your daughter for them to take with them? Then, if your Mither wishes to, she can come back with you safely escorted and stay with us until you take her back. What do you think?" I asked. "Sounds like a bonny idea, very scary, but bonny," Gillchrest said. "What do you think Grigor about going to MacLachlan lands next door to the Campbells and the old castle?" Padruig smirked. "We'd need to take one of his dogs with us, given that there are Campbells nearby with their hounds. If he gets tired running, he can rest in the cart. That's my condition. That's if you're serious about my daughter lad and she you. Are you both serious or are you both wasting our time?" Grigor answered seriously and they both nodded their heads in agreement. "And then, with Mr MacGregor here making so much effort, you are expected to overcome your fear of horses and take riding lessons with my Granddaughter, Beth Fraser at Stratherick after the journey? She is patient and knowledgeable enough to teach you. Do you agree to taking riding lessons?" Padruig Dubh had lain down his conditions. "Aye, Sir," he said obediently. Poor thing, I was feeling sorry for the lad, knowing the damage early experiences can have on a child.

"Lad?" said Padruig questionnally, "Just a thought. Why could only you hear the horse whinnying and not your Ma?" he asked. "Ma said that she never heard or saw ghosts that other people saw, but Da did when he was alive," he replied. "Aye, but what was this horse trying to tell you if you could speak horse?" asked Padruig. "There was a deep sorrow in the sound of it combined with loud noises of the clash of metal that I could hear," Gillcrest answered. "So, the horse was trying to tell you about the battle?" Padruig asked. "I've never thought about what he was trying to tell me," he said. "Do you speak Erse?" Padruig asked. "Aye, characters as well," he answered. "Then ask Mrs. Grant here how to talk to horses and if you hear it again, she'll tell you how to speak to that animal and he might be freed from his earthly prison. It may be terribly disturbing, but Mrs Grant can tell you how to speak to horses," Padruig said. "Just speak in Erse lad, softly, kindly and never loud. That horse was traumatized by the loud noises in the battle. You may have to speak to him for a while until you don't hear the whinnying anymore," I said. I was wondering if I should go too, but I was worried about Padruig's health and two weeks away from him was too long.

The journey was surprisingly enjoyable for the two men and it passed quickly because the lad was not a nurse, he was a scientist who was specializing in the quality of soil in order to produce maximum grain yield from our crops. It was Grigor's dream to talk about soil for hours and days on end as well as Gillcrest Og. Finally, they had both found someone to share their passion with and our oat crops benefited free of charge. When the three of them came home to Craskie, I was expecting his Mither to be a younger version of a middle aged lady, but life had not been kind to Mrs. MacLachlan. Her silvering and lifeless, auburn hair was once, probably a curly head of flowing hair but now it had lost its body and was just tied tightly back into a tight bun, which unfortunately accentuated the severity of her facial features and her weathered appearance. I'd thought that the lad must have inherited his good looks from his Da and I was glad his hair wasn't quite that auburn or maybe it had been life near Loch Fyne that had that effect on a woman's hair and skin. Her redeeming feature were her eyes but they were a cold blue, unlike his which were a pretty and soft blue. As I observe blue eyes, the more differenc I find in the shades and pureness of the colour.

We'd all agreed on a date for a wedding in Inverness and Isobel-Mairi, although envious, helped me make her sister's wedding dress due to my failing eyesight. The wedding was enormous with MacEwens and Gillcrests, as well as Clan Lachlans travelling together from Loch Fyne. It was odd to see even more folk with that weathered look. They all interacted well with the many branches of our family being the Frasers of Stratherick where Gillcrest learned how to ride a horse. Aonghus came up from university and was expecting to be the number one son, but found himself increasingly left out of his Father and new brother-in-law's conversation. Grigor and Gillcrest

Og would be buzzing away about the intricacies of soil, which in the past he had judged his Father as being some kind of soil maniac from the Highlands, only to find there were other soil maniacs with science degrees.

Our Gillcrest Og went on and won an award for his work on soil to increase the yield of our Scottish Highland crops and our crops were in the newspapers. Morag-Freya was very proud of her choice of husband and our crops were chosen as examples of the success in improvements that had been made. I thought the soil had already been perfected by our Grigor, but under scientific analysis, further improvements were made which required carts and carts of kelp from the coast that were brought in. More seaweed was the answer, so eventually Hugh Og and Isobel-Mairi were asked to take a team to the coast to cut costs and increase the quantity of seaweed in one load. It really stank, but it was worth it. We all aimed to avoid another famine and Grigor knew just how life saving his work was.

Padruig could hardly believe his eyes, but said one day, "I didn't even think that farming could be so interesting. I wish I had taken an interest and helped Grigor earlier." "We all know what your role here is and has been in the family darling. Without you, there wouldn't be a future at all. Everyone in all their respective roles that they have, look up to you," I replied. "Good try Isobel," he said with a wry smile. "Well, Gillcrest wouldn't be the man he is today if it hadn't been for you helping him get over his childhood trauma and now look at him. He truly loves his father-in-law and his wife, of course, and I am happy for them. I did want to ask you about Aonghus though," I said. "Aye?" he said quizzically. "He can't seem to understand that an educated person like himself and Gillcrest can love us unconditionally with or without a kilt and still enjoy farming. But most especially, can hold his own Father in very high esteem." "You mean the two World's theory is up the creek?" he asked. "Aye, it is," I said. "So, make it easier on my old brain Dath-thula my beloved and get straight to the point. What question are you asking?" he asked. "Why doesn't he respect you, his Father, myself or this farm life despite not having found anyone special or an alternative way of life in Edinburgh?" I asked. "Respect and love are two separate things, don't you think?" he said. "You've seen his long face when Grigor and

Gillerest Og walk off together having an in-depth conversation leaving him out in the cold, so I think there is respect for his Father, albeit through or because of Gillerest. Most definitely, he loves his Father. I can't speak about his feelings for me, because he has always been afraid of me and to keep him in line I have kept up my stares towards him if I disapprove of a word here or there that he has misspoken. His feelings for you though, I thought were of love, but similarly, through his fear of reproach from you, he retreats. You can scare a 6'10" Highlander, broad and braw. I have seen men tower over you to get permission to do this or that. You are not even 5' tall and from an onlooker's perspective it says a lot about how much respect that you command and that is not just here on Craskie. It is not the glare or stare that I can do better than you," he said smiling. "It's your presence. Most folk our age don't have that kind of presence, but we both do. I think that was why the Almighty God put you and I together in the first place," he said.

"Not many people could've tolerated me except my mates," he said. "Oh Padruig, that's nonsense. You're a simply gorgeous hunk of a man inside and out and I love you to bits. I don't know what I would've done without you if you hadn't asked me to wait for you when you were fourteen. I was the happiest lass alive and look around you now. Did you think that we would ever have such a complicated, yet versatile family? Admittedly, we had a bit of help from Ma and Da in those early years while you were with Highland companies, then Da and Uncle Allan, when you were pressed into service in New France, as well as our dear friends, Donald Chisholm, may God rest his soul, Hugh Mohr and Grigor Mohr, who turned out to be my half-brother. But that's normal in the Highlands for us to help each other out, especially family," I said.

"After we married and I just left you here on the farm with your parents only to find that you were pregnant with Patrick soon after, did you ever resent me for my not being here?" he asked. "Never, my love, it was always understood that being with the Frasers meant that you were training to be a soldier. It was normal that you would talk a lot about the Company. I didn't really get the chance to talk about anything around the farm, including our Clydesdales and I didn't think that you would be that interested anyway but I wished sometimes that I'd been able to interject and talk about the horses. But it really wouldn't have been polite to interrupt you at the time and Da didn't seem to think it mattered, so we just got on with normal work here, which included driving the teams. It was quite busy here with the crofters too. Do you wish you had known that I was working with Da as a teamster? Would it have made a difference? After all, it was just work which couldn't rival the obvious excitement you felt in your soldiering role," I asked.

Reflectively, Padruig answered, "At the time, it wouldn't have mattered if I'd known or didn't know I think. The farmwork is unsurprising but the teamstering is interesting if your passion is horses. It only became a big deal because of what happened when the Redcoats came and the horses were stolen, leaving no income there, the crofters gone and no income there, no crops, no livestock. You understand. It was part of the big picture, where my family could've starved, but you didn't starve because of the Almighty God's plan for us and your peculiar inner strength that I have to thank you for Isobel. You saved this family, not single handedly, that's true, but would they have helped you if you were a rude, unpleasant or immoral person? Nae, you are a pure soul Isobel," he said. "Oh Padruig, I've been so blessed it's true, but everyone here has worked so hard to save Craskie, Uncle Allan included, God bless his soul. I really needed him," I replied, feeling emotional thinking of everyone who had helped me in my darkest hour while resting my head on my husband's broad chest. His hand brushed my hair from my face. "You've no black hair left Dath-thula. It's all silver now," he said with such a cheeky grin. "Is it a pretty silver or that old looking silver?" I asked. "Pretty, of course. I've always been told by multiple friends, mates or colleagues that I was too lucky to have such a radiant beauty as you who had never been seen before in the Highlands. Even at your age you can attract really young men, I've seen it in their dirty eyes," he said. "That's why I asked you to wait for me or you would have been taken for sure," he said. "No-one had ever told me that I was pretty. You were the first to say it and I didn't believe it."

Deciding to leave the wedding party that was getting louder, Padruig and I went into our bedroom and locked the door, put another log on the fire and changed into our warmest bed clothes. Helen had remembered to put our bed warmer in the bed and our room had everything we would need and there was an atmosphere of love. Anticipating that we would go to bed early, she had left a kettle on the fire and a teapot sitting on a wee table with two cups. "You can be sure that when we die Padruig, the only one person we can rely on to pray for us will be Helen," I said spontaneously. "Aye, she is the daughter that everyone wishes was theirs," he said, holding me in his big arms. "You know Padruig, I think we're aging. We were supposed to solve the problem of Aonghus," I said. "Aye, but I'd rather enjoy my night with you." As the last of the embers of our fire died out, he said with passion, "Isobel, if I had been home all the time and not with the Company, can you imagine how many bairns we would have had?" Chuckling to myself, I fell into a heavenly sleep. I was the luckiest woman on Earth to have met, married and had bairns with this God's gift of a man. I thanked God for him and our life together however imperfect, it was still our wonderful life.

The Chapel

Overnight one night, I had decided that we'd build our own private Chapel because the Papists weren't going to build a Kirk nearby, no matter how often they had been asked. There was enough room in between the grain storage shed and the cemetery for a wee chapel. Padruig had approved of it, so long as he didn't have to build it. And so, I took a journey to Loch Insh on one of my big, old Clydesdales. Dismounting when I arrived, I was glad that he had a stone to climb down to. Mr. MacNachten, saw me coming and I took my saddle bag from the horse to give him a few things from our farm.

He was so pleased to see me. I glanced across at the loch and there weren't any swans. "No swans today?" I said. "Nae, nae Isobel, they migrate to Iceland every year. Your Grandson was lucky to see them all before they left", he said. "Thank you", I added, "for helping Aonghus. He is still a troubled lad, but that is not what I am here for Gillcrest. I want to build a wee Chapel on our land, like yours here and I don't know anyone who knows anything about how to do that. Do you know who could build it for us?" I asked. "Aye, I do," he said, pouring me a beautiful coffee as we looked over the scenic loch. "How many graves do you want inside it?" he asked. "Just four. Padruig, myself, Helen and Grigor. We can have plaques on the wall referencing all of the other graves in the graveyard," I said. "So, you will be needing the grave slabs?" he asked. "Aye, I would', I said. He took all of our details, obviously leaving off the date of death, which would be added later. "I can send the men over in a few days. Are you wanting the Chapel built from Caledonian granite?" he asked. "If they can access it, but I am not fussy and also there is accommodation for the workers in the house near the cemetery called Chisholm House. Hugh Chisholm is its permanent resident and keeps a clean house with two Collie dogs. The bitch might give birth soon and I have asked for one. I am getting too old to round up thirty five sheep", I said.

"How much will it cost Gillcrest? And by the way, we have another Gillcrest in the family now. His name is Gillcrest Lachlan Mac Lachlan," I said. "So, he'd be the laird of Castle Lachlan?" he asked. "I hadn't thought of that, but aye. He said that his Father had passed', I said. "Well, lairds don't live on their lands always nowadays, so I suppose he is more like a landlord?" he asked. "I don't know. I should have asked him that," I said "Is he a good lad?" he asked. "Aye, we think so. He was frightened of horses because he had heard 'the ghost horse' whinnying at the castle as a wee child and was frightened of horses until he met us. He is over it now." Looking thoughtful, he said that he has some of that Irish genealogy in his blood too and had also heard that horse. "Understandable if he was frightened. Did he hear the clash of metal too?" he asked. "Aye, all of that terrifying stuff," I answered. "I hope to meet young Gillcrest Og. I'll join the men on one of the days that I am delivering the slabs. Do you mind if I stay overnight too?" he said.

He invited me in for a quick lunch before I left, which I happily accepted and I tied my horse to the tree, where he munched on the grass. "How many pews Isobel?" Gillcrest asked. "Maybe eight, if they'll fit, four on each side," I said. "He drew up what it would look like and also asked for the information needed on the side panels with all of the names of the deceased that are in the graveyard. "Does the Chapel have a name?" he asked. "I'm no good with names. What do you think?" I asked. "One of the Saints?" he asked. "Do you want me

294

to choose the Saint?" he said. "Aye, you choose it. How long will it take do you think?" I asked. "Two to four weeks. The weather is good for it," he answered. We had a delicious lunch and I asked him again, how much would it cost. "Two-thousand pounds if you provide food and board free of charge," he answered. "The slabs?" I asked. "That's separate, so that would be four hundred pounds," he replied. "Can I give you the money now for the slabs then?" I asked and I gave him the money that I had put aside from the tree felling.

"Before you leave Isobel," he said. "Can I please ask you if you are preparing for your husband's passing?" he asked. "I don't know. Maybe I am. I have written to our youngest son Alex, who lives in Nova Scotia, to consider visiting his Father, but I haven't yet received a reply if he is coming or not', I said. "My dear Isobel, the way you have prepared yourself for every other eventuality in your life isn't like a business transaction. Losing your husband will be easier for you than you think because of your deep spirituality and deep connection to him. That won't change when he's on the other side of the veil', he said. His understanding words meant more to me than he could ever realise. "Please come to his funeral Gillcrest. It may well be chaotic as our family has many branches now, but for me, I'll need you. To me, you are the closest person to me now, other than Da was when he was alive. I can't fall apart at Padruig's funeral you see if eyes are on me to obtain strength from. I'd like it if you stood beside me if you don't mind. I know that you say you're not family, but maybe you are," I pleaded.

"Maybe I am, but I am honoured anyway at your request, so if you send word to me when to come, I will stand beside you, unless you change your mind or if I go before Padruig," he smiled and so did I. Departing the scenic Loch Insh and Mr. MacNachten on my beautiful big old horse, I was aware of just how far it was back to Craskie Farm as the air grew colder.

My old horse powerfully strode his long legs into the fading light and more familiar territory was finally before us, so then we slowed down a while, to give us both a rest. It was eerie being out alone at night and I'd wished for Hugh's companionship but knew that Padruig wouldn't have approved. Helen and Grigor would be anxious, so when my trusty horse's breathing had normalised, I asked him gently to 'take me home', which he did. The gate was open when I arrived and the driveway lights were lit, so I concluded that there was anxiety and a lot of questions to answer from Padruig. As I approached the house, it was Grigor who ran out desperately and yelled out, "Ma, where on earth have you been? I can take care of your horse Ma. Let me help you down." Gently taking my hand, he eased me down to the ground. Your horse is tired Ma, I'll take him up to his stables now. Good old fella, I heard him say sweetly to old Benny.

The Illness

Padruig was standing on the front porch with one of his unimpressed looks. 'Oh dear,' I thought, it's that bad. Helen ran out next, "Ma, I've kept your dinner warm. It's only us three awake with Hugh. Everyone else is in bed asleep. Are you alright? I've got your bath water cooking too," she said. "Thank you darling", I said and kissed my daughter lovingly. "You've got some explaining to do Isobel," said Padruig. "Come inside and get warm and try your hardest."

While eating and drinking two cups of coffee, Padruig's eyes were burning into my soul as Helen rubbed down my back and put on a warm, dry plaid over me. "Okay, are you finished?", he said. "Aye," I answered. "Then come and sit by the fire and tell me where you've been, why and who you've been with, how far you've travelled and your purpose for such a risky venture that kept you out alone late at night." It was then that I saw that Hugh Mohr, sitting in a dark corner who was holding his trusty rifle over his shoulder, Collies at his feet. "Isobel," he said, also sounding totally unimpressed "Hugh", I replied.

"Well", said Padruig, "Answers now please! If you were a child I'd be calling you naughty, but what do I call a wife who comes home at this hour of night having travelled alone to Loch Insh?" he said. Just the sound of that word 'naughty' took me back to when I received the only beating and whipping I received by my old Da. I was worried at just how upset that both Padruig and Hugh obviously both were that could result in a beating from either one of them, so I just started talking. "I was in Loch Insh today seeing Mr. MacNachten about the wee Chapel that I mentioned to you. Please forgive me Padruig,

Hugh, I didn't do it to harm you, please believe me. Padruig, you did agree to the building of the Chapel," I said. "Why didn't you tell us that you were going and why didn't you take one of us with you?" Padruig asked. "You were up at the manor house so, I left a wee note by the bed. Did you read it?" I asked. Holding up a piece of paper approximately four inches by four inches, he said, "Do you mean this one?" 'Off to Loch Insh about the Chapel. Back by nightfall. Don't wait up' it had read. "Aye, I went to Loch Insh to arrange the building of the Chapel because you said I could have it so long as you didn't have to build it. The only Chapel that I thought of was that lovely one in Loch Insh. Mr. MacNachten was very helpful and we're even getting grave slabs for yourself, me, Helen and Grigor inside the wee Chapel," I stated. "Why only us four?" he asked. "It's too small for any more. It's wee with only four pews on each side," I answered, but I knew that whatever I said, I was in the wrong and like my Da had said all those years ago, I should just take my punishment. Grigor then came in and said that the horse was all bedded and fed. "Where have you been Ma?" was the repeated question. The others chimed in, "Loch Insh". "You went that far Ma, on your own. Why?" asked Grigor. "You were all too busy. I couldn't take you away from your crops Grigor, you from the house Padruig, you from your painting and completing orders from Edinburgh Helen, and I did think of Hugh, but I thought you'd disapprove, so I do apologise. I knew coming home, up the Great Glen alone, had been something I would not normally do and it was really eerie. I won't be doing it ever again. It's way too eerie at night there. There are too many ghosts, but my horse was a trusty friend and he had done those journeys at night with Da and me before, so I just told him to 'take me home,' and he did."

Hugh Mohr was livid, "I am so sorry Hugh," I said but fearing for what kind of punishment Padruig would give me, I automatically handed Hugh the wee horse whip kept by the fire place. Taking it he went on. "You could have been killed Isobel and we would not have known where you were. Isn't that right Padruig?" My poor husband looked relieved that it wouldn't be his job to punish me, but was exhausted with the worry and went into our room, closing the door behind him. The others all left too. "I am so sorry Hugh. I wanted the Chapel built," I said pathetically. "Why?" he asked. "For funerals, baptisms and weddings. I hope that you don't mind it being so close to your place and could you please accommodate the four work-men when they come?" I asked. "Oh, this just gets worse. Now I have this task as well but I'm not doin it with a whip," he said. With only the two of us left in our lounge room, he asked me to bend over his knee, just as my Da had done when I was three years old, lifted up my dress and trying to avoid my scars, he took his leather belt and beat me several times, which was very painful. All the while, I wept and asked for forgiveness while clinging to his thighs. "I forgive you Isobel but you're never to do that again," he said. I crawled onto his lap still asking for forgiveness and he caressed me and kissed me fore-head. His voice began to tremble, as he said, "I never want to do that to you again Isobel, so when we marry, you'll follow me, okay?" he said seriously." Yes, I know, I'm sorry," I said, still clinging to him and I was afraid to let go. He kissed my lips softly and whispered he loved me more than I'd ever know but now he'd have to go back to his home. He left with a sadness in him and I hung my head in shame. I knew that I was in the wrong. Grigor decided to come back out after he heard the door close and asked first if I needed anything. "Oh, sweet Grigor, you are so much like your Father. Nae, thankyou, I'm fine." I said and he went to bed looking tragically sad. I smoored the fire and put out the candles and went to my room frightened of another beating. Padruig wouldn't look at me when I entered the room, he just started asking questions.

"Tell me about this Chapel then. How much it will cost and how long they will be here?" Padruig said, still not looking up at me. He was so ashamed of me and I'd never felt that before. I quietly answered "They'll be here for between two and four weeks and the cost will be two thousand pounds, but I have already paid for our slabs, which were four hundred pounds." "So, you'll be wanting me to pay the two-thou-sand pounds?" he asked. "Oh aye," I said. "I'm not offering," he said. "Oh," disappointed that this night was getting worse and so I wracked my brains as to where I could get it and came up with men's shirts and vests. "Okay, I'll do some sewing. Men's vests are popular now, over a shirt with a kilt. Maybe Isobel-Marie will help me thread the needles," I said, while rubbing the pain felt in my buttocks.

It was then that I started to feel an irritation in my throat and coughed a bit. "You're not getting sick now, are you Isobel? Come and have that hot bath," Padruig said harshly. I undressed then climbed into the hot bath, but I coughed more and realised that something was up. Padruig called for Helen. "Your Mither's sick. Can you help?" I was quickly dried while shivering all over, as in a fever, when she put my thickest nightgown on with long socks. "Hop into bed Ma and I'll get you one of your medicinal drinks. You'll be right by morning. Da, rub Ma's hands and feet to keep her warm." She said, but I pulled my hands away automatically. Putting another log on the fire, before she left the room, I heard her in the kitchen telling Grigor that I was not well and could he make up a vaporizer as well. Both of them came in armed with medicines that I had given them all as bairns and never had expected to use it myself. "You've just overdone it Ma, is all. Try and rest and don't think too much. Whatever you did today, was no doubt good for us here at Craskie," said Grigor. The dear boy was about to kiss my forehead when I saw the ghost of his father standing behind him with concern on his face. "Grigor", I reached out my hand past my son-in-law. "It's okay", said Padruig to Grigor Og, "it's your Da. Isobel sees him on occasion." I must have been delirious as apparently, I talked a lot to Grigor Mohr. I had told him that I had ridden through the Great Glen that night and it was eerie, and not in a good way. He had replied that he knew where I was and had stayed with me. "Not a good idea to go through there without full awareness these days. Some of the ghosts there will give you trouble," he said. "Is that why I am sick?" I asked. And he said, "Aye," but that I'd be alright soon as he had been joined by the live spirit of Gillcrest MacNachten from Loch Insh. One each side.

Helen, Grigor Og and Padruig all slept in my room that night taking turns to wipe my forehead, to give me a hot drink or toilet. It was a long night, but I was well enough by morning, but I still did not want Padruig near me. Everyone else looked exhausted at breakfast and my grand daughters were asked to do the cooking, feed the chickens and let them out, milk my goats and let them out as well as the sheep and the coos and the horses. Hugh Og luckily was doing his job, and upon hearing what had occured, took on doing all of the rest of the outdoor tasks with a very sullen Hugh Mohr, who had never hit a woman in his life.

Padruig had decided not to work on the house that day and lit fires to keep the house warmer and kept me rugged up. He had stopped his complaining and kept checking my temperature. I had not ever seen him so worried about me and he didn't leave my side, but I wanted him too. "I'm so sorry Padruig. Please forgive me," I said. "I wanted us both to be buried in a wee Chapel, protected from the snow and the icy winds and the rain, is all. Mr. MacNachten does make beautiful slabs," I said. "It's all right love. You told Grigor Mohr all the details. So, we all know now," he said. "Grigor Og or Grigor Mohr?" I asked. "Grigor Mohr", he answered. "Oh dear.. With Helen and Grigor Og in the room?" I asked. "Aye", he said dramatically. "I suppose they think that I am not right in the head?" I asked. "Well love, you weren't. Your temperature was high, but he was there. Do you remember him telling you that he escorted you through the Great Glen along with a living spirit?" he asked, "Was it Gillcrest MacNachten?" I asked. "Aye", it was," he said. "I'd asked him yesterday to stand beside me in the Chapel when you pass away, so I'd be strong enough after you die," I said "Is this all about my death then?" asked Padruig calmly. "All of what?" I asked and fell back into a deep sleep and I could feel my big horse under me once again and heard the eerie sounds in the glen and was aware that Grigor Mohr and Gillcrest were there. I had been so tired that I was almost falling from the horse and felt a pressure on one side to stop me falling and then on the other. I then suddenly woke up. "Padruig, I nearly fell off the horse out of tiredness, but both of them kept me on him." I blurted out, "Aye. I know. This is why you don't go out alone. Please don't do it again Isobel, no matter how important it may seem," he pleaded "Do you forgive me?" I asked reaching out to him. "Aye, I forgive you," he said, taking my hand. "You're not angry anymore then?" I asked. "Part of me is, just a wee part mind, but I'm just grateful that you are alive this morning, so I can't stay angry. I thought you were going to die last night, I can't lose you Isobel," he said. "Padruig, I don't think that we are going to die at the same time like we had always wanted to. But it is not me who will go first. Soon after you die, I will join you," I said. "We don't have to talk about death now", he said.

"I've written to Alex and asked him to visit, if he could, one last time, but he has not written back," I added. "He's too busy to spend months on a ship leaving his family to wolves, bears and painters," he snapped, dismissing the whole idea. "You're probably right, but I wish he could" and I sobbed quietly to myself. I felt so sad then that I would never see my wee Alex ever again. I curled up into a ball on a lounge chair by the fire, staring into it, when I heard a knock on the door. Meredith answered it and asked, "Aye, what can I do for ye?" I heard the familiar voice of Mr. MacNachten and Meredith let him in. He came straight over to me. "Are ye alright lass?" he said. "Aye, I caught a cold or some such and was a bit poorly, but I am getting better now. Padruig, do you remember Gillcrest?" I asked, not yet mentioning the beating. "Coffee or tea Gillcrest?" Padruig asked. "Coffee please with milk and sugar." Then Padruig called out to Meredith to get it as well as another hot drink for me and coffee for him and scones. "Scones is it?" she asked. "Aye, scones!" he spoke gruffly to her. "I'll put a big batch on then Mistress." And I nodded in agreement. "Himself" had spoken but Meredith didn't seem too pleased with him.

"Last night in the Great Glen..." I had begun to talk when Gillcrest indicated not to go any further when Padruig said, "It's okay, Gillcrest, we all know. She was delirious with a fever and first talked to her deceased brother Grigor not us." Padruig had started to explain when Gillcrest Mohr said, "Grigor, so that's who he was, your lost brother. We both worked together, but I couldn't stop worrying about you for the rest of the night." I took my punishment," I whispered teary eyed so Padruig couldn't hear me. "From the one who loves you or your husband?" he asked. "The one who loves me was given the task," I again answered quietly. "I knew you'd face a beating," he said matter of factly and so early this morning I got my old pony ready and we came as quickly as we could," he said. "Does it need one of my treatments?" he asked. "Show me," he said. He gently applied some ointment and took no heed if anyone came in and saw him apply-ing it. Padruig must have been shocked at its appearance as he said nothing to stop Gillcrest from attending to it. "That will take the heat and the pain out of it and draw the bruises out, so it might look worse for a while. I'll leave it with you to apply after your bath, or young Meredith here might do it," he said in a kindly sympathetic voice. "Gillcrest," I said, "I bought Highland ponies a while back, so they're not young anymore, but we only need one for our cart because we have a donkey too, so I can give you one of my Highland Ponies, so yours can have a break," I said. Of course, he looked at Padruig who said, "Don't look at me. They're hers to keep or sell." "You can, dearest Isobel, but would he like to leave your lovely farm to live in Loch Insh?" he asked. I thought about it and was aware our need for both ponies had ended a while ago and I could give him both, then they wouldn't miss each other. "The ponies will be happy in Loch Insh with you fussing over them, if you feed them and if they have each other, so take them both. No one's riding them here anymore. Isobel-Mairi and I are both with the Clydesdales. Can you speak Erse?" I asked him. "Aye," he said. "They like that too. Will you please spend the night here Gillcrest?" Smiling, I said and hoping he would stay, so I wouldn't face another beating, "I heard the Great Glen can be a bit creepy at night. Then if you would like the ponies, you can hitch one up and trot two behind," I said feeling weary again. "Could I leave my old pony out to pasture here on your lovely farm in retirement?" he asked. "Aye, sounds bonny," and he held my hand up to his face. "Isobel, your hands are too cold. Do you have some gloves?" I saw Padruig then go and get them as well as another rug. "Are you eating and drinking enough?" he asked. "You'll get cold if you don't eat enough." Then Helen started cooking an enormous lamb stew enough to feed an army. "Hugh Mohr just slaughtered it this morning Ma, I hope you don't mind?" she said calling out to me. "Nae, of course not my darling. He wanted to kill something last night. It was better that it was our dinner and not a person," I said.

"I am sorry Isobel," said Gillcrest. "I should've insisted that you stay at Loch Insh, but I was worried your husband would have disapproved," he said. "Aye and I would have," said Padruig interjecting. "I understand," he said. The huge batch of scones with jam and cream came out and did a lot to improve Hugh Mohr's mood when he came over curious to meet the visitor. Then he asked, "So, what's this about the men that are going to stay at my house while they build this Chapel? How many of 'em, so I'll know what to slaughter before they come?" At least the plan hadn't been cancelled for which I was grateful. It was all very matter of fact with our dear Hugh Mohr, who despite all of the bravado, had a heart as soft as butter. Gillcrest Mohr answered saying,"Some days two men would be there and some days four." "Well, there won't be enough room for five, so are you kipping in here wi' Isobel?" Hugh asked. "Aye, he is," answered Padruig. "By the looks of things," he continued, "Isobel's found herself another relative, but I'll nae ask questions." "The man who loves you' Isobel, is that him?" whispering to me, Gillcrest enquired indicating Hugh Mohr."Aye," I replied. "He's handsome and very tall for sure and younger than yourself. You don't mind that?" he asked. "I didn't ask him to love me Gillcrest, he was one of the Seven Glenmoriston Men, with Padruig after Culloden," I answered. "Why then did he take the strap to you and not your husband?" he asked. "I might not be alive this morning if it was my husband, so I handed Hugh a horsewhip, hoping he could do it, and I'd still be alive today, I'd prayed," I said still whispering, which I could see was starting to annoy my husband.

Seeing her Father's annoyance, Helen offered to sit with me to keep me warmer and rub my hands while Gillcrest moved onto a larger chair nearer Padruig. "How did you know that my wife needed you last night? Can you tell me that?" asked a very curious Padruig. "Oh aye. I was asleep when suddenly I thought I heard a voice saying 'Gillcrest, take me home' and I knew Isobel was in serious trouble. Getting dressed, I thought to borrow a neighbour's horse at first and gallop to The Great Glen where she was, but then suddenly standing from outside on the porch of our Loch Insh Chapel, I was just there with her as she was sliding off the horse on one side. Panicked about the other side, seeing how sleepy she was, I became aware that there was a spirit assisting her on that side too and so together we kept it up like that until Craskie Farm was in view when she seemed more awake and then suddenly I was back at Loch Insh on that same porch. It's the old Druid stone I think," he said. "Has that ever happened to you before?" Padruig asked. "Nae, not exactly like that. There has to be a connection for a start," he said. Then I said, "But I thought I asked my horse to take me home." Gillcrest responded by saying, "That can still be 'translated' if you like to one who can 'hear'. In your case, it was both your brother Grigor and myself," he explained.

Hugh Mohr had stopped eating his scones and said, "Remember how Grigor was when we were in the cave Padruig? He would always know what other worldlies were around and where to go or not to go to avoid 'em," he said. "Aye, he did. So, even in death, does that go on does it?" Padruig asked. "I am not an expert on 'other worldlies' but maybe he was. I just heard Isobel," Gillcrest concluded.

I'd never seen Padruig so interested in spiritual matters, but he appeared to calmly take it all in. He then said, "Now I know there's this Pecht connection with the two of you and Grigor Mohr as well, but hearing her voice and knowing it was Isobel. Can you explain that?" asked Padruig. While all eyes and ears were then trained on the lean and small Gillcrest MacNachten, I couldn't help but notice that he and I shared a very similar height weight ratio compared to the 6"7' Highlanders in the room. He began with, "I can try Padruig, but my story will go back to the day Isobel's Mither, Freya, married her Da, John Grant, your father-in-law. I was wee at the time and everyone had gathered at the Chapel overlooking Loch Insh for a wedding, so being a bairn, I was happy to know there'd be lots of bannocks to eat and a few of us ran around. But then everyone suddenly stopped talking and eating. The bride, Freya, your Mither, beautifully dressed in a long green gown covered in a green and brown arisaid, had walked toward the Loch alone and the fear was that the wedding may be called off. Then she sat on that stone there and began to sing Griegal Cridhe, that beautiful sad song that you know Isobel," Gillcrest said. "Then what happened?" asked Padruig. "She stood up and the swans that were on the Loch took flight as she lifted up her arms and then they landed in front of her, not unlike when your grandson Aonghus visited me. We gave her bannocks to give to them, which she did, still not knowing if there was going to be a wedding because she'd been crying you see. Mind you, so had nearly everyone else, especially your Da, Isobel. She was missing her young son Grigor, I have since concluded. Then the Priest asked your Da if the wedding was still happening and he told that Priest off for being impatient and to just wait for when his bride was ready. He really loved Freya I believe, but as bairns we were just excited about the swans," Gillcrest explained. "Then what?" I asked.

"Then she spoke something to the swans in a language unknown by me, and they flew off and then she turned as calm as ever and married your Da. But that's not the end of my story. Can I go to the privy before I finish?" I think a few people went off to the privies. I was glad that we had four at that time, the room seemed to have filled with the whole family, including Grigor Og, who had come in for the scones and cream. When the calm, slow-paced Gillcrest Mohr came back to his chair, he first asked me if I needed a hot drink and another blanket, which I did. God bless him. He covered me over ever so gently and sat back down, while Padruig repeated his earlier question. "The voice," he said impatiently. "Aye. I didn't hear that song sung in Loch Insh again, but I'd hear it from time to time in my head and it was her voice. That is to say, Freya's voice. Sometimes I could hear a child singing with her and wondered if she'd had a wee lass with John Grant and that made me happy," he said. "Hold on," said Padruig, "what do you mean exactly?" Gillcrest Mohr answered as best as he could being faced with Padruig's demands. I asked him quietly, "Could you hear Mither and I singing that song?" "Aye. I didn't know it was you then Isobel, but the wee girl's voice was trying to learn it, I thought." At that memory I couldn't stop the tears flowing down my face from when Mither was alive and trying to teach me that song. He touched my hand softly and gave me a cloth to wipe my face. He continued, "It was years then, when I realised that Freya was not with us anymore, as I had stopped hearing her singing that song. But then one day I heard an adult woman's voice singing it as sorrowfully as she had, but didn't complete the song. It stopped suddenly at "Oban, oban, oban," he said. "Oh Ma," Helen cried out. "That's when you sang part of it to Grigor and I, but I stopped you to ask you what 'oban, oban' meant." Grigor Og had decided not to return to his oat field then in wanting to know this story and at that part he said, "That was the night we all found out that Helen's Ma and my Da were half brother and sister and we were cousins. How could you hear it from Loch Insh? I don't understand how this can happen," Grigor said. Then Mr. MacNachten just said, "Neither do I lad, I just think of it as a gift from God and don't ask too many questions being afraid that if I upset the Auld ways that it would all just stop."

"Then I heard it again some time later and I knew it must be the same wee lass that I had heard years earlier singing it with the same sadness. As you know, I received a letter from Lochiel of the Camerons to visit you and talk about your ancestory and the moment you spoke, I recognized your voice. The same voice that had sung *Griogal Cridhe*. Your sorrow in losing your brother, found late in life must have been almost too much to bear and so he hasn't left you and probably won't until you join him and Padruig on the other side of the veil. I am truly sorry for your loss Isobel and young Grigor," he spoke so kindly it wasn't possible to hold back my tears and Grigor came to me and held me warmly. "Ma, I love you so much and I'll do whatever you need that Da would have done," he said.

Meredith had been waiting impatiently to call everyone for lunch and was glad in the break in conversation and said, "Lunch time everyone, come and sit at the table after you've washed your hands." There was a flurry of hand washing and feeling suddenly hungry, the mob descended on the beautiful table. "Please go and eat Gillcrest. The girls have to take me to the privy," I said, so happily he said thank you and joined everyone. Helen and Isobel-Mairi took one of my arms each, as I was still felt too weak to walk unaided. I felt dizzy outside, but glad of the privy until I tried to get up. Helen and Isobel needed Padruig's assistance. I heard Helen yell out, "Da." He came out quickly. I asked him if I could climb on his back and leaning down with his aching knees, I said "thank you darling." "Hold on tight," he said. Helen's hand was on my back keeping my arisaid from blowing up and walked with us both. "He has a gift, your friend or relative, doesn't he?" he said. "Aye, he does. He's been a gift to us," I said. "I suppose in the old days before Christianity, he'd have been a High Priest of the Druids, don't you think?" Padruig asked. "The Druids haven't gone Padruig. They're still here practicing secretly perhaps," I said. "What do they practice?" he asked. "I've no idea," I responded. "A bit of what you just heard maybe, except maybe they could teach it at one time to a following. You'd have to ask him yourself," I said. "I think I've heard enough for one day. There you go love," as he put me down. "I'll walk you to the table after you wash your hands." I was still dizzy and weak, so he took my arm and Helen took the other. Both Grigor and Hugh were watching on concerned.

I was given a nice carver chair to sit in and was covered in a warm blanket. A big bowl of lamb stew with onions, potatoes and tomatoes was put in front of me. The smell wasn't appetizing at all.

Isobel-Mairi got me a hot medicinal tea. I thanked them both and some people had already finished their stew and were about to eat the pudding that Meredith had cooked. I ate as much as I could, encouraged by Padruig, who told me I was getting too skinny. "I'm too short and now I'm too skinny, Padruig Dubh. What if I started saying you're too tall or too fat?" I jested. Everyone giggled at that. "I'm tall like you love me to be and I'm not fat," he responded. "You're right, you are as perfect as you are to me and never fat my love. You just think I'm skinny because I am not wearing all of my woollen garments is all, so you can feel the bones. I am always like this, aren't I Helen?" I implored. "You may have lost a wee bit of weight Ma. Da is right. Try and eat some bread with the stew," Helen suggested. "I'll have pudding too," I said and smiled to put everyone at ease, but I really didn't feel hungry.

Hugh Mohr piped up as cheerful as anything with all that food in him and asked what time the others were expected and did I need him to slaughter anything. I don't know if it was the overall exhaustion, the word slaughter or that we were expecting guests, but it had the effect of causing me to faint. Immediately, to my right was Padruig, who stopped my head from hitting something and he asked Hugh Mohr to help him carry me back to bed. I could hear Isobel-Mairi sobbing as I was carried off and Helen followed me in to change me into clean bed clothes and wipe my face, feet and hands with heated water. "Can I come in Ma?" asked Isobel-Mairi. "Not if you're crying," was Helen's answer, "only if you're useful." Hugh Mohr left the room, laying his hand on Padruig's shoulder in a supportive way. "Whatever I can do," he said, "just say so. Do you think Isobel would want the Collies in here? She likes them," Hugh added. "If they're clean and if you're not using them," Padruig said and then continued, "can you take care of Isobel's sheep and goats? Isobel-Mairi said she'd milked the goats, but if you could do the rest, it would be a great help." "She puts the manure over on that pile near the garden too, doesn't she?" Hugh Mohr asked. "I don't know. Maybe Helen knows. I'm not used to this, where Isobel is not giving out all of the instructions of the day and checking afterwards to see if it was all done, so there's a lot I don't know that I'm finding out," I could hear Padruig say. "Sheep manure goes near my garden Hugh," I struggled to say.

"Turn it over so the new stuff is at the bottom." "Okay Isobel," Hugh responded kindly, "I'll take care of your goats and your sheep and I'll kill a coo now to cater for whoever needs feeding, so don't you worry about a thing," I heard Hugh say as I drifted off again.

Padruig was so worried about me over the next few days that he called for the aged doctor, whom I didn't like. He was sitting on my bed and I got a terrible fright at the closeness of the man. "What are you doing here?" I asked rudely. "Isobel dear, it's me Dr. Keith, do you remember me, I saw you once when you were wee, sick just like this? You've got a bit of asthma dear, on top of your chesty condition. Coffee is better than tea for that, especially black coffee," he said. "It's Mrs. Grant to you and who told you that you could sit on my bed?" I asked. "I'm sorry Mrs. Grant, I'll sit in a chair to listen to your heart and so on. Is that okay?" he asked. I grumpily agreed and scowled at Padruig. "Collies," I called the two dogs that were sitting by the fire to sit on the bed so that he couldn't. I also remembered that he was afraid of dogs.

"Okay, so I'll leave some medicine for you," the doctor said. "What medicine?" I asked as he was leaving. "Laudanum dear. Just a few drops", he said. "I'm not taking that. It's addictive," I said. "I'll leave it all with your husband" and then all I could hear was coffee, and Laudanum, and fresh air and bed rest. How I hated that man when I was wee and I still did. 'Why couldn't women be doctors?' I thought.

Days went by as I slipped in and out of sleep. Sometimes Helen would be there by my bed sketching a drawing of what looked like a new style of arisaid. She designed one for me that wouldn't slip off and it was warmer with soft leather edges protecting it from mud, rain and snow. She also designed a skirt that was double thickness wool without trying to add to hip size, in fact it split in the middle so that I could mount and dismount easily. Word had spread of my illness and a kindly old neighbour offered to make me a pair of knee-high, leather wool lined boots with matching wool lined gloves. My granddaughter and Helen took it in turns washing my long silver hair and brushing it then taking me into the sunshine when we were lucky enough to have any. Padruig read Erse poetry to me, Gillcrest Og also read Erse poetry to me, so that I could memorise it after days in bed.

I didn't have the heart to tell either of them that I had never been fond of Erse poetry.

Then Beth came and sat and knitted like we taught her when she was wee, but I thought that she had stopped doing it. She had knitted me a long neck scarf and socks. "Beth darling," I said, "how are the ponies?" "They're all good Grandma. I've moved in here temporarily to help out with your Clydesdales while Simon and John are looking after mine. Isobel-Mairi is doing a really good job with them. She had a small delivery this morning, so I went with her. Hugh Mohr is a bit obsessed about protecting you all around the clock, Grandma. You've scared the life out of both him and Grandda doing what you did", she said. "I don't need you to be judgmental too, Beth. Go back to Stratherick if you are going to pile on me as well," I said. Shocked by my assertiveness, she apologised and told me that the builders had already started on the wee Chapel. "All the footings were done days ago, with the four graves that you wanted dug," she said with a tone and an emphasis on 'four'. I rolled over with my back to her. "Go back home Beth. You don't understand," I said. "There's one more delivery, Grandma, that I can help Isobel-Mairi with. Can I stay for that?" she asked. "Nae. There's no delivery without my permission. Go home first thing and send Isobel-Mairi in here now," I said. I was angry. This was my team. When Isobel-Mairi came in to see me, she knew that she had done the wrong thing. "I'm sorry Grandma. Beth said that we should just do it, seeing that you were asleep and poorly," she said. "So, is Beth in charge of my team?" I asked her. Slumping into a chair, realising her mistake, she apologised profusely and promised not to take the team out again without my permission. "Is Beth going back to Stratherick then?" she asked. "Aye, in the morning. You were going to inherit this team Isobel-Mairi, not Beth, she has her own horses. Do you want me to change my Will or do you still want to be a teamster one day? Being in charge of your own team, when I am dead, is a big responsibility and means not being wrongly influenced. These are precious bloodlines." As Helen walked in, I asked, "Well, where were you, Helen, when your daughter took the team out without my permission?" I said whilst climbing out of bed. "I was inside sewing your arisaid Ma, when I heard the gate opening. When I went to the front porch, they had gone," Helen said visibly upset.

"You have to be punished Isobel-Mairi, for not only disrespecting me, but your beloved Mither as well, I can't bear to see her upset. For one month, you will work with the chickens, the goats, the donkey and helping your Father in the fields. You will pick potatoes, bring in the corn and help Meredith cook and clean, but no horses for a month. Helen, do you have anything additional darling?" I said. "Aye, I do," she said. "I want to introduce her to a young man with the intention for her to be married within the year." "Married? Oh Ma," Isobel-Mairi cried into her hands. "Your Father and I have someone in mind. You need a husband." Then I said, "Please write this all down Helen and we will all sign it and date it. Now, Isobel-Mairi, where is my team?" I asked her. "They're away Grandma. Already stabled and fed and the stables are locked." I still asked Helen to get Grigor to check them all, especially my old boy. "Okay Ma," she said, "I'm so sorry that my daughter has let you down. She shouldn't be allowed to drive the team again ever until she proves her trustworthiness," said Helen. I told Isobel-Mairi to go and help Meredith now.

"Helen darling, come here, don't tell anyone, but I am still weak, so this is what we'll do. First a bath, then proper work clothes and boots, then sit in the lounge by the fire. Only you will know that I am still weak, but also, I'll have none of that laudanum that the doctor left. Please tip it all out darling. It's dangerous to have around," I asked. I really enjoyed a hot bath with Helen filling me in with everything else. "What happened to my dear Mr. MacNachten?" I asked. "He left a day after you fell really ill, taking the two Highland Ponies and leaving his old pony. He said that he needed to complete the grave slabs and hurry up the builders. So, they came the next day and started. He is due here again in two day's time when the slate roof goes on the Chapel. Also, the roof for Da's Manor House was delivered up there waiting for the builders to install it, I think," she said in answer.

Chapel Saint Columba at Craskie

Ewen MacThreinfhir came to the house a few days later carrying flowers for Helen, myself and Isobel-Mairi and dressed finely in his kilt wearing knee-high leather boots. He had been expected by our

immediate family and Hugh Mohr, still armed with his long rifle.
Gillcrest Mohr MacNachten, God bless him, had also arrived earlier
delivering the slabs for all four of
our graves built into our new
Chapel, which he suggested we call
Chapel St Columba at Craskie. He
had already built its wee sign in the
front, so I guess he took me literally when I had told him to choose
it that day.

The roof of the Chapel was on and
looking grand. The wall panels had
all of the names of those who were
in our cemetery, God rest their souls,
engraved onto a black marble stone
background. On each panel, stood St Columba looking very heavenly.
The pews were made from local wood and polished up professionally.
Padruig was so impressed. Both he and Hugh Mohr assisted me up
there, with Helen. I sat in there and wept with the joy of it and dedicated it to God. Gillcrest sat near me and asked if I had looked at
the tomb slabs yet and as I hadn't, with Padruig's approval, carefully first led me to Helen and Grigor's, explaining of course that
the date of death would be added at the time of death. Then he took me
to Padruig's which was so much longer than ours, but beautiful with
floral motifs on each corner. Then he said, "This is yours my dearest Isobel." "Oh," I was aghast, "Gillcrest" and I hugged the small
framed man. "You did this?" I said, "Aye, my family used to make
them all the time, but I hadn't been asked until recently when you
did," he said. Mine was a mixture of a Pecht theme with the cup
and rings all across the top, then running diagonally across the stone,
were my eight Clydesdale horses. They were my team pulling a carriage
with me as the teamster. Then on the bottom right hand corner were my
first three goats atop a rock. Billy and his two nannies, looking regal.
My name was written beautifully with both MacGregor and Grant,
daughter of Freya and John, wife of Padruig Dubh Grant, Sister
of Grigor MacGregor, Mither to Patrick, Helen and Alexander,
Grandmother of many. My birthdate with the death date left off.

Hugh Mohr donated a lovely candelabra to the Chapel and he frequently lit candles for his brothers Alexander and Donald in the Chapel. Patrick, our son, donated a long Turkish floor rug that ran between the pews. The Priests from Edinburgh, when they came, were

happy to donate bibles, prayer books and promised to send a Priest up once a month to start with, if it suited us on a Sunday morning and committed themselves to doing all of our baptisms, weddings, funerals and confessions. They also wanted to donate two hundred pounds to the cost of the building, which Padruig declined politely as he wanted the ownership to remain in our names on Craskie Farm and for there to be no doubt about the ownership. We also agreed that Episcopalians could also meet there once a month with the Reverend Stewart, but only if they workers from our farm. The four Priests, some old and some young, had stayed for lunch and thankfully left soon afterwards to get back to Edinburgh in their own carriage.

My dear Padruig was happy to part with his two-thousand pounds, which he gave to Gillcrest Mohr, but asked him about the stained glass windows, which were quite numerous and whether he had factored them into the final price. "Not exactly," was Gillcrest Mohr's reply. "Thought so, I've seen the cost of these things and how about I give you this?" He gave Gillcrest Mohr a wad of notes, which must have been a lot, because Gillcrest tried to return it to Padruig, who said, "Nae, nae, 'tis yours and your men. What a wonderful job you've all done, and you've made my wife happy. What price can you put on that? It's the first time that I have seen her happy like this in a while now. God bless you my dear friend. You are always welcome here," Padruig said sincerely.

Inside the Chapel, of course my mind went straight to that young man, Ewan MacThreinfhir and I hoped that our Chapel's first wedding would be Isobel-Mairi with Ewan. Being in the Chapel invigorated me then and I decided that I could walk back home, unaided and check in on my goats and sheep. They all cried out big hellos to me. "Oh, my darlings," I said, "I've missed you so much. Has Uncle Hugh been looking after you?" Of course, with the 'Uncle Hugh' part, Hugh rolled his eyes and decided that he would just go along with it, but said to Padruig, "So I suppose you'd be Daddy then?" grinning. Padruig didn't make fun of my way with beasts, he had long learned that in some way, unbeknownst to him, that it worked.

"So, Hugh, about Ewan. He seemed like a nice enough lad last night," Padruig said. "Aye, I've worked with him for two clipping seasons and he is the strongest man that we've got, so when there's a struggling sheep that doesn't much like the idea of a wash in the icy water, we get Ewan to do those ones. Strong as an ox he is," Hugh answered. "What's his friend like? Good or bad influence?" Padruig asked. "For what I need in a clipper, he's quick, doesn't injure the sheep, doesn't complain or gossip and follows orders. So, he is great as a worker. For your needs though, with a lassie involved, I'd have to say that he wouldn't be the best influence. He drinks away his wages and I hear he's been whoring too in Edinburgh", Hugh answered. "Has he taken Ewan with him to whore, I mean?" Padruig asked "Nae, nae. I wouldn't have suggested him if he'd been a drinker, a gambler, whorer and so on. I'd kill him if I caught him at it now while you're in the middle of talks between you and Isobel-Mairi. She's not an easy nut to crack. I almost felt sorry for him that night. He tried really hard. Mind you, I stuck my rifle in his back," he said.

"They're both border landers with family there. I've written to his parents and other Chisholms who still live there, to make sure that he is not already married and doesn't have a love child somewhere and also requesting their permission to court. I've added that there is no cost to them, given that they are crofters and must be struggling. Just the same, some of the border landers can be crafty and might want a slice of the pie, so to speak," said Hugh. "Do you think that they could be of that callibre from his conversations with you?" asked Padruig. "The lad has said that his Mither still attends Kirk frequently, Papist, but no mention of Da going to confession or Mass or such like. He said that his Father drinks whiskey, which was one of the reasons he left. His Da was violent with him and his Mither, so all of the other siblings left home because of him," Hugh said. "How violent?" Padruig asked. "Well Ewen stays in my house, so when he washes, you can see the scars all over his body," Hugh answered solemnly. "But if you have your doubts about him, I'd never forgive myself if he hurt young Isobel-Mairi," he said.

Broken Fingers

"Padruig, while we're chatting on this topic, there's a wee detail that you might need to know. I haven't married because when you were taken to New France, Grigor Mohr, Donald and I got together to decide what would happen to Isobel, the bairns and the land too, if you died over there or decided not to come back, which nearly happened. Grigor and Donald were already married and so it was agreed between us three, that despite the age difference between Isobel and I, that I would marry her if you had died or didn't come back. She needed the protection and we wanted to do that for you to protect your wife and bairns and the land. Now, thank God you didn't die, because it would have been a hell of a job convincing Isobel but I got used to the idea that she'd be my wife. That having being said, I'd do it again just for Isobel mind, so what you need is someone like that, who's willing to sacrifice themselves for Isobel- Mairi. I'll leave it with you", Hugh Mohr said.

"Now Hugh, I know that I'm getting on in years and I may have misheard what you just said, so I'll need to clarify it to be sure that I understood. You were going to marry my wife Isobel. Is that right?" Padruig asked. Hugh Mohr, knowing then that he was looking at the face of Padruig Dubh, which had now blackened with rage, said, "Padruig, now please don't misunderstand. It didn't happen and we were only looking out for her and remember that you're not young anymore, it's best not to throw fists around or you could hurt yourself. But if you do this time I won't hit back. I don't want you to be injured.

I'm younger and stronger than you are now. Why don't you take some time out and think about what I said clearly? It was a back up plan that the three of us had if you had died, not just because I fancied Isobel. And I'll still marry her and take care of her when you die, no matter how old we all become," he said.

At the mere mention of fancying and marrying me, my poor enraged husband tried to land a punch on Hugh Mohr's chiseled bony features, only to really hurt his hand. "Your bloody face has metal for bones!" my poor sorry man said, cradling his injured hand. I was watching on when I heard the last part of their conversation and I knew that he had to hit Hugh or else he'd explode. I sat down on a rock after all, almost in disbelief what Hugh had revealed. Taking it all in, I then wondered if Padruig's hand was broken or just his fingers. "Darling", I said, "is your hand broken do you think? Does it need splinting? Gillcrest Mohr said that he could help." Back at the house Gillcrest asked for comfrey leaves and vegetable oil and did a fine job of splinting Padruig's fingers. "Might be a week or more before the swelling goes down, but it was worth it, wasn't it? She is worth a sore hand for sure and I heard bits and pieces of what was said and I think Isobel would have stayed a widow if you'd died. There's no one but you in her heart. Isn't that right dear Isobel?" said Gillcrest. "Hugh wasn't even born when we met," I responded, avoiding the answer. "That's right, he hadn't even been born," Padruig managed to say between the "oh's" and "ah's" as Gillcrest realigned some of his fingers. "Some are just dislocated. That's a good thing. Only two are broken, but I would avoid hitting Hugh's face in the bony parts. My Da always said to aim for the soft parts, so that it wouldn't hurt so much", Gillcrest said with a smile. Gillcrest was looking thoughtfully at me realizing there was a dangerous secret that he had stumbled upon. One that Hugh was rather brave to speak of given how jealous my husband was, even at our ages.

"Good thing that the Priests had already gone Ma", said Helen. "Why is that Helen? Are you judging your Father?" I asked sternly. "Nae Ma, sorry Da. Can I help you Uncle Gillcrest?" she said. "Aye love, more comfrey please," Gillcrest said and Helen ran off to get more comfrey. "I envy you both for sure," said Gillcrest Mohr, "such an enduring love is hard to find. You are both very blessed." When Helen came in, she was followed by Hugh Mohr and his Collies and he asked if he could come in. "Maybe tomorrow old friend, while I take it all in," Padruig answered. "I am sorry family. I have never had a way with words and I cause stramashes with my big mouth," Hugh said. "I forgive you Hugh," I said. I felt pleased somehow that the most handsome man on Craskie farm would still marry me at my age, even after my recent mistake.

He turned and went home with his Collies looking sad. Hugh Mohr was sitting on the stone near the new Chapel when Grigor Og was finishing off his work in the fields. "Nice Chapel, isn't it Uncle Hugh?" he said, not knowing of what had happened. "Are you coming down for lunch?" Grigor asked. "Not today lad, I've some letters to write to that family about Ewen MacThrienfhir. What did you make of him Grigor?" asked Hugh Mohr. "I liked that he took my son-in-law, Gillcrest MacLachlan's advice about that wee soil course that they held in Inverness, so he can be more knowledgeable about aspects of farming, as well as being a farrier I mean," Grigor replied. "He's a farrier? Does your Ma know?" Hugh Mohr asked. "I don't know. We were just chatting and he said it was his stock and trade, but didn't have a forge to do his smithy work here," he answered. "Can you please tell your Ma and Da that Ewen is a farrier when you go down for lunch? Maybe we should get this lad back for a longer chat," Hugh said. "Well, strictly speaking, he's a blacksmith and a farrier," added Grigor. "If we could get my daughter interested in him with his work with horses rather than sheep, she would like him more, wouldn't she?" Grigor asked hopefully. "Aye." Hugh replied. Then both men departed with a spring in their steps.

"Ma, Da, has Meredith cooked lunch yet?" Grigor asked as he entered the house, then seeing Padruig's last stages of bandaging, he stopped and asked what had happened. I shook my head to indicate that it was improper information for my son-in-law, so Padruig said, "At my age lad, it all starts to fall to bits. Doesn't it Isobel?" and he smiled. Meredith called out, "Aye, it's been ready for thirty minutes. Wash your hands please Grigor". Meredith had become a self appointed health and cleanliness regulator. We all went to wash our hands and to eat when Grigor said that he had some important information about

Ewen MacThrienfhir just as Isobel-Mairi entered the room for lunch. "What do you know about that big oaf?" she asked. "Didn't you find him handsome sweetheart?" I asked. Helen then entered the room and said, "I did. He's a dish in a rugged masculine way." "Oh really," said Grigor, "a dish?" "Och, I didn't mean it like that darling," Helen replied as she smooched her husband. "That's better," he said as he held her by the waist and kissed her lovingly. All that kissing was too much for young Isobel-Mairi, who said, "You'll put me off my food if you keep that up Ma and Da," she said.

Asking us both how we were, Gillcrest Mohr finished up his work on Padruig's hand and he was invited to stay over, which he accepted graciously. Grigor went on to chat over lunch, that if we had a forge maybe we could have our own smithy and save money on buying tools as well as on shoeing horses. "He shoes horses?" asked Isobel-Mairi. "Aye, he's a farrier love," answered Grigor. "Can he shoe Clydesdales then?" she asked. "Why don't you ask him yourself. He is coming over again tomorrow afternoon." Grigor said. It turned out that he already had his own tools with him, just not the forge and we had just freed up a stable space. I offered that free space if it was big enough for a forge if someone could build the fire with chimney, then horses waiting to be shod could wait in the existing pen.

"Don't get too far ahead of yourselves," said Padruig. "This letter here is from the borderlands where Ewen's from and it says that the family name for that croft is Armstrong, not MacThrienfhir being an Irish name they thought. The only information I could get is that the Armstrongs, during the reign of King James V, owned vast lands and were vicious borderland fighters. The Scottish King, wanting better relations with England, had the chief and his men hung, thirty-seven men in total according to this letter. They lost all their lands to this day, so that would be why they're crofters, but the lad will need to explain if he was born Armstrong or MacThrienfhir," he said.

When Ewen arrived the next day, both Padruig and I had been resting up and enjoying reading our respective books. "Don't worry about today love. It'll sort itself out," he said to me making sure I was well enough to sit through another one of these stressful conversations. I responded by saying, "I'm just fine, I have faith that it will be the first wedding in our new wee Chapel." Ewen was greeted at the door by both Grigor and Helen and was welcomed in. Isobel-Mairi was seated looking pretty, I dare say, by the fire. She stood as he entered and said, "Hello Ewen," and he melted. At first, he couldn't speak and stumbled over his words and finally said, "Hello Isobel-Mairi. You do look fine today. Such a pretty dress too," he said.

Padruig said to me quietly, "I don't think we've any worries. They both like each other now. Let's just watch on a bit after I ask about that letter." We all drank coffee and ate scones before Padruig began. "So, Ewen, there are a couple of things that we need to clarify here today with you. Is that okay?" he asked, "Aye," he said. "Is it true that your stock and trade is blacksmithing and that you are a farrier?" asked Padruig. "Aye," he said smiling. "But I've no forge here Sir, to do me work," Ewen answered. "I have a letter from the borderlands having enquired on your background, as we don't know your family lad. In this letter, it says the family name attached to that croft is Armstrong. So, is your name MacThrienfhir or Armstrong?" asked Padruig. "Both names mean the same thing Sir, I am told. That is, it means "a strong man" in Irish or in Anglicised Scots. I was born MacThrienfhir, but Da chose to use Armstrong to be like many of the other folk living there in the borderlands. Armstrongs lost the land at the time of King James V. Homes destroyed and the like. All folk who were Armstrongs or MacThrienfhirs fought together in the vicious border wars. Da was one of them and still is, but he was a violent man in the home too. He has been in and out of prison and they probably will hang him one day. I don't have what you all have being all devoted to each other and I'd be surprised if you accepted me into your family. I am trying hard to be like you all," he answered. "What about your friend, who you work with? The one who goes whoring in Edinburgh?" Padruig asked. "I can't speak for his morals, for sure, he is immoral. He is a good worker is all and doesn't try to influence me. He knows I want to get away from the bad ways of the past and improve myself. I was hoping I could do that here but I would understand now if you ask me to leave Isobel-Mairi alone. Do I still have a job this clipping season Sir?" he asked. Both Grigor and Helen said they'd need to talk to Isobel-Mairi and Padruig and I before making a decision. Padruig said that he'd accepted the explanation of the name, but he should've told us up front that there was an

Armstrong connection. Ewen kept saying, "Aye, Sir, Aye Sir" and his head dropped lower and lower. Isobel-Mairi said, "I have some say in this don't I?" "Aye, love," said Grigor, "of course. It was our idea for you to marry soon and Ewen was recommended by Uncle Hugh. What do you want to say to this young man?" he said. Ewen looked up with wet eyes, trying to blink away tears. It was hard to look at when a big grown man like him had been brought to tears about perceived imperfection, none of which he himself had demonstrated. I really liked him and really wanted this marriage to go ahead.

Gillcrest Mohr, who was listening in intently, spoke up before Isobel-Mairi could speak, saying "Excuse me Isobel-Mairi, if I may?" and then addressed Ewen. "Son," he said, "I can adopt you as my own and give you my respectability. You can take my name too, MacNachten if you like and break away from all your borderland connections, including your friend who I suggest is moved to a farm far from here Padruig. That's my offer." I glanced at Ewen's face and saw a ray of hope appear across his handsome features and his eyes dry up in disbelief that such a kindness could possibly be bestowed on him. All eyes were on the compassionate Gillcrest Mohr then, who suggested that he take the lad to Loch Insh the following day to sort out their relationship before a legal commitment was made with my Granddaughter. Excitement was growing in the room. They left together the following morning, with Hugh Mohr having slaughtered a sheep for them. We gave them potatoes, corn, loads of neeps and kale, as well as fresh bread, butter and cheese. I felt a lingering sadness at their departure that I couldn't put my finger on it, so I asked Padruig. "Was his Father violent towards him?" Aye," he replied. "Hugh Mohr said that he is covered in scars." "What an awful story. Thank you Padruig. That was hard for you," I said. "Did you want to go and pray in our new wee Chapel?" And so, we did. Peace descended on us both and I knew everything would sort itself out with the handsome Ewen and even with Beth, who I hadn't seen since I sent her back to Stratherick. She must have been really put out. I left it all to God as I always did.

The Move

Walking back home, arm in arm, Padruig told me that the builders were coming the next day to install the roof on the Country Manor

House, and after that it would be up to Patrick to finish the interior with Henrietta and I'd be glad to see her move out of my house. They were in talks all afternoon concerning the interior, which was ultimately up to them. Their son James came over to understand his role in running the financial side of things and Beth was expected to help in the hanging of the drapes in a few days' time. Henrietta then made her displeasure known to me that I had sent Beth home when Henrietta needed her. Thank God my husband suddenly became protective of me, I thought. He told Henrietta off like I have never heard before and reminded her that Beth had no rights over Craskie Farm or Grant Farm let alone my team of Clydesdales and could never speak to me like that again. He turned to his son Patrick and said, "Son, you have to explain again to your wife that there is a border between Craskie and Grant Farms and the Manor House and that they have to honour that border as Uncle AltAn always had. Once you have all moved out, it will be invitation only or an emergency, like an avalanche that will allow your family to encroach on our farm. The Chapel, on Sundays, was the only exception and they could all still be buried on Craskie, with their names added onto the inside plaques as my wife has arranged," Padruig said.

Henrietta was pouting and demanded to know why she and Patrick didn't get a grave inside the Chapel like Helen and Grigor. "I don't have to answer that question," Padruig said calmly at first, "but I will. Firstly, Helen and Grigor will run Craskie and Grant Farms, as well as any other Craskie purchased businesses after we die without your interference. Secondly, Helen has always helped her Mither lovingly, devotedly and caringly and has never left us to live anywhere else even while suffering life in the sheiling. Thirdly, both Grigor and Helen have demonstrated loyalty and devotion to us both and the family businesses without taking extended holidays in Rome. Then there's an unquestionable trust that has always been there and on top of all of that there is the additional relationship to Grigor Mohr," he emphasised. "You, on the other hand, Henrietta left your wee bairns with their Grandma for years at a stressful time for my wife, to raise, feed and clothe, while you lived with your parents who fed and clothed you. Can you still sit there and claim the same rights as Helen and Grigor, despite my giving my son Patrick an early inheritance of that mansion at no cost to himself?" Padruig asked. "You dare to complain about a wee grave when you will live in that luxurious Country Manor House complete with luxury light fixtures and internal plumbing?" he said with a sting in his tone. One I'd recognized, years ago never to challenge.

He had only tolerated Henrietta because she could cook and keep a clean house, but 'her personality was lacking' he used to say. Henrietta knew Padruig had loads of ammunition against both her and Patrick and only decided to stop her antagonism after Patrick kicked her ankle and he said, "Da, we are both very grateful for the opportunity to own and run the Manor House with my son James and be business people going forward, but if ever the family needs me, then I am available and so is James. Aren't you James?" he said. "Of course," James said and added, "can I pop down for coffee with you on occasion Granny, or get advice on the books when I come across a sticky one?" he asked sweetly. I was listening in from across the room and first asked Padruig if I could answer honestly if it didn't hinder his exhaustive talks. "Go ahead", he said reluctantly. "James, you grew up here, my brother Grigor Mohr, taught you how to ride and we were both very fond of you. When I asked advice from him about Beth and yourself, he said to send you to college for business, which I did and paid for. He also said not to underestimate you. While Beth could breed Highland Ponies, it's true, but you had another more important role, he thought. I've always believed in Grigor Mohr's assessment of you, so it's important that you don't just work for your Father at the Manor House, but engage in a managerial role there up front, as it will be needed. You'll have staff to manage and that's not easy. So, your Father and you will need to work together and you alone are the sole inheritor of that business and its land from Patrick. Your Mither's role is advertising, public relations, cooking, running the kitchen, the kitchen staff, dining room staff, the laundry and the laundry staff that we have already pre-arranged for you," I said.

"Additionally, if Beth helps, please ask her to use the access road between James Grant's farm and the next property. That's the entrance road now to the Manor House that we have also arranged. We can't have soil from other farms, including yours, coming onto Craskie and perhaps making our animals sick. When you have guests in about a month, make it known to them that they cannot enter our farmlands due to the diseases that they have in other parts of the country," I said. "So, not even a shoe can enter Craskie from England?" Patrick asked. "That's right Patrick," I said. "There's foot and mouth disease there, that could decimate our farms. If you think I am not serious, Hugh Mohr will be patrolling the border as well as Hamish. I'll let them know that James has a free pass if he washes his shoes and explains the need to Hugh Mohr," I said "What about me Ma?" asked Patrick. "You won't need to come here son, unless there's a wedding or a funeral or attending Kirk. You will be very busy stocking up on lots of peat for a start. It's cold up there. Also, your guests cannot use our private family Chapel. If you have requests for a Chapel, you can build one up there behind the Manor House yourselves, can't he Padruig?" I said "Aye, if he pays for it himself, but I doubt he'll need one for tourists. Send them to Invermoriston or Inverness if they are desperate, just not here," Padruig said.

"Okay," I said, "if that is all you need from me, I am taking a little lie down now." I said. "Thanks Granny," said James who stood up and gave me a kiss. Such a sweet boy. I really loved the lad. Patrick and Henrietta hadn't even mentioned their daughter Sarah. It was as if she had never existed. Poor wee lass, first sent off from one boarding school to another and then a finishing school, making sure she spoke no Gaelic, only for her to fall in love with a gardener who was working in one of those big English country homes that she was decorating. Their shared interests in flowers went all the way into the local Chapel, in secret, to become Mr. and Mrs. Forsythe. Currently, she was living in Perthshire in a wee cottage on a humble wage shared with her gardener husband. The parents were ashamed of the daughter they had hoped one day would marry an Earl or a Duke or some such, as well as re-pay them all they had paid in private schooling. Without even trying, our Morag-Freya had married herself a Laird. We always invited Sarah to things, but she never came, fearing her Mither. I wondered if she would ever come to our funerals? Probably not, I concluded. Then I was so tired I slept for hours and my Padruig lay beside me for a nap too and surprisingly, we caressed each other like that until it was time for dinner. Hugh Og had brought my sheep in and Hamish was seen helping out more. Apparently, they'd had a problem with

Lilias living with them, so eventually they had to ask her to move back with her parents. She could continue working at the school, but not to disturb Hamish and Cora. That was why Hamish hadn't been seen around as much. Apparently, he'd been taking care of Cora, who was afraid of being left alone with the girl. It was nice to see Hamish again, I'd missed my wee fisher lad who was now 6'7" and broad as was braw. He had put on weight and Cora was expecting her first child very soon. "This might be our first Baptism in the wee Chapel," I said to her and she was thrilled.

We had temporarily lost sight of what was happening with Ewen and Gillcrest Mohr until after the Manor House was completed and all of the interior furnishings were in place. Patrick's family and Beth all used the side road as instructed. It was all busy up there for two weeks and I was glad that it wasn't me. "Are you proud of it Padruig?" I asked him. "Your dream house is finally completed and you're happy to stay here on Craskie?" I asked. "Aye, I'm pleased. It's an achievement like your wee Chapel," he said with a cheeky smile. "But its like asking you if it was worth the beating to get your wee Chapel. There's a degree of suffering in any achievement," he said. He was still a sexy man and sleeping beside him now or at seventeen, felt the same. He kissed me passionately and rubbed my bottom where the leather strap had been. "Did it hurt very much?" he asked for the first time, thoughtfully. "Of course, but I hurt myself by my actions. When Da put me over his knee, to spank me and whip me, he had rightly called me a naughty girl and I was devastated at his words more than the pain of the whipping. I crawled into their bed that night to hug him and ask forgiveness. I was so relieved when he told me I was still his good little girl. I'd often crawl into their bed after that, even when you and I were married," I said. "I still wanted them to cuddle and kiss me. Didn't you sleep with your parents?" I asked. "Nae, the opposite, I had to grow up fast to 'become a man' they said," he said. "After you and I had sex did you tell them?" he asked. "Aye, the first time I was in pain still and bleeding. Do you remember the blood? So, once you had left they both put me in a bath and bathed me so it wouldn't get infected and it took away the pain. After that they would always ask me, so I told them the truth and they bathed me each time. Why are you asking this now?" I said. "Because of the beating. Do you want to talk to Hugh Mohr about the beating then?" he asked. "It might take away the pain," he said as he kept rubbing my bottom. "I'd like you to keep doing that, then I will feel better. Do you still love me Padruig?" I asked. "Aye of course I do, then I'll have to rub you some more to convince you," he said and before long, I was giggling as we ventured into the night exploring our love anew. "I still want you to talk to Hugh though. He has ideas," he said. "It's hard for me to look him in the eyes now. I have shame but if you insist I'll talk to him," I said.

The next few days saw a slowing down of activity at the Manor House and they were ready to welcome their first guests. Not my kind of life at all, but I hoped it was all going to make them some money. It would certainly give them prestige living in a fine country home. They had an opening night, which we reluctantly attended and came home early. Hugh Mohr and Hamish were standing guard on our border, God bless them, even we had to wash our shoes before walking back onto Craskie. I was helped delicately so as not to unbalance me. Hugh Og said, "Can I help you back Mistress? Your husband on one arm and me on the other?" Padruig approved, in case we tired out on our way back in the cold air. "Weather coming Mistress," he said. "Stoke up your fires and I'll close up your shutters and check all the animals," he said. "I'll send Meredith back lad to yours as soon as she's finished up," I said. "God bless you Mistress."

It was a stormy cold night, with blustery wind that could blow over trees. At breakfast, Grigor was anxious to check everything and open up the shutters again. He told us it was a bit of a mess, but they'd all fix it. No trees down this time but a lot of branches which was always great fire wood. "Is the Chapel alright?" I asked. "No broken glass?" I asked. "Nae, nae. The shutters covered over the glass and the roof's still good Ma. No leaks that I can see," he said. "Alright, can you ask Hugh Og please Grigor to take the cattle over to another part of our pasture and bring them back later? I sent Isobel-Mairi down to the apple trees to see how many apples were blown off and she came back with two buckets of apples. So, can you cook up apple pies today sweetheart?" I asked. "Visitors might come." "Oh, really? Who?" she asked. "Not sure, but you might want to do your hair and put on that new dress your Ma made you." She cooked frantically so that we had four huge apple pies and she ran off to wash and change.

Hugh Mohr and my Padruig had overcome their misunderstanding, but Padruig's hand was still healing when we were inundated with hungry men who could smell the apple pies. Meredith hurriedly had cooked up the coffee and was busy serving up apple pies when a knock came at the door. As beef was being prepared for the later meal with loads of potatoes, Meredith was still busy in the kitchen. Isobel-Mairi took the opportunity to answer the door, but whoever it was, had left her not only speechless, but almost frozen on the spot. I think her Mither must have seen her run to the door and went to help her speechless daughter.

It was the awaited, handsome Ewen, accompanied by dear my Gillcrest Mohr who had finally bought himself some new shoes. "Please come in gentlemen," I heard Helen say and at the same time, Grigor hastily came to see who it was. Padruig seemed to know, as did I, but what had they achieved? This was going to be interesting. Padruig stood when Gillcrest Mohr entered the room. "Welcome my friend, there's apple pie if you're hungry and coffee. Ewen," he said, "are you hungry lad? There's a few folk you haven't met yet." He took Ewen over to the table and introduced him to Hugh Og, Hamish and "you know Hugh Mohr." They all seemed pleased to meet each other. "Are you one of the clippers?" asked Hugh Og. "Aye," replied Ewen. Then Grigor said out loud, "He's a farrier, a smithy no less." The men were very impressed at his qualifications as Ewen tried to play it down in his way. Padruig and I, with Gillcrest, thought it better to sit at the table and join in what was to come next as Helen and Isobel-Mairi watched on all ears and wide eyed. It was obvious that she didn't think of him as an oaf anymore, but a gorgeous looking young man and single.

Gillcrest Mohr started chatting at first over how lovely the apple pies were and asked who had cooked them. Shyly, Isobel-Mairi said, "It was me. I cooked them." "Did you?" said Ewen, very impressed. "You're a fine cook Isobel-Mairi for sure." She smiled and relaxed at that and sat between her Mither and Father at the table in great anticipation. "So, Gillcrest, my friend," said Padruig, "do you have news from Loch Insh?" he asked. "I do," he responded. All ears were waiting on the news from Loch Insh, but it hadn't stopped them from devouring the apple pies. I tried some too and they were good. She's a good cook, I thought.

Ewen MacNachten

Relaxing into what was now a familiar family environment with all of its many different personalities, our dear Mr. MacNachten commenced his well thought out statement and said with some pride in his voice. "Young Ewen here is my son, all legal, so he has my name. He is now Ewen MacNachten with no ties to the borderlands. Of course, there's not much to inherit when I die, because I rent my croft there at the loch, but there's my business if he wants to learn the craft. Now it is over to you Grigor, Helen, Padruig and Isobel, if you'll accept my son as an applicant in marriage to Isobel-Mairi MacGregor," he said.

I saw Helen nudge her husband to respond, so he stood up and in front of all of us said, "I, Grigor MacGregor, in front of these witnesses, hereby officially accept the application for marriage from Ewen MacNachten to my daughter Isobel-Mairi MacGregor, the outcome of which, however, is yet to be determined. If both parties agree to marriage, my wife Helen and I agree also and for the wedding to be held in the new Chapel Saint Columba at Craskie. May God bless the outcome of the efforts of all the parties concerned." We were all then asked to sign a document outlining thus far as witnesses. Then he added, "No other males can approach my daughter now from this day forward until this matter is concluded. Thank you Ewen. Thank you, Mr. MacNachten," he said as he sat down again as a proud Father. I saw the familiar mist marking the presence of Grigor Og's Father. He was proud of his son and proud of his granddaughter and so it had received his blessings. As usual, Padruig sensed I was looking beyond Grigor Og and my hand had stopped moving. He spoke quietly then to me, almost in a whisper, "Does he approve?" "Aye, he does," I said. Finally, Padruig saw the benefit of seeing some ghosts at least.

"This might be our Chapel's first wedding," I said very quietly. "I hope so," he said, "then there's only Aonghus to go." Secretly, Padruig had ordered a forge from Fraser's Trading Post, which was hidden in the spare pony stall. So, he then arose to speak. "I'll nae interfere with whatever trade young Ewen here wants to pursue going forward, but there is a forge for a blacksmith now inside the spare pony stall, still awaiting assembly. The yard is suitable for the horses waiting to be shod. If you are interested Ewen, you can be the official farm blacksmith," he announced. "Horses from other farms can't enter Craskie now as you know, as we have strict quarantine control. That won't prevent Ewen from going to the farms to shoe other people's horses as well as ours, provided he, when re-entering Craskie, goes through the whole quarantining process, including the horse that he rides."

"Gillchrest Og MacLachlan, my Grandson-in-law, is the head scientist now located in the nearby Invermoriston Hospital and has need for scientific tools also to be made from time to time. He is now permanently based there with a house provided for him with my Granddaughter Morag-Freya. Tools of many kinds will be needed even axes and shovels and knives, I am sure, to keep Ewen busy and if he has spare time, perhaps he can also assist with my wife's Clydesdales as I understand Hugh Og is now the head teamster. It will be up to my wife who does what with her team. Don't make the mistake of not getting Isobel's permission always concerning the Clydesdales. Thank you," Padruig said.

Hugh Mohr, having finished his delicious apple pie said, "Come on Ewen, I'll show it to you and you can say if it's any good or not," he said with a very cheeky grin, happily leading the recommended strong young man out to the stable where the forge had been hidden. It must have been alright, because over the days and weeks that followed, more tools were seen hanging from the roofing of the stall and there was lots of banging. Then, one by one, Hugh Og brought down my Clydesdales when Ewen was ready and on my instructions. All eyes were on him. These horses had big hooves, but a man that strong with a Clydesdale had no trouble at all. All their hooves and shoes needed attention, but overall, he was impressed at how well kept my Clydesdales were. He checked their feathers around each hoof expecting to find that I hadn't looked after their feathers, but I had of course.

There was a lot of bang-ing and hissing when he was making the big shoes, but it really impressed Isobel-Mairi. Her month was nearly up and so after they had all been shod, I had to come up with a plan to allow her to work with the Clydesdales somehow along-side Hugh Og again. As both Ewen and Isobel-Mairi spoke more to each other and observed each other's gifts and talents, their love grew. One day, he was better dressed and not wearing his leather apron

or chaps and asked me if he could talk to Helen, Grigor, myself and Padruig and Mr. MacNachten, or Da as he called him, in order to ask for Isobel-Mairi's hand in marriage. She said, "Aye." And a wedding date was set in my trusty calendar.

I wrote to the Catholic Priests in Edinburgh and asked them to con-duct a wedding, possibly a baptism too and definitely a number of confessions. Preferably, also to bring prayer books in Gaelic and the old Gaelic Bible too — which they did. We received a pile of old Gaelic prayer books and bibles, no longer in use, and the young couple were married. Cora's baby, named Donald Alexander, was baptised and around fifteen people went to confession, including Padruig, Hugh and I.

Aonghus had finally brought along a lady friend whom he had met by chance while visiting Gillcrest Og and Morag-Freya in Invermoriston. She was a nurse also and lived in the nursing accom-modation at the hospital. They shared some interests, like tennis, so the four of them played doubles at the Invermoriston hospital tennis court. He had introduced her as Annabel Cameron, unrelated to Lilias' family. While Father Michael was still there, the Priest commented that he may need to come fortnightly if it suited us, with how much demand there was. Even married couples were asking if they could renew their vows. We considered it, but it had all been done properly in the first place, so we only talked about our funerals, which would be in the near future, which everyone refused to believe.

I also took the opportunity to ask the young Priest about an old musical instrument that the early Papist Kirk once used in the Kirk and it was called the Hurdy Gurdy. The organ replaced the hurdy gurdy, so I asked could we have one if there was one just lying around idle. The nice young Priest, whose name was predictably Father Michael, said he'd never heard of that instrument, but he'd take a look when he went back to Edinburgh and ask those who might know what it was and where to look for it and where we could get it at no cost. "That'd be grand," I'd said. He chatted to Aonghus, who was around the same age and had asked his occupation.

Aonghus had already graduated with his law degree and had been offered the Malcolm Law Office in Inverness by our old lawyer. Surprisingly, he'd been going to decline the offer, but upon meeting Annabel in Invermoriston, he wanted to be in close proximity to her, as well as us. Our poor old lawyer was too old now to keep up the pace and was happy with his achievements. He thanked both of us for our business and returned the remainder of Padruig's pay from Quebec. He really wanted his business to go to Aonghus MacGregor, of whom he was so fond, having never married and not having had children of his own. In fact, he was very fond of our whole family. No cost was mentioned in buying the business and so I was yet to find out about that, but I invited him to our home always in his retirement and said he was welcome.

In bed that night, as usual, we read a little before blowing out the candles. I turned to my husband and said happily, "Another marriage Padruig." "The miracle is, sweet Isobel, that Aonghus turned up with a pretty lass. Annabel with one 'l,'" he said. "Aye, she is pretty and did you take notice how black her hair was? Like ours," I said. "Aye, maybe she's from the Ewen Dubh Cameron branch of the family. A distant relative of mine. He had that same black hair too. She is not as pretty as you though Dath-thula," he said and blew out the candles with that smile on his face. "Darling," I said, "who were the lad and lass with the wee bairn talking to James?" I asked. "That must have been Sarah, his sister, and her secret husband, Duncan Forsythe. Now can't you concentrate on my gorgeous body?" he joked. We could still make heavenly love, even in our eighties and I thanked God for that gift. Slower was even better than when you're young and too hasty, even with Padruig's sore hand. He asked me if I'd spoken to Hugh yet but I hadn't.

In the morning when I awoke and Padruig was still sleeping peacefully. I didn't want to disturb him, but I ran my fingers through my dearest's hair and caressed his face then covered up his big arms so he wouldn't get cold. Lighting our bedroom fire, Helen knocked very quietly and told me that Hugh Mohr had taken care of the sheep today and would be busy cutting up a big coo for everyone. I was reminded I needed to have that talk. He was becoming accomplished at tanning now too, so there'd be a line of coo hides, strung up in their various stages of development to become a nice floor rug one day. Hugh Mohr would keep the head of a coo and eat the brains himself, when all of us refused to. He said the Prince once ate coo brains and cooked it for them one night mixed into a bannock mixture. It sounded horrible, but it also sounded like survival food. I doubt that Prince Charles Edward Stuart ever told his friends in France or Italy about how he had had to survive covered in lice, let alone eating coo brains mixed in with flour. Padruig said it was quite good, but he'd always been easy to please unlike Donald Chisholm, who had been a fussy eater and always taste tested the food and hated Cora's cooking. Padruig, on the other hand, would just eat it. You'd know though, if he really liked it by the smile in his eyes, so I always aimed for that smile to please my man. I asked him one day if the Prince really did eat coo brains and he said aye, it was true and told me the whole story. Somehow the image of Bonnie Prince Charlie didn't match the brain eating chef who carried the head himself until they ate. [12]

My New Arisaid

One day it occurred to me that we had so many grandchildren in our immediate family, that their partners and their children's names were becoming harder to remember, so I had started writing them down in a wee book just in case I forgot. Like Annabel with one 'l,' Aonghus' new love. And Duncan 'Forsythe, Sarah's husband, the mysterious gardener from Perthshire. I still didn't know their lad's name, so I guessed a name and called him John after my father even if it wasn't. I wasn't likely to see them again, I concluded.

Helen had finished all the details on my new arisaid, which had netting inside the headpiece to hold it in place on my head. It really was a clever garment and I suggested that she try and sell one in Inverness for a pretty penny. She didn't want to, because it was just for me. The whole outfit was intended to keep me warm all over. When the boots and gloves came too, I was delighted and I felt a bit too flash and maybe a tiny bit shy, so I asked Padruig if I was too flashy? He said, "Absolutely not. That's gorgeous. I love it. God bless Helen and that lovely gentleman." I didn't even know his name, so Padruig invited him to morning tea. Just two old men by the fireside. It reminded me of the night that Uncle Allan and Da sat together by the fireside and reminisced. He was a veteran of Culloden and had known Padruig Dubh well and was honoured to make his wife something that would keep away the cold. He departed with our honey and our blessings.

One oversight in Gillcrest Mohr's explanation of his adoption of Ewen though, was that he had also visited Fort Augustus to consult with the same Captain whom we'd dealt with over the stolen goods by the Irish. The visit was to inform the Captain that borderlanders by the name of 'Armstrong' could lay siege upon Craskie Farm due to whom they think is still their son working there and having married Grigor and Helen's daughter, Padruig's Granddaughter Isobel-Mairi MacGregor. He produced the legal certificate of adoption of Ewen, now named Ewen MacNachten, a respectable lad and a blacksmith. If the troops were ever to see a suspicious group of Armstrong borderlanders, he had requested that they be stopped and turned back to the borderlands.

The Captain was very familiar with the reputation of the Armstrongs and said that he and his men would stay armed and ready and would very happily turn them around. Any resistance, however, from them might result in transportation or worse depending on what Mr. Armstrong did in response. I found this out belatedly, over lunch one day when Padruig let us all know and to be watchful. I loaded Padruig's old guns up in the attic again and aimed them at the gate so that if they ever tried taking one of my family members, one of the rifles might just go off. Hugh Mohr had informed Padruig that the letter that he'd received from the Armstrongs was none too pleasant and thank God Gillcrest Mohr had the foresight to legally adopt him. The letter was abusive, threatening and of course, full of demands.

Hugh Mohr, Hugh Og and Hamish were on full alert night and day taking it in turns. Ewen was informed of what our plan of action was to which he agreed. We advised him to stay away from the gate and remain on the property for now. Thankfully it wasn't too long before the troops stopped a whole carriage load of armed Armstrongs. They were all charged at the Fort with carrying arms with intent to storm Craskie Farm. Having a copy of the adoption papers, the Captain was able to prove that they had no grounds to be there. The Armstrongs were kept overnight at the Fort prison and we were informed by a soldier at the gate whom Hugh Mohr dealt with. The whole group of ten men were being sent up to Inverness for the hearing the following morning, concerning the decision on each man's fate.

Mr. Armstrong, with his prior violent history and also having resisted arrest, was hanged as we all had expected and the rest were sent to New Holland, mapped by Lieutenant Cook whom Padruig had met in Quebec. The colony was New South Wales and completely undeveloped, so they probably regretted the day they charged off from the borderlands armed with evil intentions. I pitied whoever were the native peoples of that nation. Padruig wrote to the fort and thanked them for their diligence in protecting our community, his Grandson-in-law and Granddaughter. It was accompanied with three geese in a cage for them to have a cook-up. They chose to only eat two of them because we'd often see that goose chasing soldiers around their fort as well as fending off strangers. "Better than any guard dog," the Captain had later said to Gillcrest Mohr.

Word spread like wild-fire that we had our own Smithy and orders came in to Ewen thick and fast. Ewen became a general hardware maker, competing with John, as well as a farrier whose skill was in very high demand. He was also making nails, which interested Hugh Mohr, all kinds of hinges and door latches, andirons, hooks and cranes for fireplaces. There was a huge demand also for iron cooking utensils, such as ladles, dippers, skewers, knives, trivets, pots and kettles,[52] which started to bring lady customers from farms as far away as the Cameron lands. There were many items needed also for buggies, wagons, carts and hand cultivating tools. I frequently saw Grigor Og having parts of his plough mended. Ewen was even asked to make an anchor chain

for a fisherman. Gunsmithing was always enquired after, but Padruig asked him to wait a while longer in case we broke the law, not to say that he wasn't interested. Ewen was, however, able to make bayonets secretly for the heavy rifles, swords, dirks and skein dubhs that we all kept hidden. Everyone on the farm carried a knife of some kind, even me. All the while shoeing hundreds of horses, he had to replace his own tools as well. There are hammers, pincers, punchers, tongs and swages. Specialised tools that anyone came and asked for such as Gillcrest and his science things were frequently being made. I never asked what for.

Ewen approached me one day over coffee and asked if he could build himself a wee croft somewhere on the property for himself and Isobel-Mairi, paying rent of course on a long lease, provided everyone agreed. I didn't want any of my forest disturbed and we couldn't spare any grazing land or the crops area, so it left us with three options. The most popular location was to build another cottage next door to the existing teacher house, which was on Helen's land. Helen agreed and so did Grigor and offered to help build it provided that Hamish and Cora didn't mind having a neighbour. They were excited at the idea and also offered to help and a lovely wee cottage made of stone with a slate roof went up within the month. Even Patrick gave them furniture that he hadn't needed as well as leftover drapes and a Turkish floor rug. We all chipped in with cooking utensils and Ewen made his own set of kitchen knives for Isobel-Mairi as well as an enormous iron cooking pot. He was planning to eat a lot. I gifted them with new china, not expensive like mine, but very pretty. Helen had been making them a doona filled with goose down and goat hair. It had patches of different tartan stitched together from all of the orders they'd made and sent to Edinburgh. Hugh Mohr had been working on those coo hides for ages and finally had three stitched together with leather stitching for one of their rooms. Their lovely fireplace was the 'piece de resistance' decoratively made by Gillcrest Mohr, with Pecht engravings in each piece of stone. It was so unique and such a beautiful gift to his newly adopted son, of whom he was so proud. The chimney had been completed by Hugh Chisholm. Cora had planted flowers all around their cottage and gave them a few chickens too.

Isobel-Mairi was a different young woman being married and in her own home. They'd invite her sister around as well as their new partners to show off their new home. There was a spare room if anyone needed to stay over, which they did on occasion, separating Annabel over to my place as they were not yet married. It was obvious though that Annabel was very keen on Aonghus and he had taken over the law business after Padruig had given the old lawyer £600 to keep all of his old clients. Good will, he called it. So, he renamed it 'Malcolm MacGregor Law Rooms'. Quite catchy, I thought.

So, in our family we had a head scientist, a head nursing sister, a lawyer, a horse breeder, a blacksmith and an up and coming politician in Simon Fraser who'd had a Post Office built for us just up the road. Padruig didn't have to go far then for his pension. The road was widened as I'd requested with a three-foot-high rock wall on the other side, except where the wee burn flowed through and a wee bridge allowed it to flow on its way. My Helen was next to be launched in her Art Gallery I thought. Of course, there was our James, who was a brilliant book keeper and business manager and kept it all on track up at the Manor House. These days Patrick was selling himself as a gentleman, while he shot deer with the tourists. I was still to hear back from my son Alex who I always missed.

The Hurdy Gurdy

One week, an English tourist came to the border to complain to both Hughs about the dreadful noise coming from the Chapel one Sunday morning. It was the hurdy gurdy and Gaelic hymn singing, which was beautiful, but to him it was pure ugliness. He told Hugh Mohr to shut us all up. Of course, Hugh didn't and told the man to return to his place of residence and complain to the owner, being Patrick Grant. But then, the Englishman saw Patrick and James coming out of the Chapel once it concluded. "There he is," said Hugh Mohr. "One of the singers no doubt." Both Hughs enjoyed riling up the old Englishman, who stomped off and got mud in his shoes and swore terribly. It then began to rain heavily, so both Hughs went inside their warm house, but that old man would've been soaked right through. They didn't warn Patrick or James as they departed across the border and left them to it having a bit of a laugh.

Meredith had been learning the hurdy gurdy, but found that her harp was more to her talents and so surprisingly Ewen gave it a go, as it was played in his Kirk when he was a wee lad. The Kirk tried to help keep the lad away from his father, I think and also got him to sing. So, when he sang and played in the Chapel on that Sunday, we were all very surprised, but his wife wasn't. She was just proud. He was a big fellow with a big voice and Cora harmonized with him as best as she could and even the Priest sang along, so we all tried our hardest. We found ourselves really singing loudly and uplifted, so I suppose that is why it drew a complaint, but we didn't care. There wasn't much that our Ewen couldn't do.

Over lunch Aonghus and Annabel announced their desire for betrothal if it gained Helen and Grigor's approval, which it did. Padruig and I just looked at each other, pleased as ever. He said, however, "Where will you live Aonghus? Inverness or Invermoriston?" "I would like Annabel to stop working as a nurse in Invermoriston when we marry Grandda," he said. "She has agreed to help me with the secretarial work in my new law office and we would both live there in Inverness in the house attached to the law rooms, serviced by Mrs. Ann Shaw, the housekeeper. There's a wee stable out the back, which came with a pony and cart. We might have to modernize the laundry like you did Grandma and buy some new furniture," Aonghus said. "And drapes" added Annabel. "They smell a bit mouldy," she said. "Aonghus, you could ask Patrick if he has any drapes left over, because they purchased too many as it turned out and he gave his sister drapes for her new place and Hamish and Cora too," I said.

Hugh Mohr and Hugh Og were there and told the story of the English tourist, which got a lot of laughs, but hoped that Patrick would still be in the mood to part with drapes. "If he's not darling," said Helen, "I'll make you drapes. That's easy and Annabel can choose the colour then," she said. So, getting out my trusty calendar, a date was set provided her parents approved. We invited them over for afternoon tea with Grigor, Helen and Annabel on a day that suited everyone's work commitments. "I can take a day off," Annabel said. "If it's to talk with Ma and Da about marriage and Aonghus can bring his pony and cart and pick me up," she said. I couldn't help but notice how organised this young lady was and having a qualified nurse as a wife would certainly help them with raising children. No doubt she would keep his paperwork in perfect order, I'd thought.

New Farm

The days passed quickly awaiting the afternoon tea, with only one other unexpected disruption when the two young men, also Grant family from two properties away, came to see Padruig. Since their father, James Grant, had died, the property had fallen into complete disrepair and the young men hadn't planted any crops. We were shocked. Nearly all of their stock had been eaten by the young men who clearly didn't have farming as a priority and wanted to sell the run down place and move to one of the New France colonies inland from the Americas, now independent from Britain. It may have been Tennessee, I wasn't sure, but in the hills where Indians had once been in large numbers. They asked Padruig if he could buy the farm from them as they only needed enough money to pay for their fares. Padruig wasn't going to steal from another Grant family, so first he established exactly what was on offer. Basically, it was just land. The lads didn't want it sold to the English and wanted us to buy it if we could.

Padruig's only remaining available cash, apart from his wages, was the government compensation money given for the life of poor Aunty Margaret MacDonald. That was only £1500. "Lads," he said. "All I have is £1500, no more, paid to me for Aunty Margaret. If the fare for you both can be covered by that amount and you have no regrets, then that's my offer. I'll not be offended if you decline, as it is low, I know, for which I am sorry." The two lads both looked at each other pleased with that amount. It was obviously more than they had expected. "We accept," they said almost in unison. A bit shocked, I took over and said, "We'll get our Grandson, Aonghus MacGregor, who now did our legals, to draw it up legally for them to sign and then set a date for that meeting." We then owned James Grant's run-down farm. "We do need the grazing land Isobel," Padruig said. "Aye, I agree. For the coos. They'd love it, going there each day and back again. Would Ewen take them there and back in the evening do you think, before he starts up his banging I mean?" I asked. "Aye, maybe Ewen and Hugh Mohr with his Collies. There's sixty coos love. Too many for just poor Ewen." "Isobel-Mairi could help too," I said. "That's a good idea." So, it was arranged, our coos had extra grazing lands.

"Well, I'll get onto it darling," I said. I organised Aonghus and the paperwork with the two lads, Craig and Bruce Grant. We offered the old house to salvage between Ewen, Hugh Og and Hugh Mohr. We thought Ewen might want to add on two more rooms and an extra privy to his house in case they had a lot of bairns. Hugh Mohr sold bits and pieces as an income. Craig and Bruce Grant obtained a land grant in one of those colonies and apart from bears, they liked the wilderness. They married Indian women I heard. Our coos grew so fat and healthy that when we did sell a few at the market, it brought a very nice income that repaid Padruig the money that he had outlaid. When I gave it to him after the sale of the coos, he rejected it at first, but then decided to put it all together with the last of his wages so he would leave me a "rich widow" he said jokingly. He asked me again if I'd spoken to Hugh yet and as I'd kept putting it off, I said I'd go then.

Hugh was busy tanning, so I excused myself and said "Hugh, do you mind if we speak a while, Padruig has asked me many times. I'm sorry if you're busy, I can come back another time," I said. "Come into my house, Isobel, out of the wind. I've been expecting you, he said. I followed him into Chisholm House, which I had never seen the interior of and wasn't expecting a spotless, well kept home. "It's lovely in here

Hugh," I said. He was washing his hands thoroughly, so his back was to me when I spoke. The collies were pleased to see me and I patted them but he wanted them in another room, and closed the door behind them. I was getting nervous, I confess. Hugh felt different and somehow more mature and he didn't have any cheekiness about him at all. I knew I needed to ask forgiveness again as we hadn't seen much of each other after he had been given the task to punish me that awful night. "Well?" he said, "what do you want to say?" he asked obviously waiting for me to have all of the dialogue. I became a bit tongue tied. "Will you please forgive me Hugh?". He automatically lifted up my dress to see how it had healed and without planning to cry, floods of tears came rolling down my face and I begged him not to hate me as he meant so much to me. He had an arm chair that looked comfortable and sat in it. I felt so isolated and alone without his usual friendly responses. Would he totally reject me now? "How long has it taken you Isobel to come to me after handing me the whip that night?" he asked. Gingerly I approached him and knelt on the floor in front of him and said "Too long I know, I couldn't face you with my shame," I said. "Lay across me," he demanded. Laying across him he began feeling my scars and the bruises as well as all the red marks that hadn't gone away. Hugh kept rubbing my bottom and said the pain would go away now, then he lifted me to his face height. "My name Chisholm has to be added to your tombstone now Isobel", he said with an authority I'd never heard in him before and I agreed it would. That seemed to make him happier, as he then lay me on the couch and began to satisfy himself like a man starved of water in the desert. Reaching my climax he then entered his manhood inside and thrust again and again. "Do you love me Isobel? Tell me now, I have to know," he demanded. "Yes, Hugh. I've loved you since the loch," I answered. "You're going to be mine, Isobel". My hands explored his handsome face, his lips, his eyes, such a beautiful blue. It was agreed that I would live and care for Padruig in my home, while Hugh would have access to me without his knowledge, then after Padruig's death, he would marry me and move in to my house, so the family should know soon. "I suspect Grigor knows already since our swimming lesson," I said. "I'll talk to him first then", he said. I held him tightly, it was like a dream remembered. His soft lips constantly kissing mine, I was so relieved that I was at long last forgiven and loved again. While standing, I loved feeling his hand inside me and rubbing me back and forth with his other arm held me across my breasts." You have always been known as the most beautiful woman of the Highlands, even with silver hair you are more beautiful than any woman I have ever seen," he said. Then kissing my face all over, his tongue seeking out my mouth and exploring, both hands squeezing my breasts he pushed my head down to his manhood and put it in my mouth for his pleasure. I had never done that before, so I was a bit unsure of myself. "Have you never done this?" he asked. "Nae, I'm unsure what I am to do?" I said. He showed me what he wanted me to do and what would make him happy. "Your husband never asked you to do this?" he asked. "Nae, my Father would sometimes ask me to play with his in the bath when I was wee but that's all. I was a virgin marrying Padruig you see and I was bleeding and it hurt every time he came home until after I'd had my first child". How old were you when you first married?" he asked. "I was nearly forteen years old, so thirteen and his manpart felt very big then, but I had some growing up to do as well. I'm a bit embarrassed to tell you that. I'm sorry I'm not very experienced for you Hugh, I'll do what you ask if you show me". I said. He held me so tight never wishing to let me go and kissed me lovingly. "You are perfect for me, my darling Isobel. Just lay your beautiful body on top of me," he said and we both fell asleep together. Woken suddenly from a blissful sleep, my heart raced when I heard," Ma, Hugh, Da's coming! You'd better get dressed now!" I heard Grigor saying with a large degree of stress and urgency in his voice. He helped me put on my boots, while I put on my dress and Hugh got dressed just as Padruig arrived. I sat at the wee dining table opposite Hugh wiping back my hair back from my face and hoping that it wasn't messy, while Grigor was making tea for us all as the anticipated knock came on the door and in walked Padruig. "Hello Da, just in time to join us for smoko. Coffee or tea?" smiling, he asked. "Tea today lad' he said. Hugh invited him to sit down in a friendly tone. "Milread's made some biscuit Grigor, let's party. They're up there in a tin with Bonny Prince Charlie on the front?" said Hugh smiling at the irony and we all sat and ate all of Milread's biscuits and drank tea and the atmosphere was friendly. "Did you have anything you needed Padruig, I don't ever see you here?" Hugh asked. "Just my wife, then we'll take our leave but thankyou for the hospitality," he said. And Padruig and I left arm in arm strolling back to the house visiting my goats and sheep on the way there. We left Grigor and Hugh to fill each other in and hoped it would all be accepted by my beautiful son in law.

Of course, life doesn't always run as smoothly as you'd like it. Nursing sisters have patients who die, scientists have experiments that fail, lawyers lose an occasional fight in the courts, but that's life. As long as the good held the balance, which it did. Padruig's hand healed, but he still loved his friend, Hugh Mohr. With John Campbell MacDonald long in the ground, it left Hugh Mohr as the last of the Seven Glenmoriston Men after himself. Padruig had never heard again from his beloved Prince Charles Edward Stuart and I wasn't surprised, but he still loved him, which I confess I had never understood. Not even my late old Da understood after the overall damage the Prince had caused our culture permanently. Da never forgave the Prince and my husband never stopped loving him. I think I hated him, but daren't upset my husband's feelings so I never told him that. I was the last of my generation of women left to tell the story as we knew it, but often silenced for the good of peace. Some things were best left alone in a marriage. I always knew where my limits of persuasion reached with Padruig and it stopped at Prince Charles Edward Stuart, unless I was happy to hear the story he had to tell in a positive light. I couldn't forgive the loss of the Gentle Lochiel and all his Camerons and then the men of Glenmoriston and Mither. The rest was endless. 'May God give me a forgiving heart,' was my continuous prayer.

It had become increasingly obvious that Hugh Og and his wife, Meredith, would need their own home. When Padruig bought the 'New Farm' from the Grant lads, I had first put the idea to him of Hugh Og building his own place on that land keeping it more secure from southern land grabbers and giving them more privacy for themselves. He had agreed in principle, but wanted to be certain while also obtaining Grigor's agreement on it. His concern was that the MacKenzie family still hadn't made peace with Meredith and Hugh Og and didn't want a future problem.

On the books, the new farm's name became "New Farm" and therefore part of Craskie and Grant Farms to be inherited, after Padruig's and my deaths, by Grigor and Helen MacGregor. They both agreed to having a long-term tenant on the land so long as it was built at the rear of the land, thereby maximising the grazing area. Hugh Og Chisholm and his wife, Meredith, were agreed upon provided they built the home themselves and paid a minimal rent to Craskie Farm and also guaranteed that there would be no future problems with Meredith's parents. Their jobs on Craskie and Grant Farms would still be secure and they agreed to the terms, including keeping the peace.

Having Hugh Og as head teamster working with my Clydesdale team suited him location wise as it was an easy walk to the stables from there. Stable workplaces had their hierarchies, but ours seemed more hierarchical than most. Hugh Og and Isobel-Mairi were at the top of course, then Bruce Mackay the groom, then Dougal the junior groom, but the addition of the new young lad Charlie MacKichan to work on the manure piles on all three farms, had earned him the title of "poo boy" from the others. I asked Helen to write him down in her wee pay book as "apprentice soil specialist" to work under Grigor instead of Hugh Og and it gradually stopped. He was only eleven years old and was paying for his own schooling.

His first task was to move the huge pile of manure out the front of New Farm to the back into two large pre-made wooden contraptions separating the older manure from the new. I'd ordered the kelp from the coast to add to it also and knew Grigor would need it soon. The very large pile inside Craskie Farm was so large that it couldn't take anymore, so the lad had to cart chicken, horse, sheep, coo and goat manure everyday up to New Farm. Hugh Og made another wooden contraption for the manure on Craskie having two sides for the old and new as well and Charlie worked hard for tuppence a day and was able then to pay Cora for his school lessons.

After the kelp arrived, I let Grigor know over dinner what had been achieved with all of the manure and he was relieved. He had two fields that he needed fertilised the very next day. "Who's Charlie?" he asked. "He's your apprentice soil specialist, son," I said with a smile. "What would I do without you Ma?" he said and gave me the biggest wet kiss and it was then that I knew he had accepted what he had seen that day. He knew about Hugh Mohr and loved me the same. I told him that the other lads had been calling Charlie 'poo boy', so that in the pay book he was titled 'apprentice soil specialist,' but I told Grigor that there was no reason why he couldn't train the lad up to understand the basics of agriculture and the role that manure plays. Thinking about it, Grigor liked the idea of an apprentice and he certainly needed the help and the two of them seemed to get along well when I saw him giving the young wee lad instructions. The young lad thought the world of Grigor who he called 'Himself'.

Over coffee one morning Hugh Mohr said that he'd followed the young lad one day when he had finished work. "Why did you do that?" I asked. "He's hungry all of the time, Isobel, and runs out of energy too fast, so I figured he wasn't eating at home. First, he went off to his lessons at the school, so I thought I'd have to wait too long. After he left, I asked Cora about him. She said the lad was tired and couldn't concentrate on his lessons. I don't think he's eating, I've concluded," Hugh Mohr said. "Where does he live?" I asked. "By Loch Craskie in a wee croft," he said. "So, Isobel, find out if he's eating," he added. "Hugh, God bless you for caring. We'll just give him breakfast with all of us and lunch if needed without embarrassing him." The food made such a difference to that lad and he was well mannered to all of us and very grateful and washed up his bowl every time. There were a growing number of deliveries required of the team as time went on and their work had to be divided between the ploughing under Grigor's control and the deliveries under Hugh Og's control. The final decision would be Grigor's, who was the only one who really understood the crop cycle and its needs, other than Gillcrest MacLachlan. He was also the only one in the family who knew about 'the man who loved me'. I wondered when he would tell Helen or if he thought it wise not to.

The new cottage being built on New Farm for Hugh Og and Meredith was made of stone with the assistance of his brother Hamish and Ewen. Luckily, he was still able to salvage the windows and window frames for his cottage from James Grant's old house. Meredith put pressure on her husband for internal plumbing and a wee bathroom was built. Water was piped underground from the burn up at the mountain end, so poor Hugh Og had to dig an enormous trench to please his wife. She also insisted on a modern style laundry like the Manor House, with its coppers and fires. Both Cora and Isobel-Mairi helped Meredith set up the interior of the new home and Meredith's parents actually proved their eventual acceptance of the marriage and gave them new furniture, consisting of a double bed, dresser, drapes and two couch chairs, which they had delivered all the way from Kinlochewe. I think that episode had finally been put to rest and I was pleased for them all. Helen said that if her art gallery opening was a success, she would also donate a slate roof for them to replace the thatch roof that they had begun with. Meredith continued working in the house while Helen did more work on her art. From the Drover's Road, you could see the quaint stone cottage at the back of the property with smoke coming from its chimneys. New Farm was established.

Hugh Mohr rented out the room that Hugh Og and Meredith had lived in, to the young groomsman, Dougal MacDougal and his sister, Milread, who had been living in Chisholm country in a tiny croft. They negotiated cheaper rent if Milread cleaned house and cooked. She had recently joined the wool waulking group, as she was a skilled spinner and owned her own spinning wheel.

Hugh Og and Hugh Mohr built a very sturdy front gate at the entrance of New Farm and fence builders were once again employed to build a 5' high rock wall on Drover's Road as well as between New Farm and its neighbouring property. Sheep were coming, we had been warned, in huge numbers and we wanted to protect all of our perimeters, both physically and legally. Owning New Farm, we could not be thrown off it or be replaced by sheep. We asked Aonghus to confirm these legalities with our old lawyer, who was surprised at first, but gladly went over all of the paperwork with Aonghus and agreed that all was in order, but suggested that Ewen's house be listed as an additional teacher house, to give it that added protection. This would mean that Isobel-Mairi would need to do the wee teaching course to have her name registered as a teacher and occasionally teach in the school, perhaps acting as a substitute teacher while her child was young. I always liked to cover myself from multiple directions from hard-earned experience and therefore I also asked John and Simon Fraser to put it politically to the powers-that-be that our properties remained safe from any southern land grabbers. The old lawyer did mention that because our farm had been in the newspaper as a model for crop improvement and greater yield, that our connections with Gillcrest MacLachlan should be exploited to protect our farms in that way also.

Annabel's Parents and Grandfather

Annabel Cameron's parents arrived in a nice carriage to display their wealth, I thought and they didn't much like the quarantining of the wheels of the carriage and the horses hooves as well as their own shoes before entering Craskie Farm. "Bit extreme," was their first comment. I was used to these remarks, but they continued anyway and if they wanted to come off the Drover's Road that's what was required. We explained the precautions were due to the diseases down south which usually frightened them into cooperating. They were dressed well, but in English attire, no tartan. I'd expected them to be wearing tartan for a wedding discussion. My Padruig and Grigor were both beautifully dressed in their tartan kilts as were Aonghus. Helen had made Annabel a lovely tartan dress with matching arisaid, so we all looked quite different culturally, except for Annabel's grandfather who was proudly wearing his kilt. Padruig was very pleased to meet a veteran Cameron from Culloden and they sat and talked together by the fire with their backs to us and talked endlessly, leaving the rest of us to deal with pre-marital affairs.

In essence, there was no objection to the partnership because Aonghus owned his own law firm with a house attached in Inverness. Respectability was obviously high on their list of prerequisites as well as wealth and lawyers could make a lot of money if they chose to. They didn't even object to their daughter giving up nursing to work with her future husband, if it happened. Being a proud people, however, they stipulated that Aonghus appear before Lochiel of the Camerons, whom he knew well, on Cameron lands to officially ask for the hand of their daughter. "Oh Da," said Annabel. "Aonghus knows Lochiel. That's just silly," she said. "Cameron traditions silly?" he exclaimed. "I don't think so," he said. She tried to object, but to no avail. "It's no problem," said the old gent by the fire. "Let's all go now, Lochiel's at home. I saw him as we rode by," he said.

All of us that could fit, climbed into that carriage, Padruig and the old gent continued their conversation when we were in the carriage, which finally pulled up in front of Lochiel's farm, much to his surprise to see all of us. Smiling warmly at me and Padruig for helping the Camerons, he waved us all in and gave his home help instructions for coffee or tea for his unexpected, but most welcome guests. Annabel's Father had refused to listen to her about the whole history and began his whole tale of the young lawyer Aonghus MacGregor, son of Grigor MacGregor, grandson of the late Grigor MacGregor and Padruig Grant. "Don't forget Isobel of Glenmoriston," smiled Lochiel. "Now, that's a pedigree you'd be proud of. So, what do you want of me?" he asked. "Well," continued the stuffy Father, whose name was Donald. "I am to part with my only daughter with a large dowry, so how can I know for sure of this family's legitimacy without your inside knowledge and approval Lochiel?" he asked. "How much is this dowry?" asked Lochiel. "£2500," he answered, "and her teeth are all good and there is no history of miscarriages on either side of the family or mental illness," he stated proudly. I admit that this was one for the books and I would definitely write it in my diary. Glancing at Annabel though, who usually was full of self-confidence, she was deflated, embarrassed and withdrawn. Suddenly, she had become like a vase you'd examine to buy in a shop. She saw me looking at her empathetically and wanting to cry, but she held on and I nodded to her to hold on patiently. It would be over soon. Lochiel, always the cheerful one said, "Is that all for this beauty that I see before me? You've had time to put aside more than that Donald. You've spent thousands more on your sons at university," Lochiel stated. "That's true," his wife said unexpectedly, "It should be more to be the same as our sons. That would be £4000 and we have that. Why can't we give her that as a dowry, then she can decorate her new home beautifully and even buy a horse and a new carriage?" Not expecting the tables to have turned on him, Mr. Cameron said he could happily part with £4000 if Lochiel suggested it and we'd all sign on it today if he thought the family were respectable enough. At that, Lochiel directed his conversation to the elderly grandfather. "What do you think Grandda. Are the Grants and the MacGregors of Glenmoriston respectable enough for the Camerons of Lochaber? We already owe them a debt for returning one property owned by a Cameron family from a thieving ex-Redcoat. Then there's the history of Padruig here and the Prince, returning him safely to Badenoch where the Gentle Lochiel was being cared for after Culloden, who subsequently fled to France with the Prince," said Lochiel. "The Prince?" asked Donald Cameron. "Aye, the Prince. Padruig here is one of the Seven Glenmoriston Men, or have you not heard of them?" asked Lochiel. Trying then to save face, he said he did of course and he apologised for any rudeness on his part and was just wanting to make sure that his daughter was going into a good family being that she was his only little girl. "You're not losing me Da," said Annabel. "You're gaining a lawyer in the family," she smiled. "You and Ma can visit us when we're living in Inverness, can't they Aonghus?" she asked. "Of course. Your Ma might want to help you decorate. I leave the interior up to you ladies. Decorating is not my gift I am afraid," Aonghus responded, already expecting that all had been approved.

So, in conclusion, Lochiel said, "In front of these, my witnesses, I approve of the marriage between Aonghus MacGregor and Annabel Cameron for the dowry amount of £4000 to be paid by the wedding date. Isobel, do you have your trusty calendar?" Lochiel asked. "I do," I answered. So, the date was set. "Where will this wedding be held Isobel?" he asked. "We have a new private Chapel now," I answered, "called the Chapel Saint Columba at Craskie on our property, so provided everyone adheres to the quarantining and the washing down of carriage wheels, horses' hooves and shoes upon entering our farm, all will be well," I said. "Oh, that is grand to see someone taking these diseases seriously," Lochiel said. "Thank you Lochiel," said Padruig. "I hope you'll be at the wedding. Isobel is very proud of her new wee Chapel," he said smiling. Padruig then took my arm and the two of us with the old gent walked slowly to the carriage. "I'll go up top," said Aonghus, "to make room." So, they dropped us all home at the gate with Aonghus.

Annabel left happily with her parents. On their way home, Donald Cameron apparently said to his wife, "Why didn't you tell me that she was Isobel of Glenmoriston? Everyone knows about her." Mither and daughter decided to leave that one alone. "She's built her own Chapel Ma," Annabel said. "Aye, I heard she almost died in the process. Caught a bad cold on the way home. I'm looking forward to seeing it. None of us have our own private Chapel. Should we think of that Donald?" she asked. "I'll have a look at it first. Is it Papist then?" he asked. "Aye, of course it is," she said. "The Priests visit every fortnight now to keep up with the weddings, baptisms and confessions. It'll be weekly soon," she said. Word had spread that if a Kirk had been built locally for the general public, it would have been a very popular Kirk. What a shame the Catholics didn't try and rebuild one in our area. The coast was too far to go and it was a run-down building unfrequented by many now and the Priest there was old and unenthusiastic, I had been told.

The wedding dress this time, thankfully, was not my responsibility. Annabel's Mither was very pleased to make it. I was not sure what to buy her as a wedding gift as she was not short of things, so I had to ask Helen for some inspiration. "I've got the same problem Ma. I can't think what they'd need from us," she said. In bed I told Padruig that Helen and I couldn't think of what to get them and could he please advise me. He answered me matter of factly. "For Aonghus, one of those fancy pen and ink pot thingies you see in lawyer's offices and for the lass, a book on Erse poetry." So that's what Padruig and I did while Helen bought a wee vase for them both from her earnings from the wool waulking. Both gifts were really well received and much loved by them, especially the pen and ink set for Aonghus's lawyer desk.

I went on to say, "Also darling. I needed to talk to you about a sensitive topic concerning my Will and my team of Clydesdales. I have an idea, but would like your approval and if you disapprove, that's okay." He looked perplexed but realized I was especially careful now not to displease him. "What I want to do is split the inheritance of the team into two parts. One part being the bloodlines and authority over it and the other part being the physical horses themselves, their tackle and the big carriage. This part also includes management of them, the staff and the running of the stables," I said. "This sounds complicated," he responded. "Aye, but hear me out. You can't sell one without the other, so if Isobel-Mairi inherits the bloodlines and works as a groom or a teacher while having bairns, Hugh Og could safely inherit the team and it's daily management, without being able to sell it," I said. "So, you want to leave the team to Hugh Og, is that right?" he asked. "Aye, but I don't want us to lose them again like before. I want to protect the bloodlines," I said. "How will Isobel-Mairi feel about that?" he asked. "At present, she's all caught up with having a bairn and can't run the team. She knows that. But it still gives her part ownership and involvement for a later time." I then added, "Do you think Hugh Og is the right person as I do?" I asked. "I do," he said confidently. "I think it's an ingenious decision. Write it all down clearly and explain it to them both. Make sure it's in your Will, so there's no future problem. Otherwise, I love it. Isobel-Mairi is too immature at this stage to run the team, but Hugh's been working horses for years. I approve, my clever darling." So, it was made clear and all parties were informed. Hugh Og was also given a wee pay rise to accompany his new status as 'Head Teamster' and I do believe that the young man who had come to my door selling fish all those years ago was a contented man.

Work and The Play

With all of us on the farms having been so work focused, Hugh Og and Hamish took Ewen off to go fishing for a bit of a break and to teach him what they knew about the fishing in the local area because they found something that he actually couldn't do. Those young men had continued to do that and brought back fish for all of us, free to me they said but I had insisted on a wee payment, which was lovely for us all. Helen also came up with an idea of a play with Morag-Freya, Isobel-Mairi, Hugh Og, Ewen, Simon and Dougal and had invited us all, of course, to come along and watch their play. She said that they had arranged to entertain us and it was supposed to be about the River Ness and the Loch Ness Monster, for which they'd even made props. Helen and Morag-Freya took it in turns narrating. In our audience was Gillcrest MacLachlan, who was wide-eyed and excited to see what Morag-Freya was going to do in the play. Aonghus appeared bored at first at the idea, accompanied by a friend of his from his university days, as well as Annabel, but he quickly became interested. Hugh and Padruig were both curious and so was I.

Helen began speaking:

"A long time ago, after Saint Ninian had been here in The Great Glen, in a time before our ancestors, Saint Patrick walked the path of the Great Glen to try and convert the people who lived here to Christianity. After Saint Ninian and Saint Patrick, Saint Columba came along, sent here to this region by the Irish. Expecting to meet a barbarous people, as he walked the Great Glen beside Loch Ness, he instead came across a very large procession. He must have spoken their language because he asked them what they were doing. Those ancient people answered that it was a funeral of one who had been killed by the monster of the Loch."

Morag-Freya was dressed in a cassock, dressed as Saint Columba and had Simon as one of her followers also dressed in a cassock and said to him, while holding a big staff,

"Follower. Throw off your cassock and jump into the loch," Morag-Freya said.

"Why?" the follower, Simon, asked. Holding up her staff again,

"So, we can convince these people of the power of our God," she said convincingly.

"Oh, okay," said Simon, the follower, who threw off his cassock, revealing his English underwear and pretended to jump into the loch, when a monster that they had made, appeared moving along, wanting to eat him, held by the new groomsman, Dougal. Then standing atop a chair, holding up her staff once again, she said,

"Be gone Monster! Be gone!" and Dougal took his monster quickly out of sight. Then, Hugh Og and Ewen, representing the funeral goers, were supposed to look surprised by covering their mouths and going, "oh" and "ah. This Priest must have a message for us."

Then Helen said:

"This was Part 1 of our play," so we all applauded their efforts. Padruig was hoping it was all over, but then he said, "That naked Priest probably scared off that monster for good."

"Part 2 announced," said Helen, much to our surprise.

"The King was pleased with the folk of the Great Glen for some battle we don't remember, so he gave them land in Argyle," said Morag-Freya. This had everyone's attention. "They built a castle called Dunderave Castle and their last ruler was Nachtain. They blended in there for a while and were the Clan MacNachten until the Campbells did what Campbells do and took their land and killed most of them."

349

Then the actors of the play all bowed and thanked their audience and it was all over, leaving us a little awestruck. It had been so simple for Morag-Freya and Helen to act out a story of an ancient mysterious people, who weren't really that mysterious if they were written in Papist records and Scottish records of some kind, as having been given that land.

'Why were they given the land?' was the obvious question and so it was asked and it was Gillcrest who then answered as best as he could. "Those people who settled there were previously unknown to those of us in Argyle, according to my records, but they had forged a good relationship with the MacDougals, who were anti-Bruce at the time with all of those battles. The MacNachtens were aligned with the MacDougals and almost defeated the Bruce. No one really knows why they changed sides, but it is thought they probably did it to keep their lands and the castle. But the MacDougal connection may still exist." The young lad, Dougal MacDougal, our young groomsman came inside holding his Loch Ness Monster to listen.

"So, none of them had the Irish connection like you did?" Grigor asked. "That's right. We have proof of our travels from Ireland to Argyle and there's a stone in our wee Chapel of one of the boats that brought all of us to Argyle, but those people were not of Irish descent, although they may have intermarried at some later time. They spoke Gaelic with a bit of a lilt in an accent not dissimiliar to Mr. MacNachten. It wasn't their native tongue, was the conclusion," said Gillcrest. Amongst those of us listening, it left more questions than answers. 'Why had they all left the Great Glen?' especially if their monster had been killed already. 'Where did they bury their dead?' 'Where did they live?' And so on.

"Aren't you forgetting something?" asked Aonghus. "All of what we now know as Scotland was Pictland or Pictavia. Just the same, I thank Helen and Morag-Freya and their actors for a mighty fine play." Then surprisingly, Aonghus' friend stood up and said, "My name is Fergus MacDougal. I am a friend of Aonghus' from the university and I'm just visiting. Aonghus left the Pict Club, but I didn't. So, I can add a wee bit more to your story Morag-Freya, if you don't mind?"

No one seemed to mind, so we heard him out. "Saint Columba, who I see you've aptly named your wee Chapel after, was indeed here in the Great Glen and continued on to our favourite town, Inverness. Although, preceding Saint Columba had been Saint Patrick and Saint Ninian, all trying to convert the Picts, or Pechts if you prefer. Inverness was the seat of power for the King of the Picts by the name of Bridae, although some historians say that just beside Urqhart Castle was his true seat of power which would explain why they were in the Great Glen. Evidence of a Pictish castle was found there and obviously mostly destroyed. Saint Columba met with the King wherever that actually was and the Picts were successfully converted to Christianity, some historians say. This is evidenced by the stones where you see a change in the artwork where there is a cross on one side and the usual Pict symbols on the other side of the stone. So, it is more like they added a god, but that is only my opinion. The Monks attached to Saint Columba were Celtic. That is not the same as the Roman Catholic type of Monk. They lived and worked alongside the Picts in poverty with wives. Yes, they had wives," said Fergus.

"The Romans had tried to defeat the Picts and had brutally killed over ten thousand of them or more, but had never defeated them. They would simply dissolve into the misty hills and regroup and use guerilla warfare against the Romans until they left. It made no difference as to how many walls were built to contain the northern rebel tribes, the Romans were never going to win against the Pechts but their numbers seem to have been somewhat reduced. It is a shame we didn't use guerilla warfare at the Battle of Culloden following the advice of Lord Lovat." The statement that the young man made got Padruig's attention and he looked across at him differently and thoughtfully.

"Bridae was a very successful King and ruled for a long time. I will bring the line of succession with me next time, if you invite me back. The Picts were then under attack, mainly from the Northumbrians from the south and the Picts also had their own internal disagreements about their new religion that many didn't accept such as on the Isle of Mull and the Isle of Eigg, where the Picts killed the Missionaries and destroyed the Monasteries."

"It is my understanding so far, that the strongest King of the Picts however, was Aonghus, although opinions differ on that. King

351

Aonghus had formed an Irish style of governance to better defeat the Northumbrians from the south. At one point, the Gaels, or Scots, who had come into Argyle, joined with the Picts to ward off southern attacks. King Aonghus even produced a rule of war called "The Law of Innocents," to protect women, children and the clergy. Without giving exact time lines as an historian would, the next slaughter of the Picts came from the north through the Orkneys who were the Vikings and they decimated those northern Pictish populations. Aberdeen evidently was a large population centre of the Pictish peoples but it is unknown exactly how their end came about. It is not surprising that there are few people today to tell their stories of their old religion, thought to be Druids, but most historians are of the opinion that those who survived were disguised and are indeed part of the Clans system or Septs of other Clans and simply blended and therefore, never completely went away. With the Clearances that we are currently facing, add to that together with the losses of Culloden would have added to their losses also. I don't think we will ever know now how many of those people of our ancient ancestory are left among us now," he finished while looking at me imploringly and sat down. It left me feeling a great loss and sadness when I personally experienced our ancestors in our forest on our own property and felt the need more than ever to protect what was left in our tiny part of Scotland's Highlands.

"So, Gillcrest," said Aonghus, "you can't just go on claiming that Argyle is ancestoral lands to the MacLachlans when the Pechts were there first and no doubt very annoyed at losing their land to the Irish people only later to be given a wee island," he said. It had the look of a political bun fight in our loungeroom for a while there with a MacGregor feeling feisty. "It's not Gillcrest's fault who took them all on a boat from Ireland and who killed the MacNachtens. He's a good Laird of his land now," said the defensive Morag-Freya. Isobel-Mairi then decided to weigh in in defense of the MacNachtens. "You're unfair Morag-Freya, think of poor old Mr. MacNachten and how it must have felt to lose all of Alba, that's what they called it," she said. "Good one Aonghus, look what you've started now," Padruig mumbled quietly to me.

"May I speak?" I said. Shocked into silence finally that I would say anything on the topic, the family were all listening. "It is true what Fergus said, Bridae was a King of the Pecht in either Inverness or beside Urqhart Castle as there is old evidence there of the original Pecht castle, down from Urqhart Castle. However, Bridae was certainly not the first King and in the annals of time, you will need to look further back. The Pecht are the indigenous people of this land. Many of us still carry some Pecht blood, some don't. The first King of the Pechts was said to be Nachtain. That's where the name MacNachten comes from. Spelled in so many ways, it would easily confuse a novice, such as Naughten. This shouldn't put off a true follower of this passion. Nachtain's people had been decimated by the tens of thousands and had developed strategies of war to defeat the Northumbrians.

Nachtain and his Pecht fighters fought in a famous battle called The Battle of Dun Nachtain. The English call it something else. Historians located the battle at the wrong site. Have you ever wondered why there was an old Druid gathering place there at Loch Insh? Have you wondered why Mr. MacNachten lives in Loch Insh? And why the swans have reverence for certain people? The battle of Dun Nachtain was near Loch Insh and Nachtain was their King although in their way they may not have called him that because Kings and Queens were not their way of organisation.

The history is one thing but in understanding an ancient people and their spirituality is another. If you pray, as I do, ask for guidance from our Creator to be led into a deep spiritual understanding of our Ancestors, for that is who they are. 'Our ancestors.' Not the Irish, not the Vikings, not the Gaels or the Celts although as my husband would say, 'we Scots are a blend of many peoples,' but that is not "the ancestors." Respect them, their beliefs, their names and include our ancestors into your families without animosity toward those who were here first. Other nations have "First Nations People' and so does Scotland. And that is what I wanted to say, and please forgive me any offence. My husband and I would like to retire now. Thank you, Helen, for a lovely play." Meredith got up to make refreshments. Others bolted for the privies. Simon had the time of his life and was not the slightest bit interested in the history, just the drama.

Then Aonghus stood up, not wanting refreshments and said, "There is more to this. Both Fergus and I have visited a Glen in Argyle called Kilmartin Glen, which dates back to 5000 years before Jesus was even born and well before the Irish settled there." I was hoping to go to bed, but waited to listen to Aonghus, as did most everyone else, except Simon. Even Hugh Mohr was interested, now that it was getting argumentative. "There are huge burial cairns and standing stones there, of all of the ancient people who lived here first. My question to you Gillcrest, isn't about what the Campbells did to the MacNachtens, but what you Irish arrivals in your wee boats did to all of those people who were an enormous community with their burial belief systems."

"Their old or first religion seemed to have been based around the Solar System. We still have remnants of those old traditions today. Can you answer us here, Gillcrest, what the Irish did to the native inhabitants of Argyle, before giving themselves titles, like the Duke of Argyle or Laird of this or that?" asked an angry Aonghus. "There were no MacGregors there, why does it mean so much to you?" Gillcrest asked. "Because we are part Pecht, us group of MacGregors and so is your wife," answered Aonghus. I had never seen my Grandchildren facing off like this and had never imagined that this topic of conversation would become so heated, but I didn't take sides and I didn't blame Aonghus at all.

He went on, "Grandma, if you don't mind, can I ask this question before you go to bed?" he asked "Aye," I said. "If there was a large population of Pecht people in Argyle, as the evidence shows, why then was the Battle of Dun Nachtain that you speak of, near Loch Insh?" he asked politely not wishing for me to banish him again on bad manners. Realising I had put myself in this position, I had to answer him and did so to the best of my ability, I just imagined that poor King and what he'd had to do to defeat those vicious Northumbrians and said, "I am not a scholar, so please do not quote me at your university gatherings, but I imagine that Nachtain had to gather everyone from every corner of Pictland, as it was then, from the very northern most regions to the southern most regions in order to win the battle against the Northumbrians. As Fergus mentioned, there was a strategy and they tricked the Northumbrians into following a small party of them on horseback into the deep, deep forest, where only they would be familiar. The Northumbrians, believing they would defeat this very small group of people, followed them. Those Argyle Pechts that you mentioned had left Argyle to join Nachtain to achieve what I am about to tell you. Suddenly, the Northumbrians found themselves surrounded by tens upon tens of thousands of those Pecht people from every corner of the land that he, King Nachtain, had gathered to himself. I don't know exactly how all of that was achieved of course. Perhaps your friend Fergus can look into all of that. Dun Nachtain is indeed a very controversial battle and was won by the Pecht and the Northumbrians did not bother them again after that. The English have tried to confuse its very existance by giving the wrong place and I doubt would ever acknowledge all our earlier Kings who were Pecht. But, obviously if there are other details concerning Argyle, if people were killed there by the Irish and not in other battles, Gillcrest would need to look into that. I really hope that isn't the case. I would like Isobel-Mairi and Ewen to name their baby, Nachtain Grigor MacNachten. The name will therefore stay in the family through our grandchildren and live on. Will you do that Ewen and Isobel-Mairi?" I asked. They agreed heartily to be involved in something bigger than themselves.

"Would anyone mind now please if we go to bed?" I asked. Hugh squeezed my hand, surrepticiously. It was sad to part with him and each day was getting harder, the warmth of his body close to mine was what I looked forward to every day. "What an interesting night that was," said Padruig. In bed that night Padruig was still humoured by the naked Priest jumping into the Loch and was sure that the monster would never come back after seeing such a sight as that. "It goes to prove," he said, "that even monsters have morals," he said. "Are the Irish circumcised?" I asked him. "What kind of question is that?" he asked. "A logical one," I answered. "It may have made a difference if the Irish monks were circumcised or the Pechts were and whether the monster had a preference for one or the other for dinner that night." He rolled over feeling a little sick. "Have you seen an Irishman naked?" I asked him. "Isobel, I am not answering that question about who is and who isn't circumcised," he said. "Why not?" I asked. "I don't want you thinking of other men's body parts." Rolling back over towards me with a glint in his eye, he said, "Only mine. So, just tell me if you like mine," while he blew out the candle.

"Padruig, there's something I want to tell you," I said quietly. "Now?" he said questioningly. "It's not a serious matter, but would you like to come into the forest with me tomorrow for me to show you something?" I asked. "Would you have shown this already to Grigor Mohr the day I arrived back from London?" he asked. "Aye," I said. "How did you know that?" I asked. "I had arrived back from London early. The cart dropped me off at the Drover's Road and I was walking in, excited to be home and I saw you walk to the edge of the forest and I thought this was unusual and so I went to follow you to tell you I was home. When I got closer I saw you greet Grigor Mohr affectionately on the tree line, immediately jealous, I followed the two of you quietly to see where you were going and what you could possibly be going to do in the thickest part of our forest, fearing the worse of course. I should've felt guilty for spying on you both, but I didn't. I wanted to know if you'd been having an affair in my absence. What I saw was the two of you, the happiest I'd ever seen you both. He was emotional, as were you. You were both of one mind, one soul even. It was a love I had not seen in either of you. Being the jealous man, you know I am, I wanted to kill you both and felt for my dirk and was just about to do it when suddenly I was attacked from behind by Hugh Mohr who saved both your lives. He dragged me out of the forest and told me to stay next door and return the next day in better clothes. He explained that you were brother and sister, which I didn't believe at first but it all added up and I could see on his face that it was true. I am sorry Isobel, but how could I have known he was your brother if even the both of you didn't know? I left Craskie Farm, and stayed over night with James Grant and re-entered the next day. Then I pretended that I had just arrived. Hugh had even fetched my dirk so you wouldn't find it and took it to his house and explained what happened to his brother Donald who was horrified that you could have both been killed that day," he said "I was afraid it would be misunderstood and we told you as soon as we were all together. That explains why you didn't look happy for us. Thankyou for telling me," I said reflecting sadly over such an innocent meeting with a brother who I still adored.

"It was Hugh who was always right about you. He told me not to leave you that day we all saved ourselves to live in the cave, then Mither was killed, the farm was burned down and I could have lost you all. Hugh still wanted me to check on you after Grigor Og had seen Helen. I haven't been a good husband," he said. "I was ravished at the Fort by six dragoons and kept it from you Padruig, and bayoneted, so we were all insincere with you too. I told Da not to tell you as well as Uncle Allan and Morag who had to stitch the wounds up. It was Uncle Allan's idea to say the injuries were from his coos, not the soldier's bayonets, else you would get yourself killed by going up to the Fort, so we are both at fault, don't you think?" I blurted out. Padruig's face painted a mixture of disbelief and horror. "No-one could have prevented that, not even you and I had two men trying to help me. You couldn't have changed the outcome, I just didn't want you to look at me differently, so we could still be husband and wife," I said. "But it was temporary wasn't it anyway with you leaving to go to New France, us without a house and not enough food. That is when Hugh saved me. I was walking to drown myself in the loch when he came along on his horse and saw me walking there and asked me where I was going. I didn't want to live without you Padruig and he had to carry me back unwillingly to the shieling. Morag and Uncle Allan were on loch duty to stop me from going near the loch while the men built the house. That's why they made the arrangement of who would marry me. Please forgive Hugh for that.

They were certain you were never returning, either because of your death or by choice. You had your reasons I know that now, but I was unable to bear it again. If you can't look at me now as your wife because of what I have told you then please tell me now" I said. Padruig's eyes filled with tears of sorrow that I had never seen flow from him before and wouldn't have previously believed it possible unless I had seen it with my own eyes. "Isobel, you are my wife, until I die at least and I am responsible for you and for what has happened to you. I understand why you all wouldn't have told me or I would have gone to the Fort, as you say and no doubt died still leaving you alone. I am sorry that I barely sympathized with you over the injuries on your buttocks," he said. "You said that I had an ugly bottom that you couldn't bear to look at," I reminded him. "Aye, I did. Those are bayonet scars?" he wanted to confirm. "Aye, one of them was very deep, so with the ravishing which caused a lot of bleeding and the wounds, especially that one, Da and Uncle Allan had trouble

357

stopping the loss of blood, so they had to get Morag to help, provided that she also told no-one. Da thought I would die," I said. "Do you mind if I look at them now?" he asked. "Oh, dear God, Isobel, why couldn't I see that?" he said as he examined each one. "Please forgive me Isobel" he asked. "Of course, you know I will," I said and he reached out to me to hold me to him. "Do you still love me with that knowledge?" I asked. "Aye. More than ever before. Will you come to me and let me love you?" he asked as I lay with my husband of so many years and he asked if he could make love which we did beautifully. "I don't want to share you with Hugh, but it pains me to say that I do want him to marry you after I die to care for you. Do you agree?" he said. "I agree," I said.

"I just have one question before you fall asleep," I asked. "Did you shout at me because of what occurred a few days after what happened in the forest with Grigor?" I asked. "Aye, one reason. I told the Reverend about it when you were getting the rose bushes from the Housekeeper. He didn't believe that you would have had an affair that whole time I was away. He called you a very loyal and long suffering wife. But I do know that you have a little hidey spot in the forest with your Pecht stone and I have told no one of its existance, so don't worry, your secret is safe with me. We don't need to go there tomorrow though. I've already been back there to see what it was that you and Grigor were so interested in. You told him things you could never tell me, didn't you?" he asked. "Aye," I said. "I found solace there by accident by tripping over the stone. The ancient ones would keep me company as a child. These are the things Aonghus doesn't understand yet, nor his friend Fergus, but Grigor Mohr did. God bless him. I hope one day that Aonghus or someone else in our family, taps into this ancient part of ourselves, long gone," I said. "How did you see them?" he asked. "That's hard to describe, but I felt safe there and the property feels safe with them there. With the stone there, I mean." I answered. "Padruig I haven't told you this before but I also hid there too when your Father and your Uncles all came to investigate who I was after I had promised myself to you and said that I'd wait for you. Da said that some Clan Grant men were coming to see if they approved of a marriage with me to his son, Padruig Grant and Da was surprised that someone wanted to marry me already. I was only thirteen then. I said that you never mentioned marriage but he wasn't pleased that I hadn't told them of my promise to you, as marriage was the obvious outcome. When I saw them coming into Craskie, I got very frightened. They were all so big and tall and mean looking, so I ran away as fast as I could' I said. "Neither Ma or Da knew where I was" I said and your Father was very angry Da said later to me. You must have told your family about me, so they wanted to see who it was you wanted to marry. So, he asked Da a lot of marital type questions, like Da's occupation and so did your Uncles with their scary faces. They did say that I was very pretty, like my Ma but they still wanted to meet me in person, so Da would have to tie me up if necessary, they said." Padruig broke out in raucous laughter at the story of his scary relatives and my running away from them all. "You were brave to tell your Da about me," I said. "I told them what I told you that you were mine and no-one else was going to get you just because I was being sent to Lord Lovat's to train. I knew what I wanted so that was that, so he had to make it happen while you were still young and living with your parents. I wanted you before you were forteen," he said.

"So, what happened when you were hiding. Did they look for you?" he asked. "I thought they'd left, so I came out to make sure they had gone and I couldn't see anyone but then I was grabbed by one of those mean Uncles who said "I've got her" who held me by my arm tightly and dragged me home, then handed me to your Father "I ran into Da's arms crying and more scared than ever before," I said. Still laughing, Padruig said "So long as I got you, I didn't care how." Your Father said it's a good thing I was scared of him, so I'd be a good wife to his son and added that I was very small. He squatted in front of me, looking into my eyes, then he said, "Isobel, do you want to marry my son, Padruig and if so, would you give him children when he comes and goes from his military training?" he asked. "Aye Sir" I said. He held my chin with his thumb and forefinger and said, "You are enough, its true and turned my face this way and that then lifted back my hair to see if I had nice ears. He told my Father to hold onto me so I wouldn't run away again, then we went inside the house. He commented that my breasts appeared too small to breast feed babies. Da disagreed and said that I was still growing. "Ma" I said, reaching out to her. "Behave yourself lassie," Your Father said. "I was taken into another room where each one of the five men examined me. Talking amongst themselves while I sobbed non stop. Eventually, they were all satisfied even though I was a bit small and they approved a marriage within the year. "Your Father told my Ma and Da that I was theirs for you and I saw my poor Ma had been crying too." Da said, "She stays here while he comes and goes from his military training, with us". I slept all night with Ma and Da in their bed and cried on and off apologizing to them for not telling them." Da just held me to himself and said "you're my little girl not theirs, Isobel". I concluded the story and then Padruig and I finally slept. I didn't like to remember his relatives.

Ewen Visits Loch Insh

Ewen asked Isobel-Mairi if he could spend the weekend with his Father at Loch Insh, as he was getting old and he was concerned about him, not to mention all of the issues that had come up on the night of the play that bothered him about his poor Father's history. Realistically, he would be gone for three to four days, so Isobel-Mairi stayed with us and helped cook and clean. She was much quieter these days. I asked if she could help Hugh Og with a Clydesdale delivery and she agreed, so long as Hugh Og was in charge. On occasion, he'd give her the reins while he was loading and unloading and she was enjoying the feel of it again while her husband was learning a little of Mr. MacNachten's craft. He didn't have much time left on God's Earth and had already made the slabs and stones for both Ewen and himself and left me a letter requesting they be buried beside each other at our cemetery at Craskie Farm. Then the old man taught him a lot about the Druids and the swans and the signs to look for in the Auld ways.

It was precious time together. His funeral was just one week later. It was a real loss to us all and Ewen cried his heart out. When he embraced me for solace, it was like a soft old bear hug. He was truly broken-hearted, but Isobel-Mairi's pregnancy soon after, lifted his spirits again. Gillcrest MacNachten's name was chiseled into the wall panel alongside all of those who had been a part of Craskie Farm life.

A community like no other, many said, that brought clans together from all over. On the day of his parting, the swans had honked and honked, making a terrible noise in the night, so the local folk there knew that the old man had passed away. On his grave slab, was a single swan. It stated, "Gillcrest MacNachten, father of Ewen MacNachten, Second cousin to Isobel of Glenmoriston."

The old pony left with us by Mr. MacNachten died the same week as he did. Grief will do that to horses. Such a sweet old pony. It was sad to see him go, but Ewen had brought back the two Highland ponies from Loch Insh that I had given to Mr. MacNachten, so there was only just room enough for them all. Uncle Allan's pony died shortly after that too and so we planted trees where the bodies lay up before the entrance to the Highland Manor. A raspberry tree over Blaze's body, a mulberry tree over Mr. MacNachten's pony's body and a lemon tree over Uncle Allan's pony's body.

Ewen also brought back his father's tools of trade, grave slabs and head stones left to him, which we temporarily kept behind the Chapel, but the tools were used by both Hugh Mohr and Ewen to engrave the names onto any future stones. I already knew that Hugh was going to add the name 'Chisholm' onto mine once we were married. The wedding date for Aonghus and Annabel was postponed a week while folks recovered from the loss.

I was visited by James and Beth, delivered cautiously by Hugh Mohr looking worried at first, so I invited them all in patting Hugh's Collies. "Such good Collies," I said as I lovingly fondled their faces. "Come by the fire," I said and asked for coffees all round. "Now what can I do for all of you?" I asked. Hugh stayed to watch over me. James started by wanting to sound generous in offering the Manor House's dining room for Aonghus' wedding, provided we supplied the meat and farm fresh vegetables. So far, that had sounded reasonable, but I was waiting for a catch. "And at what cost?" I asked. "No cost Grandma," he said. "It would be a wedding gift to provide the space, as well as the rooms free of charge for anyone coming any long distance," James added. "That does sound generous. Was it Patrick's idea?" I asked "Aye, it was," he said, sounding pleased with himself.

Then Beth said, "But you'll need to provide Meredith to cook too Granny." "Meredith you say? My cook, who already works two houses? So, no to that request and let me guess, that was Henrietta's idea?" I said. "Aye, it was, but you'd still need to supply staff," Beth said. "Would I?" I said. "Out of interest, will John, Anna, Simon and yourself be at the wedding?" I asked. "Oh, aye," she said. "We're all sleeping in the guest rooms," Beth said. "So, in Stratherick, you have a cook and a maid in each house, don't you?" I asked. "Aye," said Beth. "On that weekend, you won't be there in Stratherick, so why not bring your cook and maid?" I said, "then that solves the staffing, doesn't it?" "My cook's in her fifties. She can come with the maid. John's cook is frightened of boats, so that rules her out," Beth said. "What's your cook's name then?" I asked. "Patsy," she said. "Then tell Henrietta that Patsy and your maid will help, okay?" I said. They both left gossiping to each other and Hugh Mohr was pleased. "Can Patsy stay in your house overnight please Hugh?" I asked him. "Aye, she can."

Padruig was getting visibly tired of all the big occasions, but was relieved to see the last of his Scottish grandchildren married and the reception was very nice and preferable to going all the way to Inverness. We left early, but we observed that Patsy had already left and was having her shoes cleaned by Hugh Mohr at the border who was looking unusually shy. She leaned on his big arm and said something to him that embarrassed him. I saw her still leaning on his arm to enter his house and I had my concerns about Patsy.

A Patriarch Dies

My son Alex arrived the next day from Nova Scotia. The Patriarch of all our farms was my husband, Padruig Grant, who had stood by his family, his men at Culloden, the cave and Quebec. I knew I was losing him in his final days, as he spent more time in bed reading his beloved Erse poetry and talking to Alex. He started taking tiny meals in bed, as it was harder for him to get up. He made sure both Aonghus, Grigor and I all knew the legalities and feared he wouldn't see the opening of Helen's Art Gallery, but insisted that it still go ahead, now in its final stages of completion. He didn't quite make it. One morning, my darling Padruig Dubh, just didn't wake up. I howled a grief so deep it could be heard all over and everyone knew Padruig Dubh Grant, a great among men, had finally left this Earth to be with Grigor MacGregor, Alexander MacDonald, Donald Chisholm, Alexander Chisholm, John MacDonald and all of his compatriots from Drumossie Moor. Poor Hugh Chisholm was the last of the Seven Glenmoriston Men still living.

The funeral was enormous, with people coming from all over Scotland. The procession started from in front of Fort Augustus winding its way through the braes of Glenmoriston. At the head of the procession were my Clydesdales with me and Hugh Og and Ewen proudly holding the Clan Grant flag, all in Grant regalia. The coffin was carried first by my Clydesdale team, until it eventually reached Craskie Farm. Behind the team walked his two sons, Patrick and Alexander Grant. Patrick carried a Clan Grant flag and Alexander carried the Clan Grant Nova Scotia flag. Behind them walked Clan Gregor led by Grigor MacGregor carrying the Clan Gregor flag given to him by his family on that sad occasion. His cousins all walked behind him, numbering thirty. Behind Clan Gregor was Clan Chisholm proudly led by Hugh Mohr wearing his green and maroon Chisholm hunting tartan, followed by forty of his clansmen. Behind Clan Chisholm was the old Clan Nachten flag carried by Isobel-Mairi, who walked with her sister and the people of Loch Insh. Behind them were a large contingent from Clan Lachlan, Clan Neil and Clan Gillcrest. The Clan Lachlan flag was carried by Gillcrest MacLachlan for the first time, which his Mither had given him and was wearing their tartan. There were over one hundred from those different clans from Argyle, including Clan Campbell. Behind them was Lochiel of the Camerons carrying the Clan Cameron flag with around eighty Camerons, including Lilias' parents and the Septs of the Camerons including Clan Martin. Behind Clan Cameron were the MacPhersons from Cluny numbering forty followed by a small group of MacDonalds representing the deceased MacDonalds of Glenmoriston. In amongst the Clans were sedan chairs for the elderly. Behind them was Clan MacKenzie of Kinlochewe, followed by the disbanded 78th Fraser Highlander Regiment of Quebec, led by John Fraser, carrying their flag and wearing their military uniforms accompanied by pipers that rang out through the hills. Then at my request, were the soldiers from Fort Augustus in formal attire marching up the rear and armed in case of conflict.

Our New Farm came in handy that day to park many of the carriages and carts and to graze their horses that had come from far and wide. As my Clydesdales were turning into Craskie, sensing the solemnity of the occasion, they stopped momentarily. "It's okay Hugh," I said. "Let them be sad too." I spoke quietly to them in Erse to calm their hearts. Our beauties, once I took the reins, moved slowly forward on my request but 'were reluctant to see Padruig enter the ground is all,' I explained. With their heads drooped they carried the coffin as far as the stable door where it was prearranged for them to be unhitched by Dougal the groom and taken inside their stalls and fed and watered. Their heavy task having already been accomplished.

The coffin was then to be carried by Patrick, Alex, Hugh Mohr, John Fraser, Grigor MacGregor and Lochiel of the Camerons. Nothing untoward occurred and the Captain of the Fort said he'd been honoured to be involved and gave me his sincerest condolences. Our old lawyer came limping into the farm still wearing his wig whilst I stood outside the wee Chapel. "Oh, Isobel dear, what a loss!" he said and wiped his face and went inside and hoped to find a seat. There had to be chairs brought down from Patrick's Manor House to accommodate additional seating inside and outside the Chapel.

It was said that day that no one had seen a display of Clan Tartan and Clan flags since Charles Edward Stuart was marching on London, the difference being the solemnity unmatched by any other funeral by size and clan identity to date. One of my husband's achievements can be said that his funeral broke the fear of clan identity once and for all. No one was ashamed to display flags of many clans all arranged first outside the Chapel and then taken inside to line the walls. The pipes played as we entered the Chapel.

My two Granddaughters stood either side of the elderly Priest, who had come due to its importance and the young Priest stood at the door to repeat the words spoken by the elderly Priest as a crier to the large gathering outside. Isobel-Mairi repeated the Mass in sign language to those who were deaf and Morag-Freya was on hand for any medical emergency. Extra chairs were fitted inside because so many folk were old. The man with the missing eye was there and he sat with his fellow Cameron veteran who I was sure I had seen before in a time long passed. Only one other surviving veteran of Culloden was present.

My Granddaughters were in matching Grant tartan and Meredith had been playing her harp for a while to calm people's hearts as they entered the Chapel. I sat on the front pew where I could see my husband's tomb and just wished that Da or Uncle Allan or Grigor Mohr or Mr. MacNachten were there to strengthen me, but they weren't and the loss felt so much greater unsupported. Alex sat to my left and Patrick to my right, but Ewen came and said he'd promised to be there, so Patrick moved over closer to Helen and Grigor.

I was told later that a few tourists were staying up at the Manor House and were watching on. Some of us ladies were in black, most were in traditional tartan with flags flying and bagpipes playing, so it was obviously quite an historical event, which was written up in some London newspaper I was told, but didn't believe at first. Apparently, the headline was "Highland Clan Chief Dies." That was rubbish for a start. Stupid newspapers rarely got it right. I had invited our own local Inverness newspaper to ensure that there wasn't nonsense being spread about. They knew me and our lawyer from the days of the 'bawbees' and just reported it exactly how it was. With so many people attending, I became aware that in building the Chapel, I had forgotten to build privies. They would all have to use the four privies by the house or wander off into the bush.

Padruig had agreed to being carried in a coffin, but wouldn't be buried in one. He was afraid that on Judgement Day, he wouldn't be able to get out and wanted to be able to move the tomb lid to meet his Judgement, he said. So, his body was in a beautifully made shroud and his plaid and so was lifted out from the coffin with the men blocking vision from the Chapel mourners. He was entered ever so gently, given his weight and height, into the ground and the tomb was closed. Alex was crying when his Father's tomb was closed, as was I, then he came back and sat beside me and I held his hand tightly as my poor lad was inconsolable. He was as tall as his Father and much bigger all over with a goatee beard and moustache, which was still black with only a few silver hairs. He was really handsome and his blue eyes were just like his Father's.

The Mass went well as Mass goes, but when the Priests reversed their positions, the young Priest spoke of the time he had spent with my husband and his admiration for him was evident. The old Priest repeated all of this to everyone outside. He told his life story as had been told by us all and it drew so many tears. I just had to hold on until they left, I thought, but then we all had to go outside the wee Chapel while everyone gave their condolences. Down at the house, my poor Helen and her daughters had rushed down with Meredith and Cora to hand out food and drink to all the mourners who drifted in and out of the house for hours it seemed.

I wanted to go back to say a final farewell to my husband and asked Ewen to take me quietly and unnoticed. He stood at the Chapel door while I sat beside Padruig's grave and wept. I talked to him as if he were alive and hoped he was comfortable. I told him who had come to his funeral and about the many clan flags there were and I then lay beside his tomb on the cold floor and fell asleep where I could meet him and I saw his beautiful face, young and pain free and happy and smiling at me. We both reached out to each other only to be awoken by Ewen, who was picking me up and wrapping me in his plaid to keep me warm. He called me Granny just like his wife now and said, "Granny, I am taking you back to the house now to put you to bed if that is alright?" Grigor was there and had come looking for me. "She can't do any more socializing," said Ewen. "Can Helen help her to bed do you think Da?" he asked. I am sure I heard him say Da. That was so nice that Grigor's son-in-law called him Da. There was a mutual respect between the two men.

It was a sad walk back to the house. Some people had already left, like the Fraser Highlanders and the troops. The MacGregors and the Camerons were about to leave as well as the MacKenzies, Meredith's family. Upon seeing me so pale and tired, they touched my hand and said nice things and went on their way picking up their horses and carriages from New Farm.

The Apology

After the funeral the following morning, I cautiously approached 'the man who loved me', Hugh Mohr and said, "Dearest Hugh, please hear me out. I want you to take on an extra task on top of what you already do that takes an additional wage from Craskie, the title being 'Keeper of the Graves, the Chapel and the Forest.' It would pay you one pound a fortnight on top of what you already get." Looking surprised, he asked me what the job entailed. I mentioned a few things, one of which was having to keep out those who can't be buried here because there simply wasn't the room any more. Caring for the graves and maintenance of the Chapel, as well as ensuring it was locked every night after everyone was finished praying in there. In addition, there would be the digging of a grave when needed and I informed him about the few spare headstones out the back.

"You may also need to be the spokesperson with the Priests, Father Michael and Father Francis, once I pass away, so that you know which one or both are coming and when. From the young Priest, you could get more old Papist stuff off him for free, like Baptismal bowls, collection bowls and a holy water font. But, I have to stipulate that as this Chapel is my design, I do not want a naked Jesus hanging off the wall or a cross of any kind as it represents torture and they will keep asking you to put one there. Be sure to say no. Make sure they get their wee pay when they leave out of the collection, but if anyone here is known to be in poverty, they also share in the collection. The job includes maintenance of the Chapel."

His response was, "Well I can do it. I already do it. But £1 a fortnight. Is that all?" he asked with his familiar cheeky grin. "Well, how about £1 a week then?" I offered. "Okay, that sounds bonny. So long as you tell Helen to write my new title in her payroll book. What was it again? 'Keeper of the Graves, the Chapel and the Forest.' So, if anyone wants to know anything about the Chapel, they have to consult with me first." He stated with some pride. "I can see that you will do a fine job Hugh. And there is just another wee matter of the building of two privies to be built behind the Chapel. I've got the money with me now that I can pay you separately for them. Do you think you could do that?" With that I handed Hugh £100 and he said, "I'd call that chat a success, Isabel of Glenmoriston," said the cheeky fella. "I'll start on the privies today. Could've done with one on the day of the funeral. Is that when you realised you'd forgotten to build privies?" "he asked "Aye, I had forgotten to build the privies. Do you think two's enough?" I asked him. "Aye, we're not going to have a funeral that size again," he said. "I was thinking one for men and one for women with one of those wee slide locks, with a sign on each door in Gaelic stating 'Women' and 'Men,'" I said. "Do you want a wee palisade between the two or anything?" he asked. "Why would you need a palisade?" I questioned. "Well, Isabel, not all men are gentlemen like myself and they may want to take a wee keek at the ladies, if you know what I mean." Rather taken aback, I responded, "Then best put a palisade between the two. I'll leave it up to you, Hugh," I said.

"And the forest?" he asked. "It's the last of our native forest on this land with native birds finally returning," I said. "I don't want any more of its trees taken down. Naturally, if one falls in a storm, it's a gift from God to use where needed, but no felling. The shieling that we used to live in is to be closed and never used, but not destroyed either," I said. "The forest?" he said again. "Is that all I am protecting?

Wildlife and trees, Isobel?" he persisted. "There's a special part of the forest that I want no one to enter, especially anyone representing museums," I said. "Museums?" "Aye. Please Hugh. Protect it with all you have, I believe it keeps us all safe here," I said. "What does?" he asked. "I'll answer it this way. You are the protector of that forest after I die. When you enter the Chapel, there is a spirituality in there isn't there?" I said. "Aye," he answered quizzically. "Then what you are protecting is a spirituality of another kind, connected to my ancestors. Can you do that without mentioning that aspect please? Your role can be explained as a Gamekeeper if you like, to keep out poachers and Patrick's tourists," I explained hoping that that would be enough. But I should've known.

"Show me, Isobel, and I'll agree," he said. Almost crying, I wiped a tear away and reluctantly agreed and led him to my secret place deep into the forest to the Pecht stone. Upon seeing the stone, he was overwhelmed. "You have my word, Isobel, on my soul and I'm sorry I made you do this. Please forgive me?" he said, placing his big arm around me, we kissed each other. "Do you still want to marry me Hugh?" I asked, looking into his big blue eyes. "I'd be so lost and lonely without you Isobel, please marry me," he asked with such sincerity. I have waited so long for you and I have bought you a wedding band that I want you to wear once we marry," he said. "Will you wear my ring?" he asked. "Aye my darling, I will marry you and wear your ring." I said caressing his beautiful face. "My dearest, Isobel, just tell me when you are ready then we can handfast right away and I can move in with you. Grigor has agreed already," he said. "Can I take you back home now? You must be tired." He carried me kissing my lips occasionally all the way home to my fireside. "God bless you my lovely Hugh," I said and rested.

Attached is a copy of the letter I wrote to Helen regarding Hugh's new role.

Dear Helen,

Our payroll for Craskie Farm now includes a new title for Hugh Mohr Chisholm:

"Keeper of the Graves, the Chapel and the Forest."

Please pay him weekly out of the Craskie Farm £1 per week and refer any questions regarding burials/funerals to him. If you are asked, due to size constraints we have to limit burials in our cemetery to only family and close friends associated with Craskie Farm. Ask the Priests to deal with him on any upcoming wedding, funerals or baptisms. There'll be three keys for the Chapel. Hugh will have one and both you and Grigor will have one each. Please let Grigor know that Hugh will also be the Protector of the remaining old forest to prevent any more felling, poaching or trespassing. Thank you darling. The young Priest can probably stay at Ewen's house or yours while he's here. If both yours and Ewen's houses are full, ask Hamish to accommodate the Priest.

-Ma

I had hoped not to see Beth for a long time, however sitting by the fire later that morning after speaking to Hugh Mohr while the cleanup took place all the way back to the fort, I had been resting and just thinking about what I would do, when she came. "Can I come in?" she asked. Meredith stood between her and I until I gave my answer. "It depends on what you're here for Beth," I said. "Tell Meredith then and I'll make up my mind." Meredith came to me saying that Beth wanted to apologise for her previous behavior, her disrespect and hoped I would accept her condolences because she had loved her Grandfather too. So, I said "Aye, come in so long as you don't stay long." Meredith sent for Hugh Og and they both kept a watchful eye over Beth. "I am leaving for Stratherick today," she said. "Even my cook doesn't want to come back with me." "Anything else?" I asked. "I am sorry Granny. You were like my Mither growing up and I have been rotten to you. My Mither, Henrietta, isn't a pleasant person, but you know that. I was lucky to have lived with you and Grandda and had riding lessons from Uncle Grigor. Can you please forgive me? My father-in-law won't talk to me for being rude to you and taking out your Clydesdales. Things won't get back to normal with Simon either unless it's all good with you, especially now that it's in the papers."

"What's in the papers?" I asked. She produced the Inverness Times Newspaper – morning edition with the heading reading, "Teamster, Isobel of Glenmoriston, Leads Funeral Procession for Padruig Grant." The article said:

Isobel MacGregor Grant, taught from childhood by her Father to be a teamster of eight Clydesdales, led her husband's funeral cortege through the braes of Glenmoriston from Fort Augustus to Craskie Farm to the Chapel of St Columba at Craskie. Priests, Father Michael and Father Francis from Edinburgh held the service. A procession of Clan flags not seen since 1745, proudly blew in the breeze, carried by men wearing their clan tartans, came to mourn the 85-year-old veteran of Culloden in 1746 and the first Quebec campaign of 1759.

Known famously as one of the Seven Glenmoriston Men, he out-witted Redcoats and helped take Prince Charles Edward Stuart to safety in Badenoch with Alexander MacDonald, Grigor MacGregor, Alexander Chisholm, Donald Chisholm, Hugh Chisholm and John MacDonald. Refusing the £30,000 offer to hand the Prince over to the authorities, he ensured the Prince's safety, as did many others.

Padruig Grant is survived by his wife Isobel MacGregor Grant, his eldest son Patrick Grant who now owns the Hart of the Highland Manor House, his younger son Alexander Grant, who resides in Nova Scotia and his beloved daughter Helen Grant MacGregor and her husband Grigor MacGregor, who now own Craskie Farm, Grant Farm and New Farm. Together they now own five properties thanks to the careful rebuilding of Isobel of Glenmoriston and the foresight of her famous husband, Padruig Grant, never to be replaced, may God rest his soul.

Together, Isobel and Padruig Grant have been pillars of this new Highland society, rebuilding the community in which they lived. Responsible also for establishing the newly reinvigorated Glenmoriston School, the Helen Grant MacGregor Art Studio and Fraser's Trading Post owned by John Fraser of Stratherick. Isobel also had the Drover's Road widened and a Post Office built nearby, thanks to her Grandson-in-law, Simon Fraser. Well-known also for *ground-breaking soil science studies, producing better crops with higher yields, Padruig's son-in-law, Grigor MacGregor, has worked hard, hand in hand with his son-in-law, Gillcrest MacLachlan, Head Scientist at the Invermoriston Hospital. This output of all local crops has resulted in double the yield since the interest in the science of soil began, hoping to prevent another famine.*

Being responsible for building The Hart of the Highlands Manor House, Mr. Padruig Grant has been solely responsible for increasing tourism into our Highlands, bringing much needed cash to struggling families and employment for local people. All his children and grand-children have been happily married and this family will only continue to influence future generations.

This community thanks both Padruig, may God rest his soul and his devoted wife of 70 years, Isobel of Glenmoriston.

May he rest in peace
Mr. Kenneth Menzies
The Editor, Inverness Times Newspaper – morning edition

"I see," I said. "That's quite the story, but at least quite factual. Beth, now that you're here, I think you need to apologise to Isobel-Mairi, don't you think?" I said. "She has lost her confidence to be a teamster now because of you. I'll forgive you when she does and please take Patsy with you when you leave. She then went down to apologise

to Isobel-Mairi, who wasn't pleased to see her either. Apparently, she begged for forgiveness like her life depended on it and so, being a softy, of course Isobel-Mairi forgave her, but told her to stay away from the Clydesdales permanently and have no business with them.

To this she agreed and Ewen brought her back to me confirming the acceptance of the apology. "Alright Beth, learn your place is my best advice to you. You have a nice home in Stratherick, a good husband and a good horse business. Build on that. You're forgiven. Now I am tired. You'd best leave and be on your way with Patsy," I said and they left.

Hugh Mohr

After I had visited my goats and sheep, I felt much better. I milked a nanny and was carrying a bucket of milk when Grigor rushed up to me saying, "Ma. That's too heavy, I'll carry it for you," he said. "God bless you Grigor. How was it seeing all of your relatives?" I asked. "It was okay," he answered. "They were polite and sad too and pleased to be part of our family. Thank you, Ma," he said. "Well, they are your blood, aren't they?" I said. "If you need to invite any of them here, just first give me notice, so that I can go to my bedroom and read, but I don't mind if you want to catch up," I said. "Ma, we've already caught up, but thank you. Everything I need is here," he answered. "Grigor, you're a good lad. You've always been a good lad and I love you dearly. Helen is so lucky to have you as her husband as I was with Padruig. Has Hugh spoken to you yet?" I asked. "Aye Ma, I understand why you love each other and I approve of the marriage and so will Alex. My Father also would have agreed," he said as he kissed me gently on the cheek.

He carried the milk to the kitchen and handed it to Meredith and morning tea was available, so we all had cakes and coffee, which were lovely. "New recipe?" I asked. "Aye, Patsy gave it to me," she said. "That's nice. She's gone back to Stratherick with Beth," I said. More hungry men came in pleased to see cakes, so Hamish, excusing himself first, asked if he could have some morning tea. "Of course, my dear lad. Sit down, when have you ever needed permission to eat?" I said.

Relieved at some levity, the mood was lifted and then Hugh Mohr and Hugh Og arrived with the two dogs.

"Work's all done Isobel," said Hugh Mohr. "Those people left a mess all the way to the fort. Those horses sure left a lot of manure behind them," he said. "I hope you didn't waste it Hugh?" I asked. "No, it's on a new pile though on New Farm with the coo manure," he answered. Meredith piped up and said, "Patsy left with Beth." "Oh? Did she?" he said nonchalantly." Hugh and I retired again to the fire and we started to chat.

"You know Isobel, the first day that I saw you and wee Alex was at the front of the farm as we were all escaping the Redcoats from Culloden Field. We were saving ourselves, but what was going to happen to you was my concern and still is. Padruig and I had an argument in the cave and I said to him, 'How can you leave your wife and bairns?'" "My dearest Hugh," I said. "In those terrible times, all I thought was that if he was safe, I could go on, no matter what happened to me, but if he had died, I couldn't have gone on. I drew my strength from Padruig too, you see? Just as you did," I said.

"Your face as you rode away, was the face of a shattered man who had seen unimaginable horrors and I knew that you would need Padruig to guide you through it. Which he did. Look at you now. Padruig was proud of you Hugh because he trained you and helped you through that time and kept you all safe, may God rest his soul. Aye, you were right that the Redcoats were behind you and so eventually they would come here and that's how we lost Mither, but the rest of us survived hiding in the shieling. All I could think of while hiding from them was 'thank God Padruig is safe. We'd known each other for a long time and knew our limits with each other as well as our needs. Sometimes the need is to do what he did that day. It was a brave and hard thing for him to do," I said. "Aye, I suppose," Hugh said. "None of us are perfect Hugh. We all just try our best before God. Look at you and me, we've tried our best is all," I said unconvincingly as Hugh took my hand. We had lost our inhibitions with the family being in the same room for which I was so relieved. "When are we going to tell all the family that we will marry?" Hugh asked. "Both Grigor and I wanted to tell them now, but Alex isn't here yet, so do you mind if we wait for Alex? We think his influence may be important,"

I asked. "I hope that doesn't take long, I'm wanting you Isobel," he said and I couldn't stop smiling. "What are you smiling at then, cutie?" he asked. I didn't get the opportunity to answer as Alex did come down finally.

Alex had slept in Patrick's old room and slept in until he smelled lunch calling. Meredith had cooked up a huge pot of stew with loads of vegetables to accommodate whoever might turn up. First, Alex asked his sister where or how he could bathe and she lit his fire and put on an enormous water boiling pot over it and asked him to drag in a bath from one of the other rooms. "Do you want me to wash your hair Alex?" she asked. A bit shy, he covered himself in the water while she washed his hair. "Do you want a trim too after your bath?" she asked "Aye," he said. When he came down for lunch, he was clean and tidy with shorter hair and a trimmed beard. "It's so nice here," he said to Helen and Grigor over his lunch. "Ma, you've all done an amazing job. It's all beautiful," he said "Aye it is," they said.

"Hugh built most of this house with his brother Donald," I added. "Did you Hugh? Well done, I love it," he said. "The front door was built by Grigor Mohr, and Grigor Og has something to say to you all, don't you Grigor?" I said "Oh aye?" said Grigor. Nervously at first, he stood up as did Hugh and I, who was armed with ribbon and ring. Walking then rather formally over to us both, he asked for the ribbon and ring and announced to the confused family waiting on what was to take place. He then asked Alex to come over near us as well, so he did and stood to my right. Grigor took the ribbon and tied both our hands together at our wrists with Alex announcing we were hand fast until a formal ceremony would take place and his face was gleeful.

Grigor announced, "In front of these my witnesses, my mother in law, Isobel Grant, is hereby handfast to Hugh Chisholm till death do they part. Amen." He asked Hugh to put my ring on and Hugh took my hand and placed the ring on my wedding finger and asked Alex to cut the ribbon, which he did. "Ma is now to be known as Mrs Chisholm to outsiders and Hugh will move in here with Ma until she passes and given the same respect as Da had." There was silence in the room at first, but my wee Alex, God bless him, congratulated us both with kisses and hugs and said he was thrilled to have Hugh as my husband, but didn't know what to call him. Hugh said, "Just call me Hugh".

Grigor was naturally so happy for us both and hugged and kissed us with one of those wet kisses of his. "What if I want to call you Da?" Alex asked. Hugh was shyly emotional at the thought and said that he could. Grigor asked the same question, so he too called Hugh, Da. All the ladies at the table had tears in their eyes and came to us both and congratulated us. Meredith just looked on in shock. When things quietened down, Alex then filled me in with all his news from Nova Scotia.

"As you know Ma, we lost two bairns, but went on to have two more. One of my sons, Archangel, is religious and has joined the Priesthood in the Roman Catholic Church. One of my daughters, Isabella is married to an immigrant Scot with two wee bairns. My two youngest, a son and a daughter, wanted to come here with me. My wife Therese has never forgiven me for the death of our eldest daughter, Therese, who was taken by the bear because I was with her at the time. We weren't happily married after that but the business continued to run well. The oldest ones are all settled there and so is Therese, who has another love interest now. I asked Therese if she'd agree to dividing our land in half and selling what would be my half, so I could buy a property here with my younger two children provided she was happy to relinquish the children into my care permanently. They're here with Therese's family at the moment. Can I borrow horse and cart to pick them up?" Alex asked. "My Grandchildren are here?" I exclaimed. "Och, Alex" I was overjoyed. "How much luggage do you all have?" I asked. A Clydesdale team of two was decided on and I asked Hugh Og to drive the team as there were no deliveries today. The proud Father went to collect his son Alexander Og and daughter Jean. Jean was 20 years old and unmarried and Alexander Og was 22, also unmarried. Poor Padruig had thought all of his grandchildren had been successfully married, but there were two more to marry off.

When my grandchildren entered through my front door, the Priests were still packing up to leave and so there were introductions first, to the Priests, who were happy to meet even more Papists. The collection on the day of the funeral amounted to £1000, I donated a further £50 for the travel, Patrick sent down a further £50 and so did Alex and Grigor. In total, the Priests earned £1200. They thanked us all for the beautiful food and accommodation and said they'd pray for us all and light a candle for Padruig at their Kirk in Edinburgh. Before the Priests left, I asked them if they could bring some of that black stuff they called black diamonds that you can keep your fire going longer from a town called Culross to which the young Priest happily agreed. As the Priests left in their carriage, we waved them off and the gate was finally closed again. Both Hugh and I had told them that there'd be another wedding on their next visit. When they asked for the names, they raised their eyebrows at the couple being Hugh and I but they agreed and wished us both well.

I was so thrilled to meet my Grandchildren "Alex and Jean. I am so please to meet you," I said. They had the best manners I'd ever come across with a pleasant accent and Jean gave me a big smile, "Grandmother," she said. "You can give Granny a hug," I said. I hugged them both and they slowly melted into an emotional greeting unexpected even by their Father. "We are so happy we have a Granny. So sorry about Grandpa," they said. "Your Da will take you to his grave in the wee Chapel and you can pray there anytime," I said. I then asked if they could share a room and they said they did anyway and so they were both put in Beth and James' old room upstairs. They loved it. It had a nice view and was near the family library. "Can we please use the library Granny?" they asked. "Yes of course," I replied.

Meredith had time to show them around the house and where the privies were and the laundry and left the outdoors up to Helen, who showed all three of them around. Jean loved the goats. "The coos are due to come back about 4:30pm," I said, "so don't be afraid when you see sixty big orange coos with horns coming in through the front gate. They're our family too," I said. Alex borrowed Padruig's horse, now ownerless, and pleased at the attention and so I gave him indefinite use of her, provided she could still spend time with her offspring. She was a lovely chestnut mare.

Alex looked around our area for a property for sale and spoke to farmers and asked if anyone was interested in selling. The only property for sale was the one upon which also sat the Post Office, which was not ideal. "Ask Lochiel," I suggested. "He'll know," I advised and so with Lochiel's assistance, he found a nice property that bordered both MacDonald lands and Grant lands. Lochiel was happy for Padruig Grant's son to own it on their border.

The farm was owned by people wanting to migrate and was in very good condition, with a well maintained large two-story home with servant's quarters, large stables, goat enclosures, coo pasture and forty coos, vast oat crops, potatoes, corn and kale crops as well. There was a grain storage shed, smaller than ours but adequate, as well as potato storage and the cost was almost the right price. He was short £1000, which I gave to him so that he could buy it. His father would've wanted that. I didn't need to be a rich widow. His family would be able to move in once the legals were all completed by Malcolm MacGregor Law Rooms, Aonghus's law firm. It was only in Alexander Grant's name, excluding Therese. He hoped his son would inherit it and work with him and his daughter could cook for them, until she married, he hoped. She had worked previously as an interpreter to a law firm and the law courts in English, Gaelic, Algonquian, Dutch, Latin and French languages. I surmised that she may be interested in more than cooking.

I advised Alex to get a farmhand, as the work is quite hard and the hours long, so he asked us to recommend someone. Farmhands that could be trusted was the hardest part of farming, I had found. So, I asked Hugh's advice. "He needs a dog, I can sell him a Collie soon and I'll ask around," he said. I knew Hugh scared most men, so they wouldn't get involved with us unless they were trustworthy given our reputation after the Irish thieves were transported and the Armstrong bandits too.

The Elusive Sarah

I was unexpectedly visited by the long-lost daughter of Henrietta, the elusive Sarah and her husband, Duncan Forsythe and their bairn Robin. They had been waiting for an opportunity to pass on their condolences before leaving the area, they said. Meredith didn't know who they were, so called out "Mistress, there's a Sarah and Duncan Forsythe to see ye." "Thank you, Meredith," I answered. "That's James' and Beth's sister with her husband and child. Can you invite them in and make up some jam and scones please?" I asked. "Aye. Better be a big batch then," Meredith said.

"Grandma," Sarah said. "I am so sorry about Grandda and for not coming to see you or telling you we were married. This is my

378

husband, Duncan Forsythe. Da let us stay up at the Manor House that Grandda built for two nights. We've never seen a funeral such as that and my husband here is sorry he didn't meet Grandda. I was too afraid of Ma, you see," she said almost without taking a breath. "I understand you'd be afraid of Henrietta. Imagine how her staff must feel," I said with a smile. They relaxed a bit with the shared understanding of her Mither's character. "Henrietta's father was a drunk dear," I said. "He hurt Henrietta's Mither and that is why they left the bairns for me to raise with Grigor Mohr's help, who taught them both how to ride. I taught them their lessons, but you'd never know that now," I said. "I never saw you again after you were born. You were packed off from one boarding place to another. Poor wee bairn', I thought, but she didn't want you to be like us, speaking Gaelic," I said.

"So, Duncan and Sarah," I said. "Are you returning to Perthshire now?" "Maybe Mistress," said Duncan, "although me job's finishing up there," he said. "So, you don't need to return then?" I asked. "That's right Mistress. I wasna born in that part of Perthshire, I was born in Perth and most of me immediate family live in Aberfeldy. So, Mistress, who's Clan MacNachten?" he asked. Shocked at the question, I answered, "They are from Loch Insh. My Grandson-in-law was adopted by Gillcrest MacNachten, a dear old man who was my second cousin." "So, weren't they Druids?" he asked. "I am sure that is none of our business," I responded and then went on, "Ewen is Catholic and plays the Hurdy Gurdy beautifully," I said. "Would you like to stay overnight and meet the rest of the family?" I asked. "Aye, Mistress," he answered. I then asked Meredith to get Hugh Mohr to meet Duncan Forsyth to see what he thought of him. "Well," he said, "it would save me a lot of trouble if he took that job with Alex, but Duncan, you'll have to know your place around here. If you apply for work here, knowing who's boss is paramount, especially if it was Alexander if he's anything like his Father demanding a high level of respect and obedience. Are you wanting to work around here?" Duncan was already looking unimpressed, but Hugh Mohr continued on.

"Alexander has high standards that any worker would have to meet up to and carry the family name with honour. Isobel, maybe he should do that wee soil course in Invermoriston first that everyone's doing for maximising crop yields?' That's what I'd do if I were you Duncan. It's a two-week course run by your Grandma's Grandson-in-law, the scientist Gillcrest MacLachlan," Hugh said. Duncan was looking pale and Sarah was looking very doubtful. "That's a good idea Hugh". You can borrow the donkey. Frederick's his name, old and noisy, but a good character if you give him a carrot first, then he won't bite you," he grinned, knowing that Frederick was going to bite him for sure. "How much is the course, Hugh?" I asked. "It's free. Funded by the government, so there are no more famines like we had before. You remember Isobel?" he said. "Oh aye." What was Hugh up to I wondered, but I was already enjoying this marriage.

"Meredith, can they have your old room for the night? No one's using it." "Aye," she said. "I'll put another bed in there and stock up the peat," she said. "Look Isobel. Alex is back!" We both stood side by side watching my son riding in. "Och," said Hugh Mohr, "he looks just like Padruig did when we lived in the cave. He even had that little beardy thing," Hugh said. "Did he?" I asked. "I didn't know that." "He shaved it all off before you saw him. He didn't want you to think he was scruffy-like," he said. "You know Isobel, he has that same bravado and confidence that Padruig had and ego too mind. He didn't mind a bit of admiration," he said. "Who from?" I asked.

Realising he'd put his foot in it again, he said, "Well, he liked it if the ladies thought he was braw, even if he wasna as good looking as me, but he only had eyes for you. A more faithful man you'd never find. I told him that he wasna so handsome as me and it was just that long black hair that he thought made him braw, so I sat across from him threatening him with me clippers in the cave I did. You knew we had a wee burn that ran through the cave? Well, I sat on the other side of it and teased him with me clippers and told him that in his sleep, I'd cut it all off and he'd wake up and no one would think him braw no more" he said "You didn't?" I exclaimed. "All the fellas laughed and so did he thinking I was just joking, but in the morning when he woke up, all that long black hair was just lying around in the heather. I'd clipped it all while he was asleep. When he woke up, he couldn't believe his eyes at his hair just lying there on the heather. He felt his head 'What have you done?' he roared and I swear I thought he was going to kill me, so I ran like the wind and hid until it was safe to go back," he said laughing still pleased at his achievement.

Then changing the subject, he asked, "So, Isobel, what's going on with young Alex's marriage? Can't get divorced, can he?" he stated. "We'd have to talk to the Priests and the law and see if the marriage can be made null-and-void is one option," I said. "Wouldn't that make the bairns bastards?" he asked. "I don't know. I've never thought of that. Surely not. I suppose first we should ask him if he is legally separated in Nova Scotia," I said.

My tall, straight, proud, smiling son suddenly appeared on the porch after stabling the Chestnut, picked me up and twirled me around. "Whoa, whoa," said Hugh Mohr. "She's delicate! Stop!" Of course, Alex kept kissing me totally ignoring Hugh's concerns. "Ma," he said joyously. "It's all gone through. I own it already," he said. "Congratulations son, I am so happy for you," I said. Then a wee child held his hand and said, "Are you Uncle Alex. I'm Robin." He picked up Sarah's child and said, "Well, hello there Robin. Aye, I am Uncle Alex if you are my sister's bairn." Then Sarah came forward and said, "He's your Great Uncle lad. I'm Sarah," she said to Alex, "Beth and James' sister and this is my husband, Duncan Forsythe from Perth. I saw you at Grandda's funeral. Please accept our condolences Uncle Alexander," she said. "Thank you," is all he said. "Meredith's made scones son. Would you like some?" I said to him. "Oh aye, after I've washed my hands. I have to tell you, this farm is everything I've dreamed of, I just need a farmhand," he said.

"Duncan here is finishing his job in Perthshire, he says, and wants to do the wee soil course in Invermoriston. He is unemployed and a gardener by trade," I informed Alex. "Well, Duncan," said Alex, "we'll need to talk, won't we? Are you staying here with Ma?" he said with boldness. It threw Duncan off a bit, who said, "Aye Sir." Hugh Mohr was grinning that he'd taken his advice already in showing Alex respect and it was obviously needed anyway. They decided that if Duncan passed the soil course with Gillcrest writing a reference of some kind, then he'd think about it but with no promises. Hugh said to me quietly, "I don't think you need to worry about Alex, he's no fool but ask him about his marriage situation," he said. "Oh, later please Hugh. I do need a rest now," I said. He then picked me up like

I was a dry leaf and gently took me to our room, all the while kissing his new wife on the lips then stoked the fire, left the Collies with me and said he'd be back. When he closed the door, I heard him yelling at everyone to be quiet while I rested. "Quiet!" he shouted.

I awoke to my new husband having already taken off my bed covers and was holding my legs gently apart and rubbing my legs with his hands first then exploring further he put his big hand over my private area then searched for my clitoris which he found. Unable to stop my squeal of joy when I came he continued on licking, sucking and giving me and then his fingers began exploring inside. I was small inside even after having three children but he was assessing his size with mine and then said. "Will you have me wife?" he asked. "Aye", I said and my new husband of only a few hours first teased me, putting my hands on his manhood to show me what he wanted of his wife. I held them in my hands like they were so precious to squeeze ever so gently, massaging then suddenly he thrust his whole manhood inside me many times letting out a loud groan as he came. I couldn't hide my pleasure and enjoyment of sex with him and just wanted more and more." I knew you'd like that as he kissed it and I moaned in absolute pleasure. You are a perfect sexual match to me and I can do anything now you're my wife," he said. Like the starved sexual beings, we were, we didn't stop exploring each other and what made us both happy with our experiments of joy. "I won't be able to leave you alone now; the family will have to get used to a bit of noise or go outside," he said grinning while he explored further at every inch of my body as I did with his perfect manhood. I had never done things like he asked me to do or to be done to as Padruig's wife and it was so exciting. His penis was larger than Padruig's, so he wasn't too careless as to hurt me. He was a considerate lover as well as adventurous. After using the bed chamber, we both had a hot bath together, sensually washing each other's private areas and I lay on his hairy blonde chest while he wiped my face. "You are so beautiful Isobel," he said and wanted more after drying each other. He wanted to towel my buttocks and told me how beautiful it was. Lifting me up at my knees to face him, he entered me in the standing position and we made love in that position. Carrying me to our bed still with him inside, he ran his arms up the side of my body then sucking my breasts until he came, groaning in pleasure. He sucked each breast vigorously and massaged each one sometimes squeezing them just going into the realm of pain before stopping. "I love your breasts," he said. "I've wanted to suck them since the day I first saw you and now I can. It's heavenly, my lovely one, to feel you and suck you and enter you and to hear your little squeals of joy or moans," he said. "Just watching you sleeping, I go hard and I want to make love to you," he said. "Hugh, would you think less of me if I told you that I wanted to rub up against your manhood just to feel it go hard but I didn't want you to know how much I wanted to touch it. I wanted to put my hand under your kilt just to feel it and know how big it was," I said. "There was one time when you stepped back and I was there behind you and you must have felt its hardness and I moved it side to side so you could feel it and you didn't move away. There was a wall behind me and I couldn't move away even if I'd wanted to," he said feeling very pleased at what I'd said. "Aye, it was when you were working here on the house. I didn't want to move away from your hardness that day, so I moved my buttocks a wee bit," I said coyly, but can you just imagine what Grigor Mohr or Donald would have said if they knew. "So, you have loved me longer than you have said?" he asked. "Aye, I would have dreams of you every night with your beautiful blonde hair," I said, then tears flowed freely." I did love you Hugh but I had to be faithful to Padruig, even though you all thought he was dead, but the day you touched me at the loch, I knew I couldn't control my own feelings much longer," I said. "How long have you loved me?" he persisted. "The day you stopped me from killing myself. I didn't want to ever let you go. When you left the shieling that ter- rible day, I knew," I said. "Can we sleep like that with me clinging to you if you don't mind?" I said. "By the way, wife, Donald knew, he caught me taking a keek at you from the rooftop. He tried to put me off saying you would be too small for my big one," he said smil- ing at the knowledge that his was a big one. "Will you suck it now for me Isobel?" I did whatever he asked me to do and taking it into my mouth I carefully caressed it with my tongue, sucking and lick- ing until he came. I loved it. My new husband and I slept with me clinging to him every night until I knew my last day was coming. We did get comments the next day about 'staying up late' and making wee noises, but I think Grigor was keen to have sex with Helen that night and after that Alex made a remark that he would miss all the love making sounds at night when he moved out to his new farm. His children were getting an education from both Grigor's bedroom with Helen and ours, which got noisier every night.

As it turned out, the laws in Nova Scotia allowed Alex and Therese to divorce. "Will you remarry, do you think?" I asked him. "Probably Ma, not while I am getting the farm going, but hearing the night time sounds in this house has made me want a woman again," he said. "Okay, but just a warning, seeing as you're close to Cameron lands," I said "Aye?" he said, quizzically. "There's a single lass, named Lilias, who we do not recommend. She's still teaching at the school, but she is an awful person," I said. "Okay, I'll take it as a warning not to involve myself with Lilias." From the kitchen, Meredith called out, "She's fat, ugly and racist." "No worries Ma. I will not bring Lilias home." I shuddered at the thought. "Have you met Milread yet, Dougal's sister from our wool waulking group, pretty as a picture she is and a great spinner. I've forgotten her age, but around twenty I think?" I said. "Not yet Ma, can you introduce me to her and I'll tell you what I think abut Milread," he responded positively. Hugh put his arm on Alex's shoulder and said, "She lives in my house with her brother. I can take you there and get you two paired off I reckon," he said. "Thank Da, when I get all my work done, can you take me there?" he asked.

"Son, I've been meaning to ask you if you wanted to visit Aunty Morag's grave? You too Grigor, if you haven't already been today?" I asked. He was puzzled why in particular that Alex needed to visit his Mither's grave, so he said he'd like to come with flowers and so did Helen and Hugh. "Climb aboard Ma," Alex said and I rode on his back up to the cemetery with Hugh watching on protectively, passed our wee Chapel that felt quite different these days. It definitely felt occupied.

As we approached Morag's grave, Alex put me down gently and we walked hand in hand to the grave side where he fell to his knees and began to weep surprising onlookers, but not me. "Oh, Aunty Morag, I couldn't help you. I am so sorry. I hope you're in a good place now with Uncle Grigor, God rest both your souls," he said through the sobs of a wee bairn. I sat beside him and I spoke to Morag in Erse as I always did, saying that wee Alex was here to visit her and that his heart was at ease now that she was. I told her the news of Padruig's passing and I hoped that they'd all see each other. Grigor and Helen and Hugh were all confused at first but then Helen suddenly remembered that horrible day hiding in the shieling. "The shieling. Aunty Morag. We could hear your suffering from the wee shieling where we were hiding. Please forgive us," she cried putting her hands over her mouth, as we all did that terrible day. Grigor, poor man, was lost for words at gaining an understanding as to what had happened to his Mither and I sadly knew that Helen would have to explain everything to her husband later on, which she did, as well as me having to explain it all to Hugh, who also had no knowledge of Morag being ravished by the redcoats.

I saw Grigor and Alex speaking in depth by the fireside that night and I guessed that Alex had told him that he couldn't get the sounds out of his head until he went to Nova Scotia, which finally silenced the screams. Our dearest Grigor had never known of his Mither's suffering and neither had Grigor Mohr, as was the way with some women who were too ashamed or afraid of losing their husbands. Grigor came to me and asked me, "Ma, was this commonplace in those times?" he asked sorrowfully. "Aye, Grigor, very common," I said cautiously. "You see those rose bushes along the path with names under them? They are just the close friends I knew who it happened to. Some husbands knew and some didn't. Your Ma has a whole rosebush and it was only when she passed and was removed from your property, that I could sleep without hearing your Ma's suffering. She spared both you and your Father. It was incredibly brave. She learned a way to bare it by calming herself knitting. They are the silent heroines just there. It was fortunate she already had you," I explained rather inadequately. Poor Eilidh was left unable to bear children after the ravishing against her. Around here in Glenmoriston it went on for a lot longer than in many other places because of the fort and their horse races. I stopped myself from telling him that I too was ravished just on a different day but knew it would come soon. From that day beside Morag's grave, Alex and Grigor formed a strong bond between themselves and they loved each other which strengthened both of their hearts. I was very relieved at that outcome. Grigor could've been disappointed in me for not telling him, but he wasn't. I couldn't bear disappointment from my beloved son-in-law. It had been up to his Mither, Morag. May God rest her soul, Amen.

Being brothers-in-law, Alex and Grigor consulted continuously on farming and the latest in farming developments and catching up with who was who in the family, when Alex asked Grigor, "What do you think of Duncan?" "I don't know him at all or his wife, so other than us being related to his wife, I can't speak for his knowledge or ability or even if he's a likeable character. One of our keys to success here at Craskie has been having likeable people, like Hugh Og and Hamish. They're very likeable and become like family. So, if you like him and you think he can work hard, you could put him on a trial for a few months for him to prove himself, but even then, some staff had worked here for years and then turned and followed Irish itinerants to steal from us. It was in all the papers. We caught them all in the stables by accident. It could've turned very bad, had Hugh Mohr not shown up with his trusty rifle and threatened to shoot their leader. I don't want to paint a picture of doom and gloom, but I also don't want to be overly positive about a complete stranger to us from Perth. The fort advised us to get references for any new staff after that incident, so I would first get a reference from his current workplace and ask why that job is finishing up," Grigor said. "Thank you Grigor, that's good advice. So, should I wait until he finishes doing his soil course while living here and hopefully get the response before the two weeks is up?" he asked. "Or go there myself?" he added. Grigor responded by saying, "Now that could go badly for you. We don't know that territory or anyone there," he cautioned. "But, ask Ma."

Over dinner that evening, I was asked about that trip to Perth and I said, "Nae. Too risky son and anything could happen like accidents, robberies, who knows?" I said. "Write a letter now and take it to the Post Office, then wait is my advice," I said. Thank God he took my advice. The following day's newspaper included the usual storm damage, but robberies also along the Perthshire route. I'd found myself now in the position as an advisor against risky trips. I didn't miss the look that Hugh Mohr gave me and he wanted then to add on his piece considering he'd had to punish me after my risky venture to Loch Insh. So, in a serious Fatherly tone he said, "Alex your Mither took a risk that could have cost her her life by venturing off on her own to Loch Insh to have the Chapel built. If she didn't have her ghostly helpers, she wouldn't be here now. She is speaking with knowledge, as am I because I was given the task of punishing your Mither, by her choice or your Father would have killed her." Hugh said. "I'm familiar with my Father in that mood, he never liked me much growing up, so thankyou Da. Should I also keep looking if there is someone better than Duncan?" Alex said, "Aye, definitely," Hugh said. "Someone who is not so cocky son. Cheeky is funny, but cocky isn't. He's cocky," I said. We had been reminded of that night once more, but no-one wanted to be reminded of that night, especially poor Helen who was looking grave but I knew that Alex would need it explained later.

"Son," I said, "what I'd like you to do is visit my grandson-in-law in Invermoriston. He teaches the soil improvement course there at the hospital science department. Have a cup of tea with him and ask him about whether he'd have a student there that he'd recommend, because students need good grades and are unlikely to upset the Professor. He may have the right person or persons right there. Pray about it in the Chapel son and ask God to solve this problem for you. Every night here, even in the hardest of times, I handed it all over to God, but if you want my personal opinion, I believe that Sarah and her husband will go back to Perthshire and what exactly they're after, I am unsure. He may think that there's inheritance to be had. Hold off employing him, even part time. Having them under the same roof these few days, I've trusted them less, not more, if that helps. By comparison, my grandson-in-law, Gillcrest MacLachlan is very trustworthy and a good lad. He is likeable, even if he and Aonghus face off against one another occasionally about Irish settlement, he is devoted to his craft and his family, even his lands back in Argyle. You know he is the Laird of the MacLachlan lands I suppose by now? He acts as a landlord, but deals with it all despite his young age, God bless him."

"Do you want Ewen to take you to Invermoriston in case you get lost before he starts shoeing horses? Invermoriston is bigger these days and Ewen knows his way around and he is a lovely lad?" I said. "Aye, Ma. I'll take your advice and I'll take Ewen. You're so full of love. I've missed you so much," he said and hugged me warmly. "Meredith's making your favourite dinner tonight son," I said pleased with my plans. "Just for you and Hugh or we'll run out of chickens mind," I said. "You do still like chicken darling?" I asked. "Oh aye," he said smiling from ear to ear.

The farm was settled in Alex's name and he changed its name to 'Loch Garry Ranch' and the Cameron family moved out leaving furniture, which they couldn't take with them and Alex even gave us a big couch. It was a large green velvet three-seater with high arms at each end and solid oak lion shaped feet. The Cameron family obviously had specific taste. Alex struck a deal with Gillcrest MacLachlan and was given a student of farm science and animal husbandry for the practical part of their studies, free of charge, who would work and live with them for a year. If the student passed their practical year with Alex, he would write a report back to the university. He then had hard working young men who were enthusiastic, eager to please and honest. The deal worked well for Gillcrest, Alex and the students and I sent Sarah and Duncan back to Perthshire after Gillcrest failed Duncan in the soil course.

With all of Jean Grant's qualifications in translating and interpreting to date having been overlooked, her cousin Aonghus offered her a job in his Inverness law office on Thursdays because he had clients needing an interpreter for various languages. The Inverness Courts also went on to employ her on Fridays as their official court interpreter, mostly dealing with Gaelic to English and vice versa. Jean said that she only wanted to work those two days because it is so well paid, which enabled her to purchase all of the gear needed for training her wee yearling, including a lovely big blanket for the cold nights. She stays with Aonghus and Annabel in Inverness from Wednesday evening until she finishes work Friday evening when Alex picks her up. When her Father takes her in on Wednesdays, he stays overnight also, so they can all catch up and he returns back to his farm the following morning with items that he needed to purchase in Inverness anyway, including the geese that I recommended he buy. When buying the geese, apparently there were lots of younger women who gossiped incessantly about the new blood in town and were heard commenting on how handsome he was. Jean looked forward to going back home as she also enjoyed cooking for her Da, her brother, Alexander Og and the student. One of the agriculture students was admiring her and vice versa, but Alex was keeping a close eye on that as he had high hopes for his accomplished and dignified daughter.

I was drained after thinking in depth over Alex's new farm issues, so when he and his lovely son Alexander and Jean moved out, I thought I could get more rest, but before Ewen left that morning upon returning from Invermoriston with Alex, I asked him how Isobel-Mairi was today and he said that she'd had a bad night with her back. "It was aching her real bad Granny," he said, "so I rubbed her back with the cream Da gave me for pregnancy back ache and it helped a lot. Da said that it was an Arabian recipe that had dates in the mixture," he said. "Ewen lad, how was she before you left to go with Alex?" I asked. "Och, Granny, I am worried about her. Her back was a wee bit better, but she was in pain and her belly was tight and then not tight again." Panicked, I realised that she was in labour.

"Ewen, go immediately now and carry your wife here quickly with her shroud," I said. "Meredith, ask Mary the washer lady if she can help me deliver a bairn. I'm not strong enough for it. Tell her I'll pay her an extra shilling. Helen, put on a huge pot of water to boil please," I ordered in haste. Hugh Mohr then came in and saw all the flurry. "What's up Isobel?" he asked. "I think Isobel-Mairi is having the bairn darling. Can you keep the dogs out and keep anyone from coming in the front door, except Ewen and her? Tell Grigor, when he comes, to use the side rear door quietly and leave his boots outside and wash his hands. Meredith, put as many floor rugs on the floor near the fire with a clean sheet over the top. Alex, son, move that couch you gave me over to be underneath the window, then cover it with sheets as well as cover the window and then you'd best go home son," I said. "Okay Ma," he said, completed the tasks and went. "Oh Alex, take the chestnut son," I said "Thanks Ma," he called back.

Ewen arrived running, carrying his wife carefully with his face panicked. She was obviously in labour. "Sit on the floor Ewen with your wife between your legs, your arms underneath hers and don't worry if she swears at you or comes out with really bad language. She may even say she hates you. This is normal okay?" I said. "Just do what we tell you," I said. Mary came in looking very serious. "Need my help Mistress?" she asked. "Aye, Mary, I'm not strong enough to catch the bairn in delivery. Can you help me or are you queasy?" I asked. "Not queasy Mistress. I'll help the poor wee lass." Looking at Ewen, she said, "It's gonna hurt. He's a big fella." I examined Isobel-Mairi like I'd done a thousand times before and the bairn was already crowning. "Isobel-Mairi," I asked, "did your waters break already? That's that gooey stuff," I asked. "Aye," she shouted. "It won't be long then. You're already two inches in diameter," I said. "Ewen, when I tell you, lift her to a standing position. Mary, can you safely catch him?" I asked. "Aye, of course," she said. Isobel-Mairi was screaming like a banshee and her Father came running from the oat fields worried sick only to find Hugh Mohr blocking the front door. "Side door, Isobel said." Then he ran to the side door, hoping not to embarrass his daughter.

The animals on the farm were reacting, I was told later, with empathy to the lass and a big boy was delivered and was held by a very strong Mary. "Water, Helen," I said and gave Ewen a cool wet cloth to wipe his wife's face. "You pig, you rat, you dog, I hate you, it hurts," she said and thank God he smiled and wiped her face as gently as could be. As the placenta came out, she yelled again and again and I asked him now to place her on the couch where we delivered the placenta and tied the umbilical cord. I proceeded to press down on her to ease out any blood clots. "Nae, nae, Granny, stop!" she pleaded. "It's nearly over darling. You have a healthy son. Helen was cleaning her grandson lovingly and wrapping him up tightly and warm and then gave him to his Mither and said "Your son Isobel-Mairi and Ewen. Congratulations." I am not sure who cried first, but I think it was Ewen and then surprisingly, Mary. Ewen and their baby were enraptured with each other, so I kissed Isobel-Mairi on her forehead then hugged Helen, Meredith and Mary. Grigor had passed out on the kitchen floor, so Helen had to help him. It had been an emergency birth. "Let Hugh Mohr know, Grigor," but unbeknownst to me, Grigor was on the floor and so Mary went. "Hugh, it's a big boy. Healthy and fat. The Mither is well too. Grigor is on the floor. Can you pass on the word, especially to Cora please?" Mary said matter of fact. Then Ewen said boldly, "His name is Nachtain MacNachten," then Isobel-Mairi said, "Nachtain Grigor MacNachten please husband and I am sorry for calling you those names," she said. Baby Nachtain must have weighed at least about 9 lbs. without weighing him, but I measured him at 21" in length.

We put a sign on the door announcing the birth that day. I felt it was time to part with my Pecht brooch, given to me by the lovely Gillcrest MacNachten, now that in death he had a son, a daughter-in-law and a grandson. Going into my room to get out my precious tin from under my bed, I felt suddenly exhausted but took it out just the same, fearing I'd forget. Parting with it felt oddly strange, like I was parting with something more than a brooch. Helen had the Clan Gregor brooch, I had the Clan Grant brooch as well as a wedding ring and they would have the ancient Pecht brooch to be handed down to their oldest lass. It would be for the husband Ewen to give to his wife as a gift for giving him a healthy bairn. When I gave it to Ewen that day, I explained its importance and who it was from and how ancient it was and he was visibly touched. "Your wife has the Pecht blood on both sides, so it's appropriate you give it to Isobel-Mairi for giving you this gift from God. But you must take care of this. It is fragile and don't let your children play with it. It can hold her arisaid in place nicely. May God grant you all a happy and healthy life, my lovelies," I said. I left Meredith and Mary to clean up, giving them both an extra shilling and then added, "Ewen, you have to do your family's washing for at least a month. Isobel-Mairi, keep clean and change the cloths regularly. You will bleed a lot at first, so no exercise or horse riding. Now, let me rest and Meredith, can you please feed this nursing mither some broth?" He was baptised when Father Michael came next bringing along also, the black diamonds from Culross that the monks had mined there. It was an entire cart load, which he said may last us a year if we were thrifty. God bless Father Michael.

After the emergent birth of my first great-grandchild, I started to feel that I had lived for too long, through famines, drought, the clearances, the '15, the '45, losing Ma, then Da, losing all of the crofters, the unexpected disappearance of my husband and the incredibly difficult farm rebuilding process after the complete destruction of our property and culture by the English then the glorious re-marriage to my lovely Hugh Mohr. I was aware that there were pockets of our community who disapproved of my re-marriage but my immediate family were all that mattered. Both Padruig and I had been satisfied with our determined and combined efforts to rebuild not only our farm, but our community and our culture as well. I knew I would be happy to hand over to a competent new generation, bringing their own particular skills into a new world constantly changing but for the love that kept me alive. The wee bairn, Nachtain Grigor with his chubby pink cheeks, fluffy brown hair and blue eyes may never know me or some of our old ways, but he will be safe in his parents adoring arms. I slept for hours after that.

Wool Waulking, the Garden and Padruig's Tomb

Helen still held the wool waulking at our place during each clipping season with her two beautiful daughters, their singing voices heard all across the farms. I wasn't expecting a visitor when the gentleman from the funeral, whom I'd recognised from somewhere, visited. Meredith was busy with the wool waulking and so I answered the door. It was Annabel's Grandfather, John Cameron, who had known Padruig from Culloden. He said he had wanted to wait a respectable time before coming to give me his condolences in person. He carried with him flowers and a pot of honey from his own bee hives. The old gentleman had ridden on a big bay horse, so I ushered Dougal to stable her while we chatted in the house. "Please come in. I am sorry if my house is a bit noisy, but its wool waulking season," I said. "Aye, I heard the singing from the Drover's Road, Mrs Grant," he said. "Its Mrs Chisholm now," I said to a shocked John Cameron. Gathering himself together he said that the singing was quite lovely. "I don't mind it at all, but I would prefer a quieter place to talk, maybe later in the Chapel?" he asked. After we had coffee and cake, we strolled to the Chapel where he lit a candle for Padruig and reiterated how sorry he was at his passing, but surprised that I was already re-married.

Then he said a few surprising things. "I read the newspaper about the funeral and how you were taught to be a teamster by your Da, John Grant. He was very protective of you, given you were Padruig Dubh's wife and when you delivered that time in Badenoch in '45, we were all told to keep our eyes off you. Cluny made sure that we all behaved ourselves, mind you, it was dark and you had your plaid covering your head. I couldn't believe that you were managing a team of eight Clydesdales, as calm as could be and those horses were only listening to you," he stated. "So, that's where I've seen you before, in Badenoch?" I asked. "Aye," he said. "You and your Da delivered some important things that night but he never claimed he was a Jacobite despite having Cluny's trust," he said. Feeling awkward, I said that "Da wasn't a Jacobite and nor was I. We had a business to run and that was all. Whether it was oats to the fort, or those heavy drums to Badenoch, it was just business. We were careful to stay out of the political arena and I never asked Da what was in those enclosed drums. That was Da's business. I just had to drive the team," I said defensively.

"John, where is this conversation going? I appreciate you coming with condolences for Padruig, but asking about Da and his deliveries in 1745 is making me feel uncomfortable and it's irrelevant now. What do you want to know exactly?" I asked. "I am sorry, Isobel, if I have made you feel uncomfortable, but I will ask. Were you delivering gold to Cluny for the Prince?" he demanded to know. "Oh, John you are one of those treasure hunters. Nae, is the answer and I am going back now to the house and I suggest that you take your horse and leave. I don't want bad relations with Annabel's family. The last I heard, that gold was at the bottom of Loch Arkaig. You could ask the MacPhersons or MacKintosh clans," I said.

As I stood to leave our Chapel, I became aware just how alone and vulnerable I was at the top end of the property without Hugh Mohr today, who was busy wool clipping. Grigor might be close by, but I felt insecure and I had been a bad judge of character to be alone with him. Internally, I pleaded, 'Oh Padruig, I need you.' Then suddenly, from behind me as I was walking out, a loud metallic clashing sound came from above Padruig's tomb. John Cameron recognised the sounds of swords in battle and he spun around to see where the noise was coming from and looking very afraid. Whatever it was that John Cameron heard or saw that day, had the effect of terrifying the old man. He ran passed me like the devil was at his heals and he was as white as a ghost. He didn't stop until he took his horse and galloped off Craskie Farm. What a bizarre event. I strolled over to Padruig's grave. "Darling? Are you in there?" I asked. "It's okay," I said, "he's gone now, but thank you for helping out. That was very impressive," I said. Even in death, my husband could impress me like no other.

I strolled back to the house to where it was all happening. The wool waulking was a big job, but Hugh Mohr, Hugh Og, Hamish and Ewen did the washing of the sheep first and all of the clipping. They had been oblivious to John Cameron's visit. There were a few new lads there too learning the trade from them down by the burn, but I had forgotten my glasses, so I couldn't see them

clearly. I wasn't sure who they were. Mairi, long deceased, God rest her soul, had been right. Helen, her daughters and all of the wool waulking women could hardly keep up with the orders from Edinburgh and were making a healthy income. Milread, Dougal's sister who had just recently joined the wool waulking women, brought along her own spinning wheel, which was much faster than my old spinning wheel had been. It was a much cleverer invention I thought. She was a real asset. Mairi's daughter Cora, had taken over her Mither's role in the wool waulking group and she still remained the lead songstress for this traditional task. Jokingly, I said to her one day, "You'll have to sing a beautiful song for me beside my grave on the day of my funeral young Cora. Your voice gives me goosebumps."

Helen also took over my large garden and the glasshouse that I'd had especially built, including the herbs, the lavender plants and the tomato plants grown from seed from New York, thanks to Padruig. What we didn't eat of the sweet red fruit, we sold at a wee market stall that Helen's children had run as wee bairns and the two girls continued to do so as adults at Fraser's Trading Post next to the school, which was very popular. I really love tomatoes in stews and even on plain bread with butter. Da had refused to eat them at all at first, but gave in to eating stews with tomatoes gradually, but never trusted them raw. It must have been nice for Padruig to have been aware that not only was the family blossoming once again, but also the community coming alive with people moving back in to Glenmoriston.

The lavender plants had been given to me by the Reverend Stewart's housekeeper all those years ago and I had planted them in between the rose bushes in one line, but that had only made up half of them. They had grown thick and tall reaching the height of the rose bushes on each side, so it gave our entry to the house an attractive appearance. The scent was glorious from both the lavender and the rose bushes.

I planted the remaining lavender bushes in a row in front of the porch, as well as a few big hydrangeas that I had been given and I placed one at each end. I loved their huge flowers. The lavender bushes never needed to be fertilised or cared for, they just multiplied. After twenty years, they had covered the ground between our driveway right the way through to the tree line, but stopped before the hitching rail. Padruig would sometimes call them smelly weeds that would take over the farm one day, until he ben-efited from the oil extract from them to ease his headaches in his last days. I'd dab it gently across his forehead and temple. "Are these those smelly weeds?" he'd say with a smile that he could still produce, God bless his soul. Helen now regularly extracts the oil from the plants and both the oil and the flowers were sold at our growing local markets. I thought they were beautiful and it kept the manure smell from taking over the farm.

Over breakfast each morning Hugh Mohr would always ask if see if there was anything I needed before he started his day especially the clipping season. The day after John Cameron's visit, I told him what had happened the previous day and that I had found myself alone with everyone else down here. So, I have learned my lesson from that experience not to do that again. I told him, however, how Padruig had 'helped out' and despite not being an overly spiritual person, I thought, he was very pleased at Padruig's intervention and somehow not sur-prised. He said, "I am going to light a candle for him again today, God bless him. Isobel, please don't leave the house without one of us. You never know, Padruig might be angry with me for not looking after ya properly." "Don't be ridiculous Hugh," I said. "Then can you take young Dougal if you're going to the Chapel or the stables," he said.

"I don't know Dougal very well. It would be uncomfortable. Besides which, he is supposed to be working with the horses," I added. "Okay," he conceded. "Then just come and get me," Hugh said. "Hugh, it's not likely to ever happen again. My only concern is Aonghus when Annabel tells him," I said. "Oh," he said. "That could be a problem."

"Can we agree then that when Aonghus visits next, that you will send for me and I'll have me gun," Hugh said. "Okay, I'll do that," and I smiled but then added, "My dearest, do you really think that you would shoot someone with your rifle one day, or is it just the threat of it?" I asked. With that cheeky look of his, he answered, "That's what they'll never know now isn't it?" he said. "If a rifle was facing in your direction or poked into your back, would you take the chance that it was a bluff?" he asked. "That's a good point Hugh. Padruig thought you were bluffing when you were threatening to cut off all his lovely black hair while he slept in the cave, but you did hack it all off with your clippers. So, it brings me back to my original question. Would you use your rifle when you are threatening to or not?" I asked looking directly into his big blue eyes. "Aye, I would Isobel, if it was a threat to you, but not if it meant killing one of your children or grandchildren or Grigor" he added with serious and honest conviction. "Hugh, you are my last best friend, my lover, my companion and my husband. Can you please promise not to actually kill anyone? If you did that, then I would possibly lose you to the hangman. You won't have to be patient for too long, I'll be joining Padruig soon, I think," I said. "Can you please just bluff, for a while at least, unless the situation is like the night one of those Irish thieves could have killed us all. You are still my hero from that night Hugh," I said.

"You have asked me so nicely, Isobel, I like the 'my hero' bit the best," he said as he chuckled away to himself. "On one condition then," he said. "Aye", I said warily. "I need a new large bonnet for this freezing cold weather and this one's too old and it no longer keeps the damp out or me head warm. With your own hands, you have to promise to knit me a large new bonnet in green and brown wool with a double woolen lining that won't fall off me head with a wee leather edging and I'll no kill anyone till after you pass away. Is that a deal?" he said. "Aye. Is this old one the right size?" I asked. "Can

I take a wee look at it? Are you wanting it the same design as this old one but knitted?" I asked. It revealed his beautiful mop of thick yellow, blonde hair that fell to his shoulders. "Hugh, your hair is so blonde and beautiful", I said. "Before I'd seen your hair, I'd always imagined it to be black like Padruig's. "You should grow one of those little beardy things like Alex and you'd look really handsome," I said. "And I'll make you your bonnet, I'll just take its measurements." Happy then that no one would be killed by my blonde Hugh Mohr for the time being, he left sounding out, 'my hero, really handsome and blonde', to himself. I made him two large bonnets to chose between depending on the weather, one out of green tweed with leather edges and the other as he had described. He grew a wee beard and didn't even threaten to kill anyone. I liked the green tweed bonnet the best and he loved them both.

After years of preparation on Helen's part, the opening of the art gallery, which she named Helen Grant MacGregor Art Studio, was one of the highlights of my adult life, aside from their weddings and the births of my grandchildren, my great-grandchild Nachtain and my second marriage. Everybody was wondering about Beth's new bairn's hair colour and talking about what name Beth would give it. If it was a boy she would name him John Simon, John being after my father and Simon's father. If it was a girl, she had decided to name her Simone Anna Isobel Fraser, but not hyphenated like Helen's children. To be honest, I didn't really mind, so long as the wee bairn was healthy and I didn't have to deliver it.

The Art Gallery Grand Opening

Many tourists from The Hart of the Highlands Manor House attended the Grand Opening of the Art Gallery on 17th May 1788, as well as neighbours and friends and colleagues from miles around and in total, an unheard of £20,000 was earned by our artist daughter in one night. Even Padruig wouldn't have expected his daughter to have been the wealthiest out of all of us. Enclosed is a copy of the invitation that we sent out and an itemised list of all sixty pieces of Helen's magnificent artwork for sale or perusal. Admittedly, "The Polar Bear Trilogy" had been sketched by her Father and was sold

397

as such and because it had been actually sketched by *Padruig Dubh* himself, it sold for £350, as did his "*Pack Wolves in Quebec*" and his "*HMS Panther.*"

When *Gillcrest MacLachlan* and *Morag-Freya MacLachlan* arrived at the Grand Opening of *Helen's Art Gallery*, they were first awestruck by the two tall standing lights at the drive entrance on *Drover's Road* making it clear where to go. The pathway up to the door had been raked over and over, so it was as smooth as it would ever get without putting down cobblestones. Greeted at the door by our smiling uniformed security men, *Hugh Og* and *Hamish* and upon showing the invitation, they went in to a brightly lit art gallery.

Gillcrest had never seen *Helen's* work before and was aghast. He had been told that he had first choice on a painting called "*The Bombing of Castle Lachlan*". He had helped *Helen* get all of the technical details correct as well as *Loch Fyne*, but when he saw the finished product, he was very impressed at what a great talent his mother-in-law truly was. Other *Clan Lachlan* members had come too and were staying at either the *Manor House* or with *Morag-Freya* in *Invermoriston* and they had commented on how perfectly *Helen* had captured the light reflecting off their loch in the painting.

Gillcrest and *Morag-Freya* really honoured the occasion by wearing formal attire. His jacket and waistcoat matched with a white linen shirt underneath. The tartan kilt also matched, but the jacket was plain grey tweed and the kilt was a grey based tartan and he wore knee-high boots with matching sporran. *Morag-Freya* matched her husband, wearing a long tartan dress the same tartan as her husband's kilt, but her arisaid was grey with tartan frilled lacey edges and she wore leather ankle boots. They looked like a confident couple who had a future and he definitely looked like a *Laird* for the first time.

He purchased "*The Bombing of Castle Lachlan*", but I can't remember its price. They then wandered around mingling with everyone and looking at everything and then I noticed him stop suddenly in front of "*The Irish Dog.*" That painting had been sold already to an Irish tourist. *Grigor* was nearby, so *Gillcrest* asked him had he seen this dog before. It was then that *Grigor* and I locked eyes, realising that our scruffy dog must have indeed been his father's escapee bitch, which was now long in the Earth. "Aye, she was a stray bitch that kept following Ma and Uncle Allan around and even when we asked around for its owner, no one came forward, so she stayed with me actually," he said. "Ma wanted me to have company in the oat fields. She was a good old dog and even caught her own food. I hope she wasn't your Da's lost bitch Gillcrest. Was she?" Grigor said beautifully. "Aye, it's her, but I am so happy to know that she was cared for for all those years and loved by you, Da. Thank you," and he hugged his father-in-law.

My grandson-in-law, Simon Fraser and his father John Fraser, paid £1400 for the painting called "Murder of Fraser of Inverallochy"; along with its poem, which they were going to proudly display in the foyer between the two parts of their lovely country house in Stratherick. Looking heavily with child and somewhat happier, Beth bought "Learning to Ride with Uncle Grigor" for her stables in Stratherick. John also bought "Fraser's Trading Post" to be hung in Fraser's Trading Post.

Who will remember Fraser of Inverallochy?

Buried in the English telling of Dromossie Moor

Buried in time to be forgotten

Fraser of Inverallochy bravely led his clansmen

Into a clash of metal against metal

Still alive while all around his men fell

His death was a murder ordered by the Black Prince

No, I'll not commit murder Wolfe said,

So, another emptied his gun into his heroic and defiant heart,

Into Fraser of Inverallochy

After paying for his paintings, John then came up to me to speak a while in order to enquire after my wellbeing since Padruig passed away and my subsequent remarriage to another of the Seven Glenmoriston Men. "I've lived a little too long," I answered honestly in response, "though I am pleased to see Padruig's dream realised of our daughter Helen being launched onto the wider stage. He always knew there was more to Helen. Her expression in the artwork really touches one's soul, no matter the topic," I said, to which he agreed. John went on to say that, in gratitude to us all, he and Anna had a few wee gifts for us for Craskie Farm. The first one being a pole light to be erected on the border between The Manor House and Craskie Farm near Chisholm House to enable him to patrol that border a lot easier with light. His expression indicated that he would not accept refusal, so I allowed him to continue.

Completely surprised at his generosity, he went on to say, "My wife Anna also has a few wee gifts for the Chapel if we can bring them over tomorrow. She thought you may like candle holders erected on the inside walls. Would you like that?" he asked. "Oh aye," I said, "at night time I admit it is very dark in there," I replied. "In addition," he went on, "I want to give you, two tall free-standing pole lights for the front of your house to light it up at night, but if you want to put them elsewhere on the property, that is up to you all. So, in total I am giving you three pole lights including the whale oil and Anna is giving you six candle holders complete with the candles, but your men may have to attach them to the walls. For the outside wall of the Chapel, I wish to include a portable torch light attached to the building itself, like you have on the stable. What do you think?" I responded humbly, "May God accept your charity in the name of better religious practice John. May you both enjoy long and healthy lives and a good place in the Afterlife. Amen," I said. "You have both been good friends to both Padruig and I as well as Hugh and the community of Glenmoriston and I am forever grateful for that. I just have one question John," I said. "Aye?" he asked. "Do you want your bible back that you taught Padruig the English with?" I asked. "Nae, nae," he said. "You keep it," and with that they kissed my cheeks in the European way, took their purchases and departed into the cold night in their lovely horse-drawn carriage with Beth and Simon.

The elderly Bishop Gordon from London, his wife and the old doctor, Dr. Browne, who had treated Padruig on his return from New York, were invited and purchased "The Seven Glenmoriston Men" for the Episcopalian Manse in London. The old doctor brought his son along with him who was also a doctor, Dr. Browne Junior and he was a very bright and intelligent man. Dr. Browne Junior had purchased the land beside and behind the Post Office to set up a new Medical Practice in Glenmoriston. The local doctor had retired finally much to my pleasure. Mrs. Margaret Gordon spotted me and said, "Oh Mrs. Grant or should I call you Mrs. Chisholm now? Congratulations by the way. It is so nice to meet you in person at long last. This is my husband, Bishop Gordon and the good doctor who saved your first husband's life and this is his son Benedict," she said.

Benedict was excited to be in Scotland and upon arrival had seen the old doctor's practice was for sale and so he bought it much to the shock of his Father, who had expected him to practise medicine in London. In buying the land attached to the Post Office, he was going to be more visible, he said and would have a practice built next door to it. He explained that the land behind the Post Office was large enough for a very large two-story home to invite a wife into one day with a tall hedge and extensive gardens, he thought. I was very supportive and told him of the types of farm accidents that occurred in the area, as well as emergency childbirths like the one in my own house. I asked him to also consider building an Emergency Room attached to his house for medical emergency events before the patients could then be transferred onto Invermoriston Hospital. He was very grateful for local input and knowledge and thanked me for the suggestion, which he thought was brilliant. I then introduced him to Gillcrest from that hospital who could give him more working knowledge. "Welcome to Glenmoriston," I said and sat down.

Morag-Freya was curious and listened in to her husband's conversation about the hospital, then added that if the new doctor was building a Waiting Room and an Emergency Room for local people, he would need paintings suited to the local clientele to relax them, such as the "The Scots Dumpies", "The Goats" and "Black Faced Sheep" paintings. Helen hadn't yet sold those three paintings, but Dr. Benedict Brown agreed to buy them and paid £200 each for them then they departed to stay at the Highland Manor House with a Malcolm MacGregor Law Rooms business card in his pocket to settle the land deal. It was clear that Padruig's dream was being realised just in how much money the family was set to earn from this one English Doctor.

Morag-Freya had come up to me saying, "Granny, where's Aonghus? I need one of his business cards." I'd answered, "Aonghus is with Annabel visiting baby Nachtain at Isobel-Mairi's house while Ewen is occupied here, but I have one of his business cards that I can give you, for the Doctor I presume?" and I gave her one of Aonghus' business cards.

Our elderly former lawyer was able to come with his man-servant and was gifted his portrait as payment of a debt, called "Portrait of a Lawyer", as well as purchasing "The Day the Dragoons came to Craskie Farm" for £1250. Alex bought "The Crofter's Mournful Departure" and a painting called "Ma and Da" and Patrick bought both "The Hart of the Highlands" and "The Hart of the Highlands Manor House" to be proudly displayed in the Manor House. The MacPhersons came and purchased "Cluny MacPherson" for £500. The current Lochiel of Clan Cameron came and purchased "The Cameron Charge" and "The Gentle Lochiel" for a total of £2000. Later, I saw Lochiel talking head-to-head with Gillcrest MacLachlan, looking as equals despite the age and clan differences. What a lovely sight they were, with Lochiel also presented in full Highland dress and it brought back a feeling of nostalgia in my heart. I saw some of the English tourists staring. Lochiel even wore a blue bonnet with a white cockade. It was the only one in the room. He had confided in Gillcrest that had there been a traditional portrait of the Prince, he would have bought it, so Gillcrest said quietly, "There is one, but it's at home. If you still want to buy it from Ma, make a time to come around and she will gladly sell it to you," Gillcrest whispered. "I understand why you wouldn't want that one. Did you know that he was also covered in lice too?" he said pointing to the painting on the wall called "Prince Charles Edward Stuart Bearded and Barefoot."

I took this opportunity to ask Gillcrest about the MacNachten conversation that we'd had on the night of the play and approached them both and pulled up a chair. "Excuse me gentlemen. Can I have a moment of your time please Gillcrest? Totally unrelated to art I'm afraid," I said. He nodded in agreement and said, "Of course Granny." "Can you please tell me what you may have learned of the MacNachtens who lived in Argyle?" I asked. "Och, I can only tell you a wee bit, Grandma. They were granted lands in Argyle, as you know. Where they were before that is said to be somewhere in The Great Glen, but the Pecht came from all over, so I am uncertain as to where the MacNachtens were from originally. The more I've looked into it, the more complicated it has become. I have found, however, historical references to them in Ireland that might help." I was surprised that historically they would've walked the same land as us, but it would explain my fairy stone. He went on, "They did build Dundarave Castle on Loch Fyne as Morag-Freya has already stated and it's a nice castle. They were, however, right in the heart of Campbell and MacDougall country. I am told they became aligned initially with the MacDougalls and for a time, were anti-Bruce and fought alongside the MacDougalls against the Bruce. You already know that story.

They appeared to get along with the Campbells by necessity for a long time, as did we but that all ended with the Campbells taking over their lands and their castle. Basically, they ceased to be a clan about eighty-years ago and most of them had been either killed or displaced. Earlier, however in the 1500s, a separate branch had been formed in Ireland by marriage, so there may be descendants there. I am sorry for the loss of Mr. MacNachten, Granny. I really admired him. Is it true that he was your second cousin?" he asked. "Aye," I answered. "That's all I know, thus far," he concluded, "but I will look into it further for you," he said in earnest. "Och, if you're going to look into it lad, look into it for Ewen's new bairn, Nachtain and yours too when they come along, God willing. They still carry the Pecht ancestry from the MacNachtens through their Mithers, their Grandfather and me." Both men then looked at me like it was the first time they'd seen me.

"There's also an ancient place there in Argyle somewhere, called Kilmartin Glen I believe, with very large burial cairns, standing stones and the like, according to Aonghus and Fergus. So, it also raises the question of who the Martins or Marthains were and if there's a connection between the Marthains and the MacNachtens or if indeed they were one and the same. Can you enquire also about Kilmartin Glen please Gillcrest?" I asked. Then Lochiel, looking rather sheepish said, "Kilmartin Glen you say?" "Aye," I answered as I turned to him. "Well, I might have records of that name Marthain or Martin, but it's really old. It would take me a while because some of our records were destroyed in '46 when the English laid waste to Achnacarry. But not all was totally lost," he said. "Why would you have Argyle records?" asked Gillcrest. Both men then looking like someone had stepped on their respective Laird toes. "It's Cameron records concerning the Clans that joined with us in the early days and that name rings a bell, is all I'm saying Gillcrest. From memory, without looking at my records, MacMartins are linked to the Camerons by the fact that the MacMartins of Letterfinlay of Lochaber are an ancient race who later went to make up Clan Cameron as we now know it, initially through marriage, I've been told.

Clan Martin, of course, is the Anglicised form of the name of a very ancient people. It could be more accurately described as the tribe of Martin, Martin having its variations like Marthain, as you said Isobel. It's also thought it could be Naughton or Nachtain because of the oral traditions of our ancestors as well as the language differences and we are unable to be certain of the spelling. Druidism is also a factor where records were intentionally kept secret. From Cameron records, it shows it was the late 14th Century that they joined with Clan Cameron then after the Battle of Lochaber in 1429, they became a Sept of Clan Cameron and were considered the most loyal to the Camerons of Lochiel. I'm no historian, so I'll do my checking and you do yours Gillcrest and I apologise to you Isobel for not disclosing our connections to our ancestors also. They never went away you see, the ancient is within us. I recognised it in you Isobel, as did Mr. MacNachten and we refer to them as ancestors and not a separate people from us," he said.

Gillcrest was flabbergasted at the information overload and appeared deflated with his lack of knowledge, possibly even worried that his Irish ancestors could've been the cause for a massacre in Kilmartin Glen. I heard Gillcrest mumble that he was pleased that Aonghus wasn't there and I said, "That's right he and Annabel are visiting his new nephew Nachtain and they're staying over at Isobel-Mairi's house. They went on a special shopping trip to Edinburgh with Annabel's Mither for the bairn and they've bought him all kinds of things, which should make Isobel-Mairi very happy." Lochiel then leaned in and said to me, "I hope that you will sleep peacefully tonight Isobel, knowing what I've told you. Gillcrest here, on the other hand, may not," he said. "God bless you Lochiel. Thank you."

It was then that I remembered John Cameron and the Chapel incident. "Lochiel," I said. "I have to apologise to you if John Cameron was offended when he visited me last. He left our wee Chapel in rather a hurry, but I should explain," I said. "Aye," he said. "I wasn't expecting John to raise business matters going back to 1745 concerning Da's team of Clydesdales and it turns out John is a treasure hunter and believe me, we have no connection with the missing gold that he is still looking for, obviously," I said. "What?" said Lochiel. "He did what? Oh, Isobel, I am so sorry. Aye, he is known for that, but I didn't expect him to bother you with it," he said. "Well, that's okay," I stated, "Padruig dealt with it" then both men looked at me quizzically and I realised that I shouldn't have said that and I excused myself.

Before Mr. MacNachten passed away when Ewen was spending time with him, the two of them had sketched Loch Insh and the swans in various stages of swimming or flight and Ewen had given the sketches to Helen to see if she could paint it before the opening, which she did. It was truly beautiful and was called "The Rise of the Swans – Loch Insh" and it attracted a lot of attention and a bidding war, so that Ewen couldn't afford it. I approached Helen and told her I'd give her the money at home for that painting, so that Ewen and Isobel-Mairi would have that precious memory of his adoptive father, Mr. MacNachten.

My memory is failing me without consulting the books, but that is what I remember. I kept the "Padruig and Isobel Grant" portraits for myself and I also took the painting "A Wedding – Grant MacGregor", with Helen's blessing, as her and her husband were now the new face of Craskie Farm. I wanted the portraits hung on an obvious wall as you enter my house with Helen's wedding painting beneath it to give the home that old-world and generational feel about it. I didn't pay her for those paintings as I didn't want her to sell those ones ever, as they would now stand as history of Craskie Farm. I also asked my dear daughter if I could have my "Clydesdales on Grant Farm" painting and the "Old Men by the Fireside", so that I would have Da, Uncle Allan, Padruig and my old boy all around me and she asked Hugh Og to take them off the wall immediately and they were all taken down to the house for me. "God bless you Helen," I said. "I love you Ma," she had responded.

An English tourist purchased the "Golf in Scotland" painting and "HMS Panther" and a visiting Islander from Skye bought "Flora MacDonald" and "The Prince's Escape Map". "Hugh – the Last of the Seven Glenmoriston Men" was bought by a well-dressed middle-aged lady representing the Council in Inverness, which did a lot for Hugh Mohr's ego. The MacDonalds from Glencoe made the journey across to buy a few items, one of which was "Signage – Keep Out".

The new owner of the Post Office bought "The Braes of Glenmoriston" for the Post Office and the "Home-Made Vase of White Roses" for his house. One of the tourist ladies bought three of the still life paintings and the Inverness main library bought "Padruig in Culloden Battle". The people that we were selling the wool garments to in Edinburgh came and bought "Highland Men During the Clipping Season" and "Wool Waulking in Four Stages" for £3000.

The Grandson of the late President Duncan Forbes, who had also dressed formally, had accepted our invitation, much to our surprise. He had hoped to buy "Padruig on Culloden Field", but had missed out, so instead purchased "Palinurus in a Storm" to be hung in his office at Culloden House. He said that he would return to our art gallery with other business people who might be interested, to which Helen replied, "Please give me a year."

It is hard to explain the excitement and the many different feelings amongst the people who were astonished at Helen's artwork, some of whom were in a hurry to pay for fear they would miss out on the one they had loved the most. Grigor was hoping that "Grigor and the Ox" would not sell and he stood in front of it most of the night, so that no one could see it because he loved Charlotte the ox so much and he wanted his wife to just give him the painting, which she did as a wedding anniversary gift on the condition that he made two busts of her parents out of stone one day.

Hugh Mohr also did a similar thing to that. He was supposed to stand at the door as a security guard with Hamish and Hugh Og to make sure that nothing was stolen, but instead he kept on going over to the painting of himself and the Collie dogs, block-ing its visibility from the visitors. He looked quite distressed at the idea that his Collie dogs would end up in someone else's house and he didn't have the

coin to buy it, so I bought it for him. His shoulders were so broad that no one could see it and he would scowl at anyone who looked at that painting. So, once again I approached Helen and said, "Sweetheart, I'd like to buy "Collie Dogs and Hugh" to be given to Hugh at the end of the night. But I don't want you to tell him who paid for it. I'll leave the money for you in an envelope on the coffee table at home. "Aye Ma", he said. "Did you want it hung in our house too with the others or leave it to Hugh to decide?" she said. "Best leave that up to Hugh or he will know I paid for it," I said.

The Italians that had made the journey across from the Continent were able to coincide their visit with the opening of the Art Studio, accompanied by our local Priests, Father Michael and Father Francis. There were two representatives from Rome who were par-ticularly moved by the painting of "The Old School House" and purchased this item as a reminder of its Papist roots and congratulated me personally on building the Chapel St. Columba at Craskie. They also took one of the still lifes, "A Wooden Bowl of Home-Grown Tomatoes." Both Fathers Antonio and Marcus from Rome were later seen standing in front of the painting "Dougald MacCulloncy: The Prince Bearded and Barefoot" and one of them stifled a giggle. "Father Antonio. That is him, I recognise him. It represents his suf-fering in his escaping. Can't you see? Only those who helped him like Mrs. MacGregor's Father, would have seen him in this poorly condi-tion," he said. "Well then, Father, I think we should buy it, don't you? For historical reasons," Father Antonio said. "Yes, let's buy it Father. How exciting," said Father Marcus. When they left they were chattering away to each other in Italian, carrying their paintings and still excited at their find as they made their way up to the Manor House, with Fathers Michael and Francis trailing behind.

I saw the MacDonalds of Glencoe talking to Helen at the opening, asking her why she hadn't painted the massacre of Glencoe or the magnificent Ben Nevis. She is such a lovely diplomat and answered that they surely could do a better job than her, for it wasn't where she grew up even though she knew their stories and as for painting the iconic Ben Nevis, there simply wasn't the time with a new grandchild, wool waulking and running the farm. When they realised just how busy she was, they apologised. She offered to do their portraits if they could come to the Old School House on a day in about six months' time. Grigor, by then, had become intensely protective of his wife.

And so, on it went until 9pm when the MacDonalds finally left. "They sure can talk, those MacDonalds," said Hugh Mohr. Out of the corner of my eye, I noticed Patrick ushering folk up to the Manor, but I had been preoccupied. "The MacDonalds said that all expenses there and back would be paid, plus £500 if she could do the painting if it were a wee one, but if it were a large one, then £800 was their best offer if I was able to capture its essence," Helen said. I wondered if they were related to Alexander MacDonald, my husband's deceased best friend.

While ushering guests to the Manor, I observed that Patrick was departing with the painting called "Ma and Da"; which was a painting of myself and Padruig reading books before bed. Alex had already purchased that painting, but as Patrick was walking away with it, he was stopped by his brother. "That's mine Brother. I paid for it," said Alex. This sent Patrick into a jealous rage and at first, he wouldn't part with it. I had to intervene with Hugh Mohr and Hamish. "Patrick dear," I said, "you were the older brother who picked up wee Alex on the day the dragoons came and ran with him as fast as you could to the shieling. You are his older brother who should still love him like that. Please give him back his painting darling?"

I said. He did so reluctantly, apologised and left without so much as a congratulations to Helen.

Morag-Freya came up to me shortly after that and said, "Granny, have Aonghus and Annabel bought baby Nachtain presents already? Because I haven't bought my nephew anything yet. What do you suggest?" she asked. "Frederick – the donkey,'" I replied pointing at the painting, "for his bedroom." "Oh, that's a wonderful idea," she said. "Will Ma charge me the price that's on it?" she asked. "Aye,

she will." "Oh, well. Gillcrest," as she called her husband over. "Can I have some money please?" she asked him. "Aye, what for?" he asked. "It's for 'Frederick,'" she replied. "Why do you want to buy Frederick?" "It's for the wee bairn, for his bedroom," she explained. "Och, that's a bonny idea. When are we going there to visit?" he said. "Can we go there tomorrow?" "Aye. Don't worry I'll pay Ma for it," he said. "Oh, thank you darling," she said and kissed him on the cheek. "Will Ma charge us the same price?" he asked. "Aye, Granny said it'll be £200." "Oh," he replied, "maybe she'll give us a family discount." And he walked over to his mother-in-law to negotiate a family discount for "Frederick", which of course she gave him when it was explained that it was for her grandson. "Frederick" went home with them.

Hugh Mohr took the lead concerning the dangers of having this large amount of money in the house or even travelling to the bank with it. Gillcrest suggested splitting it up that evening to go between the banks at Invermoriston and Inverness where he could take half wearing his scientist garb, therefore looking like a struggling scientist and unlikely to have anything of value on him and bank it for Helen in her name in Invermoriston in the morning. Half was then entrusted into Gillcrest's care and half went into Hugh's care to go into the Priest hole temporarily. It had been decided that early the next morning, the other half would need to be escorted by Grigor, Hugh Mohr, Hamish and Aonghus into Inverness. Hugh Mohr was going to be armed as was Grigor. They were serious about protecting a lifetime's work from thieves. Ewen had prearranged to shoe a horse coming in from another property, so he was going to remain at home working, as were Helen, Meredith and Mary at the house. Hugh Og Chisholm, Bruce MacKay, Dougal MacDougal and Charlie MacKichen were going to be staying on the farm to attend to the animals as usual.

Invitation
For
The Grand Opening of
The Helen Grant
MacGregor Art
Studio

PLEASE JOIN US AT
The Old Glenmoriston
School Building
Old Drovers Road
Glenmoriston

Enclosed is a list of all
paintings for purchase or
perusal of 60 items of
various sizes and styles

Don't be late!

6pm opening
7pm closing
Cash only

Anyone whose
relatives appear in the
war scene, takes
precedence over others
to purchase.
Any children attending
are advised to peruse
animal paintings at the
rear to minimise
potential distress

17th May 1788

You are invited to peruse
and purchase glorious
artwork from our revered
local artist Helen Grant
MacGregor, sponsored by
her parents Isobel and
Padruig Grant

Helen Grant MacGregor Art Studio

Still Life

A Wooden Bowl of
Home-Grown Tomatoes
Home Made Vase of
White Roses
Wooden Bowl of Corn
Wooden Bowl of Neeps
Head of Oats

Portraits

Padraig Grant
Cluny MacPherson
Isobel Grant
The Gentle Lochiel
Padraig and Isobel Grant
Oval Portraits
Flora MacDonald
Portrait of a Lawyer

Landscapes

The Braes of Glenmoriston
Loch Ness in Mist
The Great Glen in Snow

Wildlife

Pack Wolves in Quebec
The Arctic Fox, the Arctic
Hare and Polar Bear Trilogy
The Hart of the Highlands
The Rise of the Swans

Domesticated Animals

The Clydesdales on
Grant Farm
Our First
Highland Ponies
Our First Black
Faced Sheep
Highland Coos
The Soote Dumpies
An Irish Dog
Frederick the Donkey
Blaze the Horse
The Goats
A New Kid
Grigor and the Ox
Black Faced Sheep
Collie Dogs and High
Helen with Black Faced
Sheep on a Windy Day
Milking the Goats

War Themes

HMS Panther
Prince Charles Edward Stuart
Bearded and Bare Foot
The Day the Dragoons Came to
Craskie Farm
The Crofter's Mournful Departure
The Prince's Escape Map
Prisoners in a Storm
Padraig Dubh in Culloden Battle
The murder of Fraser of
Inverallochy
The Seven Glenmoriston Men
Hugh Chisholm – the last of the 7
Glenmoriston Men
The Cameron Charge
The Bombing of Castle Lochlan

Miscellaneous

The Old School House
The Shieling
Our Completed House
Fraser's Trading Post
The Hart of the
Highlands Manor House
Signage – Keep Out
Golf in the Highlands
Curling in the Burn
Harvest Time
After the Harvest
Grigor MacGregor, the
Ponies, Beth and James
Highland Men During
Clipping season
Wool waulking in
Four Stages
Old men by the Fireside
A wedding –
Grant-MacGregor

The Envelopes

I had meandered slowly on my own with Hugh's two beloved Collies that he had entrusted into my care back to my Craskie home that I had loved so much since it had been built from the ashes of the burnings. Feeling a little short of breath, I was glad the night was over. Inside was just Meredith, tending the fires and to my night clothes. Very surprised at the presence of the lovely dogs, she fed them and I sent her home to her husband's house. I laid out a comfortable mattress by the fire for the Collies and was completely alone except for the loving presence of my husband. The dogs had other ideas as I climbed under my covers. They leapt up onto my bed and stretched out to sleep there with me, but then I remembered the envelopes numbering one to eighteen.

1. To Helen – payment for the painting "Hugh Mohr and the Collie dogs". 2. To Helen – payment for Ewen's painting "The Rise of the Swans". 3. To Alex – passing ownership of the Chestnut mare to Alex and the yearling for his daughter, Jean, to train. 4. To Hugh Mohr and Hugh Og – to have the use of those vacated stables for their horses. 5. To Helen and Grigor – Instructions to install lights arriving from John Fraser today. Two tall ones in front of the house directly beyond the porch. One tall one on the border near Chisholm House. Six candle holders to be installed in the Chapel. 6. Instructions for my passing at time of death as follows: Helen, Mary and Meredith to wash my body then dress in prepared shroud and Helen's arisaid. To be buried in my tomb within 24 hours. No procession. Family members and close friends only. Small notice in the paper. Catholic Priests requested to hold a funeral Mass in our Chapel as well as Nachtain's baptism at a convenient time for the general public. 7. Bank Helen's takings as soon as possible. 8. The two paintings of Padruig and I are to remain in the Craskie Farm House on the walls and not to be sold. 9. To Aonghus – to legalise the lease agreement on the house on New Farm between Grigor, Helen and Hugh Og Chisholm. 10. To Aonghus – to legalise my will request regarding the Clydesdale team: Isobel-Mairi owning only the bloodlines and Hugh Og Chisholm, owning the team requiring both of them to work together and unable to sell the team from Craskie Farm. Team to be known as "John Grant Teamster". 11. Hugh Mohr inherits Padruig's old Fraser bible. 12. My sheep to never exceed thirty-five

in number with Hugh Mohr taking over the responsibility of them. 13. Hugh Mohr's paid titles to include: a) Craskie Farm butcher and tanner; b) Farm overseer and security c) Keeper of the Graves, the Chapel and the Forest. 14. To Alex Og Grant — to be given my Grant brooch. 15. To Grigor — when my old boy dies, please bury him near Blaze and the two wee ponies and plant an orange tree on top of him and allow wild birds to eat from all of the fruits up there. 16. To Helen and Grigor: To legalise ownership of Chisholm House to Hugh Mohr Chisholm transferring its lease to ownership. 17. To Helen: You may keep all of my sewing equipment and any of my clothes. 18. To Helen — any cash remaining in the tin under my bed, please use for my expenses and any of my outstanding bills. If there is any left over, keep it for yourself and my darlings Grigor Og and Hugh Mohr.

Going back to bed, the Collies were very comfortable and kept my feet nice and warm. I was so pleased for Padruig that finally our daughter had been launched very successfully as he had dreamed of, all those many years ago when he bought that old school and I knew he'd be so proud of her now.

I heard news today that Charles Edward Stuart had died and still the Pope hadn't recognized his claim to the British Throne and I agree with that. If only he had taken the advice he was given at the time and stopped at the Scottish border and restored Scotland's independence once again from England and become just a King of Scotland. That may have worked, instead of facing losing Holyrood house or all our historical personages, Kings, that the English can then lay claim to, which would be unbearable. He had outlived everyone who had helped him, except Flora MacDonald. So, I thought, she did get her moment of glory in outliving him. What a waste it all was. "He was just a man who had a great deal of power, who betrayed and took advantage of the Highlander people." [2] Could Helen's paintings really make a difference to future generations, who will probably forget our languages and traditions? Even though Charles Edward Stuart may be seen on walls wearing our Highland dress, so too will the "Seven Glenmoriston Men" or the "Murder of Fraser of Inverallochy."

Our lands will carry the scars of what has happened here and the solemnity may never leave, even though we have done our best in our small corner of the Highlands. Like Glencoe holds onto its tears and

Culloden holds onto its ghosts, when the mist rolls across the moor, it still connects with all of the souls carrying our culture to all corners of the World. I felt tired, really tired and lay my head on my pillow and reached out to my dear Padruig who was waiting for me. I knew then, it was indeed my time and I thanked God for helping me and my family survive and thrive in these our Braes of Glenmoriston and waited to be reunited with my Padruig.

Isobel.

Entry by Hugh Chisholm
Craskie Farm
17th May 1788

I am writing this entry for Isobel on the night of her passing. We'd cleaned up the Art Gallery after the last of the people left with their paintings. Taking my own "Collie Dogs and Hugh" painting that an anonymous person had gifted to me. I was thrilled to own it. My Collies had gone home earlier with Isobel and were safe with her. Hamish had gone home to Cora and his bairn and Ewen to Isobel-Mairi and their new bairn and it only left Grigor, Helen and I to wearily blow out the last of the candles and put out the fire. It had been toasty in there all night with that many people and the fire going. The three of us locked up the Old School House after checking all the windows and doors and then doused the big standing lights by the Drover's Road. What a success Helen's Grand Opening had been. How did Padruig ever come up with these ideas? I'll never know, but I'd wished he had been here to see it.

As we approached the Craskie Farm gates, I heard my Collies howling. They were both howling like never before with a grief having beset them. Opening the gate, I saw Isobel in a distant mist in a white lace-edged night dress walking alone toward the Chapel. Her bare feet didn't appear to be touching the ground. "Do you see that?" I asked both Helen and Grigor. "See what?" they both said. I knew then that Isobel had passed away and was going to join Padruig. Her ghostly apparition turned toward me and then entered the Chapel through its walls, confirming my dreaded conclusion and I ran to the house.

Going into the house with the Collies still howling so loudly, I entered the bedroom. Helen must have thought that I should just quieten the dogs down. They were happy to see me, but they were licking Isobel's face with no response. Isobel's arm had fallen off the side of the bed, she was white and very cold to the touch. Lifting up her cold arm, the full realisation that she was actually dead hadn't yet sunk in and stupidly, I tried to wake her up even though her beautiful blue eyes were wide open. I didn't want to believe that she had left me, left us all. She hadn't been sick or in pain, she hadn't had an accident or expressed any discomfort in her body. Why had she passed away? Then it just hit me. "No, no you can't leave me."

"Oh Isobel, oh my God," I cried and cried. "Please God, don't take my wife from me. Isobel, you are my oldest and dearest friend on this earth. How can I live now without you to love everyday? I confess my tears will not stop rolling down my face and I am helpless and so lonely when your voice will not respond to mine. You are with the others now aren't you my dearest? Please greet my brothers Alexander and Donald and your brother Grigor Mohr, but especially Padruig and all the others for me. Please tell Padruig I did my best for you my lovely one. Tell him I have loved you and protected you with my heart, my soul and my body. Oh, my darling Isobel, I will be so lonely now without you my beloved. I watched you sleep just this morning and traced my finger over the lines in your forehead. I wanted to memorise the curve of your lips and smell the sweet fragrance of your breath as you slept. The only sound that could be heard were the birds when I woke you up to make passionate love to you and now you have gone. We didn't know that that was the last time we would ever make love. I have loved you for so long and will go on loving you until we meet again. I have chiselled my name on your tomb so you take my name as well as my ring with you. You have married two of the Seven Glenmoriston Men, Sister to one and you have loved, understood, defended and cared for us all when no others could and I am the last of the Seven Glenmoriston Men. Who will care for me now? All my family are dead, oh dear God, Who? Isobel my forever lovely?'

I heard the sounds of Grigor and Helen entering our room, too afraid of what they would learn. Poor Helen collapsed near my Isobel onto the bed weeping inconsolably for her Mither, who had protected her through so many terrible times. Grigor asked me not to leave them as well and to stay and live with them all until my death, for surely the loss of Isobel and I would be too great for the family in one night. He and I wept as I held him. I knew that I had an obligation to them who had accepted me as their Da and Grandda, as well as to Grigor Mohr, my brother in arms and Isobel's brother. Leaving my beloved's home permanently to live in Chisholm House for now at least wasn't an option.

There was an old bible on my side of the bed with a note attached in Isobel's handwriting. "Dearest Hugh. Padruig would want you to have this. Isobel." In accordance with all of her instructions, I left the ladies to their tasks with Isobel and walked back slowly to Chisholm House with my bible and my painting, this diary and the dogs and waited to be called on to take Isobel to her grave. Dougal had been sent on horseback to get the news to both Alex and Patrick and the English Doctor from the Manor House. A death certificate would be needed, so we could bury her as she had instructed. I will return to the main house if they wanted me there to care for them and protect them as my family. For now, the silence of Chisholm House was an agony that I needed to feel. I would read Isobel's story in her diary.

This diary had fallen on the floor by Isobel's bedside and so I sign it off for all of us mentioned in these pages including me. There are so many instructions left behind in many envelopes for different matters. There'd never be another Isobel of Glenmoriston. May God forgive me and all of us for our shortcomings, our mistakes and our sins for the things we may have done or eluded to do. Amen.

Signed,
Hugh Chisholm
The last of the Seven Glenmoriston Men

Isobel of Glenmoriston
Isobel's Story

Author's Notes

In researching this story, I designated the task to my daughter, Fatima to not only map the Prince's escape route but also include all of the names of individuals involved with assisting Prince Charles Edward Stuart's escape from Scotland to France in 1746. In this effort we hope we have not excluded anyone. Other topics that have come up during the writing of this story became quite complex, so I have done my best to research both Scottish wild and farm animals, of which previously I knew nothing, the Clans of that period who lived around Glenmoriston and some beyond, as well as the many issues faced by Highlanders especially. I would like to thank my daughter Fatima for her technical support and her fact checking on geography, dates, times, expected life spans of farm animals and distances between places. This humble work would not have been possible without both of my daughters in their respective roles. Thanks also goes to my daughter Halima, who has patiently completed many of the artistic illustrations as has Fatima in their different formats. Thanks also goes to Mr. Iain MacIlleChiar from the Gaelic Society of Inverness for his very kind support.

Real People and Places

Sport

Military Campaigns

Poetry, Music and Song

Agriculture

Legalities

Architecture

Real People and Places:

1. The Prince's Escape: the people involved from Culloden through the Highlands to the Hebridean Islands on to France

2. Letter from Prince Charles Edward Stuart to Clan Chiefs 28th April 1746

3. Complete list of real historical persons mentioned in the text and full list of characters

4. Character Names – both Fictional and Historical

5. Alexander MacDonald of Glenalladale

6. Flora MacDonald's Statement 21st June 1746 (1722-1790) Member of Clan MacDonald of Sleat

7. Donald Cameron of Lochiel

8. Padruig Dubh Grant of Glenmoriston

9. Ewen MacPherson of Cluny

Sport:

1. The History of Golf

2. The History of Curling

Military Campaigns

1. The 1759 Quebec campaign on the Plains of Abraham led by General Wolfe in New France

2. The Rising of 1745 and the Battle of Culloden

Poetry, Music and Song

1. On Ederchaillis' Shores – Poem by Mrs. D. Ogilvie

2. The Red Wolfe Is Dead – Poem by Zaynab El- Fatah

3. The Hurdy Gurdy

4. Wool Waulking Song – unknown

5. Poetry from Poems of Os'Iain translated by James MacPherson

6. Who Will Remember? Poem by Zaynab El-Fatah

7. To Grigor and Helen – Poem by Zaynab El-Fatah

8. Grigor of the Mist- Poem by Zaynab El-Fatah

Agriculture

1. Scots Dumpies

2. The Highland Coo

3. Blackface Sheep

4. Crops

5. The Scottish Highland Pony

6. Scottish Collie Sheep Dog

Legalities

1. Tartan Proscription law

2. Act of Union 1707

3. Act to Annul Suppression of Name Gregour or MacGregour

Architecture

1. History of the Palace of Holyroodhouse

Real People and Places:

1. The Prince's Escape: the people involved from Culloden through the Highlands to the Hebridean Islands on to France

2. Letter from Prince Charles Edward Stuart to Clan Chiefs 28th April 1746

3. Complete list of real historical persons mentioned in the text and full list of characters

4. Character Names – both Fictional and Historical

5. Alexander MacDonald of Glenalladale

6. Flora MacDonald's Statement 21st June 1746 (1722-1790) Member of Clan MacDonald of Sleat

7. Donald Cameron of Lochiel

8. Padruig Dubh Grant of Glenmoriston

9. Ewen MacPherson of Cluny

1. The Prince's Escape: the people involved from Culloden through the Highlands to the Hebridean Islands on to France (12)

1. Edward (Ned) Burke (d.1751) guided the following people from Culloden Battlefield to Gorthleck house to see Lord Lovat Simon Fraser (d.1747 exec.)

   The Prince

   Lord Elcho

   Sir Thomas Sheridan

   O'Sullivan

   O'Neill

   Mr. Alexander MacLeod, aid-de-camp

2. Donald McLeod of Gualtergill in Skye (Palinurus) (d.1749 aged 72) captained the 8 oared boat across to North Uist, along with

   Murdoch MacLeod (son)

   The Prince

Sir John William O'Sullivan

Captain Felix O'Neill

Captain Allan MacDonald of Clan Ranald

Clergyman of the Church of Rome

Boatmen:

Rhoderick MacDonald

Lachlan MacMurrich

Rhoderick MacCaskgill

John MacDonald

Alexander MacDonald

Edward (Ned) Burke

3. Flora McDonald (d.1790) accompanied the Prince across to Skye, along with

Neil MacDonald MacKechan

John MacDonald (Glenalladale's cousin - helmsman)

Duncan Campbell

MacMerry and

Alexander MacDonald

4. Old Alexander MacDonald of Kingsburgh (d.1766) accommodated the Prince in his home and coordinated with:

Donald Roy MacDonald and

Lady Margaret MacDonald arranged Malcolm MacLeod of Raasay

5. Captain Malcolm MacLeod of Raasay (d.1761), took the Prince across to Raasay and back to Skye accompanied by

John MacLeod and

Murdoch MacLeod (Laird of Raaza's sons) with boatmen:

Sgt. John MacKenzie,

Donald MacFrier

6. Old Iain Dubh Laird of MacKinnon (d.1756) and

John MacKinnon (d.1762) Malcolm MacLeod's brother in law

7. Angus MacDonald of Borrodale

Captain Alexander MacDonald of Glenalladale – Borrodale's nephew

8. Captain Alexander MacDonald of Glenalladale (d.1761)

The Prince, guided by

Donald Cameron of Glenpean

Lieutenant John MacDonald brother of Glenalladale

Lieutenant John MacDonald son of Angus MacDonald of Borrodale (cousin)

9. The Seven Glenmoriston men with Glenalladale as interpreter

Padruig Grant - aka Padruig Dubh of Craskie - nephew to Allan MacDonald

Alexander MacDonald (d.1751) of Aonach

Hugh Chisholm (sons of Paul Chisholm, tenant at Blairy)

Alexander Chisholm (d.1751)

Donald Chisholm

Gregor MacGregor

John MacDonald (Campbell) of Craskie

Hugh MacMillan (happened upon them)

10. Donald MacDonald of Lochgarry

   Dr Archibald Cameron

   Ewen McPherson of Cluny

   Donald Cameron of Lochiel

   McPherson of Breackachie

11. Donald Cameron of Lochiel (the Gentle Lochiel) took the Prince to Eriskay at Lochaber to meet a French ship

   Of his travels, the Prince is quoted as having said:

"We spent nights in Raasay, Elegol, Mallaig, Borrodale, the Braes of Morar, Loch Arkaig, Corriescaradil, Glen Shiel. There were awful midges at Strathcluding, Corrie Goith, Glen Carrick, Fasmachoil, Glengarry, Braes of Glen Kinney, Ben Alder, Achnacarry. I had blisters on every inch of my foot and let me tell you if I never see another midge again, it will be too soon" [2]

2. Prince Charles Edward Stuart's letter to the Clan chiefs on the 28th April 1746

After 11 days on the mainland, the Prince fled by boat to the Outer Hebrides, but first he wrote a letter to all clan chiefs explaining why he was running away.[2] He said *"When I came into this country, it was my only view to do all in my power for your good and safety. This I will always do so long as my life is in me, but alas I see with grief I can at present do little for you on this side of the water for the only thing that can now be done is defend yourselves until the French assist you. I am of little use here, whereas my going to France instantly, however dangerous it may be, I will certainly engage the French Court either to assist us effectually and powerfully or at least to procure you some terms as you would not obtain in other ways. My presence there, I flatter myself, will have more effect to bring this sooner to determination than anybody else. My departure should be kept as long private and concealed as possible on one pretext or another, which you*

will fall upon. May the Almighty bless and direct you" – 28th
April 1746.

Map 4. Escape Route of
Prince Charles Edward Stuart – April to
September 1746

3. Complete list of real historical persons mentioned in the text

Burke, Edward (Ned) of South Uist d.1751	MacDonald, Alexander of Glenalladale of Skye d.1761
Burton, Dr John of York d. (unknown)	MacDonald, Alexander of Aonach d.1751
Cameron, Dr. Archibald (1707 – 1753)	MacDonald, Flora of Sleat 1722-1790
Cameron, Donald of Glenpean	MacDonald, Allan Uncle of Padruig Dubh
Cameron, Donald of Lochiel (1700-1748)	MacDonald, Sir Alexander of Skye
Campbell, Lord John 4th Earl of Loudoun (1705-1782)	MacDonald, Alexander of Kingsburgh on Skye d.1772
Campbell, John MacDonald Os-Iain of Craskie	MacDonald, Angus of Borrodale
Chisholm, Alexander d.1751 of Blairie	MacDonald, Flora wife of John MacDonald d. (unknown)
Chisholm, Donald of Blairie d. (unknown)	MacDonald, Isabel wife of Alexander MacDonald d. (unknown)
Chisholm, Hugh (1728-1812) of Blairie	MacGregor, Gregor d. (unknown)
Cook, Lt. James (1728-1779)	MacIntosh, Alexander of Stratherick
Cumberland, Prince William Duke of (1721-1765)	MacKinnon, John Dubh of Skye Laird of d.1756
De Montcalm, Gen. Louise Joseph (1712-1759)	MacKinnon, John of Skye d.1762
Drummond, Lord John 4th Duke of Perth (1714-1747)	MacLeod, Norman of Skye Laird of (1705-1772) "The Wicked Man"
Forbes, Duncan of Culloden (1685-1747)	MacLeod, Donald of Gualtergill in Skye (Palinurus) d.1749
Forbes, Bishop Robert of Ross and Caithness d.1775	MacLeod, Cpt. Malcolm of Brea, Isle of Raasay d.1761

Fraser, Jenny MacPherson of Cluny d.1766	MacPherson, Ewen of Cluny (1706-1764)
Fraser, Simon 11th Lord Lovat (1667-1747)	O'Neil, Cpt. Felix
Fraser, Simon Master of Lovat 1726-1782	O'Sullivan, Sir John William (1700-1760)
Fraser, Simon of Balnain (1729-1777)	Stewart, Rev. John of Inverness
Gordon, Bishop Robert of London	Stuart, Prince Charles Edward (1720-1788)
Glenmoriston, the Laird of Clan Grant	Stuart, Prince Henry Benedict
Grant, Alexander (1734-1813)	Stuart, King James II exiled
Grant, Elizabeth (1764-1823)	Stuart, James Francis III (the old pretender)
Grant, Isobel of Glenmoriston (1702-unknown)	Threpland, Dr.
Grant, Helen d. (unknown)	Wolfe, Gen. James (1727-1759)
Grant, James (1768-1834)	
Grant, John (1685 – d. unknown)	
Grant, Robert	
Grant, Padruig Dubh (Patrick) (1701-1786)	
Grant, Patrick (1732-1793)	
King Louis XV of France	
King George II of England	

Disclaimer: In naming historical personages, we have endeavoured to ensure correct spellings due to Gaelic usage as well as accuracy of dates where available. We invite the reader to do their own research. We apologise if there are errors. We are Australian and do not have any known affiliation with any clans in Scotland or Canada.

4. Character Names – both Fictional and Historical

Algonquian hunter – Indian who Padruig befriended in Quebec

Armstrong bandits – group of men from the lowlands

Bowles, Frederick– Captain of Dragoons, ex-Fort Augustus, murderer of Freya Grant

Browne, Doctor Senior – the doctor in London who treated Padruig

Browne, Doctor Benedict – son of Doctor Brown Senior. Buys medical practice in Glenmoriston

Camerons, Lochiel of the – Charles 21st & Donald 22nd Lochiel, lived in Achnacarry, adjourning lands to Grant lands. Assisted Alexander Grant in purchasing a farm property on the border. Married.

Cameron, Lilias – temporary maid with poor character. Moved on to teaching and sent back home to live with her family.

Cameron, Annabel – wife to Aonghus MacGregor. Nurse. Traditional Cameron family.

Cameron, John – Grandfather of Annabel and treasure hunter

Chisholm, Donald – one of the Seven Glenmoriston Men. Husband of Eilidh. Son of Paul Chisholm. Brother to Alexander and Hugh. Children unknown.

Chisholm, Eilidh – wife of Donald Chisholm. Ravished and sickly.

Chisholm, Hugh Mohr – one of the Seven Glenmoriston Men. Son of Paul Chisholm. Brother to Alexander and Donald. Lived and worked on Craskie Farm after Donald's death.

Chisholm, Hugh Og – one of the fisher lads. Brother to Hamish. Son of the widow Chisholm. Husband to Meredith MacKenzie. Employed on Craskie Farm as head groom.

Chisholm, Hamish - one of the fisher lads. Brother to Hugh Og. Son of the widow Chisholm. Husband to Cora MacKinnon. Father to Donald Og. Employed on Craskie and Grant Farms and the Glenmoriston School as security.

Chisholm, Donald Og – son of Hamish and Cora. First baby to be baptised at The Chapel.

Chisholm, David – Father of Hamish and Hugh Og. Husband to Mary. Drowned in Loch Craskie.

Chisholm, Mary – became Widow MacDonald. Mother to both Hamish and Hugh Chisholm.

David, Alexander Malcolm – Lawyer to Grant family. Sells his business to Aonghus MacGregor in his old age.

Father Antonio – Representative from Rome who attend the opening of the Art Gallery.

Father Francis – Catholic Priest from Edinburgh who performed the funeral Mass for Padruig Grant

Father Marcus – Representative from Rome who attend the opening of the Art Gallery.

Father Michael – young Catholic Priest from Edinburgh, who preaches in the new Chapel St Columba. at Craskie.

Forbes, Bishop Robert – Bishop of Ross and Caithness, Episcopalian Church, Leith. Collector of witness statements of survivors' post Culloden battle through to 1775.

Fraser, John of Stratherick – father of Simon Fraser. Husband of Anna Fraser. Militarily affiliated with Padruig Grant. Owner of Fraser's Trading Post.

Fraser, Anna – wife of John Fraser of Stratherick. Mother of Simon Fraser.

Fraser, Simon – son of Anna and John Fraser. Husband of Beth Grant. Became a politician.

Fraser, Robert – 78th Fraser Highlanders, Quebec. Friend to Padruig Grant.

78th Fraser Highlanders – formed by Simon Fraser Master of Lovat. Fought in Quebec Campaigns against the French.

Gordon, Bishop Robert – Episcopalian Church in London who assisted in Padruig's recovery after the first Quebec Campaign.

Gordon, Mrs. Margaret – wife to Bishop Robert Gordon.

Grant, Padruig – b. 1701 known as Padruig Dubh. Husband to Isobel Grant. Father to Patrick, Helen and Alexander. d. 1786

Grant, Isobel – b. 1702. Wife to Padruig Grant. Mother to Patrick, Helen and Alexander. Also, Clan Gregor. Daughter of John and Freya Grant. Second cousin to Gillcrest MacNachten. d. 1788.

Grant, Patrick – son of Padruig and Isobel Grant. Husband to Henrietta. Father to Beth, James and Sarah

Grant, Helen – daughter of Padruig and Isobel Grant. Wife of Grigor MacGregor. Mother of Isobel-Mairi, Aonghus Grigor and Morag-Freya

Grant, Alexander – son of Padruig and Isobel Grant. First married to Therese and move to Nova Scotia. Six children, of whom two died and two return to Scotland with him, being Jean and Alexander.

Grant, Beth – daughter of Patrick and Henrietta Grant. Married to Simon Fraser.

Grant, James – son of Patrick and Henrietta Grant. Married to Susan Chisholm.

Grant, Susan – Clan Chisholm. Married James Grant. son of Patrick Grant

Grant, Sarah – daughter of Patrick and Henrietta Grant. Married to Duncan Forsythe. Mother of Robin.

Grant, Freya – mother of Isobel Grant. Wife of John Grant. Also, Clan Gregor.

Grant, John – father of Isobel Grant. Husband of Freya Grant. Known as Da.

Grant, Henrietta – wife of Patrick Grant. Mother of Beth, James and Sarah

Grant, Therese – wife of Alexander Grant who divorces. Six children. Went to live in Nova Scotia permanently.

Grant, James the elder – farm owner and neighbour with two sons.

Grant, Craig – son of James Grant the elder, neighbour. Sells the farm to Padruig.

Grant, Bruce – son of James Grant the elder, neighbour.

Grant, Archangel – son of Alex Grant, Nova Scotia Catholic Priest.

Grant, Jean – youngest daughter of Alex Grant, who moved to Scotland from Nova Scotia

Grant, Alexander Og – youngest son of Alex Grant, who moved to Scotland from Nova Scotia

Irish bandits – group of thieves found on Craskie Farm, including:

> **Rory O'Rourke** – transported
> **Mihael O'Sullivan** – transported
> Two lowlanders **Edward** and **John Murray**

Johnson, Captain Stanley – Captain at Fort Augustus involved in collecting the stolen goods.

Jones, Frederick – Corporal, ex-Fort Augustus. Horse thief. Clop n Drop.

Keith, Dr. – aging Glenmoriston doctor who Isobel dislikes.

MacDonald, Allan – Uncle to Padruig Grant. Husband to Margaret. Later husband to Mairi Chisholm. Advisor to Isobel Grant.

MacDonald, Margaret – wife to Allan MacDonald. Children unknown.

MacDonald, Mary – wife of Joe MacDonald. Washer lady to Isobel. Helps deliver Nachtain.

MacDonald, Joe – husband to Mary MacDonald.

McDonell, Patsie – widow McDonell. Childless. Unhappy cook to Beth Fraser.

MacDougal, Dougal – junior groomsman for the Clydesdales, brother to Milread

MacDougal, Milread – wool waulker and spinner, sister to Dougal MacDougal

MacDougal, Fergus – Aonghus' friend from university

MacGregor, Grigor Mohr – father of Grigor MacGregor, husband of Morag, half-brother to Isobel Grant.

MacGregor, Morag – wife of Grigor MacGregor Mohr, mother of Grigor MacGregor Og.

MacGregor, Grigor Og – husband of Helen Grant, son of Grigor MacGregor, father to Isobel-Mairi, Aonghus and Morag-Freya.

MacGregor, Isobel-Mairi – daughter of Grigor MacGregor Og and Helen Grant MacGregor. Wife of Ewen MacNachten. Mother to Nachtain Grigor MacNachten

MacGregor, Aonghus – son of Grigor MacGregor Og and Helen Grant MacGregor. Husband to Annabel Cameron. Became a lawyer in Inverness.

MacGregor, Morag-Freya – daughter of Grigor MacGregor Og and Helen Grant MacGregor. Wife to Gillcrest Lachlan MacLachlan. Became a nurse.

MacInnes, Alasdair – actual name Rory O'Rourke. Husband of Agnus.

MacInnes, Agnus – former maid. Wife of Alasdair MacInnes (Rory O'Rourke). Transported after the birth of her child.

MacKay, Bruce – the young groomsman for the Clydesdales.

MacKenzie, Meredith – daughter of Alexander and Ferne MacKenzie, wife of Hugh Og Chisholm. Employed in the house at Craskie as well as wool waulking.

MacKenzie, Alexander – father of Meredith from Kinlochewe. Husband of Ferne MacKenzie.

MacKenzie, Ferne – mother of Meredith, wife of Alexander MacKenzie.

MacKenzie, Felicity – secretary of David Malcolm Lawyer Rooms, Inverness.

MacKichan, Charles – 11-year-old student. Apprentice soil specialist to Grigor Og for soil movement.

MacKinnon, Mairi – widow MacKinnon. Mother to Cora. Wool waulking group.

MacKinnon, Cora – daughter of Mairi and Donald MacKinnon (dcd), wife to Hamish Chisholm, mother to Donald Og, songstress, school teacher and wool waulking.

MacLachlan, Gillcrest Lachlan – Laird of Lachlan lands. Husband of Morag-Freya. Head scientist specialising in crop yield by perfecting soil.

MacNachten, Gillcrest – adoptive father to Ewen MacNachten, second cousin to Isobel Grant, Loch Insh.

MacNachten, Ewen – born MacThreynfhir – adopted son of Gillcrest MacNachten. Husband to Isobel-Mairi. Father to Nachtain Grigor MacNachten. Blacksmith and farrier at Craskie Farm.

MacNachten, Nachtain Grigor – born to Isobel-Mairi MacNachten and Ewen MacNachten

Menzies, Kenneth – The Editor, Inverness Times Newspaper, Scotland

Shaw, Ann – housekeeper of Malcolm Law Rooms, Inverness

Shaw, Donald – the one-eyed veteran of Culloden battle

Stewart, Reverend John – Episcopalian Reverend in Inverness.

Stewart, Mrs. John – wife to Rev. John Stewart in Inverness.

Wool Waulking Women

Isobel (until retirement), Helen, Mairi MacKinnon (until dcd), Cora, Agnus (until transportation), Meredith, Isobel-Mairi, Morag-Freya and Milread

HISTORICAL PERSONAGE WHO LIVED AND DIED

5. Captain Alexander MacDonald of Glenalladale [13]

Glenalladale is spoken very highly of in Bishop Robert Forbes' book, The Lyon in Mourning, Vol III and is quoted as having said:

Captain Alexander MacDonald of Glenalladale was a very smart acute man, remarkably well skilled in the Erse language, for he can both read and write the Irish language in its original characters, of knowledge quite lost in the Highlands of Scotland, there being exceedingly few that have any skill at all in that way. For the Captain told me that he did not know another person (Old Clanranald only excepted) that knew anything of the first tongue in its original character, but that the natives of Ireland (particularly the higher parts of the country) do still retain a knowledge of it. Several of the Captain's acquaintances have informed me that he is by far the best Erse poet in all of Scotland and he has written many songs in pure Irish.

NB: The Erse language was the original language of Ireland, which spread through to Scotland via the Southern Isles. Because the Seven Glenmoriston Men only spoke erse they needed an interpreter, Glenalladale remained with the group, who had been given the job of protecting and guiding the Prince to his next destination.

The Poems of Ossian

It is our opinion that the author of some of the poetry in the Poems of Ossian could most likely be Captain Alexander MacDonald of Glenalladale, Isle of Skye, Scotland. James

MacPherson, translator of Poems of Ossian, was the nephew of Ewen MacPherson of Cluny, who was not only a leader of the '45 Rebellion, but also a contemporary of Glenalladale. Glenalladale passed away on Skye in 1761 and Cluny passed away in France in 1764.

Eulogy

January 30th 1761

Died in the 49th year of his age,

Alexander MacDonald of Glenalladale, in Moydart, a man well known of the gilded dust when no despicable quantity thereof, and his personal safety, with that of his helpless family, the weeping mother and the hungry babes, strip'd of everything, tempted his acceptance. Firm to his word and steady to every trust, his soul was impregnable as a rock amidst all the storms and tempests this fluctuating state of things could dash against him. Let all the World say what they can, Glen liv'd and died the honest man.

Interpretation:

£30 000 was offered to capture Charles Edward Stuart at the time, which was called the "gilded dust". Despite losing everything and at great danger to himself and his family, he was never able to be bribed to give up the location of the Prince

6. Flora MacDonald's Statement 21st June, 1746 Member of Clan MacDonald of Sleat (1722 to 5th March 1790) [20]

Flora MacDonald, 21st June, 24 years old. *"I did know where the Young Pretender was, but I had only heard he was somewhere on the Long Isle, but he had stayed at my brother's shieling, a wee hut on the hills. About the 21st June, O'Neill or as we call him, Nelson, proposed to me that as I was going to Skye that the Young*

Pretender should go with me. I went and stayed with Lady Clanranald for 3 days and she communicated the scheme to me. Lady Clanranald would furnish clothes for the Young Pretender as my dresses would be too small for him. The Prince was a tall and handsome man. We were frequently updated at Clanranald's house with information on where the Young Pretender was and what preparations had been taken for our voyage. Bit at the same time, we were pushed to hasten to get our affairs and readiness for going off. It was urgent you see. We did not find The Pretender in the place we had first been told, but we followed his informants to a place called Royfinish, where we found him, taking with us the women's clothing which he would be dressed in. Here we heard of General Campbell coming to South Uist and that Captain Ferguson was within a mile of us when we got this information. We sat up all night at a shieling called Cloches terrified to be caught, General Campbell having come in from Berneray and passing not far from us, put us again in great fears. However, we continued there till about 9 o'clock at night when the Young Pretender, myself and one MacKechan and five men for the boats crew, embarked and set out to sea to escape in a small boat. Lady Clanranald had provided provisions for the voyage." The Prince was impersonating Betty Burke as an Irish maid. They travelled to Kingsburgh's house and stayed for the night. Flora MacDonald continued her statement. "I had a room to myself, but The Young Pretender and MacKechan lay in the same room. At this time, he appeared in women's clothes, his face being partly concealed by the shadow of a hooded cloak. You wouldn't have recognised him. The family at Kingburgh's house never inquired who the disguised person was, but I observed them whispering as if they suspected him to be some person that *desired not to be known. I know from the servants that they suspected him to be MacLeod of Berneray, who had been in the rebellion. Kingsburgh must have suspected that it was the Young Pretender, but he never said so to me."*

The following morning, they set out to Portree where a boat was waiting to take him to Raasay. He made it to Raasay even though by then the disguise wasn't working. Two weeks later after parting with the Prince, Flora MacDonald was arrested and was taken to the Tower of London. Her family arranged house arrest in London. Prince Frederick helped her to be comfortable. Prince Charles Edward Stuart was still on the run for another three months beyond that time. [2]

7. Donald Cameron of Lochiel

Donald Cameron, 19th Lochiel of the Camerons whose seat of power was Achnacarry in Lochaber, was known as the Gentle Lochiel. He was a supporter of the Stuarts and was therefore pivotal in the Jacobite Rising of 1745. He was a great chief, admired and loved by his Camerons and their Septs as well as many other Clan Chiefs. He was a regular correspondent with the 11th Lord Lovat and of his four brothers, John succeeded him as Lochiel after his death in 1748. Fr. Alexander, who was a Jesuit Priest

died whilst imprisoned on a British prison ship captained by Ferguson parked on the Thames River in London. Dr. Archibald Cameron became secretary to the exiled King James in Italy and was executed upon his return to Scotland in 1753. His brother Evan's (1708–1750) fate is as yet unknown. During the battle of Culloden, Lochiel led hundreds of his men bravely into battle. His own injuries were terrible with both ankles smashed and was carried off the field whereupon he then took refuge in MacPherson lands until the Prince arrived having initially been escorted by Padruig Grant and then

Cluny MacPherson. It was suggested that he escape to France, where he died. He sadly never returned to Scotland. After 1746, the Cameron home, in Achnacarry, was destroyed and the property confiscated. John Cameron, 20th Lochiel, was allowed home in 1759 but the Cameron estates were not restored until 1784.

The Viscount Dowager of Strathallen is quoted as having been told that the Younger Lochiel "had refused to raise a man or make any appearance till Prince Charles Edward Stuart should give him security for the full value of his estate in the event of the attempt proving abortive." Young Glengarry (Alexander MacDonald the younger of Glengarry) confirmed that the Prince told him as much. Assigning this as the weighty reason why he had shown so much zeal in providing Young Lochiel in a regiment, he said. "For", said the Prince, "I must do the best I can in my present circumstances, to keep my word to Lochiel." [14] As Donald Cameron of Lochiel died in France in 1748 of an apoplexy, the fate of the gold he was given by the Prince to offset the loss of his clan lands, is unknown.

8. Padruig Dubh Grant of Glenmoriston

Padruig Grant, known as Padruig Dubh of Craskie, was most famous for being the leader of the Seven Glenmoriston Men who rebelled against the prevailing government after the Battle of Culloden. He lived another 40 years beyond that battle and died in 1786 leaving behind a wife, 3 children and 8 grandchildren. After returning from the Battle of Quebec in New France, he obtained the Chelsea Pension, but he also lived to succeed to his forefathers' estate in the farm of Craskie in Glenmoriston. The 78th Fraser Highlanders were disbanded in 1763 at the conclusion of the Seven Years War against the French in which he only took part in one battle. He and many other Scots returned to Scotland, others remained and took up land in Canada (New France) where upwards of 300 of them reenlisted in 1775 and formed part of a new battalion under the name of the "Royal Highland Emigrants".

9. Ewen MacPherson of Cluny

As described by Simon Fraser, 11th Lord Lovat, Ewan MacPherson of Cluny was a "thorough good natured, even tempered honest gentleman and physically he was of low stature, very square and a dark brown complexion." [17] Cluny married Janet (Jenny) Fraser, Lord Lovat's daughter, in 1742 and they had two children, Margaret and Duncan. He was therefore Lord Lovat's son-in-law and Lochiel of Cameron's cousin through his mother, Jean Cameron. Cluny had an Independent Highland Regiment under the government man Lord Louden in 1745 as the Rising began. In August he became a leader in the Jacobite army and was present for the Battles of Prestonpans and Falkirk, but was delayed at Culloden.

Both Cluny and Lochiel received the value of their lands in gold from the Prince as a condition of being involved in the Rising. Cluny, known for his honesty, is reported to have cared for Lochiel's money as well as his own. After the Prince had escaped to the Continent, he demanded that of Cluny to meet with him in Switzerland. Cluny reluctantly travelled through England and across to the Continent, despite there being a price on his head, but the Prince was wanting some of the money back for his own use. Cluny was unable to return to Scotland and died in France alongside his wife and daughter only a year later. The Prince wrongfully accused Cluny of embezzlement, despite his impeccable reputation. So, the gold's whereabouts remains a mystery, although it is rumoured that both the Spanish and French gold are at the bottom of Loch Arkaig.

Young Glengarry said that Cluny MacPhearson junior made the same agreement as Lochiel with the Prince before joining in the campaign of 1745 viz to have security from the Prince for the full value of his estate. Young Glengarry declared he had this from Young Cluny MacPhearson's own mouth as a weighty reason why he would not part with the money which the Prince had committed to his care and keeping. [13]

Sport

Inclusions-

1. The History of Golf

2. The History of Curling

1. The History of Golf

It is generally accepted that modern golf developed in Scotland from the Middle Ages onwards. The Gaelic word being gowf. The first documented mention of golf in Scotland appears in a 1457 Act of the Scottish Parliament where an edict was issued by King James II prohibiting the playing of gowf and futball as these were a distraction from archery practice for military purposes. Bans were again imposed in Acts of 1471 and 1491 with golf being described as an unprofitable sport. Golf was banned again by Parliament under King James the IV of Scotland, but golf clubs and balls were bought for him in 1502 when he was visiting Perth and on subsequent occasions when he was at St Andrews and Edinburgh.

Mary, Queen of Scots, played golf and she was accused of playing pell mell and golf at Seton Palace after her husband, Lord Darnley, was murdered in 1567 in Musselburgh, which is the oldest playing golf course in the World. The earliest known instructions for playing golf were found in the diary of Thomas Kincaid, a medical student, who played on the course at Bruntfield Links near Edinburgh University and Leith Links. Diary entry 20th January 1687 "After dinner I went out to the golve" [24]

2. The History of Curling

Curling is a sport invented in Medieval Scotland with the first written reference to a contest using stones on ice coming from the records of Paisley Abbey, Renfrewshire, February 1541. Curling stones are solid pieces of granite shaped into a round shape with a concave top and bottom. Stones currently obtained in Scotland from Ailsa Cave meaning Fairy Rock and this is a bird sanctuary owned by the Marquis of Ailsa.

Military Campaigns

Inclusions-

1. The 1759 Quebec campaign on the Plains of Abraham led by General Wolfe in New France

2. The Rising of 1745 and the Battle of Culloden

1. The 1759 Quebec campaign on the Plains of Abraham led by General Wolfe in New France

The city of Quebec was held by the French in the mid-1700s and they were confident the English could not penetrate the well defended natural cliff faces inside a web of rivulets that had been made intentionally difficult to navigate by the removal of buoys. When General James Wolfe (1727-1759) sent his Highland Regiment of Frasers up an impassable cliff face, the French General Louis-Joseph de Montcalm did not at first believe the reports that 4000 odd British army personnel stood on the Plains of Abraham ready to challenge him to the city's occupation. On 13th September, 1759, a battle took place and the French were defeated. Both Wolfe and Montcalm died as a result of injuries from this battle.

Whilst still a major, Wolfe had fought under the Duke of Cumberland at the Battle of Culloden. "A General ten years later, he was dispatched to New France (Canada) and died on the Heights of Quebec. Simon, Master of Lovat, en route to Culloden, would be one of his senior officers: the Frasers accompanying him would serve Wolfe and King George II with courage and loyalty. Serving also would be Inverallochy's younger cousin, Simon, and the Fraser lairds of Culduthel, Balnain, Belladrum, Errogie and hundreds of Lord Lovat's ordinary kins-men now fleeing into the hills" [17]

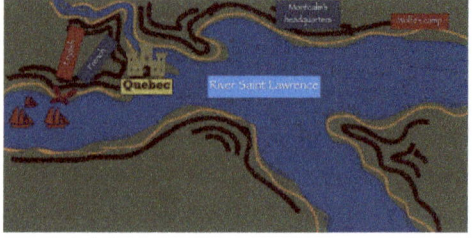

From the book, 78th Fighting Frasers in Canada, A short History of the old 78th Regiment of Fraser Highlanders 1757-1763 by Colonel J.R. Harper, on page 57, he is quoted as having said:

"Joseph Trahan on the French side said:

'*he would never forget Frasers Highlanders flying wildly after them with streaming plaids, bonnets and large swords, like so many infuriated demons.*'"

Fraser Highlander losses at the Battle of the Plains of Abraham, according to Colonel J.R.Harper were as follows: Captain Thomas Ross of Culrossie, Lieutenants Roderick MacNeil of Barra, Alexander MacDonnell, son of Barrisdale, Captains John MacDonnell of Lochgarry, Simon Fraser of Inverallochy, Lieutenants MacDonnell, son of Kepoch, Archibald Campbell, Alexander Campbell son of Barcaldine, John Douglas, Alexander Fraser, Ensigns James MacKenzie, Malcolm Fraser and Alexander Gregorson; 7 Sergeants, 131 rank and file wounded. [22]

"The French Garrison capitulated on September 18th, 1759 but the main body of the British troops didn't march to the city until September 29th." [22]

"The Royal William" was the name of the ship that carried Wolfe's dead body along with Sgt MacLeod who had a shat-tered shin bone. Colonel John Hale who carried the dispatches to the King of England was then put in command." [22]

2. The Rising of 1745 and the Battle of Culloden

On the 23rd July, 1745, Prince Charles Edward Stuart, the oldest son of James Francis Stuart, born in exile as heir to the Kingdoms of England, Scotland, Wales and Ireland, arrived on the western Scottish shores at a Highland place named Eriskay.

Borrowing money, the Prince had fitted out a French naval ship named The Elisabeth, which was compromised in a skirmish with an English vessel, HMS Lion enroute to Scotland. The Prince was on the smaller vessel called The Doutelle. The Elisabeth had to return to France, leaving the Prince with a few guns, a small amount of money and seven people to overthrow the British government.

Despite local pleadings for him to return to France, the Prince chose to stay and rose his father's Standard at Glenfinnan on August 15th to march toward Edinburgh. The first Clan to agree to support him was the Camerons, provided he gave them the value of their lands should it be an aborted mission. This also applied to Ewen MacPherson of Cluny. The Prince had success with Edinburgh, Falkirk and Prestonpans as more Clans joined with the Jacobite cause including Frasers of Inverallochy, Frasers of Beauly, Clan Grant, MacDonalds of Glencoe, Clan Chisholm, Clan Farquharson, Clan MacLachlan, MacIntosh, Stewart, MacGillivray and many others.

The Prince had advisors Lord George Murray, Captain O'Sullivan (Irish) and Lord John Drummond. He also received advice from Simon Fraser Lord Lovat, but didn't follow it. The Prince's plan was to march on London, which most disagreed with, but they did get within a few miles of London before turning back and returned to Scotland where they amassed near Inverness at Culloden Field, Drumossie Moor. The small now depleted force of Clans met with the Duke of Cumberland's army and were decimated within an hour. Cumberland's army then killed all of the wounded on the field and stripped all their bodies naked. They then went on to rape, pillage and kill innocent men, women and children of Inverness and beyond to where ever they thought the Prince had escaped to, burning everything down in their wake including Castle Dounie of the Frasers and the Hebridean Islands.

Unsuccessful in finding the Prince, Lord Lovat was decapitated and atrocities can be read in "The Lyon in Mourning" [12] by Reverend Robert Forbes. This was the last battle fought on British soil against its own people and to this day, the victors have not claimed victory. The Clan structure was destroyed, the Highland way of life, also Gaelic language prohibited, as well as the carrying of weapons, the playing of bagpipes and Highland dress all being outlawed. Scotland has never recovered from Culloden and its subsequent Clearances of its people.

Those in the world who ultimately have benefited from the mass forced distribution of Highland people throughout the British colonies in the 18th and 19th Century is that the culture, language, dress, music, poetry, dance and traditions have endeavoured to be preserved.

Poetry, Music and Song

Inclusions-

1. On Ederchaillis' Shores – Poem by Mrs. D. Ogilvie

2. The Red Wolfe Is Dead – Poem by Zaynab El- Fatah

3. The Hurdy Gurdy

4. Wool waulking song – unknown

5. Poetry from Poems of Os'Iain translated by James MacPherson

6. Who Will Remember? Poem by Zaynab El-Fatah

7. To Grigor and Helen – Poem by Zaynab El-Fatah

8. Grigor of the Mist- Poem by Zaynab El-Fatah

1. On Ederachillis' Shore

"On Ederachillis' shore,
The grey wolf lies in wait-
Woe to the broken door,
Woe to the loosened gate,
And the groping wretch whom sleety fogs
On the trackless moor belate,
The lean and hungry wolf,
With his fangs so sharp and white,
His starveling body pinched,
By the frost of a northern night,
And his pitiless eyes that scare the dark,
With their green and threatening light,
He climbeth the guarding gate,
He leapeth the hurdle bars,
He steals the sheep from the pen,
And the fish from the boat-house spars,
And he digs the dead from out of the sod,
And gnaws them under the stars,
Thus, every grave we dug,
The hungry wolf uptore,
And every morn the sod
Was strewn with bones and gore
Our Mother-Earth had denied us rest
On Ederchaillis' shore." (37)
        - *Highland Minstrelsy, by Mrs. D. Ogilvie* [26]

2. The Red Wolfe Is Dead

"No more do we see the grey wolf
On Glenmoriston Braes,
It is said they are all dead,
But the wolves in colours red
Were here in numbers abound.
The red wolves dug up our dead,
In frost and rain, they stripped them all,
Their bodies lay frozen,
No rest for them or us to mourn,
The red wolf stole our sheep

And our fish and goats and cattle too,
No gate or door could stop
The red wolf but death
In a frozen land
Called "Abraham's field",
The red Wolfe is dead.
Some peace is afforded us
As we lay them all to rest again"

- By Zaynab El-Fatah

3. The Hurdy Gurdy

The Hurdy Gurdy is a Medieval wheel instrument originating from France and it dates back 1000 years and at the time of its original use was ten times its current size. The instrument was first used in the Catholic Church. Its function being liturgical. It preceded the pipe organ, which was popular in the Church around 1390 to 1400 and therefore it was phased out of the Church. The name means string instrument of the wheel. The wheel acts as a bow on a violin and the older ones look like a music box. Pictured: Jim Kedross [25]

4. Wool Waulking song

English	Gaelic
She's my love,	Hu ri ri o hu o Ro-ho I o hi o
My life is she	Gaol ise, goal I E ho hu o hu o
	Hu ri o hu o Ro-ho I o hi o
Love for Anna	Gaol air Anna Ni-n Nill

Daughter of Neil,	E ho hu o hu o Hu ri ri o hu o Ro-ho I o hi o
I am pregnant	Mi torrach, mi trom E ho hu o hu o
I am heavy (with child)	Hu ri ri o hu o Ro-ho I o hi o
Not by some ordinary Lad is my pregnancy	Chan ann le balach Mo throm E ho hu o hu o Hu ri ri o hu o Ro-ho I o hi o
But by the darker-haired Young man,	Ach leis an Lasgaire dhonn E ho hu o hu o Hu ri ri o hu o Ro-ho I o hi o
Son of the Laird of the ships	Mac fir Bhaile Nan Long E ho hu o hu o Hu ri ri o hu o Ro-ho I o hi o
With whom warriors would rise	Leis an eireadh Na suinn E ho hu o hu o Hu ri ri o hu o Ro-ho I o hi o
My hair is curly, My hair is brown	Mi dualach, Mi donn E ho hu o hu o
Good and sharp my eyes, Melodious my voice,	Mi gur bior- Shuileach, binn E ho hu o hu o Hu ri ri o hu o Ro-ho I o hi o
I am like the thrush on the tree I am like the cuckoo of the forest	Mi mar smeaoraich An craoibh E ho hu o hu o Hu ri o hu o Ro-ho I o hi o

447

I am well-proportioned And I am curvy	Mi mar churhaig An coil' E ho hu o hu o Hu ri ri o hu o Ro-ho I o hi o
She's my love My love is she	'Mi cuimir 's 'mi cruinn E ho hu o hu o Hu ri ri o hu o Ro-ho I o hi o
Love for Anna, Daughter of Neil.	Gaol aor Anna ni'n Nill E ho hu o hu o Hu ri ri o hu o Ro-ho I o hi o Hu ri ri o hu o Ro-ho I o hi o

5. Poetry from Poems of Os'Iain

"I have met the battle in my youth,

My arm could not lift the spear when danger first arose,

My soul brightened in the presence of war as the green narrow veil

When the sun pores his streamy beams, before he hides his head in a storm

The lonely traveler feels a mournful joy

He sees the darkness that slowly comes" ....

"we are in the land of foes; the winds have deceived us Dar-Thula!

The strength of our friends is not near nor the mountains of Etha

Where shall I find thy peace, daughter of mighty Colla".

"Thy face is like the light of the morning

Thy hair like the raven's wing

Thy soul generous and mild like the hour of the setting sun,

Thy words the gael of reeds...

Dar'Thula with the dark brown hair

Thou art lovely as the sun beams of Heaven."

- Translated by James MacPherson, 1805

6. Who Will Remember?

Who will remember Fraser of Inverallochy?

Buried in the English telling of Drumossie Moor

Buried in time to be forgotten

Fraser of Inverallochy bravely led his clansmen

Into a clash of metal against metal

Still alive while all around his men fell

His death was a murder ordered by the Black Prince

No, I'll not commit murder Wolfe said,

So, another emptied his gun into his heroic and defiant heart,

Into Fraser of Inverallochy

- By Zaynab El-Fatah

7. To Grigor and Helen

To Grigor and Helen,

May love flow through and from you

Into each other

Receive God's gift, unlike any other

One that calms on a windy night

One that warms on a chilly day

One that protects the heart

And cannot be dejected

When the wolves are at the door

May your children be strong as you are

And carry this your love

Into each other and into every generation

So, safety is in your company

Comfort is in knowing you

Let this be your legacy, we pray.

- By Zaynab El-Fatah

8. Grigor of the Mist

It's true to say that Grigor, son of Grigor

Could recite the names of all the Scottish Sith.

His Grandmother taught him no English

Important only was the knowledge of the unseen.

Escaping as a deserter

Joining with the Seven Glenmoriston Men to live in a cave

Needed was he with that knowledge, through the mist

But of his sister, he knew naught.

Captured by the Redcoats imprisoned was he,

Not short of friends to break him out

Yearning always for his lost Mither

And the sister of whom he knew naught.

Taking a ride on a teamster with a lass at the reins

Her face, her voice he still knew naught

Married to his best friend, black hair like his Mither's

No recognition as the sister of whom he knew naught.

The song of Grioghal Chride broke the night air

His heart pierced as an arrow of the Mither long gone

His sporran held the key all along, A carved wooden
Clydesdale,

Of a team driven by the sister, Isobel of the mist,
brought to light.

- By Zaynab El-Fatah

Agriculture

Inclusions-

1. Scots Dumpies
2. Highland Coo
3. The Blackface Sheep
4. Crops
5. The Scottish Highland Pony
6. Scottish Collie Sheep Dog

1. Scots Dumpies

The Scots Dumpy Chicken is a
traditional Scots chicken dating
back to the 11th Century. Records
for the following 700 years are
not all verifiable and they were
introduced into England at some
point. The breed then almost died
out, but fortunately a family had taken the Scots Dumpies to
Kenya and had a large pure breeding population over there.
These were then reintroduced to Scotland and the numbers
are now on the rise. They are known for their short legs, which
makes them walk in a waddle fashion. Most commonly they
are speckled black and white with a bright red comb and only
four toes. The eggs can be white or creamy white in appearance. The hens carry quite a lot of weight by comparison to
other chickens, so the meat is tender to eat. They were probably taken to the American colonies.

2. The Highland Coo

The Highland cow/coo of Scotland is the oldest registered
breed of cattle in the world, identifiable by its long horns and

flowing red locks. They are raised primarily for their meat, as it is lower in cholesterol than other forms of beef.

A hardy breed, they can withstand conditions in the Scottish Highlands and islands, the long hair is a double coat with an oily outer layer and a downy undercoat. The bulls can weigh up to 800kg and the cows 500kg and the milk is very high in butter fat. They are not ordinarily kept as a dairy cow, except for personal use. Their long fringe covering their eyes is called a dossan.

On the Western Islands, they tend to be smaller and they bred black ones as well. They used to be kylos. Today they are all call Highland coos.

The earliest mention of these coos is the 6th Century and they've been bred in many other parts of the world since then. During the 18th Century, thousands of the Highland cattle were taken high in the hills of Strathspey by their owners to fatten. Markets were in Falkirk, Crief and Carlisle and buyers came from England. The Highlanders lost most of their cattle by government theft in the 1700s, sold then in England at cheaper prices. At one market in the 1800s, £30,000 changed hands, therefore cattle thievery remained a problem.

3. Blackface Sheep

In 1503, James IV of Scotland established a flock of 5000 Black Faced Scottish sheep, otherwise known as Scotties at Ettrick House. Earlier records in Catholic monasteries, reveal that they were bred possibly in the 15th Century for the monks' garments. Later records in the 17th and 18th Centuries, show

that the breed was known as Linton Sheep in England.

The Scottish Blackface is an old and primitive breed originating in Scotland that were able to withstand marginal grasses in shocking weather in the Highlands. This breed is highly disease resistant, smarter than average sheep, highly protective of their young, who use their horns against threats such as wolves, dogs, pigs and fencing. The ewes lamb easily and are strong and energetic. Both ewes and tups (rams) grow horns. Ewes usually lamb in May. In June, the hogs are clipped. In the 1700s only, hand clipping took place by men, where a gifted clipper could remove the entire fleece in one piece. The sheep were washed in a fast-moving stream before clipping. Soapy water was sometimes needed to remove any dirt, called scouring. It was then carded to separate the fibres to break up clumps and tangles, also called combing. The fleece is then lain out on the heather to dry. As each fleece dried, the women would work the wool by hand to break it up. Urine was used to fasten dyes. Dyes were usually prepared by the stream in a large pot placed over a peat fire. In the steaming water, colourful leaves were infused. The muckle wheel was invented, making spinning easier. Later easier again, when the foot treadle was introduced. Wool waulking songs varied from place to place to keep the momentum of women's work. (Ref: BFI National Archives, Edinburgh, 12th December 2017, Wikipedia. History UK.com and www.scotlandinfo.eu Scotland Info Guide, History of Cloth Making and Wauking)

4. Crops

Crops commonly grown were oats, corn, kale and later potatoes. Potatoes were introduced into Scotland due to failed crops after Culloden in 1746 and the following famine that ensued. Oats grown in Scotland have a nuttier flavour than oats grown elsewhere, but Scotland is generally a favourable location to grow oats. In the 1700s the Scots people ground the  oats by hand into a fine texture before soaking and cooking for parritch/oatmeal.

5. The Scottish Highland Pony

The Scottish Highland Pony lived in the Highlands long before people ever did, so it is unknown exactly how old the breed is. The Highland Pony doesn't usually grow taller than 14hh, with short legs and a stocky well-rounded body. It often has a dark stripe down the middle of its back and comes in a variety of dun colours, as well as chestnut, with a long mane and tail. It has a double layered coat of hair to weather the cold and rain. With its pleasant temperament, it is a popular pony to ride, but its numbers have diminished over the years.

6. Scottish Collie Sheep Dog

The Scottish Collie Sheepdog traces its Celtic history back to 4000BC according to the Scottish Collie Preservation Society

on its website scottishcolliepreservationsociety. com. Both rough and smooth Collies originate in Wales. The Welsh breed being much smaller. The Highland Collie was a large dog, very strong and aggressive, bred to herd Highland sheep. The word "Collie" meaning useful in the 18th Century, the rough Collies natural home was in the Highlands of Scotland where he had been used for centuries as a sheep dog. "He is lithe active dog, deep chest with lung power, neck strength, he has sloping shoulders and well bent hocks, indicating speed and his expression is of high intelligence." His coat is waterproof and he has an incredibly intense sense of hearing enabling him to predict the coming of high winds and the bleating of sheep covered in snow. His acute sense of direction is well known. They are sometimes orange, black and white and other times, just black and white.

Legalities

Inclusions-

1. Tartan Proscription law

2. Act of Union 1707

3. Act to Annul Suppression of Name Gregour or MacGregour

1. The Proscription Regarding Tartan

After a number of Acts of Parliament designed to disarm Highlanders, came the Act of 1746 (19 Geo.II, c. 39) which reads as follows:–

"...and be it enacted by the Authority aforesaid, that from and after the First Day of August, one thousand seven hundred and forty-seven, no man or boy, within that Part of Great Britain called Scotland, other than such as shall be employed as Officers and Soldiers in His Majesty's Forces, shall, on any pretense whatsoever, wear or put on the cloths commonly called Highland Clothes (that is to say) the Plaid, Philebeg or little Kilt, Trowse, Shoulder Belts, or any Part whatsoever of what peculiarly belongs to the Highland Garb; and that no Tartan or party-coloured Plaid or Stuff shall be used for Great Coats, or for Upper Coats; and if such person shall presume after the said First Day of August, wear or put on the aforesaid Garments, or any part of them, every such Person so offending, being convicted thereof by the Oath of One or more credible witness or witnesses before any court of justiciary, or any one or more Justices of the Peace for the Shire or Stewartry, or Judge Ordinary of the Place where such an offence shall be committed shall suffer imprisonment without bail, during the space of six months and no longer: and being convicted for a second offence before a Court of Justiciary, or at the Circuits, shall be liable to be transported to any of His Majesty's Plantations beyond the Seas, there to remain for the space of Seven Years." [22]

2. Act of Union 1707

The Acts of Union, passed by the English and Scottish Parliaments in 1707, led to the creation of the United Kingdom of Great Britain on 1 May of that year. The UK Parliament met for the first time in October 1707 [51]

3. Act to Annul Suppression of Name Gregour or MacGregour

"Act. At the Parliament Begun and Holden at Westminster the 29th Day of November, 1774

"An Act to repeal Two Acts made in the Parliament of Scotland, the 28th day of June 1633 intitled Act anent the Clan Gregour and the 15th day of June 1693 intitled Act for the Judiciary in the Highlands, so far as relates to the Mac Gregors; and to revive an Act of Parliament of the 26th day of April 1661 relative to the people called MacGregours.

"Whereas in the Parliament of Scotland being the first Parliament of King Charles 1 holden at Edinburgh the 28th day of June 1633 an Act entitled Act anent the Clan Gregour, ratifying and approving all Acts of Council and of Parliament made theretofore against the Clan of MacGregour, and ordaining the Clan of the people of the name of Gregour or MacGregour, and every one of them on arriving at the age of Sixteen to give Security to the Privy Council of Scotland for their good behaviour and obedience, and the said Clan Gregour should take to them some other surname; and that upon their failure to appear, it should be lawful to any of His Majesties Lieges to take and apprehend them to be presented to the Privy Council, there to be taken order with, and if it should happen any of the Clan Gregour to be hurt, mutilated, or slain the Party so doing and their accomplices should no ways be subject or liable to Law therefore, nor incur any Pain of Skaith in body or goods, and should be free of all pursuit, Criminal or Civil, and the same should be holden as good service done to His Majesty, and that for the better extinguishing and extirpating the said Clan, no minister or Preacher within the Bounds should at any time hereafter baptise or christen any male child by the name of Gregour and that no clerk or notary at any time coming should make or subscribe any Bond or other security under the name of Gregour. And whereas in the first Parliament of King Charles the Second holden at Edinburgh 1661 bearing date the 21st day of April in that year, whereby His Majesty who formerly designed by the name of MacGregour had during the troubles carried themselves with such loyalty and Affection to His Majesty as might justly wipe off all memory of their former miscarriages, and take off all mark of Reproach put upon them for the same, and His Majesty being desirous to reclaim his subjects from every evil way and to give all due encouragement to such as lived in due obedience to His Majesty's authority and Laws of the Kingdom, therefore His Majesty with advice and consent of His Estates of Parliament, rescinded, cased and annulled the Thirtieth Act of the First Parliament of King Charles the First, intitled Act anent the Clan Gregour and declared the same void and null in all Time coming; and that it should be hereafter free to all persons come of the name of Gregour or MacGregour, and enjoy all Privileges and Immunities as other subjects, notwithstanding the said Act or other Acts or anything contained to the contrary"....page 451. [34] Full restoration of the name occurred in 1774.

Architecture

Inclusions-

1.   History of the Palace of Holyroodhouse

1. History of the Palace of Holyroodhouse

King David I founded the Palace of Holyroodhouse as an Augustinian monastery in 1128.

In 1501 James IV cleared the ground close to the Abbey and built a Palace for himself and his bride, Margaret Tudor – the sister of Henry VIII. Only a fragment of the gatehouse survives today.

In the twentieth century, King George V and Queen Mary continued restoration and renovation work on the Palace, which they regarded as a family home. They were instrumental in bringing Holyroodhouse into the twentieth century, installing bathrooms, electricity and lifts. They also began the tradition of Garden Parties being held at the Palace. [50]

Finance

Inclusions-

1. French and Spanish Gold

In the text of this story there's mention of French gold, Spanish gold, Cluny's gold and the Cameron gold. Both Clan Cameron and Clan MacPherson were legitimately paid by Prince Charles Edward Stuart for the value of their lands should the Jacobite Rising prove abortive and as such, the moneys would be paid in compensation. It is rumoured that due to his ill-health, Lochiel of the Camerons entrusted the Cameron money into the safe keeping of Ewen MacPherson of Cluny. Neither man died in Scotland and it is unknown whether is remained hidden in Scotland or spent on the unfortunate crofters whose homes were lost.

The other gold being referred to, being French and Spanish, arrived too late to assist in the Rising and it is unknown as to its whereabouts. The strongest rumor is that it ended up at the bottom of Loch Arkaig, whilst some of it was stolen. To this day, people still search for the lost gold of Spanish, French or MacPherson origin to no avail. With many theories, all unproved." The French and Prince Charles' father all wanted it back in 1746 due to a large debt left by Charles Edward Stuart.

Bibliography:
Isobel of Glenmoriston

1. Aggarwala, Rohit T. (2013) "One such place in North America": New York, Boston, and Halifax as British Naval Bases, 1743-1783, https://www.cnrs-scrn.org/northern_mariner/vol23/tnm_23_339-365.pdf

2. Annie and Jenny (2021) Over the Sea to Skye: Bonnie Prince Charlie's escape; Episode 50, The Stories of Scotland Podcast – https://www.youtube.com/watch?v=PsAA9z7IpoI 21st August 2021

3. Bannerman, John (1998) The Beatons, Birlinn, Edinburgh, UK.

4. Bird, Jaguar (2018) The Picts: Scotland's First People - History, Spirituality & Battle, Jaguar Bird Channel, YouTube, https://www.youtube.com/watch?v=OwQCRaG6t78

5. Burton, Noel (2009) Battlefield Quebec Full Movie, TheGrapevineTV Channel, YouTube, https://www.youtube.com/watch?v=Osj47uHJkUs

6. Caitlin (2019) Highland Cows and 8 Fun Facts you need to Know about these Legendary Beasts, www.highland-titles.com

7. Cadwallader Colden, Wikipedia, https://en.wikipedia.org/wiki/Cadwallader_Colden edited 8th July 2022

8. Clans, The Scottish (2021) 5 Interesting Things about the MacNaughtens!, The Scottish Clans Channel, YouTube, https://www.youtube.com/watch?v=Pr8rtK8zu9Y

9. Craig, David (2010) On the Crofter's Trail, Berlinn Ltd, West House, Edinburgh, U.K.

10. Ewen MacPherson of Cluny https://en.wikipedia.org/wiki/Ewen_MacPherson_of_Cluny

11. Exploring Scotland's History (2020) Castle Lachlan, McLachlan Clan stronghold, Exploring Scotland's history Channel, YouTube, https://www.youtube.com/watch?v=YTWrdSj7OmQ

12. Forbes, Rev. Robert (collected 1746-1775) (published 1895) The Lyon in Mourning, Vol. I, edited from 1746-1775 Manuscript by Henry Paton MA, Forgotten Books, University Press, Scottish History Society, Edinburgh, UK.

13. Forbes, Rev. Robert (collected 1746-1775) (published 1895) The Lyon in Mourning, Vol. II, Edited from 1746-1775 Manuscript by Henry Paton MA, Forgotten Books, University Press, Scottish History Society, Edinburgh, UK.

14. Forbes, Rev. Robert (collected 1746-1775) (published 1895) The Lyon in Mourning, Vol. III, Edited from 1746-1775 Manuscript by Henry Paton MA, Forgotten Books, University Press, Scottish History Society, Edinburgh, UK.

15. Fraser Highlanders, Fraser Highlander Attack on Quebec, Electric Scotland, https://electricscotland.com/history/scotreg/fraser/f2.htm

16. Fraser, James (2009) The New Edinburgh of Scotland Vol I: From Caledonia to Pictland, Scotland to 795, Edinburgh University Press Ltd, Edinburgh, Scotland, U.K.

17. Fraser, Sarah (2013) The Last Highlander, Harper Collins Publishers, London, UK.

18. Fummey, Bruce (2020) St Columba: The Saint Who Made Scotland, Scotland History Tours Channel, YouTube, https://www.youtube.com/watch?v=zfhesEWpok8

19. Fummey, Bruce (2021) Why You'd be Crazy Not to Visit Kilmartin Glen, Scotland History Tours Channel, YouTube, https://www.youtube.com/watch?v=VB2jRL_DqKM

20. Gilles, Alan (2007) The confessions of Flora MacDonald, Copy of the Declaration of Miss MacDonald. Apple Cross Bay, July:12:1746, https://sites.google.com/site/culduie/theconfessionsoffloramacdonald

21. Gregor's Lament (2017) Griogal Cridhe - Scottish Gaelic LYRICS + Translation, M. Máire Ní Shúilleabháin YouTube Channel, https://www.youtube.com/watch?v=scc-XXZDvdE

22. Harper, J. R. R. (1966) The 78th Fighting Frasers: A Short History of the old 78th Regiment or Fraser Highlanders 1757-1763, DED-SCO Publications Lmt, Laval, Quebec, Canada.

23. Heroes and Legends (2021) Captain James Cook: The incredible true story of the World's Greatest Navigator and Cartographer, Heroes and Legends Channel, YouTube, https://www.youtube.com/watch?v=H6Fz88l2vlo uploaded 10 July 2021

24. History of golf (2022) Wikipedia, https://en.wikipedia.org/wiki/History_of_golf

25. Kedross, Jim (2018) Hurdy Gurdy expert, Illinois, U.S. https://www.youtube.com/watch?v=gYJg9cLk1us

26. Liath Wolf (2020) Baobhan Sith: Vampiric Beauty of the Highlands (Scottish Folklore), Liath Wolf Channel, YouTube, https://www.youtube.com/watch?v=MMF0x6kbBXk

27. Liath Wolf (2021) Cù-sìth: The Faerie Dog of Scotland (Scottish Folklore), Liath Wolf Channel, YouTube, https://www.youtube.com/watch?v=UyhFtH09Xew

28. Liath Wolf (2022) Morag Daughter of Donald: Haunted by the Daoine Sìth (Scottish Folklore), Liath Wolf Channel, YouTube, https://www.youtube.com/watch?v=UbNt_NgGBcc

29. MacGregor, A. A. (1937) The Peat Fire Flame: Folk-Tales and Traditions of the Highlands & Islands, The Moray Press, Edinburgh and London, U.K.

30. MacInnes, K. (2018) Gaol ise Gaol i - Scottish Gaelic Lyrics & Translation, M. Máire Ní Shúilleabháin YouTube Channel, https://www.youtube.com/watch?v=avLl yNs3ROQ

31. MacPherson, James (1736-1796) Fragments of Ancient Poetry, Collected in the Highlands of Scotland and Translated from the Gaelic or Erse Languages, Franklinn Classics, USA.

32. MacPherson, James (1807) The Poems of Ossian, Volume the Second, T. Bensier, Printer, London, UK.

33. Moffat, Alistair (2010) The Highland Clans, Thames and Hudson, London, UK.

34. Murray MacGregor, A. G. (1901) History of the Clan Gregor, from the public records and private collections: Compiled at the request of the Clan Gregor Society Volume II, William Brown, Edinburgh, Scotland, U.K.

35. Naval History Homepage (2011) Service Histories of Royal Navy Warships, https://www.naval-history.net/xGM-Chrono-10DD-49P-HMS_Panther.htm

36. Nevin, Michael (2020) Reminiscences of a Jacobite, Birlin Limited, Edinburgh, UK.

37. Ogilvie, D. (2021) Highland Minstrelsy, Liath Wolf Channel, YouTube, https://www.youtube.com/ watch?v=L2kl-BmosSQ

38. Pictish Language (2021) Pictish Language, Stones and Symbology: Who Were the PICTS of Scotland?, Celtic History Decoded Channel, YouTube, https://www.you-tube.com/watch?v=z1ziNAis2Ew

39. Pittock, Murray (2016) Culloden, Oxford University Press, Oxford, UK.

40. Prebble, John (1966) Glencoe, Clays Ltd UK Penguin Books, London, UK.

41. Prebble, John (1963) The Highland Clearances, Clays Ltd UK Penguin Books, London, UK.

42. Province of New York, 1664–1776: New York prior to the formation of the United States https://en.wikipedia.org/wiki/Province_of_New_York

43. Scallon, R. (2018) Hurdy Gurdy (The Medieval wheel instrument), Rob Scallon Channel, YouTube https://www.youtube.com/watch?v=gYJg9cLk1us

44. Scotland Info Guide (2017) History of Cloth Making and Wauking, BFI National Archives, Edinburgh, History UK.com and www.scotlandinfo.eu

45. Scottish Collie Preservation Society (2019) SCPS is a registered 501(c)(3) Non-Profit Organization International Registry, https://www.scottishcolliepreservationsociety.com/

46. Secret Scotland (2019) Kilmartin Glen - the Archaeological Highlights, Secret Scotland Channel, YouTube, https://www.youtube.com/watch?v=URqj7F6VzTo

47. Snake River Fur Post (2008) Great Lakes Indigenous People and the French, Minnesota Historical Society, https://www.mnhs.org/furpost/learn/french

48. The Gaelic Society of Inverness (1871) Comunn Gaidhlig Inbhir Nis, https://www.gsi.org.uk/

49. The Gaelic Council of Nova Scotia (2021) Comhairle na Gàidhlig, https://www.gaelic.ca/

50. The Royal Household (2022) History of the Palace of Holyroodhouse, Royal Residences: The Palace of Holyroodhouse, https://www.royal.uk/royal-residences-palace-holyroodhouse

51. UK Parliament (2022) Act of Union 1707, https://www.parliament.uk/about/living-heritage/evolutionof parliament/legislativescrutiny/act-of-union-1707/

52. Watson, Aldren A. (1968) The Blacksmith, Ironworker and Farrier, Norton paperback edition reissued (2000), New York, U.S.

53. Watson, Dr. Aaron (2021) Connecting the Dots: the Rock Art of Kilmartin Glen, Kilmartin Museum Channel, YouTube, https://www.youtube.com/watch?v=Yyn3vm 2L9Vc

54. wm Alan Ross (2015) Seven Glenmoriston Men, wm Alan Ross Topic Channel, YouTube https://www.youtube.com/watch?v=5YTlif8F4p0

55. Woolf, Alex (2007) The New Edinburgh History of Scotland Vol. II: From Pictland to Alba 789 to 1070, Edinburgh University Press Ltd, Edinburgh, Scotland, U.K.

Printed in Australia
AUHW010928060323
375265AU00004B/4